A Tough Act to Follow

A Tough Act to Follow

by Max Wilk

W · W · NORTON & COMPANY · *New York · London*

The text of this book is composed in Times Roman, with display type set in Lydian
Bold Italic. Composition and manufacturing by the Maple-Vail Book Manufacturing Group.

First Edition

Library of Congress Cataloging in Publication Data

Wilk, Max.
  A tough act to follow.
  I. Title.
PS3545.I365T68   1985   813'.54   85–5669

ISBN 0-393-02219-6

W. W. Norton & Company, Inc., 500 Fifth Avenue, New York, N.Y. 10110
W. W. Norton & Company Ltd., 37 Great Russell Street, London WC1B 3NU

1 2 3 4 5 6 7 8 9 0

For
Dawn,
Jessie,
and Emma—

—The Sunshine Girls.

Good evening, ladies and germs,

for my next number, I should like to render—
render meaning to tear apart—
the famous ballad, "I gave her the ring, she gave me
the finger"

Hey, you, where are you going with that case?
I'm taking this case to court!

These are the jokes, folks!

Order in the court! Order in the court!
Thanksh. I'll have a small beer!

"Good evening, Honeymoon Hotel. Two hundred rooms—
ninety-two honeymoon couples, and the others just rehearsing . . ."

Hey, you, where are you going now with that ladder?
I lost my case and now I'm going to a higher court!

Then it was Halloween, and my mother used to hold
me up to the window—
Too cheap to buy a pumpkin, eh?

And now the famous ballad, "Curfew Shall Not Ring
Tonight,
My Mother's Asleep In the Belfry."

I know you're out there, folks, I can hear you breathing . . .

I've seen better heads at a cabbage patch.

She was so knock-kneed and he was so bowlegged, when they stood up to be married they spelled OX!

Onward, onward, through the muck and mire—
Hiya Muck!
Hiya Mire!

I love that joke, it was one of my father's jokes.
What are you, one of your mother's?

Hey lady, are you feeling hysterical? Or is he feeling yours?

> "Oh I wish I was in the land of cotton,
> Meals are bad, hotels are rotten,
> Keep away, keep away, keep away from
> Dixieland!"

Speaking of inflation, I just heard pumpernickel has gone up to pumperdime—

You know, when I told that joke in Chicago, you could hear them laughing across the street?
What was playing across the street?

> *A wild sort of devil,*
> *But dead on the mattress*
> *Was my Gal Sal!*

For my finale, I will now sing "Till We Beet Again."
Beet? Isn't it meet?
No—I'm a vegetarian!

—and I had a room that was so small that

He was so rich that—

—and I said "Doctor, I've got this
funny thing that—"

And the booking agent says, "What kind of an act is
that?"

. . . You want opera? How about the "Havabanana," from
Carmen

or *"I'm Carmen, Virginia"*

yes, you're a wonderful, wonderful audience
And My Partner And I
want you to
Know—
FADE TO BLACK.

A Tough Act to Follow

Eileen Tighe:

The Egyptians wrapped their dead in sheets. We preserve ours differently. Our archaeological artifacts come in much neater packaging. The first time the shades of Jody Cassel surfaced into my consciousness, she emerged from a plastic video cassette-box, frozen in time on a scratchy kinescope. Preserved by the miracle of Minnesota Mining technology since 1952, hardly a mummy, there she was, very much alive. Yelling and cracking terrible jokes, making faces, dancing and singing, a time traveller from the recent past.

Maybe it would have been simpler for me if I hadn't fallen for her, and she'd stayed quiet, stored away on that videocassette in Bernie Lorber's collection.

It was a couple of months back, one of those rare Sunday nights here in L.A. when I didn't have much happening.

No screening at the Academy, or at the Directors Guild, nobody had invited me to a dinner party, I was very much alone in my place. Freddy, my current every-so-often sleep-over, was back East doing a couple of commercials his agency had assigned him to do with a New England background. That morning I'd played tennis, and gotten rid of a lot of my tensions, stored up from a week of conferences, arguments, and negotiations. I'd finished the *New York Times* Sunday crossword, washed my hair, done some cleaning up, spoken long-distance to Albie, my son the student, and now it was time for reading.

There, on my desk, staring accusingly at me, was the pile of film scripts submitted by agents, in hope that my employers, based on my recommendations, would smile favorably on, or buy, or option. All those poor bastard writers, who'd sweated out those endless pages, rewritten, polished, edited—then had their fantasies neatly xeroxed and bound. There they were, waiting for me to reach out and tap them on the shoulder, to say, "I dub thee— Sir Producible."

They never stop coming. This town floats on a sea of submitted scripts, Venice with properties sailing by. And what was sitting here in my place were the ones winnowed out by my two bright young readers—these they considered Possible. So out of guilt, I usually try to plow through at least two or three each weekend.

I'd finished the first one, a strange mixture of love and sex and comedy featuring an old private eye and a beautiful young industrial spy working Silicon Valley, when Bernie Lorber called to dish a little Sunday gossip.

"Come over and have dinner with me," he suggested. Selim, it seemed, was off in Idaho—(*Idaho!* Lord—it was incongruous to think of that thin little decorator slogging through the frozen North.)—he was doing the preliminary survey of somebody's ranch house hideaway for a complete face lift—("He will probably end up with something very butch," said Bernie. "Early Rugged.")

Bernie and Selim have kept house together for years. Their latest one is a huge old monster of a '20s mansion down in Hancock Park which they bought a couple of years ago, and are doing over, room by room; when it's done, they will certainly sell it for a huge profit to some rich, insecure couple whom they've romanced at one of their customary tax-deductible parties. Then they'll take the cash and reinvest some of it in another dump somewhere unfashionable and go through the process all over again. It's the game Bernie calls Musical Houses.

Since Bernie sounded wistful that Sunday night, I decided I wasn't enjoying being alone here any more than he did. The scripts could wait until later. I climbed into jeans and a sweater, found some decent wine to bring along, and drove down to be his visiting Florence Nightingale.

. . . Lord knows, there have been dark nights of the soul when Bernie has done the same for me.

We've known each other for years, ever since New York, when he kept his antique shop on Third Avenue, before he met Selim, and I was still the nice middle-class married lady commuting from New Jersey for lunches, matinees, and shopping. Bernie consoled me through those very tough months after my separation from The Boy Wonder of Wall Street. He encouraged me, massaged my ego all through the divorce and the aftershock. A woman in trouble usually brings out the best in gays.

So we've kept in touch, especially after we both migrated out here. Oh, yes, there are times when Bernie's wit can be cruel and as sharp as a laser-knife, but he's reliable, and I respect his judgment. Selim may be the truly talented side of their partnership, Pacific Interiors, but it's Bernie who keeps the financial side of the firm healthy. Sharp? Nobody is ever going to run a benefit for those two. The only loophole, or tax shelter, or gimmick they haven't taken advantage of, yet, is to be able to file a joint return. ("Don't worry," Bernie confided in me once. "The Gay Lobby has it on the top of its Priority List. All we need is to get one or two of the Senators on the Finance Committee to come out of the closet.")

We're back to Jody Cassel.

Bernie had thrown together a very tasty pasta salad, with some cold marinated chicken, there was good cheese and fruit, we uncorked my wine, and we sat in the kitchen—that vast room they've done over—and ate, just the two of us. We could have been the servants in a pre-war English movie.

We dished the gossip, he filled me in on who was doing it with and to whom this past week. Which affairs were breaking up, whose finances were shaky, and which career was on the way up, or down.

When we finished, he suggested we take our coffee in the den. "I want to show you something," he said, smiling. ". . . Something special."

I followed him through the long center hall until we got to the den. *Den?* It's as large as a small airplane hanger, a relic of the affluent 20's when ceilings were fourteen feet high, and floors parqueted, and everyone hired plasterers to festoon your rooms with elaborate moldings, around the ceilings and above the mantelpiece. By today's standards, it's a ballroom.

The boys haven't gotten to redo that room yet; it's furnished with various pieces of furniture left over from previous houses they've had. On the floor there's a huge Persian rug they haven't yet been able to unload on somebody. What they really need is to find somebody who's remodelling a mosque. There are a few nondescript graphics and pictures on the walls—all for sale—and in one corner, a TV, which is hooked up to Bernie's favorite new toy, his videotape machine.

In the bookshelves he has a huge collection of tapes, not merely the shows he's taped off the air, but all sorts of rarities which only a true fan treasures, stacked in neat rows.

Where he acquires them, I don't know, but there's obviously a wide network of people like Bernie, all over the country, who pass these things back and forth. He loves musicals, the ones which go back to the beginning of "talkies," with long-forgotten performers. Two-reel comedies with Laurel and Hardy, Thelma Todd and Patsy Kelly, people like Charley Chase. Early Marlene Dietrich films, Bette Davis pictures from her Warner 1930s and '40s days, "society" dramas with people like Kay Francis and Ruth Chatterton, William Powell and Robert Montgomery. Judy Garland musicals, of course ("The Mother of Us All," he once said.), and a lot of other stuff, some of it truly classic, others merely camp, most of it forty or fifty years old.

Why always old movies? What is this fascination with the

past? I asked him once, and Bernie thought about it, and said ". . . Because they're restful."

Restful?

". . . All their problems are so godamned simple," he explained. "You *know* everything is going to be solved by the end of the seventh reel. Now I ask you, in times like these, who could ask for anything more reliable than that?" Then he grinned, conspiratorially. "And don't forget, Selim gets all sorts of ideas from the decor."

He offered me a joint, which I turned down. Not because I don't enjoy one every once in a while, but because I was feeling quite relaxed enough. Soon I'd have to go home like a dutiful production executive and plow through another one of those waiting scripts before going to sleep.

Bernie was rummaging through the carefully stacked rows of cassettes. "So which ghost are we planning to exhume tonight?" I asked. "Carole Lombard? Pola Negri?"

". . . Minor talents at best, compared to this one," said Bernie, holding up a cassette. "This is a true artifact—took me months to get it. Sit back, Mrs. Tighe. Thanks to the miracle of Japanese technology, we are about to turn back the clock to another, better time."

He snapped off the lights.

"Who's the star?" I asked.

"You will see," he replied, and tapped the "Start" button on his remote control switch.

The light was on up on the screen, and then a disembodied voice said "This . . . is the Dumont Network!" Then there was the sound of bright, tinny jazz music. The voice spoke again, this time as we faded in on a pair of curtains. "Ladeez and gentlemen . . ." There was a drum roll, a cymbal crash. ". . . The makers of Zingo Toothbrushes—and Easo, for your stomach, bring you . . . TIME FOR JODY, starring Jody Cassel!"

The curtains parted, the picture was grainy and harsh, the

camera work quite jerky and hesitant, the setting obviously cheap, a couple of pedestals with artificial flowers.

"What is *this?*" I asked.

"A kinescope!" said Bernie. "Recorded off the screen—"

Three boys in tails and two girls in abbreviated dance costumes emerged, and went into a brief, syncopated dance.

"Why are we watching?" I asked.

"Keep your eye on the third boy on the left!" he commanded.

I squinted at the picture. Making out what was going on up there was difficult; all the dancers seemed like tiny automatons.

"Who dat?" I asked.

"Oh God, he was so young and beautiful!" sighed Bernie. "Dummy—it's *me!*"

The dancers were going through an intricate routine—*Bernie*—there? One of those lithe young boys in tails? I'd never suspected he'd ever been a TV performer—a dancer—and then, promptly, I warned myself—*don't laugh, be careful how you react.*

"Little old Bernie," he said. "In the warm, pulsating flesh . . ." He sighed. "Time certainly marches on, doesn't it?"

"You were *good,*" I said, finally. But I wasn't sure I was watching the right dancer.

". . . And here she is—the toast of TV—Jody Cassel!" cried the announcer.

On the screen, the camera was moving in for a close-up—and out from the wings raced . . . someone in a bear suit? Yes, it was definitely a bear costume. And now, right after the bear, there emerged a brassy young girl, in an elaboarte flowing cape, wearing a blonde frizzy wig, waving a baseball bat! She proceeded to corner the bear—and now she was beating the animal furiously on the head with her bat. "Back to the Bronx Zoo, you bum!" she cried. "Goldilocks doesn't play house with bears!"

The bear ducked away, ran out past the cameras, into the audience, which cheered and applauded.

The comic Goldilocks turned to the audience. Two of her teeth were blacked out, her nose was obviously false, and she

wore heavy glasses. "Who could blame that poor bear from running out on me?" she demanded, and burst into a loud, braying
laugh. "Wowowweeweewo!" she chortled, and clasped her hands
above her head like a victorious prizefighter. "Now you know
why Goldie ate lox, right, gang?" There was an answering laugh.
"How are you tonight, folks? Say you're okay!"

"We're okay!" came a few scattered voices from the audience.

"Louder!" demanded the girl, hands on hips like a cheer-
leader. She began to jump up and down—"Gimme a J—gimme
an O—gimme a D—gimme a Y—and what've you got here
tonight? *JODY!*"

The audience roared back—*"Jody!"*

Leering happily, Jody ripped off her cape and blonde wig,
tossed away the glasses and the bat, to reveal herself now in a
football player's garb, complete with shoulder pads, a huge *J. C.*
covering her bosom. "We've got a great show here tonight, folks—
the finest guests money can buy, which isn't saying anything—
and funny stuff—and let's get started with the opening, and this
time, gang, let's get it right!"

The music hit, and in tandem with the three boys and the two
dancers, Jody Cassel, in her ridiculous outfit, began to do a dance,
if you could call it that, to the brassy beat of an old song called
"You've Got To Be A Football Hero,"

". . . God, what energy!" I remarked. "Who is she?"

"You don't remember her?" demanded Bernie. "How quickly
they forget. She was a big star—for about half an hour there—
the hottest—but stop looking at her—*look at me*—wasn't I thin
and gorgeous?"

I stared at the screen, on which Jody, every so often squealing
and screaming, was being tossed back and forth by the dancing
boys—trying to stiff-arm her way out of their reach. *Now* I could
make out Bernie—much younger, thinner—and yes, very attractive—

"You're terrific!" I told him.

". . . Yes, sure," he snarled. "I'm the one she kept on hitting—look, see? The bitch—I had black and blue marks for a week—when she was out there, she never gave a damn what she did, as long as she got the laugh—'' He reached over to pick up his remote control, ready to turn it off. "Okay, enough of Memory Lane . . . I can tell you're bored with Early Bernie—''

"No, no, leave it on,'' I said. "It's fun!''

"You want more of Miss Crazy?'' he asked. "I don't believe it—to me, you've always seemed somebody with *taste* . . . ''

On the screen Jody was executing an intricate series of steps, tripping here and there, taking pratfalls—but every time the girl stumbled, somehow she got a laugh. She fell down again, she tripped—stuck out her tongue at the dancers, made rude gestures—and everything she did got more guffaws.

"Look at that klutz!'' said Bernie. "Couldn't dance for shit!''

"But listen to the audience—they *love* her,'' I said. "She can't do anything wrong for them . . .''

"Oh honey, in those days, you could make the audience laugh with anything,'' he said, scornfully. "They were just so damned grateful there was anything *alive* up there on their mighty nine-inch screen—''

"How long ago was this?'' I asked.

"Sorry,'' said Bernie "I never reveal my age.''

"Don't be coy,'' I said. "I know how old I was when my folks got their first TV set, and that was . . . let's see—1952—''

"Listen, toots,'' said Bernie, snappishly. "*I* can handle being middle-aged, it doesn't threaten me, but you—you're in a youth-oriented business, remember? You can be easily replaced . . .''

The dance up on the screen came to a crazy, wow finish, a pileup of dancers onstage, with Jody underneath, fighting to get out, and finally surfacing through that mass of bodies, waving at her audience. ". . . Don't go way.!'' she yelled, trying to catch her breath. ". . . After . . . I get . . . a blood . . . transfusion . . . we'll be back!'' She stuck her tongue out like a naughty kid on a playground. *"Love you all!"*

The screen went to black, and then, there suddenly appeared a middle-aged actor-type, grey-haired, in a white jacket, a doctor's mirror on his head. "Folks," he said, "I have important news about gastric acidity. Look over here." The camera panned to reveal a large glass vessel, shaped like an intestine, suspended in mid-air. "Now, watch as that food you've eaten reaches your stomach," he continued, and the camera moved in close on the glass. A foamy white mixture began to pour down through an opening at the top, and to fill the glass container below. "See what happens when you overindulge?" intoned the huskster. ". . . Heartburn . . . Stomach Acidity . . . *Distress!*"

"Now can I turn this off?" Bernie demanded. "It's enough to turn anybody into a vegetarian!"

"—Wait, *wait*—" I said. "Tell me about Jody Cassel."

He punched the sound button, and mercifully the huckster's voice vanished, but we were left with a picture of some alkaline solution as it poured down to the rescue, in that glass cauldron . . .

". . . What the hell do you want to know about *her* for?" he asked, and there was more than a trace of impatience in his voice.

Yes, of course—he had treated me to this private showing, this antique precious relic of his youth, lord knows where he'd found it, to show me *himself*—young and beautiful, an intimate sharing of something he cherished . . . and all I'd done was to start laughing at Jody Cassel. Completely ignoring him. Very foolish of me.

"Because it's a whole new you!" I told him. "I had no idea you were such a marvelous dancer, Bernie. I am impressed."

". . . I wasn't bad, was I?" he said, softly. "Had three or four good years. A couple of Broadway shows—summer stock, and then a lot of this TV stuff."

Alas, time had not been generous to my friend. All that was left of that beautiful cheerful dancing boy was, above the jowls, the familiar wicked grin. Dorian Gray Bernie wasn't.

"Honestly," I confessed, "I've never had the guts to get out there and perform on a stage, in front of an audience. I'd be scared out of my wits. It must take a special kind of courage . . ."

"Not guts, honey," said Bernie. "Mainly chutzpah. You've got to dare them. *Here I am*—out in front of you—you better love me, or else!"

". . . So why'd you quit?" I asked.

"Not me, *this*," he said, tapping his knee. "Tore the cartilage doing a lift. Some cow of a leading lady. Goodbye show biz. Nobody needs a crippled gypsy; I hung up my Capezios. I was too lazy to teach and too nervous to steal, so I opened up the antique store and never looked back . . . But for a while there," he added, sadly, lapsing into Marlon Brando, ". . . *I coulda been a contenduh . . .*"

On the screen our tour of the intestinal tract was over, the show was on again, and now there seemed to be some sort of a magician up there at work. A swarthy little man, grinning, wearing a Turkish fez, standing at a table, bringing forth baby chicks, an endless supply of them, from beneath a series of cups, saucers, tiny bells. Then he walked out into the audience and produced them from ladies' handbags and mens' pockets. Then he came back and popped chicks from the instruments of the orchestra . . .

"Does Jody come back?" I asked.

"Are you serious?" asked Bernie. "This was *her* show. Watch."

Within moments, the magician was back on the stage, and his assistant was wheeling out a large papier-mâché egg. Now the magician covered it with a large cloth, waved his hands, tapped it with his wand, and whisked away the cloth—to produce, now dressed in a giant chicken outfit—Jody!

". . . It goes downhill from here," said Bernie.

Off went the magician, and his supply of chicks, and now Jody was standing, in that ridiculous outfit, and now she was obviously telling jokes.

"Turn on the sound," I said.

"Masochist," he muttered, and tapped it.

". . . I won't say I'm ugly, *but*," Jody was saying, "I sent my picture to the Lonely Hearts Club, and they sent it back. They said they weren't that lonely!'' The audience roared. "You've heard of the Before and After pictures in those beauty ads?'' she asked. "Well, I'm During!'' Another roar. Jody grinned triumphantly. "So I went down to the Navy Yard, and I finally ended up with a sailor. He'd been at sea for two years and he was desperate! That made him even with me!'' Another laugh. The orchestra struck up "Anchors Aweigh.'' *"Hold it!''* yelled Jody. "We went out to dinner, and afterwards, he said 'How about coffee in the library?' I said 'Okay—' so I went all the way downtown to 42nd Street, and he never showed up! Hey, you think I went to the wrong library?''

". . . Henny Youngman in drag,'' said Bernie, as the orchestra struck up a military march. The dancers came out in sailor outfits, there was a drill routine with a lot of saluting and marching, and now I saw Bernie again, Bernie the Young, he was the sailor who hoisted Jody onto his shoulders and carried her off, as she waved madly at her audience and yelled ". . . I'll send you a postcard, folks! Wowwowweeweewoh!''

Then we were into another commercial, this time for a toothpaste guaranteed to be gentle to tender gums.

"That's enough,'' said Bernie, hitting the sound button.

"You were very good in the sailor number,'' I said. "What do you do next?''

". . . Ah, don't try to butter me up,'' he said. ". . . Actually, I don't appear again until the finale. Before that, the bitch has her solo spot.''

"Solo?'' I said. "She's been on solo for twenty minutes . . .''

"Oh, you noticed?'' said Bernie.

"Leave it on,'' I coaxed. "I want to see the closing.''

". . . What is this sudden fascination you've developed for Miss Monster of 1952?'' he demanded.

. . . I wasn't sure. The novelty of it, perhaps. Or was it the raw energy, the nerve, the sheer, unadulterated brash Jody Cassel was demonstrating? This blurry shadow from years ago, forcing herself on the world, obviously insecure and unaware of the classic rule—*less is more*—but funny, oh, absolutely, a born clown.

On the screen, the young woman smiled, showing us her perfect teeth, we went to black, and then, the curtains parted to reveal a ramshackle set which seemed to represent a nightclub. A dance team, he in tails and she in a long gown, appeared in the shadows, and went into an intricate, stylish routine. The lighting was poor; I couldn't make out faces.

"Is that you?" I asked.

"You need an eye exam, honey," he said.

Then the camera dollied over to a doorway, and there, standing in a spotlight, appeared Jody Cassel. Not in a comedy outfit, but now wearing a long gown, her hair combed back—(how could she have made a change so fast?)—and she'd begun to sing.

"Put the sound on," I suggested. "I thought she was a comic."

"Oh, she could do anything," said Bernie. "Or so she thought."

He tapped the button, and we heard her now. It was a 40's ballad, one of those real, heartthrob torch numbers, her man had left her, she was bruised and battered, her dreams were all shattered, and where did she go from here?

". . . Now she's ripping off Lena Horne," said Bernie. "Oh well, if you're going to steal, steal from the best, right?"

Her voice was deep and husky, but good, remarkably good. She was really selling that song, making those ordinary rhyming lyrics into something honest and heartfelt. The camera had dollied in until her face was in close-up, she wasn't pulling funny faces, she was singing it absolutely straight, she was almost close to tears, she built it up to a dramatic finish. Amazing.

There was spontaneous applause.

Blackout, and then there was some sort of a finale, with all the cast coming out on stage, obviously there hadn't been much time to rehearse the end of the show, but in some haphazard way, they carried it off—the magician, the dance team, everyone joining in, and here was Bernie again, with the ensemble, waving and smiling—

"*There* I am, selling like mad!" he chuckled.

Now Jody was elbowing her way into the front of the group, waving her arms. "Until next week, then!" she yelled. "Just remember—I say—*Jody loves you*—and what do *you* say?"

"We love you!" yelled a few brave voices.

"*Louder!*" she commanded, stretching out her arms to them.

". . . WE LOVE YOU!" came the echoes, obediently.

"That's what I want to hear!" she told them, happily. Now we could see tiny beads of perspiration on her forehead; it didn't matter, she was obviously on a high. Tonight she'd conquered them, made them all hers. The orchestra struck up a bright up-tune, and Jody began singing, joined in by her ensemble, as the closing credits began to roll, somewhat unsteadily.

". . . From the bottom of my feet, I love you!
To the top of my head, I'm yours—you're mine.
Come around again next week and I'll tell you—
Having you love me is simply divine!"

Somebody had come out onstage to hand Jody a bouquet of flowers; she sniffed at them, and then, spontaneously began to toss them at the startled ensemble beside her, throwing blossoms at the dancers, they began lobbing them back at her, and now it was like a snowball fight amongst a bunch of kids—we went to black, and the network logo came on, and the announcer identified the station.

End of tape.

The room was suddenly silent.

"Talk about milking bows," said Bernie. He pressed the rewind button.

". . . Tell me about her," I said, as we waited for the technology to do its job.

"What's to tell?" he asked. "She came and went . . . and I certainly hope she saved her money."

He took the cassette out of the machine, and stowed it carefully into its plastic coffin. Jody Cassel, a crowd-pleaser thirty years ago, a peculiar shadow of vanished history, fixed in time, went back to her assigned place on Bernie's shelf.

". . . Moving right along," said Bernie, "let's see something professional."

I know enough about my friend to sense he needed placating, so I agreed. "Whatever you want to show," I told him.

He picked out a tape of Fred Astaire and Ginger Rogers, doing a batch of their incredible dance numbers, taped from some PBS special recently, and we both sat back and enjoyed true excellence.

". . . Now that's dancing," said Bernie, softly, when it was over. "If you can't be *that* good, forget it."

It was time to go home to my script-pile.

He escorted me through the echoing hallways to the front door, opened it. We embraced. "I loved seeing the family album," I told him. "You've aged very well."

"Bullshit," said Bernie, fondly. "Don't try snowing me, I'm a master. I don't think I'll ever show that damn tape ever again. Too traumatic."

It was a damp night, with a hint of fog coming in.

". . . One question about Jody Cassel." I asked.

He grimaced. "Listen," he said. "I'm not really bitter about her. Christ knows everyone in this so-called business has an ego problem, or else why are we in it instead of selling shoes, right? But I just remembered something that poor sad bitch said, one night, when she was throwing a big temper tantrum at rehearsals, telling everyone how to stage her numbers, rewriting the gags, cutting everyone out of her scenes so she'd be solo, stepping all over the world—Finally, she stopped everything, grabbed a mike and said 'Pay attention.! The first fifty years of this century were Charlie Chaplin, okay—but the *next* fifty years—it's Jody Cassel!' . . . Now, what does that tell you about her problems?"

". . . Plenty," I conceded. "Poor demented lady . . . Whatever happened to her?"

"Oh, who *cares?*" snapped Bernie.

And I went home, leaving him alone with his library of *temps perdu*.

Jody Cassel didn't resurface in my conscious for some time after that night at Bernie's.

Things suddenly heated up at my office; we abruptly went into a period of preproduction frenzy. Three coproduction deals—we refer to them as GOs—count 'em, three—which had been stalled for months in various stages of on-again, off-again, will they or won't—all came to life simultaneously.

Things were jumping. There were conferences, the phones and the Telex never stopped, and we were all cranked up, the adrenalin flowing—and then the rug was pulled out from two GOs. The bankable star we'd been waiting for on the first venture decided he didn't want to risk making a film in Mexico City. He loved the project, but his objection was to the altitude and its effect on blood pressure. Not his, his current lover's.

Then, the financing which had been lined up for the second coventure, previously arranged with a Swiss consortium, turned out to be connected with a mysterious commodities-futures manipulator, who vanished over one weekend, leaving his New York firm belly-up. By Monday, a lot of his trusting investors had lost their shirts, and our second GO was left waiting at the church.

We still had a viable third GO—for development of a two-hour film for one of the cable networks. But when the smoke and dust had settled on the battlefield, we were only batting .333.

Par for the course, in this business.

If the alumnae magazine of that elegant ladies' college I attended ever surveys me to find out what my current job entails, I'll have to think over my reply carefully. Here at Interfico, my letterhead lists me as "Senior Production Executive."

What I really am is a well-paid radar screen.

Interfico—International Film Development Corp—isn't exactly a production company. Nor are we distributors. We're a product of I.R.S. regulations—a hybrid, devised by tax-lawyers. We thrive on a pool of capital, supplied by various anonymous investors who've been steered to us by *their* tax lawyers. In some of our deals, we may "participate" from the first dollar with producers. Sometimes we invest "first monies," which they then use for "further development." When projects arrive at the next stage of production, we may "joint venture," which means further financing. We're flexible. Each deal is different. Confusing? Certainly. Putting together one of our GO ventures is as difficult as building your own Rolex watch from a hobby-kit . . . without instructions.

We never go door to door, selling ourselves like the polite loan sharks we are. We don't have to. Hopeful partners-to-be come courting us. Since we're solvent, with ample cash to invest, and we currently have "points" in a couple of current films, one that's doing nicely on cable TV and videocassettes, and the other almost in the black, we are an attractive honey pot for the dozens of hopeful bees who swarm through L.A.

Most of the time, for me, it's not so frenetic. I sit upstairs in my elegant office, on the twenty-second floor of this Westwood tower, watching through my hermetically sealed windows as the daily wave of smog comes over the Santa Monica mountains and blurs my view of that endless moving snake of traffic on Wilshire below. I listen attentively to the latest pitch being made to Interfico by some hopeful producer, or packager, and then I take his material—books, plays, scripts—and I "evaluate."

I also go to parties and pick up random pieces of information on who's preparing what "property." Regularly, I gossip on the phone with publishers and agents and book-packagers back East, who sometimes tip me off to a new book that's hot, or a play that might be a new "possible." (. . . but *only* if and when it's melded with the right bankable star and/or director. That's always primary. Don't let anybody snow you with that old saw—*the play's the thing*. No way. It's the elements you add to the stew pot which will make your ragout edible. Otherwise, you're strictly dealing in broth.)

Once every week, we have a staff meeting, and then we sit down with our own lawyers, our business people, and I present my evaluations . . . the material I think is possible.

Sid Budlong presides; he's my boss, who's only in his mid-thirties but is already feeling the hot breath of youth at his back. Sid spends a lot of time racing back and forth between coasts, or over to Europe, storing up notes and data on his latest toy, the minicomputer, which he schlepps everywhere in his Italian attaché case.

At the end of that meeting, will have made further decisions—reevaluations of my evaluations. *Pass*—or once in a great while, *P.F.E.* (Pursue for Future Evaluation)

For every P.F.E.—and nobody needs Sid Budlong's sophisticated gadget to spit out these numbers—there have to have been at least forty-odd *passes*. And out of every ten or so P.F.E.'s—*if* all the pieces fall into place—we might arrive at an honest-to-God GO.

. . . and then again, we might not, as the events of the past couple of weeks proved.

I know the odds against a GO—so do all those hopeful producers who come up to my office lugging their scripts, and yet, despite the immutable statistics, my phone keeps on ringing, manila envelopes continue to arrive by messenger, and my lunchtime appointment calendar is full of dates at which I will be wooed, for at least the next three weeks.

. . . Human ambition is a strange and wonderful phenomenon. Since you could obviously do better at Vegas or Atlantic City, what keeps them coming?

A couple of days after our weekly meeting, while Sid Budlong was back in Europe, trying to get another set of ducks in a row so that our batting average could move up from .333, I had a long and pleasant lunch with Ozzie Kaufman downstairs in L'Etoile, the elegant imitation nouvelle-cuisine restaurant he fancies down on Melrose.

Oz is a very special character in my life. He was one of my few contacts in town when I first came out here to change my life-style and seek my fortune A.D. (After the Divorce). He steered me into my first job, which was reading scripts for a production company owned by one of his clients. I've had three other jobs since then as I moved onward and upward, but we've stayed in close touch.

. . . Okay, so it isn't merely friendship. Oz is a very valuable person to know in this frenetic jungle town. He's a vestige of the old days; he's an agent. But not just an agent; he's legendary. He represents some of the best talent in town; he's their father figure, and they all swear by him. He's certainly eligible for Social Security, but he's trim and well-dressed in his Carroll & Co. suits. He still puts in gruelling eleven-hour days as if he were every bit as young as the killer sharks who swim in the same waters.

Oz continues to operate a tiny "boutique" of clients all his own, up at that mammoth conglomerate talent agency, OCM, and he's been around this so-called business ever since the dim days of the past, when making movies was a private poker game, run year round by seven major studios. In the years since then, the business has proliferated into an urban sprawl, populated by a horde of tax lawyers, business managers, and Harvard Business School graduates who represent the owners, corporations back East. Most of them under forty.

"Your hair is grey and you don't use Grecian Formula 9. You've never had a face lift. You never hide your age. How do you survive?" I once asked him.

"Oh, I'm the Jewish Satchel Paige," he confessed. "I never look back. If I did, I might find the stiletto in my back, and that could be depressing."

We sat there at the restaurant and exchanged horror stories. For every one I had, Ozzie had a choice one of his own.

". . . Of course it's frustrating," he said, picking away at his poached salmon. "You can always quit—and go into real estate."

"No thanks," I said. ". . . and I'm too old to become a call girl . . ."

"You're never too old!" said Ozzie. "Maybe *me*—but not you."

". . . Thanks, dear," I said. "You're good for my ego."

He nodded. "So tell me, when are you going to become a producer?"

"Me?" I asked. "I should turn into one of those pathetic creatures who charges into my office, dragging a script behind him, whispering 'Take me, take me.'? Never."

"You'd be good at it," said Ozzie. "Don't tell me you haven't considered putting together your own package."

Perceptive bastard. Of course I have, and he knows it.

"How about you?" I demanded. . . . Why had *he* never succumbed to that burning desire which impels the lowliest agent-trainee at the William Morris Agency . . . to be the man who calls the shots, rather than merely selling them. ". . . All these years you've never wanted to be a power broker? A Ray Stark— a Freddy Fields—"

". . . Don't forget Lew Wasserman," said Ozzie. "Oh sure, I've thought about it. But a long time ago I learned the agent's trade secret—ten per cent of other peoples' Somethings is always worth more than a hundred percent of your own Nothing. But for *you*—it's wide open out here. These are the Years of the Female. So when are you going to do something about it?"

"I *am* doing something," I said.

"Not as much as you could," he said. "A shrewd mind in a very sound body—"

". . . Why, Ozzie—at *lunch?*"

"—Let an old man dream, he grinned . . . It's amazing how things have changed here," he said. "When I first got out here, this was strictly a male ballpark. Oh sure, women were stars—"

"Sexual objects," I said.

"The greatest," he said. "Maybe once in a while a talented lady could get to be a screenwriter—"

"—Usually on soap opera weepers," I said.

"Exactly," he said. "But direct, or produce a picture? Forget it. You could count them on the fingers of one hand. Women's

Lib? That was when they'd dress Roz Russell up in a tailored suit, and she would charge into the board of directors meeting—and say things like 'Gentlemen—I'm your new boss—any objections?' But after six o'clock at night, off came her tailored suit, and she went into her Adrian dress . . . a highly paid peon.''

"Some of them must have fought back," I said. "What about them?"

"Oh, they made some points," he said. "You know enough about the sexual wars to know how successfully *The Taming of the Shrew* plot works. *But,* in the tenth reel, the pushy broad always gets slapped down and into the sack. That's how it was here. Always."

"Ozzie, we do not use the term 'pushy broad' any longer," I reminded him.

"I stand corrected," he said. "Pushy person." He patted my arm. "I repeat—in my opinion, it's time for you to become a boss."

. . . Something was ticking over in my mind, triggered by his analysis of the war between the sexes, show biz style . . . The image of that young girl, Jody Cassel, grinning, mugging, thrusting herself at the audience, years back, in a desperate wooing of their mass love, defying them not to adore her . . . And what had become of her?

"Ozzie," I asked, "did you ever hear of a lady comedienne—"

"—*comic-person,*" he corrected me.

"—named Jody Cassel?"

He blinked. Sipped his iced coffee; slowly shook his head.

". . . From thirty years ago," I said. I told him about the half-hour kinescope I'd seen. "She'd be about fifty now—seemed to have a lot of talent—"

Ozzie grimaced. "They *all* have talent—at the beginning. It's how they handle it makes the difference between long-term or short," he said. "Jody Cassel? . . . Wait a minute—I think she came out here and made a couple of comedies—or was it musicals? And I think she used to play Vegas . . ."

"You're not doing bad for an old-timer," I said. "Is she still around?"

"Why do you want to know?" he asked, ever the agent. "Thinking of using her in a picture? *That* would be strictly 'Love-Boat' time . . ."

I shook my head. "Then what is it?" he asked, probing away. "A show biz story? Forget it. They're out. These whiz kids who run the studios never heard of your lady—or anybody else since 1976. They think the Beatles are prehistoric!"

He gracefully permitted me to pick up the check and sign— which shows how well Ozzie has adjusted to the new mores.

". . . This week, we're making movies strictly for the eleven- and twelve-year old market," he sighed, as we walked out to the Valet Parking attendant. He handed the parking ticket to the youth on duty.

". . . and next week?" I asked.

"Check with me Friday and I'll have the latest trend," promised Ozzie. "Now—think about the Roz Russell bit, honey— you'd be a good producer . . . I'm very serious."

"You're good for my ego," I told him, ". . . but I always get nervous when an agent tells me he's very serious."

"See?" grinned Ozzie. "You're learning—pushy-person."

"How' this? I'll turn producer when you tell me you'll be my partner."

Ozzie climbed into his waiting Jaguar—not a sleek new one, but that well-cared for early-'60s saloon, which is truly his style. "Never," he said. "My wife wouldn't tolerate it. She'd feel threatened."

Later that day, I sent my secretary out to pick up some sort of a history of TV. I wanted to find out exactly where Jody Cassel fitted, in that long-gone scene that raced past our eyes so fast.

She came back with a pictorial history, something for fans to browse over as they wandered down Memory Lane, its pages crammed with a parade of forgotten stars.

Turning the pages was an increasingly depressing experience.

Talk shows hosts. Elegant hostesses. Commentators, movie has-beens taking a final shot at the brass ring, ''kiddy-lures,'' Uncle This or Aunt That—soap-opera stars. Endless half-hour idiot sit-coms which had sputtered into life, flickered briefly, and van-ished. Musical shows, large and small—variety hours and half-hours—proudly presented dramas, half-hour detective sagas . . .

. . . All of it born of enthusiasm, launched in pain . . . now in limbo.

What a waste. For thirty-five odd years now, that glass-eyed monster in the corner of the living room—that miracle presented us by Dr. Lee De Forest, in hopes that he would improve man-kind's condition—all it had spawned was this ragtag procession of cops, doctors and nurses, plainclothesmen and Western sher-iffs, mingled with an endless supply of daffy mothers, mischie-vous brats, and idiot fathers—and the boss—always coming home for dinner unexpectedly—(with hilarious consequences).

True, here and there were the rare, worthy moments of achievement, scattered about like prizes in a vast, endless pile of Cracker Jack. But who remembers?

I finally found Jody Cassel, under the category of COMIC LADIES. It seemed her Dumont half-hour had flourished for sev-eral months—in the 1950s that was success!—and the following season she'd been starred in her own show on a major network. A sitcom, called *"Dew Drop Inn"*—in which she played the part of a madcap New York stenographer who'd inherited part own-ership of a diner up in Cape Cod—(with hilarious consequences).

There were photos of Jody, in outlandish get-ups—in one she leered happily at us through a face covered with flour as she emerged from some sort of an oven. In another, suspended above a fishing-dock, holding on for dear life to a rope. A full season on that show? In an era when comedies came and went by the week, not bad. In fact, a definite hit. The following year, she was successful enough to have a full hour, of which she was the hostess. That, too, had been an audience-pleaser.

". . . In years following, Jody went to Hollywood," said the text. "She appeared in several films. She did guest appearances on L.A.-based shows, and appeared in Las Vegas. In 1961, she was signed for a new comedy series, to star herself, but after a succession of unfortunate misfires, the show floundered and was not renewed."

That would bring us to . . . what? The author had no further information. Had Jody retired?

I had my secretary call AFTRA, to check on her membership status. *"Inactive,"* came back the word. Was there any address? No, nothing since 1964.

Strange. Stars don't usually vanish so abruptly, without some reason . . . especially when they've managed to carve out a niche for themselves.

What sort of reason had pushed Jody Cassel over the edge?

I had to put Jody Cassel on hold for a while. Sid Budlong reappeared from a trip to London, bringing with him another potential GO, this time with a British conglomerate, and for the next few days, there was a considerable amount of muted frenzy at Interfico.

Then, unexpectedly, I picked up another vague but tantalizing clue about the lady, from, of all people, my part-time bed partner, Freddy Snyder. He was back from his latest commercial "shoot" in the East and was over for dinner and a little therapeutic dalliance on a Friday night.

Freddy is a contemporary, and we have a carefully uncomplicated relationship. We've kept it that way by mutual agreement. He's separated from his wife, and can't afford any other life style until his kids have grown up. She lives up in Northern California, painting and teaching, with custody of the children. Between their visits, he can get terribly lonely down here. I empathize. I know about lonely.

He has to go on earning a good living doing commercials and hoping that some day he'll get a shot at a feature, or a two-hour TV film. He's damned good at what he does, but then, so are plenty of other directors around this town, with whom he's in competition. Meanwhile, he can't afford to take a gamble on some independent venture; he needs the cash flow, so he continues doing half-minute productions . . . and hoping.

Sleeping with Freddy isn't quite the mechanical process it sounds. He's a thoughtful, accomplished lover, and since I'm not the world's greatest cook, I assume he must enjoy our nights together . . . as much as I do.

He was eating late breakfast on my terrace and leafing through the pages of that fat TV-history book I'd brought home from the office. I brought out more coffee; the book was open at the pages devoted to Jody Cassel, paper-clipped for reference. He was staring at her. ". . . Hey, I remember this one, I think," he said. "What's with her?"

"I'm not sure," I said. "How did you know her?"

". . . Never in the Biblical sense, thank God," he said. "She was a pistol, this one—"

"Tell me!" I urged.

". . . So long ago," said Freddy, stroking his greyish beard. "Let me think. It was some kind of a compaign from way back when. I think it was when I was still in New York—an assistant. This was a series of spots we did for some big TV special—"

"What year?" I prodded.

"Oh, Eileen, what the hell," he complained. "It was so long ago. Who can remember? They're all a blur. I know it was a big sponsor—General Motors . . . or was it General Electric? But Jody Cassel, *her* I remember. A total pain in the ass."

"She must have made a real impression on you—if you can remember that much."

"Oh yes," he said. "See, most of the time when you get a performer in to do commercial spots, they're so damned greedy to get that big fee and those residuals, they're delighted to take the money and run for the bank. Not this character. She had some chip on her shoulder, believe me—"

"Hostile because she was making commercials—and it was

a comedown, maybe?'' I speculated.

"Sure, that was part of it, I guess," said Freddy. "She was the kind of pushy, ballsy performer who knows everything. What angle the camera should use, how we should focus the lights on her, oh, she was driving everybody crazy that day."

He lit his pipe and exuded a cloud of fragrant smoke. "You know, she had a thing with a prop—yeah—*now* I remember—she had to pour something out of a crystal pitcher, and we kept doing it over and over again—and in the middle of a take, it slipped—she spilled everything on herself. Then she started cursing, and stamping her foot, she went into a rage—a real temper tantrum—just like a spoiled kid, you know? Well, we couldn't help it—she'd given us so much trouble all day—we started laughing." He grinned. "Amazing—the minute we did that, *she* started doing a bit—like Fanny Brice doing Baby Snooks, you know? She went on for about five minutes, with her shtick—and she had us all in stitches."

"A funny lady . . ." I murmured.

Freddy stared off at the skyline below us and sipped his coffee. "Yeah, but you know, she was sad. I mean—here was this dame who'd been some sort of a name, a star, just a few years back, and now she was fighting for every little piece of space . . . Jesus, there was so much *desperation* in her."

"You're pretty ambivalent about her," I said.

"That's because middle-age is making me more tolerant," he said.

The sun had emerged, and down below, there was the sound of *plop-plop, plop-plop,* as the morning tennis games began.

". . . Tell me, was she sexy?" I asked.

"Maybe to somebody else—not to me," he said, smiling. "Listen, I don't mind assertive women—in fact, I'm very attracted to them." He ran his hand over me. ". . . But with somebody like Jody Cassel, if you went to bed with her, she'd either be directing the action, or turning it into a comedy bit—or demanding a retake."

His hand continued moving.

". . . I wonder what happened to her," I said.

Freddy put down his pipe, and began to undo the buttons of my blouse. ". . . Who cares?" he asked, and kissed me.

And for the moment, I dropped the subject of her past to concentrate on my present.

*   *   *   *

In the upper echelons out here, nobody reads. Who has the time? Lawyers read contracts, and you can hire people to read books and scripts. They'll do the summations, the synopses— boil everything down to a couple of pages, or even one, with an attached recommendation—*No* or *Possible*.

From then on, every day, we handle the properties with *Possible* attached to them. But from then on, they have to be digested to a point where they could be Western Union telegrams. How else, when you're confronted with a harried exective, a deal-maker, who says "Okay, let me have it in High Concept."

So, you fire away with one-sentence digests. "Retired-CIA-man-prevents-Third-World-holocaust." Or "Young-girl-raped-by-psycho-hunts-for-rapist-discovers-he's-a-neighbor," or "Pro-foot-ball-player-turned-thief-to-support-drug-habit-meets-therapist-who-straightens-him-out," And then we wait to see how that grabs him, or her. Sale—or no-sale—possible, or forget it?

It's that bald. Because, within moments, you get back equally instant reactions. "Tired." "It doesn't do anything to me." "Too heavy." "Old-fashioned." . . . or this month's latest catch-phrase . . . *"Too soft."*

. . . Can somebody please define "hard" for me?

Upon these foundations, believe it or not, cursory though they are, eventually there emerges an *E.T.*

. . . Also a *Heaven's Gate*.

Ah well, nobody ever said this was an easy business. You want something rational, go sell shoes.

So, assuming I found any plot-line, then how would I sell Jody Cassel? *High Concept it, Eileen.*

"Young-girl-with-talent-for-comedy-breaks-through-male-dominated-showbiz-succeeds-but-then-fails . . . *why?*"
How would that grab them? Too grim, maybe? I didn't need Sid Budlong to remind me people do not pay $5 at the box office, or $6 to rent a videocassette, to sit through a failure-saga. Also, Eileen-baby, too old. How do we hook the kids, who are the primary audience? Go back to when Jody was fourteen, and document her earliest struggle, à la Deanna Durbin, or Judy Garland . . .
No, that's been done.
I didn't have a hook. Not for today's market.
So Jody Cassel went back on *Hold,* while I minded the store at Interfico, preparing my daily quota of Western Union messages.

Until I ran into Ozzie again, a couple of weeks later, this time at one of those lavish, mindless cocktail party receptions in a Beverly Hills office-suite.
It was the usual publicity-do, this one to announce a deal for a big new cable TV project, based on a historical novel that had just been sold for a TV series, some big promotable blockbuster about three generations of a family who'd pioneered the Northwest. Since the agent for the book had me on his Active list, there I was, mingling with the mob of greats and near-greats, the movable feasters who're always around, all of them making kissy-face, sipping white wine or Perrier, gobbling the canapes (Washington State smoked salmon—delicious) while looking over each other's shoulder to spot the nearest press photographer, also checking to see if George Christy of the *Reporter,* or the man from *Daily Variety* had arrived, to take down their names for tomorrow's story in the trades.
Ozzie surfaced, embraced me, and steered me to a quiet corner, where we took advantage of some chic Italian office chairs to sit and watch the passing parade mill by. "So," he said, "how's my prospective producer doing? Come up with a good salable project yet?"

I had to confess I hadn't.

"So—take the traditional route," he said. "Find a disease—they're always bankable."

"They're all taken," I told him.

"Okay, then, try a social problem. I had a writer in this morning pitching a script at me—a-lady-who-left-her-husband-to-take-a-job-as-fire-watcher-in-a-Montana-tower."

". . . What's her social problem?" I asked.

"She's lonely," he said.

"It doesn't grab me," I said. "Not unless she maybe falls in love with a bear."

"Now *that's* for Disney," he said. "Thanks. Did you give up on that old TV star you were asking about?"

"Jody Cassel?"

"I may forget names, but I don't forget subjects," he said. "I've been thinking—maybe there *is* something in early live TV—it's a pretty interesting background—if you find the handle. Ever hear of Teresa Contini?"

No, the name meant nothing to me.

"You and she ought to talk," he suggested. "She's an old TV hand, goes back to the earliest days. Very tough lady—but talented. Been out here as an executive, but she's got the itch to produce again, so she's going back to New York, on a big fat daytime soap. Knows where all the bodies are buried, so, let me see if I can set up a date for the two of you—"

"You mean, she's looking for an associate?"

"You looking for another job?" Ozzie asked.

"Why—should I be?" I replied, my radar suddenly turned on. Did Ozzie know something about Interfico I hadn't heard yet?

He shook his head. "I only mean—you should pick her brain . . . she might be able to help you about that Jody dame, who knows?"

". . . Why not? A very constructive suggestion," I told him.

"Don't be so surprised," said Ozzie, patting me fondly. "What are agents for? Now, enough of this altruism. I have to go try and scare up some commerce . . ."

That night I looked up Teresa Contini in my illustrated TV history. Yes, indeed, she was truly an old hand. She'd started back in the early days of "live," and eventually progressed to producer on one-hour dramas. Then she'd worked steadily with Dick Hatch. ". . . the innovative director-producer who'd been responsible for developing many writing talents, in the years when the finest TV drama was seen on the legendary Royal Playhouse."

. . . But in all of Teresa Contini's credits, I could find no mention of Jody Cassel.

So what could Teresa Contini, a producer of drama, tell me about a lady comic? Obviously, Ozzie's suggestion was worthy, but a time-waster; when his secretary called the next day to give me Teresa Contini's home number, I wrote it down, and then nearly tossed it away.

Which would have been a big mistake.

The Contini house was a couple of blocks below Sunset, on a quiet street once zoned for single-family houses, but now invaded by massive, outsized apartment houses. Her address was that of one of the last survivors, a Moorish-style two-story hacienda, on whose front lawn the real estate agent's sign was now covered over with SOLD.

She met me at the door, wearing a Levi skirt and sweater, a short lady with cropped black hair, streaked with grey. Not fat, but sturdy. Age? Hard to tell, but if she had credits going back to the '50s, then she had to be well along toward her own Golden Years . . .

"Hi, Eileen Tighe," she said. "Come on in—and excuse the mess. Godamn movers will be here tomorrow, and we're behind schedule." She looked California, but her voice still had that New York accent.

She led me into a living room that was partially dismantled. Some furniture was already crated, there were movers' cartons piled in the corners, open boxes filled with books, manuscripts, framed photographs; it was as if we were in a warehouse. "I'm a pack rat," she said. "Can't throw anything away. Why do I have to drag all this crap back to New York, can you tell me? Want coffee—maybe a beer? The booze is all packed—"

No, I wasn't thirsty. "Find yourself a place to park," she said, indicating the one or two club chairs that were still unpacked. I sat down; she lit a cigarette and joined me. "Let's get down to cases," she said. "Ozzie said you're looking to do a picture on early TV?"

"Ozzie is a little ahead of himself," I said. "I'm actually—*researching*—"

"Well, I made some oral history about the early days," she said. "Kid came out from U.S.C., tape recorded me—I don't really enjoy all that reminiscing, you know? Makes me feel so damned old." She grimaced. "You could go down there and listen to Teresa do her dog-and-pony act about how I contributed mosaics to the grand design which has become such a major medium—"

From upstairs, there came a female voice, calling. "Ter-*ree?*"

"What?" she called back.

"The summer clothes?"

"*Pack* 'em!" yelled Teresa Contini.

"But it's December," complained the voice.

"They have four whole seasons back there!" reminded Teresa.

". . . So should I pack them separately?"

"Would that make you feel more secure?" called Teresa.

". . . You're always so sarcastic . . ." replied the upstairs voice. "I asked a simple question . . ."

Teresa smiled briefly at me. ". . . Good help is hard to find these days," she said. "Let's get the show on the road. What do you want to know?"

". . . I've done some checking on your career," I told her. "You have very solid credits."

"Of course," she said. "Ancient history. All of them—and ninety cents should get you on the subway. Where should we start?"

I took a deep breath. ". . . How about with Jody Cassel?"

She stared at me. Blinked. "I thought you wanted to talk about me," she said. "How did *she* get into this?"

"You knew her?"

"If you can call it that," she said, without enthusiasm. "Why're you asking?"

"I'm interested in her," I said.

"You look like a sensible lady," she said. "Now I'm not so sure."

"Did you know her well?" I persisted.

"As well as I needed to," she said. "Which was plenty."

Silence descended on the room.

I tried again. "Is she still around?"

Teresa Contini lit a cigarette. "I don't know," she said, "and I really don't care. Why should *you?*"

It wasn't going well. I explained about the kinescope I'd seen, and the few fragmentary bits and pieces I'd picked up about Jody. She sat there, stony-faced. ". . . I gather she wasn't one of your favorite people," I said.

"Perceptive, aren't you?" said Teresa.

"What sort of a girl was she?"

"Jody? Never a girl," said Teresa. "Oh sure, she came equipped with a female body, but inside, she was strictly a Sherman tank. She was also a pain in the ass, and a killer, and why you expect me to spend even ten minutes discussing her frankly pisses me, especially on a day when I'm up to my ass packing—"

I'd obviously opened up a large can of explosive peas.

". . . But after all," I suggested, "she was a big star for a while there, so she did have talent—"

"Oh, forget it!" she replied. "*Star.* It's such a nothing word. Soem idiot runs a hot quiz show—he's a *star.* Four baby-faces write a dumb song—*yeh-yeh-yeh*—the idiots love it—all of a sudden, they're *stars!* Spare me that word."

"But I've seen the way she held an audience," I protested.

"Okay—for a while there she was hot. Big deal," she said. "In those days, all sorts of crazies could catch on. It was such a wild new business—we were doing shows every week, we picked up talent from everywhere, there were lots of instant stars. Ah, *stars*—there's that damn word again—'' Angrily, she stubbed out her cigarette. "Well, some of them lasted, but most of them didn't. The smart ones saved their money. Today, nobody gives a shit about those so-called pioneers. Including producers,'' she added, balefully. She got up from her chair. "Listen, I don't want to sound abrupt, but please, no rambling down Memory Lane. I've got to get all this junk here ready to go—''

Okay, so I'd struck a nerve. This interview, if you could call it that, wasn't going well, in fact it was almost gone, but what she'd said about Jody was buzzing around in my head. . . . A female body, but *inside, strictly a Sherman tank.* Wasn't that sort of ambition always interesting to an audience? Even though something Jody Cassel had done to—or was it with?—Teresa Contini, years back, had induced such Pavlovian hostility. And it had certainly lasted. I took one last shot. ". . . I won't take up your time,'' I told her, "but before I go, could you perhaps give me some clue as to why Jody didn't last? I mean—it must have been so tough for her, a female comic—we don't have too many of those around, even now, maybe one—Joan Rivers, but—''

"Sure, it's tough,'' conceded Teresa. "When was it easy? You think it's been an Easter-egg roll for *me?* I've done my share of arm wrestling, and what about you? But I don't think either of us is *that* driven—''

"What was hers?'' I asked.

She lit another cigarette. "Forget it,'' she told me. "If you're trying to dredge up some romantic image of a little lost girl, buffeted by cruel forces—another Frances Farmer, maybe—she doesn't fit. Try Typhoid Mary instead. Jody was strictly a noisy, pushy kid from the suburbs, who picked up the trick of capitalizing on her own insecurities by getting laughs—usually at her own expense. But once you get to be a comic, you become a monster. People on that kind of ego trip are diseased . . . and they infect everything they run up against, and so what else is new?''

She stared out the window, obviously rerunning images of

the past through her private screen. ". . . When I think of the
nerve of that kid, doing what she did to Buddy Grimes, dumping
on Dick Hatch—"

She shook her head.

Tread carefully, I warned myself.

"Dick Hatch I know about," I murmured. ". . . But who is
Buddy Grimes?"

"You've never heard of him?" That made her even angrier.
". . . Jesus, the man has a wall full of Emmys—he was one of
the first real *playwrights* this business ever developed—" She
sighed. "Ah, screw it. I have to keep reminding myself—nobody
in this town really cares, and probably not in New York, either.
I'm sorry. I can't get used to being an artifact, you know?"

"Ter-*ree*," came the voice from upstairs. *"Guess* what I just
found!"

"Animal, vegetable or mineral?" Teresa called back, as if to
a child. "Do I win some damn prize?

". . . *Wow*," said the voice. "What did *I* say?"

Teresa walked to the front door, opened it. "You hit me on
a bad day," she said. "Us Rover Girls have to finish packing so
we can clear the hell out of Funville."

I followed her obediently to the door, but before I went outside, I took one final shot. "Where could I find Buddy Grimes?"

"Persistent, aren't you?" she observed.

I nodded. "Yes. I figure anybody you've hated this long can't
be all dull."

". . . Call the Writers Guild," she said. ". . . and if he
answers your call—which I doubt—tell him Teresa says hello."

"Thanks for your time," I said.

"Don't call us, we'll call you," she said, and closed the door.

*   *   *   *

My brief set-to with Teresa Contini was a tantalizer.

. . . What the hell could Jody Cassel have been, or done—
all those years ago? What was so monstrous, or shameful, to
induce such a powerful hate-reaction?

In a lady who certainly didn't seem to be a shrinking violet.

Covered with scar tissue as she was, from all those years of survival in a rough business, she'd obviously learned to handle herself in the clinches—and yet, drop Jody's name and she came out
of her corner snarling.

I came away from her house thirsting to know more about the
Sherman-tank-masquerading-in-a-female-body. As much as I
could.

Where next?

That night I called Bernie Lorber, and after the usual cozy in-
gossip, I switched us around to that scratchy old kinescope he'd
shown me. Did he possibly have a Source—someone who might
know where there were others, of that same period, anything else
from early TV?

Yes, he did have a Source, and he was sure there were many
more such precious relics hiding in secret places . . . "Don't tell
me you're still carrying on about Jody?" he probed.

I proceeded to lie. "It's not heroine-worship," I said. I needed
to know more about lady comics in general; we had a possible
project developing with a producer-writer, and I was hunting for
background materials. "Could I call your Source and ask him?"

"Never," said Bernie. "My Source is the All-American paranoid. He'll never tell you anything; *I* 'd have to speak to him."

"Ask him if he knows how Jody ended up or where," I said,
casually.."She seems to have dropped off the map completely.
Think she got married?"

". . . What a repulsive image that conjures up," said Bernie.
"Imagine crawling into the sack with that octopus. I'd sooner
ball Ilse Koch."

"See if the Source knows," I wheedled.

"Only for you, honey," he said. "But you really must try to
get over this obsession with *The Fabulous Fifties*. It's unhealthy.
You're in a Now business—nobody in this town gives a shit about
anything that happened as recently as last Thursday."

I went to bed, but I lay awake, thinking over what Bernie had
said. Sure, he was being bitchy, but perhaps he was right.

If I was hooked on Jody, what chord had she plucked within me that vibrated to the lady?

. . . Her sheer guts, perhaps.

The nerve, the chutzpah, to get up there in front of an audience. When I was younger and my folks took me to a matinee, hadn't I been stage-struck by the bright lights, the excitement, the golden glow in which it was all Happening? All of us in the audience, hypnotized . . . but the idea of getting up there and performing? No thanks. Terrifying . . .

Here came Jody, this noisy girl from essentially the same middle-class milieu as mine (probably the class cut-up, the playground performer who did imitations of the teachers, who kept the cafeteria crowd roaring with her antics), going on to do what *I* secretly, desperately wished I could—taking the crowd and making it want her—wrapping them up in a bundle of affirmation, we love you, *we love you!*

Was I jealous? Perhaps.

(*Why?* Hadn't I done as well—broken loose from my own middle-class milieu, made a whole new career for myself, proved I didn't need to be dependent on a husband? Wasn't I pleased I was now an executive, an integral part of this daily creative treadmill?)

Yes, very pleased with myself. I am one of the people with Access. Part of a vast phalanx of over-achievers—(perhaps a bit older than most of them) all of us running around to the appointments in the leased Mercedes, with an assigned parking space in life.

Asserting ourselves . . . *I'm on. Listen. Pay attention.*

The money's fine, so's the ego trip . . . how come we're not totally happy? Because we're still *audience.* We're not—not ever will be—this week's hot new performer (Love him, love her, *found* him, *discovered* her—Always knew he/she could make it!)

Untrue? Explain then, how we all promptly begin rooting for that same new hot whoever to fail, to crash?

Because, dummy, that's not us up there.

Question for Eileen Tighe. As far as Jody Cassel is concerned, what is it you're responding to? Her success—or her eventual failure?

Late Monday, my secretary, a new one named Agnes—they come and go around these Interfico halls like migrating birds—reported that the Writers Guild could not furnish me with any address or phone number for Mr. Buddy Grimes (officially listed as Walter R. Grimes.) He was a member, indeed, he'd been one for many years, a Permanent, but they would be willing only to receive my letter and forward it to that gentleman, and no amount of urgent persuasion would change their procedures.

Nor had it done Agnes any good to argue with the Directors Guild, which would also not give us a phone number for Mr. Richard Hatch. They did, however, provide us with his last known address, a post office box in some New Hampshire town.

Where, according to Directory Information, that gentleman's number was Unlisted.

So the next morning I sat down and dictated letters to both.

Carefully thought out at home the night before, with no reference to a Miss Jody Cassel. . . . No sense waving possible red flags in front of any bull. I'd couched my request in very tactful terms, purposefully vague. ". . . the subject of live television, in its earliest pioneer days, intrigues us as a basis for a possible project, and since you were so integral to the growth of the medium, we are wondering whether you might confer with us at some mutually convenient time. It would be so helpful if you would answer a few questions about the part you played . . . etcetera . . ." I put in my office and home phone numbers and suggested a reversed-charges call.

After the letters went off, I put Agnes to work tracking down any other official sources, collections of old kinescopes which might reveal Jody's work, either here in California, at one of the universities where they keep them, or perhaps in New York, at that Museum of Broadcasting.

During the week, there was a top-level conference on one of our coventures, one so complicated that not one, but two of our firm's lawyers showed up. When the session finally broke up, I buttonholed one of them, an amiable young hotshot named Ted Kelsey, a bearded whiz kid, as he was reassembling all his documents and stuffing them into his I. Santi briefcase.

Might I ask him a couple of technical questions about biographical material, and the laws about invasion of privacy?

"Broad subject," said Ted. "Full of grey areas. New law being made all the time. We'd need full consultation—"

Of course, but could he give me a few ground rules?

"Okay, is this a biography of somebody living—or dead?"

"Good question," I said. "We don't know—yet."

"Ah. Better find out fast," warned Ted. "Next question— are we talking about doing a documentary—PBS sort of thing, or a nonfiction biography?"

"Not yet decided, but let's assume we're discussing a possible dramatic film bio," I said.

". . . Somebody in the public eye? A politico? Media star, out of the news?"

"Was. In show business. Star," I said. "We're at the research stage."

"Well now, that opens up a big can of worms," said Ted, glancing at his Rolex. "From here on, you'd better step ve-ry carefully . . ."

He started out, and I went along with him.

". . . To begin with, you'd better get signed releases from anybody you talk to for source material," he said. "They protect you and the firm against recourse from whoever talks to you. Any stuff that's of public record? Okay. Now. Access to written memoirs, oral histories, interviews—for that you also need releases. But Big Casino is the party you're doing the script about. He's primary—if you're doing his life for entertainment purposes, and he won't agree to a release, forget it. He can blow the whistle and get lawyers who'll sue you for every dollar you've ever earned."

By now we were on our way down the hall, headed for the elevators. "It's all very tricky," I said. "Especially if I don't know how to reach my subject, whether she's alive, or dead—"

"Or married. Don't forget children," warned Ted. "They could also make you trouble. Or, if they're not of age, their guardian—and don't forget, the subject's estate. Executors can try to protect their rights—it's not like writing a book. A movie is entertainment—"

He must have seen the dismay on my face. "One sure way out," he said. "Stay away from *fact*. Turn it into fiction. Dramatize it—change the names—put on a disclaimer at the beginning—boilerplate—nobody in the movie bears any resemblance to anybody living or dead, ya-ta-ta-ta—then, if any shyster lawyer pops out of the bushes waving a complaint, you've covered your ass, see? Sorry, I've got to go—tennis date—"

The elevator doors were open. As he got in, I said "Thanks—you've been a terrific help—"

"Don't worry," he told me. "It'll show up on the bill—one hour's consultation, at least—"

. . . Change Jody's name? Easy. But her *story*—if she had one—did that change, too?

Fiction, or nonfiction. I needed more facts.

Next day, I found notes on my desk from Agnes. Yes, there were two Jody Cassel kinescopes out at U.C.L.A. She would shortly know exactly what there was of hers in New York.

There was also a brief note from Sid Budlong's secretary. He was back . . . from Paris and In. . . . could I please come to see him after lunch?

When I entered Sid's spacious office, he was seated at his elegant desk, tapping away at his briefcase-size minicomputer. He waved me to a chair. "Be done in a minute," he promised.

Sid travels incessantly. En route somewhere or returning, airborne one day out of every three, he never seems to be bothered by jet lag. No matter how elegant those European cuisines and wine cellars our executive Peter Pan indulges himself in, he also seems to remain trim and fit (damn the perks of youth) . . .

His machine chattered softly, and a page of material emerged from the mini word processor. He scanned it, nodded, set it aside. "Beautiful," he remarked.

"Your notes?" I asked.

"My expense account," he said. "Right up to the minute." He rose and strolled over to me.

"Everything going well?" he asked.

"Fine," I assured him.

"You certain?" he asked.

. . . Why this sudden interest in my well-being?

"Absolutely," I said.

Sid strolled back to his elegant desk, on which reposes his constantly changing display of electronic gadgets he picks up from duty-free ships everywhere. He picked up a small black device with a digital print out, from which protruded a metallic probe. He sat down and positioned the probe against the inside of his elbow-joint. Studied the digital print-out. "Blood pressure normal," he announced, and tucked the device away in a drawer.

"Eileen," he said, "are you happy here at Interfico?"

A warning blip showed up on my radar—a hooter went off in my head. I didn't need a digital print-out to tell me this was no ordinary conference.

"Very," I said. "Why—what's up?"

"You tell me," said Sid. "I need to use your secretary—they tell me she's busy checking out old TV kinescopes. You're writing letters to people whose addresses you can't get, asking questions about the history of TV, then you spend an hour of Ted Kelsey's expensive legal time—which gets charged to Interfico's bill—checking out the laws on invasion of privacy—" He continued to stare at me. "Every week you get a large check from us to do a job. *For* us. What does all this have to do with that job, Eileen?"

This damn office—a high-tension sieve, full of leaks!

. . . Why hadn't I thought of that? *Stupid,* Eileen. Dumb, dumb dumb—

He was waiting for my answer.

When in doubt, punt.

"I wasn't sure I should tell you about it," I said. "Not yet."

He sat there, waiting for me to continue, not playing with his Hong Kong toy now, impassive. I've been around Sid long enough to know that look. It's the same expression his face wears before he turns down a deal.

I pressed on. ". . . I came across the germ of an idea for something I thought might be a viable project," I said. "But I don't like to discuss anything with anybody until I'm sure it's something solid."

So far, I was telling the absolute truth. Was it the best offense?

"For Interfico?" he said. "In-house?"

He'd nailed me.

". . . Why, it would certainly be that," I said. "After all, it's all part of my job, isn't it?"

"I hope so," said Sid, softly. "Now, do you want to clue me on what you're up to?"

No, I didn't. But how could I elude him?

". . . Before I've got something tangible? Really, Sid, you're far too busy for me to waste your valuable time by throwing a half-formed something at you—" I was vamping. And he knew it.

"I turned off the phones," he said. "And I want to know what the hell you're spending Interfico's time on. Before you go any further. Give it to me in one sentence."

. . . You take a man's bread, you dance to his music. Okay, Eileen, go into your dance.

". . . Young girl with talent for comedy breaks through male dominated showbiz," I said. "Succeeds, becomes a star—but then fails, burnt-out rocket. *Why?*"

Sid pressed a button and his chair tilted backward. He stared at the ceiling.

"For whom?" he said, finally.

"Bette Midler." Silence. "Bonnie Franklin." . . . "Sigourney Weaver—Liza Minnelli . . . Gilda Radner?"

The chair came back up and he was facing me now. "All possible," he said. "What age group are we talking about?"

For that one, I knew the answer, by rote. "Under twenty," I told him. "They're all keyed into success—they instantly relate to all their own teen-age idols who've made it—*both* sexes—"

Still no reaction.

"But what's the connection with *now?*" he insisted. "You're prowling around ancient history—years ago, live TV—"

"Sure, but they all grew up with it," I said. "This is the TV generation—so are their parents. TV was their baby sitter—their literature—their pacifier—ever since they were old enough to snap on the set. Today they see the reruns."

"Yeah . . ." said Sid, slowly.

Then he nodded.

"How soon do we have something I can see—on paper?" he demanded.

Damnit—*he liked the idea!*

". . . No definite time frame yet," I said. "A week or two—"

"You have any writer in mind? A director?" he asked.

"Not yet," I said. "Not that far along—"

"Mmmm." Sid got up and stared out through the hermetically sealed windows, master of all the Westwood skyline he could survey. When he finally turned around to me, his face had relaxed. He was no longer the Grand Inquisitor, but calculating, conspiratorial, Executive Sid. ". . . It's a definite Possible," he told me. "But from now on, Eileen, no more Lone Eagle stuff. I want progress reports as you go along, and before you make any commitments, you and I interface. Not in committee—but head to head, *alone*—is that clear?"

". . . I could have brought it up before, but you've been so busy—"

"I am never so busy I can't be reached by *you*," he said, piously. "If we move ahead on this project, you and I stay strictly on parallel tracks."

I got the message. "Parallel tracks" meant (A) I, Sid, am your leader; (B) My project was already a *we;* (C) You can be replaced before I am; and (D) *remember (A) (B) and (C) at all times, Eileen-baby.*

"Absolutely," I said.

He snapped his fingers. "Question. You were quizzing Ted Kelsey—are we talking docudrama here, with real people involved? If so, on whom are we basing this?"

Oh no. I wasn't about to fall into that pothole. Bring up Jody Cassel, when I wasn't even vaguely certain she was the possible star? No way. "Sorry—still very much up in the air about that— I'll have to get back to you," I said.

He nodded. "I am also thinking—this whole thing has got to be kept under wraps. Too many ears. You've already leaked some of it around the office. From now on, *quiet.* When will I get to see some pages?"

Wait a minute—secrecy—and he already had me writing a screen treatment? "Sid," I protested, "it's not that simple. There's a lot of research to do. I'm going to need time, with all the other projects we have coming through—I can't drop everything and concentrate on this—I need help—and you tell me I can't use the office—"

"You're a pro—you know what to do for us," said Sid. "Hire some bright researcher. Put the pieces together. But remember, under wraps. The researcher mustn't know what we have in mind."

Which wouldn't make it too easy for the researcher, would it?

"And use a dummy title," he instructed. "Let's see—what shall we call it?" He stared into space, thinking.

". . . The New York Project?" I suggested.

"Mmm . . . Doesn't do anything for me," he said. "But we'll get a grabber later—"

On his desk, a light flashed, and his secretary's voice announced

". . . On the private line, your Swiss call."

"Good," said Sid. "Give me a minute—then put him on."

He pulled open a desk drawer, flicked a switch. Turned to me. Held his finger to his lips, came over to me. "We're recording," he whispered. "See you later. Parallel tracks, remember?"

I tiptoed out.

We.

. . . Well, it was my own damned fault for not having covered my ass, right?

I'd come into Sid's office not knowing I was teetering on the edge of being dumped, and instead, I was leaving, in charge of a possible top-secret Possible.

So . . . why wasn't I grateful for the reprieve?

Because I knew Sid. When he talked *we*—he wasn't necessarily referring to Interfico. He meant *me*. If the New York Project blossomed, who could tell? He might decide to take it and run with it on his own—and where would that leave Eileen Tighe?

. . . dangling in the breeze on unemployment insurance, that's where.

Cynical? Paranoid? Damn right.

You work in this town surrounded by Sid Budlongs long enough, you'd better begin to think in those terms.

Or else.

On my way back to my office, I cheered myself up with one thought. I had one hole card left. *He didn't know about Jody Cassel.* Wherever she was. Yet.

I planned to keep it that way.

*   *   *   *

I interviewed half a dozen researchers before I found one who wasn't young, bright, and supporting himself or herself while writing screenplays part time. Finally I found Tess Davidson, who was young, bright, but working part time on a biography of an obscure medieval composer of motets. Perfect for me; no chance of her running off with the idea for which she would be researching.

Sid wanted secrecy? I gave him secrecy.

When I gave Tess her orders, the C.I.A. would have been proud of me. I was casual and vague—I wanted background material on live TV production in its early New York days, very general stuff, an overview.

Oh, and by the way, there were a few specific people I was interested in knowing more about . . . typical of various aspects of talent. A writer by the name of Grimes, Buddy Grimes. A producer-director named Richard Hatch, and there was a performer or two in which I was interested, typical of the period, female comediennes. What could she dig up on ladies such as Joan Davis or Jody Cassel?

She went off to work, and I went out to U.C.L.A. to look at those two episodes of "Meet Me At Jody's." They set up a screening for me; I was ushered into a small cubicle with a seventeen-inch monitor hooked up to a videotape machine, and a bearded young student-assistant named Walter set up the videotape they'd made of those precious old kinescopes.

Click. We went back in time thirty years as the first of the episodes unwound. Bright comedy music, titles, commercial, and then Jody, in a diner setting, opening with a comedy song, something to do with spring cleaning, in which she got to do all sorts of funny *shtick* with mops, brooms, and other props.

Then we were off into a batch of country-type gags between Jody, the transplanted city girl, fish-out-of-water, and the local types, her supporting cast, who popped in and out of the diner. Gags about outdoor plumbing with Rafe, the town plumber, gags with the town drunk who kept spilling his black coffee on people, a scene with a stuffy old-maid New England type, very prim, who obviously resented Jody's presence here in her home town. A potential romance between Jody herself and the local cop (it was a one-man force) who'd been warned by the nasty old maid that Jody's place was violating health ordinances—all fairly traditional stuff, typical sit-com humor, one-liners, jokes that got big laughs, other that lay there and died. The only difference between the thirty-year-old show and tonight's sit-coms was that the laughs were authentic. Nobody had yet invented the laughtrack.

If a laugh-line didn't score, Jody would leer at the audience and yell "Wowoweeweewoh!" her catch phrase, and that generally saved her from dead air. It was a private joke between her and the audience, and they loved her for it.

The episode was constructed to build to a physical comedy hunk. Because the baker hadn't delivered the morning supply of bread, Jody had to get up at 5 A.M. to bake it herself, using an old cookbook from which a page was missing. That meant she misread the instructions—dumped in too much yeast, and shortly found herself wrestling with a huge blob of rising dough, which took on a life of itself and resisted her pummeling. Soon it was wrestling *her*. It became a wild piece of pantomime, and the audience began to roar. Even I found myself laughing at her wild antics. Behind me, Walter, the student-assistant, giggled. "Funny!" he commented, as she finally managed to push the stubborn mass of dough into the oven—slamming the door, then collapsing on the floor, covered like a ghost-face with white flour. Commercial break, and then the final payoff, as Jody, triumphant, opened the oven, lugged out a huge six-foot long loaf of bread to her customers, and began to slice pieces of it off with a hacksaw!

As the closing credits rolled, over Jody's triumphant leer, there came the credits. "Written by," followed by no fewer than five names, and then, on a separate line—"Special Material by Buddy Grimes."

So that was the connection Teresa Contini had mentioned. *He'd written for her.* What an unlikely combination!

. . . Might he have been the one responsible for the knock-down, drag-out scene with the six-foot loaf of bread?

Why not? All important authors have to begin somewhere, don't they?

The second episode I looked at was even more frenetic. Far less plot, much more physical comedy. Obviously the producer had decided that Jody, successful at the rowdy bits, should concentrate on pie-in-the-face stuff, so the half-hour was jampacked with business. Jody, about to go out for the evening, wrestling with a balky coffee urn, which exploded, spewing a rain of coffee grounds over her and her customers. A visit from a travelling salesman peddling frozen foods, which culminated in a mock softball game in which his wares were tossed all over the set, followed by the arrival of a local farmer with a crate of fresh chickens (yep, the freshest in the state). For a finish, we were treated to a scene in which Jody attempted to sing a ballad, "Skylark," while the live chickens, somehow released from their cages, flew all over the set!

Underrehearsed, with miscues, lost lines, and obvious ad-libs from the cast, it was a shambles, but somehow she managed to make it all work, and again her audience loved it. When we reached the end of the half-hour, there were screams of delight as she chased the chickens here and there, and then tossed them out to her fans, crying "Wowoweeweewoh!" with each fluttering bird.

The credits rolled, the list of writers responsible was even longer, but this time, I caught a tantalizing clue. No more of Buddy Grimes and his "special material." He'd departed. And now "Meet Me At Jody's" had acquired a new director. *Dick Hatch?* The same one who would go on to become the eminent producer-director, the innovator of TV's Golden Age of Drama?

". . . That is one funny lady," said Walter, as he rewound the videotape. "Whatever happened to her?"

I shrugged. Perhaps Tess Davidson would come up that answer.

"Haven't a clue," I told him, which—damnit—was certainly the truth.

"Mind me asking why you were looking at these?" he inquired.
"Yes, I do," I told him.

Which did not stop him. Before I could get out of the cubicle, Walter had informed me *he* was writing a screenplay in his spare time, and since I was an executive at Interfico, was there any possibility I could take a look at it?

No. But his was a good question.

I'd had another look at Jody's public face. She was indeed a clown, a rowdy comic, a potential Lucille Ball, and I could go on checking out the artifacts of her talent which remained, whatever other scratchy kines The Source might dig up, but that was all Outer Jody.

I'd already checked through FILMS ON TV, and her Hollywood work hadn't been all that spectacular. In 1960, she'd been starred with a couple of minor names in *Hold The Phone* ("An amusing musical romp about a long-distance telephone operator's romantic involvement with her Manhattan boyfriend and a wealthy Texas rancher, in which TV star Jody Cassel makes her film debut. Mild."), and in the following year, *Money In The Bank* ("Wild and often frantic farce in which Jody Cassel as a prim Mid-Western accountant, gets mixed up with a crew of comics who involve her in a financial swindle. Starts out promisingly enough but fizzles out badly towards the end. Fair.").

Then there would also be her filmed show, the one she'd come out here to do, which hadn't lasted. But how much would I learn from looking at all of these exhibits? What I needed to find out was what smoldered *inside* the lady!

For I knew my market. Today's audiences don't want to know about Rebecca of Sunnybrook Farm—they're hooked on supermarket check-out literature. Oh sure, the fans have always wanted to know which of their stars is doing it with whom, but this is the age of disaster. We're conditioned to a steady diet of Somebody's Illegitimate Child, So-and-So's Deadly Struggle With (Fill In The Addiction), The Night She (He) Fought Off (Fill in the Assailant), and/or the Continuing Tragedy of Joan/Rita/Princess Grace/Dear Di.

. . . Evil fascinates. Evil sells. Whatever I brought back to Sid Budlong had better be a shocker, something a writer could get his teeth into. When Sid's interest had flickered, up in the office, it was certainly not at the prospect of a 1940s Mickey-and-Judy musical. Young-girl-makes-it-in-show-biz-succeeds-and-then-fails . . . it wasn't enough.

So far, too easy. Too *soft*.

Where was the hook? Booze? Dope? Human tragedy of what sort?

If Jody, driven, talented, had made it to the top of the heap, star of her own show back there, and as rapidly as she'd made it had vanished from sight a scant few years later, there had to be some reason.

Otherwise, I was nowhere. And Sid Budlong would be wanting to know why I was wasting Interfico's time and money to come up with nothing. Sucking wind . . . zilcho? *Pass*.

Sid would certainly not appreciate that.

*   *   *   *

Walter R. (Buddy) Grimes:

After I hung up the phone, I stared out the study window. There was a parade of low grey clouds sneaking in from the Atlantic, a storm by tonight perhaps?

Teresa Contini.

. . . that hoarse voice I hadn't heard for so long, who'd brought up another relic from ancient history. Jody Cassel.

Jody the demented, the driven. Ambitious, whacked-up . . . big-mouthed, she hadn't surfaced in my life since . . . the Ugly Old Days.

Which suited me just fine, thanks.

Ah, ah, now, Mr. Grimes, please, no Pavlovian hostility. Those days are past, such reactions are childish, they demean you. Remember, you are sober, a dignified Elder Person of Status now and you must behave like one. Anyone who spends his time in Paul Stuart tweeds, at meetings with the corporates, puffing on a pipe, and nodding soberly as he passes on projects involving huge sums of the P.R. budget . . . must not permit himself to give way to childish bursts of foot-stamping. Bad for the image, Mr. G.

Minutes before, I'd been at my desk, dictating the rough of my report on some series of Italian Renaissance art films I'd spent the week screening, when the phone had rung, and I'd picked it up. I heard a voice, one which I instantly remembered, even if she hadn't said "Buddy Grimes, please."

"I haven't been Buddy for quite some time now, Teresa." I said. "How did you get my number?"

"Ah, ve haff vays, mein friend," she said.

"You never could do a Nazi, could you?" I said.

"Do it for me, then," she said.

". . . How *are* you, Teresa?" I said, summoning up my Otto Preminger. It wasn't very good, but it would have to do. I'm not as quick with the funny bits as I once was. Among the people with whom I deal, Walter Grimes is light years away from Buddy, the pushy kid who grew up in a Queens flat and was expected to serve as his old man's partner, doing the jokes, learning the snappers instead of *Silas Marner*—("Do you know Fat Burns in Milwaukee?" / "I know fat burns anywhere!" "Did you take a shower?" / "Why—is there one missing?") No, not precisely the sort of material one uses in conference at Bidwell Corp. For the substantial sums they pay me, they do not expect me to provide laughs.

Teresa said she was fine, she was calling from New York, where she lately seemed to have moved, back from the Coast, which she despised, settling in to a new job at one of the networks, a soap opera which she'd be producing.

"Sounds like well-paying work," I said.

"It better be," she said. "This show has been on for nine years, and it needs Creative Restructure. That's Network for Get The Rating Up Or Off You Go, Charley."

"They're lucky to get you," I told her. Which wasn't flattery. Teresa is a pro—shrewd, tough, organized, and obviously, since she is still gainfully employed after all these years, a survivor.

"You're right," she said. "Are you okay, Buddy? I read about you every so often, you've become an Authority . . . you give lectures, and write articles, and all that shit."

"I learned how to fool them," I said.

"Don't knock it, kid," she said. "Keep it up. Ever come into New York? I'd really love to see you."

. . . Suddenly, so did I. Teresa had been much more than just somebody I'd worked with. Why had we lost each other's presence? "Me, too," I told her. "Let's do it."

"I promise not to bore you with reminiscences," she said. "But listen, that's not why I called you. Before I left the Coast, I had a visit from some dame, name of Tighe, Eileen Tighe. You don't know her—she's with one of those film investment houses that once in a while gets a project off the ground, and she'd like to pick your brains—"

"What's left of them," I said. "Usually I get serious kids who are writing Ph.D. theses on the cultural implications of 'Klown Time With Koo-Koo.' Is she one of those?"

"Not at all," said Teresa. "Which is why I called you. This lady seems to have developed a fix on our friend Jody Cassel."

Jody?

". . . Je-*sus*," I said, finally.

"Yeah," said Teresa. "I figured you should be forewarned. I didn't give her your address, or lead her to you—I told her to write you through the Guild—"

"Thoughtful of you," I said. "Thanks."

". . . I wasn't sure you would want to discuss dear Jody," she said.

Neither was I.

"When you get her letter, it won't mention Jody, I'm sure," said Teresa. "No matter what she says, that's what she's after. Why anybody would be digging around, picking up on Jody, beats the hell out of me, you know?"

"Agreed," I said. "Couldn't she go directly to Jody?"

"Doesn't know where she is," said Teresa. "Do you?"

"Up here, it's a bit remote from show business," I said. "If I subscribed to *Variety,* I'd ask them to mail it in a plain paper wrapper."

"I haven't heard about her for years, which isn't to say I was listening for her and her 'Wowoweeweewoh!' " said Teresa.

Lord, how the echoes were coming back.

"She wants to do a film about early TV—or is it Jody she's after?" I asked.

"Jody herself," said Teresa. "Live—direct to you from New York. The Tighe lady is still at the exploratory phase. Eerie, isn't it? After all these years, the ghost walks among us. I know how you feel about Jody, so I wanted to let you know—before her letter—"

Suddenly, I didn't know how I felt about Jody. It had been so long since I'd even thought about her . . . "Listen, do you think she's still around? Jody, I mean . . ."

"Honey," said Teresa, "Monsters like Jody never die. They outlive us all. Listen, I'm serious about seeing you. Please—take my number, and call, before I disappear into the busy, romance-packed thrilling day-to-day struggle of the Dickinsons, a young married yuppy couple, struggling to maintain their happiness amid today's stressful world."

"Absolutely," I promised, and jotted it down as she gave it to me. "But we don't get down to New York too often—"

"Your marriage still holding together?" she asked.

"When last I looked." I said.

"You working on a new script, I hope? God, the crap I get to read—" she moaned. "Where are the good writers?"

"I've got some ideas," I told her. "But they don't come as easily as they used to, and maybe I'm getting too old to face the audiences any more—"

"Oh come on, Buddy," said Teresa, "this is me, Teresa— I've heard all your little excuses for not writing. Sit down at the typewriter, or the word processor or whatever it is you're using, and start writing—"

"Please, no lectures," I said. "You gave me enough—"

"Okay," she said. "Hey, I might have to call on you to be my new head writer—don't say no until I tell you how much money there is in the budget, kiddo. What I can pay you is obscene—"

"I never say no—I say 'I'll think about it,'—you taught me that," I said.

"Not me—that was Dick," said Teresa. "Our fearless leader—the General."

Dick Hatch. Another father figure from an earlier time. ". . . Where the hell is he?"

"Well, he did that big blockbuster on the Bicentennial, remember, and after that, I haven't heard much," said Teresa. "Who knows, maybe he went home to the family plantation down in Kentucky—I'm going to have to try and find him—*all right, I'm coming!*" she called, to somebody in her office. "Another meeting, kiddo," she said. "Got to run—into the Valley of Death rode the brave Teresa—keep in touch, *please?*"

After she'd hung up, I was left alone to stare out the window. I should have been working, but Teresa's call had intruded on the Renaissance. Instead of the soft grey clouds out there on the Atlantic what I was seeing was an image of Jody Cassel. In one of those outrageous outfits she'd certainly picked up in some thrift shop, a Boy Scout cap, perhaps, corduroy knickers, somebody's football jersey. Prancing up and down in a rehearsal hall, oh yes, that would be it, I'd be playing the piano as we rehearsed the material I'd written for her, now she was stopping to yell "Come on, pick up the tempo, Buddy—we can't just leave it lay there—let's get this show on the road!"

The bad old days.

". . . Ah come *on,* Buddy," she'd probably say. "They weren't that bad, now were they?"

What *did* happen to you, Jody?
. . . Was it what you wanted?
God knows, you worked hard enough to get it.

When Cristina came into the study, her daily stint at the hospital over, she found me sitting in the half-darkness of our comfortable living room, in the Governor Winthrop chair—one of her family heirlooms—with a scotch-and-water on the Chippendale side table beside me.

"Cocktail hour's a trifle early today, isn't it?" she remarked, as she took off her coat, shook her blonde hair free of that ridiculous cap they wear, and rummaged through her mail.

I'd gone for a walk on the beach, trudging across the sands, fighting those brisk October winds that brought tears to my eyes and caused my blood to pulse. In the late afternoon, the gulls flew around me, irritated by my presence on their turf, screaming whatever gulls tell each other. . . . Once I'd worked briefly for an old radio comic, what was his name? who claimed what they were saying was *Schmuck—schmuck!*

But not on this beach. These were strictly Wasp gulls.

"I'm entitled," I told her. "I had a strange phone call."

She came over, perched herself on the arm of the chair, kissed me with a gentle brush of her lips, and helped herself to a sip of my drink.

"Crank?" she asked. "Someone looking for me? A heavy breather?"

"He'd have had good taste." I said. She kissed me again. "Why thank you, sir," she said.

Even after a long day of good works, she looked particularly fetching in her prim hospital uniform. Other women look dowdy in such outfits; Cristina somehow gives hers style. It's a knack she has, inbred, comes with the territory, the indefinable self-confidence of a good-looking lady whose family has now resided in this country for five generations. . . . Not like my own, whose very name was acquired from some weary immigration official at Ellis Island, in the early part of this century, who couldn't pronounce Grimnecki, so we became Grimes.

"Actually," I told her, "it was an old friend."

When I finished explaining about Teresa Contini, and the lady in California who was searching for information about Jody Cassel . . . and Dick Hatch, Cristina nodded. "You've never told me much about any of these people," she said.

"They were in another life," I said. I finished my drink, got up to mix another, and one for her.

"Are you planning to meet with this . . . California person?"

she asked. ". . . Light on the scotch please."

"Hadn't thought about it," I told her.

Which wasn't completely the truth. All that time I'd spent pacing down the beach, I'd been pondering this sudden intrusion into my Later Years. Asking myself—did I wish to go backward in time, twenty, thirty years ago, and begin digging up all those buried unpleasantries? What the hell would be served by excavating them?

". . . Well," said Cristina, "It does sound remote to me, I mean, it's difficult for me to relate to your history, so if you don't mind, I'm going up and have a little lie-down, take a long hot bath, and then we've got to dress because we're due at the Dudleys at seven-thirty, and you know how precise she is about guests being on time . . . I mean, she's positively rigid."

"Oh yes, good old Florence the Implacable," I said.

Cristina came over to me, eying my second highball. . . . But we mustn't irritate her," she said. "After all, Roger is very much your mentor at Bidwell, isn't it?"

"I promise I'll behave, teacher," I said, and put my arm around her, pulled her close to my chair, ran my hand beneath her uniform skirt, then up to encounter the warmth of her smooth thigh, ventured to the pleasantries above . . .

"Really," said Cristina, in a small voice. But she did not move away.

". . . We can take that little lie-down together," I suggested, resting my face against her waist.

". . . You get physical at the oddest times," said Cristina.

"Amazing, for an old man, isn't it?" I said, my hand continuing to explore.

". . . We really . . . haven't time," she protested, glancing at her watch.

". . . When that happens, I'll be dead," I said, and kissed her.

Her tongue found mine, and she began to move gently against me.

". . . Not that I'm complaining," she whispered, ". . . but

are you horny for *me* . . . Or is it this old girl friend of yours
who got you so excited? Teresa whatever?''

Sharp lady, my wife.

Close, but no cigar. It was never Teresa.

After we had our very pleasant matinee, we still had time for
a little lie-down. Then we dressed, and went over to the Dudleys,
arriving a safe minute or so after 7:30.

Dinner was served precisely at 8, as is usual at the Dudleys,
and the food was dull but good, as usual, and the conversation?
Strictly as usual. Gold. Local real estate values. The Market. The
Dudleys' imminent winter trip to Egypt, with that same Harvard
alumni group they join each year, a ploy that guarantees fond old
pals as company, and saves mingling with any possible strangers.

After dinner, a casual business chat between Roger Dudley
and me as we adjourned to the study for cognac. How was I
coming along with my evaluation of the latest batch of TV projects sumbitted to Bidwell—would my report be available for pre-
sentation at next Tuesday's monthly meeting? Oh yes, absolutely,
I was coming along fine. That satisfied Roger. We adjourned to
the study and I sat and sipped his excellent cognac, and let the
small talk swirl around me.

Discount designer fashions. Tennis. A local marriage which
had just broken up. Somebody's by-pass operation.

Hey there, Buddy-boy, said a small voice in my ear, *take a
look at you tonight.* You have come a long way, buby—light
years since those days when a frantic young kid was scratching
his way around Manhattan, hand in hand with a noisy girl named
Jody Cassel. So now you're *Mr.* Grimes? An *authority?* How
about that! . . . so smug, so pleased, so content, happily married
to that good looking lady over there who's supplied your sunset
years with love, and trust funds, and antique furniture, plus an
entree to this genteel Cape Cod society. Here you sit, surrounded
by a gaggle of solid citizens, not one of whom has the faintest
notion your family name was originally Grimnecki. If your old

man were here, Buddy-boy, you know what he'd say? *Enjoy it, why not? But remember, you're in on a pass.*

As she prepared herself for sleep, Cristina asked ". . . Where *were* you tonight?"

"On duty with you at the Dudleys," I said. "Why?"

"I'm not sure," she murmured. Snapped off the bedside lamp, and slid in beside me. "Ever since this afternoon, you seem to be somewhere else. Certainly not *here* . . ."

So sharp, my wife. This time, she got the cigar.

"Yes, but I'm back now," I promised. Kissed her a fond goodnight and turned over to sleep.

An hour or so later, I was still awake, and still somewhere else, not here in 1984, in this comfortable bedroom, with the soft steady rush of ocean waves muttering outside, in counterpoint to Cristina's contented breathing, beside me in her four-poster heirloom.

I was replaying other times, on some mental video-cassette, half-remembered scenes at first, the scenes running fast-forward (backward?) through my mind, retrieved from the limbo to which they'd been consigned for so many years.

. . . Full head close-up, she is twenty or so, one of the people leaning over me as I play the piano, the old out-of-tune upright at Camp Greenways ("The Adult Resort For Fun-Loving Folks"). I am camp counselor, underpaid man for all summer seasons, musician, entertainer. Hours? I work all day, and put on nightly entertainments whenever there isn't a political talk scheduled (Camp Greenways has a social consciousness, and there are nights when speakers discuss Important Issues of The Day.) Who is she, this anxious, pie-faced girl who's fastened on me, now she's moved in beside me on the bench, as I run through a couple of the jazzy vaudeville songs I picked up from my father, who used to score with them in the days he was a number three act—guaranteed crowd-pleasers—"O'Brien Is Tryin' To Learn To Talk Hawaiian To His Honolulu Lou!"—that's one; "Take Your Girlie To The Movies (If You Can't Make Love At Home,)"—that's another.

This frowsy girl beside me laughs. She's a pest—but it's part of my job to make nice to the guests. Okay, she's a fan, she's stage-struck, she makes me play another, then persists, will I please teach it to her? and when she sings the chorus back to me, she's not bad. She's on key, she has a sense of rhythm, good, now I can go on to somebody else. No, I can't, she's not letting go of me, where did I learn all this stuff? what's my background? Oh, I'm from a show-business family? How *exciting*—now she is really impressed. She's not pretty (might be if somebody took hold of her), she's plumpish, bulging out of her summer outfits. Nobody could call this one sexy, fact is, she's a *schlepper*. Doesn't matter, what's going on here between us certainly isn't lust. (For that there are plenty of availables, Greenways is packed with them, marriageable—oh God, how marriageable—prowling singles up from the city, also lots of youngish wives left alone during the week by their husbands, it's take your pick, Buddy, you have here a smorgasbord of sex . . .)

So why is it I soon find myself hanging around with this Jody Cassel, that's her name, crazy Westchester kid who's attached herself to me, adoringly, telling me how absolutely great I am, and would I please play her another song as funny as "All The Quakers Are Shoulder Shakers (Down In Quaker Town)."

Because I need affirmation, maybe as much as she does. I need to show off, too. I've got a parody I've worked up, crazy lyrics to a pop ballad of the day, I call it "Shampoo For Everybody" (get it?), and I play it for her. It breaks her up, she loves it, will I *please* teach it to her? Oh, I am feeling great, she's laughed in all the right places, so of course I'll teach it to her, I'll show her how to phrase it, where I'm sure the laughs will come. She's a quick study, this Jody, pretty soon she's got it perfectly, and we try it, this time she's singing without me, she starts very straight, à la Deanna Durbin, but she has trouble with the high notes, the next thing I know she's switched to a hoarse growl, hey, she's kidding it, singing like Fanny Brice, with a crazy Jewish accent, what the hell is she up to? All of a sudden, around us in the camp lounge, the people are laughing! Insane, spontaneous—she's taken *my* words—and she's getting big laughs! Who could figure such a thing? She's *forcing* all these people to pay attention—to Jody Cassel!

You could never say she was shy, or reticent. Not this one. After she's done it at my upright a couple more times, getting better each chorus, now she's hooked, she's on a high. Oh, she adores having the people applauding her, approving her, from now on she'll be like some demented little kid who's been let loose on the main floor at F.A.O. Schwarz. Will I please teach her another number, will I rehearse it with her? Could we maybe to do something together, have I got some more vaudeville songs, hey, we could have fun!

I'm hooked, too. My father was a pro, he could make an audience sit up and take notice, he knew how to milk bows (until sound movies came in and vaudeville collapsed around him)—isn't that what I want to do? Sure, be as good as your old man, do I need a psychiatrist (the one who gives Tuesday night seminars on Your Sex Problems) to tell me that?

So I'm not annoyed at Jody Cassel. After a while I am enjoying all this time at my piano with her as much as she does, because I am the old pro. Buddy Grimes, giving this noisy amateur the benefit of my vast experience, smiling fondly at her crazy antics, her face-making, her dialect *shtick*—

Such a dummy. So naive. Never once understanding—you, Buddy, are nursing a viper in your bosom (while never once laying a hand on hers) Because there is no thought of getting into Jody's pants, she is much more of my pal now, a kid sister, this middle-class maiden who so obviously trusts me, worships me, follows me around, loves me for my talent. For God's sake, how could one betray that sort of adoration?

In time I'd discovered she's not even a guest, she has a job here in the camp's business office, her folks are somehow related to Mr. and Mrs. Heller, the camp's owners. Mrs. Heller is a matronly boss-lady who's plenty annoyed at first because Jody is spending so much time hanging around with me. (Later on, she grudgingly forgives me, I seem to have pulled off a major public relations stunt.) What did I do?

I made Jody a hit.

Wednesday is Talent Nite (how else would you entertain the guests without spending any money? The Hellers may have a social conscience, but they book professional acts or comics on the weekend. Mid-week, they are in the philanthropy business.) What could be simpler; I'm in charge, hey, Jody, how about trying out some of our stuff that night?

At first she says no, she wouldn't dare, she'd be scared out of her wits, she's never performed in public, but all of that is strictly window dressing, she'll do it, she'll go on—she knew that all the time. So did I. *The kid's a born trouper, Moe.* Besides, I'll be there, won't I—the old pro?

Sure, don't worry, Jody, I'll be with you all the way, I'll be backing you up, we'll be working *together*.

So on Wednesday she gets up, and she begins with a ballad, just something to get herself warmed up, and she gets a polite hand from the guests, which gives her enough confidence to come back and do her comedy number. She's found an old Mexican sombrero in some closet, and she's wrapped a towel around her like a serape. She starts by doing "Mexicali Rose," slowly, like a dirge. The audience doesn't have a clue what she's up to, and anybody else would have panicked, but not this girl, she's going to make them laugh if it kills her, she mugs, on she plows, and now we switch tempo, we're into "Shampoo For Everybody," and she's doing her Fanny Brice thing, and now come the laughs, they build, they're with her, they love her, she's *made* them love her, at the finish they're applauding her and yelling for more.

Satisfied? Happy? Yes, but only for a minute. The next thing I know she's embracing me, she's perspiring under that towel, but there's electricity coming out of her, and she's telling me

". . . Please, promise me, Buddy, tomorrow we've got to work up another number for an *encore!*"

Of course we will. We're a team, aren't we? Suddenly we're excitement. We're hot, we're successful, already we can tell that, the paying customers are crowding around to tell us how marvelous we are, even Mrs. Heller, who already figures next year she'll be saying, "They got their start right here at Greenways, don't forget it!"

Dummy, Buddy. You don't see, you don't realise what's happening? You're so proud of yourself, you think you're some kind of a road company Svengali, up here at this resort? Forget it. What you are is Dr. Frankenstein, presiding at the birth of your own particular brand of monster, not a Daughter, not a Bride, no folks, what we got here is a real, full-fledged Queen-Size Jody the Terrible. It's Omen-time!

("And togezzer, dallink, ve vill rule ze vorld!")

But you never knew that, did you? So take another bow, Buddy . . . and start writing Jody an encore, okay?

The bright red numerals glowing on the digital clock by our bed said 3:06.

Let's stop here, Buddy, and go to sleep, we're still in the fun-and-games MGM musical, hey-gang-we're-doing-a-show-here part, a fine place to switch off the tape, go to black, and get yourself some shut-eye, fold up 1951, send it all back into limbo.

3:19 Sleep wouldn't come.

Quietly I got up, found my slippers and robe, went out of the bedroom, closing the door behind me, down the stairs to the kitchen, all the appliances humming softly away, the waves endlessly rolling outside, no sleeping pills for me thank you, not at this hour. I found the canister of the Twining's Queen Mary Blend tea Cristina fancies, boiled some water, took the steaming mug into my study, lay back on the easy chair with a book . . . tea has done it before. When I've got a script jogging up and down in my subconscious, and I'm awake, I've learned to come down here and sit it out until eventually sleep comes.

I read, but nothing was registering from the pages. Another videocassette was running through my head. Time for Buck Dawes to make his entrance.

Gently, without warning, Buck Dawes tiptoes into our lives, he's here at Camp Greenways, it's Saturday evening, he works for The Office, a giant talent agency, he's been sent up here to "service" a comic for tonight's show, one of their clients ("service" means drive the car, pick up the pay check, see to it the client makes the show). The comic (who can remember him?)— some aggressive young kid who's equipped with the standard eighteen-minute monologue of my mother-in-law / the food there was so bad that / Irving in bed with his wife Selma turns over and says / talk about the cost-of-living, just the other day I / Miami Beach, Morris is swimming with his wife at the Fontainebleau and a wave comes and / jokes . . . *Jokes?* Don't argue, the audience here on the weekend laughs, he earns his fee, and afterward while the comic is in the bar getting sauced and finding a bed partner for the night, I get to talk with Buck Dawes.

He's like no agent I've ever met before. Doesn't wear white-on-white shirts, no cigar, rarely raises his voice. He wears a J. Press tweed jacket and button-down shirt, looks like Joe College, in fact, he is, a real Ivy Leaguer, believe it or not, out a year or so, but now he is working for The Office, why not a bank, or a brokerage house? Because he sees a future in show business, all sorts of things happening, this television thing is going to be big, nobody can imagine how big. He's a gentle smiler who isn't looking to get laid (at least not obviously), who uses words with two, maybe even three, syllables, gives me a sense of security, cameraderie, since he's already found out my father was a performer, he's careful to respect my background; if I'm not his full-fledged equal, he's clever enough to make me feel like one.

What is this about me and some girl named Jody, is that it?

He's heard it from some people at the bar, this Buck Dawes has sharp ears. Later we will find out how very sharp, and how fine-tuned the rest of his senses as well. Very casually he suggests, if we're funny enough to have knocked Mrs. Heller's mid-week guests for a loop twice running now, why don't we give him a little sample of what we do? Maybe tomorrow morning?

I promise to ask Jody.

For the rest of that night she's hysterical. Wakes me up at 6, insisting we have to rehearse, she's had no sleep, she's already thrown up twice.

After breakfast, while the comic is still sleeping it off, we do a private audition for Buck Dawes, we have him all to ourselves in the lounge, the cleaning crew with their vacuums aren't due for half an hour.

We run through everything, we've got about fifteen minutes' worth now, stuff we've worked up, more parodies, and a couple of patter duets. He sits there nodding, but not cracking a smile. Once in a while, his lips curl (is that good or bad?).

Only one year out of college, this boy knows; from somewhere he has learned the rules—a good agent never lets you know what he's thinking, keeps a poker face; if the people are waiting for your opinion, keep them waiting. If you're buying, the more enthusiasm you show, the higher the price you'll have to pay. If you're selling, undersell, it always leaves you an escape hatch.

We're finished, we wait for the great man's opinion.

He thanks us, very nice, let's keep in touch, now he's got to leave, the comic will be looking for him, he has another booking a few miles away, before he goes out the door, he slips me his business card, when we get to town, be sure to come and see him.

Sounds good to me. Not Jody, she's perplexed. What's happening here? He just walked out on us like that, she's suddenly beginning to puddle up, near tears, this is a big thing with her, this girl can't obviously handle any kind of rejection. Now she's angry, who the hell is he to walk out on us like that? I try to explain to her, he didn't—he liked us, he gave us his card, didn't he? That doesn't satisfy her, this girl is insistent, before I can stop her, she's out the door, headed after Buck Dawes, she catches up with him outside the dining room, it's really embarrassing, there are guests beginning to stare, that doesn't stop her, she's after him, please, Mr. Dawes, we want to know how you felt about us, you're a real pro, and we're just a couple of amateurs, now she's batting her eyelashes at him, so please, couldn't you give us a little more encouragement?

He doesn't get upset, he chucks her under the chin, he tells her, listen, I gave your friend here my card, didn't I? Keep on working, get together some more stuff, and when you come to town we'll see what happens. Then he's gone, looking for his client.

Now she's excited, *omyGod, he liked us!* A real honest-to-God agent! This girl can change moods faster than a green light can turn red, she's dancing me up and down the hall, doing a real number with me—

I'm not buying it, I'm suddenly angry, *I* liked us first, didn't I? Damnit, since when am I an amateur, how dare she put me down to Buck Dawes, after all I've done for this noisy bitch, I tell her right to her face she has a big mouth—

—Oh, she's so sorry! Now she's embracing me, hugging me hard, she wants me to know she never meant to insult me, she made a mistake, of course I'm a pro, she is so grateful for everything, her body's against mine, but it's not sex coming from her, only that same quivering electricity I felt before, waves of pure ambition, she's babbling on, aren't I tickled at what's happened for us?

Sure, okay, all is forgiven. Face it, I'm impressed myself, Buck Dawes, from The Office, it's a real foot in the door, who would ever have planned on connecting with such an outfit? Maybe he's only one step removed from an office-boy trainee, so what? it's The Office, and I've grown up knowing that's where the clout is, didn't my old man always lecture me, *Buy the cheapest thing in Tiffany's, it's always a better value than the most expensive item in S. Klein!*

It's only later, much later, when it suddenly dawns on me what Jody said—aren't I tickled at what's happened for *us?*

Us. I have acquired a partner.

Correction. I have been acquired.

. . . I woke up, chilled. An open book in my lap? I was stiff from having dozed off, in this easy chair?

The time was 6:02. I hadn't slept soundly, merely dozed, but for a while there, I'd managed to keep the memory tape switched off. Fair enough, the reminiscences were over, now we could please forget Jody Cassel and get on with the business of life circa 1984.

There was a faint white line of light trying to intrude beneath the distant clouds. Dawn, already? (How time does fly when you're having fun.)

I went into the kitchen to make myself some coffee, toasted a frozen bagel (since the nearest bagel bakery is miles from this solid Wasp area, I often toy with the idea of having a baker bussed in daily), took it all back to my study to enjoy an early breakfast.

The rest of the town was already up, out jogging through quiet roads, or riding Exercycles, lifting weights, doing aerobics, carrying on in the fine old New England tradition, *get thee to good works,* and here I was, sitting on my ass, taking in useless calories.

Try some honest labor, Mr. Grimes, now that your head is clear, purged of the past, the terrible night is o'er, any minute now they'll deliver your copy of the *Times,* before that happens, justify yourself, do a little good work on that report you were preparing, on those oh-so-piss-elegant Italian art films, for next week's Bidwell meeting.

I picked up the pages of my notes. ''. . . This four-episode production, which covers the entire Renaissance, seems demographically to limit its appeal to a somewhat fragmented audience. Give the current network TV scene, however, this set of films will certainly provide alternative programming, either for PBS or for cable. As to subsidiary benefits for a potential underwriter, one must assess the prestige values carefully—''

That was as far as I'd gotten before Teresa's call.

Hedging? Noncommittal? Absolutely.

The truth was, this Italian production was a four-hour long moving coffee table book, opulent visual caviar, which travelled from museum to church to chapel and back again, dazzling the eye and filling the ear with appropriate medieval music. But the end result was weariness, and as for that narrator, who intoned endless paragraphs of art-type prose, he was one of the leading Italian scholars, but why did he constantly remind me of Peter Sellers doing one of his imitations, this one of a leading Italian art scholar?

So why hedge? Take a position. For once, come out with it, flat out, and say . . . *boring.*

Boring! *BOR-RING!*

. . . in my ear, Jody's voice again. ''. . . Ah, come on, Buddy, let's get something going here, a big boffo, it's *boring,* we need a joke—something to wake them up, honey, I *know* you want to grow up to be Noël Coward, a noble ambition, toots, but not here on television, these are the meat-and-potato folks, Ma and Pa from TV Land, they do not understand your high-class inner rhymes, darling, listen to me (now she's doing her James Cagney) ''. . . All right you guys, from now on, no more rhymed couplets, gimme a guaranteed *wowoweeweewoh!*''

Oh, she was a quick study, that one, not only could she pick up music and lyrics at sight, but she also acquired stage presence, lost her fear, developed the guts of a burglar, and along with it, increasingly definite opinions, and why not? (as she was fond of reminding me) wasn't *she* the one who was out there, naked to the world, selling my material? sure, I could hide behind my piano, but in the end, if anybody in the audience tossed a tomato, it would be at *her* kisser! So there was bravado, but she was far from secure, all through our time at the Village Club, or on those first faltering TV shows where we cut our teeth, no matter how I argued for my clever lyrics, pointing out she was *not* naked, all she had to do was to sell them—she insisted on buying insurance, coming on with those thrift shop funny hats, the outrageous '20s costumes, the billowing skirts, (beneath which, always good for a laugh, were the roller skates, the cowboy boots, even a pair of galoshes!) and damn her, she was right, they worked.

New York, 1951, there was so much going on, frantic but exhilarating, there was a war in Korea, who knows what else, but we paid no attention, we were too busy selling ourselves to the world. Jody had finagled her way out of Westchester, I'd never know how she'd persuaded her parents to allow her to abandon a good secretarial job to try show business, but she had, part of the deal was she must share an apartment with some other reliable female types, which is how she ended up in a West 20s walk-up railroad flat with Claire . . . what was her original name? that blonde beauty who was also here in New York, from New Jersey, trying for a career in modelling (my God, I've forgotten—*she* was how we first met Dick Hatch, wasn't she?) . . . the two girls splitting a rent of $90 a month—Yes, Virginia, in those days, there were such prices!—but most of the time she was over at my place, I had a room-and-a-half in the Village, big enough for my piano and my bed, which was where we rehearsed each afternoon before we did our two shows a night, yes, we were already hired, doing an honest-to-God booking at the Village Club, no, it certainly wasn't The Copacabana, it was what they called a *boîte,* in reality a remodelled speakeasy, owned and operated by Benny Keyser, a gnomish little bald guy who'd run it since the days of Owney Madden and all the other New York hoods. He was a survivor who smoked evil Italian Parodi cigars, which dangled from his perpetual grin, a specialist in unearthing talent, he presented jazz musicians, folk singers, and an occasional new act, that was us (all very underpaid, but as Benny firmly reminded us "Here you get to be seen, *kinder,* go, be great for me.") Thanks to Buck Dawes, our mentor at The Office, we were booked for a couple of try-out nights, then a week, then a second, finally our name went outside on the board, Cassel & Grimes. (Get a load of that billing, notice whose name comes first? *Mene mene tekel, upharsin,* go look up what it means, *kinder.*)

("Since you're so definitely one of television's pioneer playwrights, Mr. Grimes, would you mind telling us how you first broke into this exciting new medium back there?")

. . . That's one I'm always asked, by any of those interviewers who's interested in my *curriculum vitae,* my early original dramas, my awards, my "contribution to" the "literature of the Golden Age." Well, up to now I've never bothered to mention the facts, have I? This is not precisely the sort of input my friends at Bidwell might want to hear, so stand back, this is a first, would you believe that Cassel & Grimes set their first feet on a TV stage because of a sick seal?

Yes, on "Video Varieties," of blessed memory, on Dumont, for not one, but two appearances, not because Buck Dawes was such a red-hot agent, who'd brought Frankie Fogarty, the producer of that live TV weekly show, down to the Village Club to scout us . . . no, because Fogarty (who loathed us) discovered that same Tuesday night he was over a barrel for his Wednesday show (yes, sometimes life does imitate Twentieth-Century Fox musicals). He had to replace a five-minute booking, Sharkey the Seal, who had developed a bad case of the trots, in Philadelphia. (God bless you, Sharkey, I owe it all to you—may you be barking out a ripe old age in some Florida Home for Senior Seals.)

"How, then, did live TV feel? What was its birth like? Mr. Grimes, sir, Can you give us a sense of the excitement, the creative thrust?"

Okay, you students and Ph.D. chasers, who've decided it's an art form that we shall henceforth treat with dignity, I'll give it to you straight—it was a shambles, nerve-racking, Heartburn Alley, in which only those with iron colons could survive. Fogarty's production (if you could dignify it with such a word) was done on the cheapest cheap, in a dirty old West Side theater, four hours' rehearsal the day of the show, when we got to his studio, nobody knew what to do with us, and neither did we, sink or swim, get out there and fill five minutes, the show itself was a thirty-minute obstacle course for performers and audience alike, Jody's palms were sweating and she tossed her lunch a couple of minutes before we went on, oh pioneers! Then we were confronted by those ominous TV cameras, which dollied in and out on us, stalking us like androids, their little red eyes winking at us, the audience, where the hell was it? Somewhere behind those cameras, all we had was a desperate floor-manager who cued us, whoever was out in the theater was effectively screened from the scene of the crime.

You think we went out there unknowns and came back stars? Forget it. (Jody later told me her own mother complained she'd been called to the phone while we were on, and missed our whole act!) No, that red light went on, those glass-eyed lenses stared at us, and we were out there, naked, alone, ulcer-time, believe me. Then we heard a scattered burst of applause from behind those damned cameras (cued by the floor-manager) and we'd filled Sharkey's five-minute spot. How were we? (*My* mother, who'd watched the show at a friend's house, said we looked like a couple of fleas on a microscope slide—and she was a fan, yet!)

Frankie Fogarty, that eminent judge of low-priced talent, that footnote to TV history, told us we stank, who the hell could understand that "Shampoo For Everybody" piece of crap? Jody was ready to go after him with her fingernails, but I restrained her, after all this was an ongoing relationship, we had a deal to do a second spot on his show the following week, that was Buck Dawes' doing, he'd fought for it ("One to learn, the second to score," was his dictum).

And so the following Wednesday, we were back, trying to score on "Video Varieties" no matter how insistently Jody had complained all week about trying to get laughs from an audience that saw only cameramen's asses, we gave it another shot, this time with Jody got up in a feather boa, a frizzy wig, and an old German helmet, since she could do a decent Marlene Dietrich, I wrote her some dialect material mixing up "Falling In Love Again" with "Mairzy Doats," once again the ominous horde of cameras pursued us, hiding us from the audience, we were on, then we were off, we slunk out of the studio, Fogarty never even said goodbye; he was an angry producer double-crossed by a sick seal, and we were back at the Village Club, our TV career was kaput, okay, fine, at least downtown there were living bodies each night who occasionally laughed at us, and Benny Keyser and his rancid Parodi cigars never looked or smelled better. (Are you keeping careful notes on this, historians?)

Daily we nagged Buck to use his wiles to get us something, anything, in a Broadway show, those were the audiences we were aiming at with my sophisticated comedy patter, if we could only have a spot on a stage, we could make it big, score like Sid Caesar, or Imogene Coca, Jody would be the next Bea Lillie, I'd be the next Hiram Sherman, sauve and amusing, right? We'd end up going through TV through the front door, on "Toast of The Town" with Ed Sullivan on a Sunday night, that was *the* way to go in 1951, everybody knew that. While we waited for lightning to strike, Buck Dawes and The Office came up with a steady TV job, believe it or not, we weren't pariahs, we were *hired!*

Trivia specialists, for $5, do you remember "Sing Us A Smash"? Another pit stop on Memory Lane, the sort of show proliferating all over the tube in those early seven-inch days, in its Golden Age, dreamed up by some hopeful Lindy's Restaurant habitaué, it was actually On, a weekly half-hour in which amateur songwriters could peddle their wares, vying for a moment of fame and glory and a giant $50 cash prize. The American Dream . . . *you, too, can be Irving Berlin.*

Beneath those hot white lights, in front of those unblinking cameras, there we were, weekly, along with a couple of other hopeful performers, doing the opening number (why is it I can still retain such garbage?) "Sing us a Smash/let us know it's a wow/Sing us a Smash/Start it bubbling now/For when you sing to us/You make it Spring for us (How about that for a rhyme, Mortie?) So sing us, sing us (big finish) A Smash!" For the next twenty-four minutes, we went on to perform those so-called works, mailed in from all over America and screened by a panel of experts, don't knock it, it was a job, and it paid a weekly salary, which fed us, and paid our rent. The sponsor was peddling some nostrum called Nite-Nite, a pill to help you sleep, but you didn't really need Nite-Nite, all you had to do was watch this show, it did the job nicely, have you any idea how many terrible songs are written out there each year? I do, because we must have sung dozens of them over those weeks until we were fired, one worse than the next. (Oh yes, we were fired, that memorable night when Jody rebelled and decided she absolutely could not sing one of those beauties straight, a wretched offering that went ''When You Walked Out Of My Heart, You Slammed The Door on Our Love.'')

She'd fought that piece all through the rehearsals, complaining bitterly that the audience would laugh her off the stage if she tried to do it straight, but nobody listened, on those live TV schedules there was never time for a conference, it was learn it fast, get up and do it, get off and go on to the next. Jody went around arguing with the people, collaring everybody on the show, right up until air time, but it was always ''Forget it, honey, just do the song, please, it's only another show.'' Nobody paid attention, so how could any of us realize this would be a momentous night, the birth of a monster? Least of all me, the midwife—

All of a sudden, show time, we're on the air, we've done the opening, nothing happening, we were running through this week's hopeful entries, then we reach our spot, we were on, me in a smoking jacket, it was like a little play, I'm walking out on Jody, she was in a long evening gown, the announcer cued us, another song! ''When You Walked Out Of My Heart,'' music hit, away we went, Jody sang the verse perfectly straight, nothing to worry about, then we were into the chorus, doing it like a duet, okay we're almost there, she got past the line about slamming the door on our love, I heard one of the cameramen snicker, then another one, now the crew is laughing, what the hell? Because my partner had raised a hand, one of her fingers has a hankie tied around it like a bandage, and she's suddenly ad-libbing *You caught my finger!* the crew is breaking up, so is some of the audience, ad-libs? who the hell had given her the right to do this to me? the song goes on, now she's leering at me, she lifted up her skirts to reveal—damnit, *her galoshes!* then she's doing a kind of clog-waltz, leaving me standing there like some jerk, staring at her as I went on singing, the floor manager is going nuts, she's waltzing around like a dervish, now the people are really laughing, oops, she fakes a trip, picks herself up, did some *shtick* with her damned handkerchief so she looked like a cowboy, when we finally reached the end of that song, she's clasping her hands over her head like a triumphant prizefighter, I'm still there with egg on my face.

Oh, there was applause, nobody had to cue it, she'd sung us a smash, a real wowser, she'd knocked the audience for a loop, but what my smart-ass partner Jody who couldn't stand such rotten material didn't know was that the terrible song she'd just destroyed for keeps had been written by a relative of the sponsor, some nit from Nite-Nite (remember this, historians, this was years before the quiz-scandals). It had been rigged, mind you, he was all set to win the $50! Not after Jody got through with it, the song lost, so did we, end of employment, Nite-Nite Cassel & Grimes, we were fired before we could take off our makeup.

All the way to her place, we argued and fought, she was contrite, like some naughty kid who's made a boo-boo, at first defensive, then apologetic, but I wasn't having any now, she'd pulled something so damned unprofessional, how dare she do this to *me?* Mea culpa, she yelled, stone me, I was bad, what else was I supposed to do, the song stank, you know that! Yes, but the paychecks were nice, couldn't you force yourself to take the money and forget your pride? I yelled back. Okay, so I blew it! she said, how could I go out there and have them stare at me, I couldn't stand them *hating me!* Ah, what stupid, self-indulgent shit, you *amateur!* I screamed back, you couldn't even be seen, the cameras were in the way! By now I was following her up the stairs to her apartment door, lugging all her damn junk like a porter, her costumes, raving at her, suddenly she was grabbing it all away from me, snuffling like some naughty kid again, yes, all my life it's my fault, I've never been good enough! she snarled, how would you like to be laughed at because you're not pretty, hey? Even your own godamned mother agrees, so now you know, pal, get away from me, Now she was really raving as she fumbled for her key, I'm Typhoid Jody, see, so now you can go find youself some beautiful girl like Claire, maybe she'll do your material straight, and make you Noël Coward, I'm an ugly amateur, goodbye, I'm not good enough for you! She started to slam the door, but I wouldn't let her, I pushed my way inside, the room was dark, no sign of Claire, she started yelling Get out, *leave me*—near hysteria. Shut up and *listen,* I told her, you're talented, you're going to be funny, you're good, but you've got to control it, stop pushing so hard, let them find you, don't make it so obvious you need them! I snapped on a light and we were glaring at each other, who could argue with her mother? she *wasn't* beautiful, now even less attractive, her eyes bleary from tears, her makeup a mess, and she wasn't listening now, I'm bad— you're good! I'm a nothing, you're a *pro,* so who needs this? I can type and take dictation, and screw you and show business, you can all drop dead, *get out!* That's when I slapped her, not hard, mainly to shut this demented creature up, it wasn't anger any longer, anybody could see this girl was almost over the edge.

You *hit* me, she said, suddenly astonished. I didn't mean to, I had to shut you up, I said, I was instantly contrite, who the hell was I to be such a damn bully, this whole thing had gotten way out of hand, I reached out and pulled that shapeless female mass toward me, she still wearing one of those ugly duffel coats, she was heaving away, whimpering, then I kissed her on the cheek where I'd slapped her, she subsided, then, in a tiny voice, she said Hey mister, you trying to make a pass?

Oh, that tore it, didn't it, I started to let go, but now she was grabbing at me, No, no, I take it back she pleaded softly, *please,* I'll shut up, she was fastened against me, we'd collapsed onto the tiny sofa nearby, now she was kissing me, I could feel the wetness of her late tears on her cheek, when we finally came apart for breath, she said in a whisper, you're nice, a talented writer, a real teddy bear . . . so what are you doing hanging around an ugly noisy broad who needs love, you can get it anywhere else? I thought you said you'd shut up, I said, and inside I heard warning bells, stop here, Buddy, this isn't any good, it won't get you anywhere but trouble, then I thought, ohmyGod, if I do push her away, she'll take it as another personal put-down, what do I do now? So give her a nice fraternal kiss, and that'll be the end of it, make an excuse and go.

Fraternal it started out, but before it was over this time there was passion, both of us, the anger giving way to another emotion, the unexpected softness of her ample body pushing against me, my hand found her breasts beneath the outer clothing, now we were struggling against each other, gasping and kissing again, oh hey, she whispered, doctor dear, if this is therapy, many thanks, but if this is for pleasure, a little faster, please?

Another joke? At a time like this? Christ! *sorry, sorry,* she whispered, and that was the last of her defenses, soon we were pulling at each other's clothes like a pair of randy teenagers, for someone who hadn't been popular with the gang at school, she was eager, willing (how stupid of them to pass her up), we wrestled each other off that rickety sofa, then we were on the floor, on a pile of pillows, our clothing tossed everywhere, the lamp was off, she insisted on darkness, but the reflection of light from the window enabled me to make out the shapes and planes of an unexpectedly lush body, nothing Italian Renaissance, but more out of Rubens, gleaming up at me, she responded to my hands as they explored, she crooned in my ear, opening herself to me, there was a soft gasp as I entered her for the first time, she held me so tightly, her eyes closed, gone somewhere into a world of her own, her head turning slowly from side to side, her legs wrapped around me, soft, suddenly vulnerable, as she met my rhythm, like some little child being fed candy she whispered ohniceohnice, *nice* . . .

Until I came, and she hadn't, then I was the one whispering sorry, *sorry.* Oh no, she replied, patting my shoulder, thank you, doctor, dear doctor, then, exhausted, we dozed, both of us covered with that ridiculous duffel-coat.

. . . Later, footsteps coming up the stairs outside, coming closer, the ancient floorboards creaking as they arrived at this doorway and stopped. Now I was awake, there was the sound of soft voices just a few feet away, a man's, then a woman's, murmurs, chuckles, soft sighs, it was obviously some couple kissing goodnight out there, I nudged Jody urgently, she stirred, listened, giggled . . . what's so funny? I asked her. That's *Claire!* she explained, sitting up, with some guy of hers trying to get her in here and do what we're doing! She pulled the coat around her, and went over to the door, yelled Hold the phone, Claire, sorry, it isn't checkout time yet! Chuckling, she began to pull some clothes on, while I scrambled around searching for mine, like in some damn Feydeau farce, Jody continuing to bawl Just give us a couple more minutes to get off, then you two can go on! Crude, sure, but it was funny, I was laughing with her, what the hell, sex is funny, even after the apartment door finally opened, and there was Claire, her roommate, that very elegant blonde girl, peering into the gloom, beside her, a thinnish young guy with heavy horn-rimmed glasses, wearing an old, olive-drab Army overcoat, both of them staring at this scene, the room a shambles, me in my hastily donned trousers, still tucking in my shirt, Jody still assembling herself, the two of us looking like refugees, as she pulled on her clothes beneath that duffel-coat, she said, Well, how teddibly nice of you to drop in so unexpectedly, she'd lapsed into a phony British accent, Claire *dearest,* she said, won't you introduce us to your friend?

Dick Hatch, somebody Claire had met in her drama class, a hopeful director, right now scratching around the same way we were . . . Poor bewildered guy, he had no idea what was going on here, all he knew for sure was, tonight was certainly not going to be his night on that broken-down sofa, nor even on the floor, not after a comedy bit like this. Talk about destroying the mood! (I remember once Dick and I discussed it later, we were arguing about some love scene in a script I'd written for him, this was long after he and Claire had got married, I argued for humor, and kiddingly reminded him about that crazy night. Believe me, I said, you were lucky, the sofa was hard and the floor even harder! Dick blinked owlishly at me behind those glasses, and in his rich Southern drawl he said Well, old son, ah'll be the judge of that, poontang is poontang wherever and whenever. Then he grinned, All ah remember figgerin' that night was that you and your friend Jody sure picked one helluva way to celebrate bein' fired!)

Almost broke, out of work, neither of us had time to brood about it, for the next few days after that ridiculous night at her place, we kept busy, we could sneak into matinees of Broadway shows, friends having slipped us passes, we'd see them on Saturday before they closed, we even got a couple of dates to play, courtesy of good old Benny Keyser, even though we weren't working at his place, he kept in touch, he'd call to ask would we do our stuff downtown at a benefit, Astor Place somewhere, good people, friends of his, a worthy cause, a fund-raiser, they needed entertainment before the speakers went on, just remember, *kinder,* you never know who might catch your act, it could be good for you two . . . Sure, why not? We did one, something about literary censorship, then another one for some out-of-the-way magazine. (Oh, we were so godamned naive, we never paid attention, it was important to try out our material, there were living bodies out there, they responded to us, applauded, that made the whole thing worthwhile.) While we waited for Buck Dawes to come up with some gainful employment, we were up at my place rehearsing, working up new bits, at least some of the time we rehearsed, remember, there was a bed there, an honest-to-God pull-down, so we used it.

Things were quite different between us now, weren't they? Jody was certainly better at performing, she had confidence in my material, certainly more in herself, as well, and surprisingly, she was able to show affection, although some times it was wild. One afternoon we were rehearsing a new piece, she standing behind me, dutifully singing away, when she got to the end, she announced, If we don't take a break soon, I'm going to catch pneumonia! I turned round, there she stood, absolutely bare-assed!

While she'd sung, she'd stripped! I collapsed with laughter, what a sight-gag! *Oy, doctor,* she said, the nurse said I should take off my clothes and you'd be right in, so now it's up to you, doc, she was on my lap, running her hands across my chest, I think I need a treatment right away, doctor, then she was yanking me upward and over to my bed, I told her "Hey, you are one voracious lady," and as we fell down on the bed, she said "So put it on my Blue Cross!"

Okay, so today memory is tricking me, but damn, those *were* pleasant days, an impromptu honeymoon, two optimists, scratching and struggling to get somewhere, to be somebody, our adrenalin flowed like wine, everything was possible, if it hadn't happened for us this day, certainly it would soon, tomorrow? maybe Tuesday would be our good news day, someday he'd come along, the man who'd make us into stars.

We stayed alive on a diet of cheap Neapolitan pasta from that basement Italian place down the street, on a treadmill of constant activity, and for dessert, that sporadic series of delicious explosions which took place on my unmade bed. (Jody did go home nights, not that she cared if Claire knew, in fact dear Claire was probably making it with Dick Hatch uptown in their place, but Jody worried her mother would call and not find her there, Jody's bourgeois upbringing nagging away, yes? Girls who gave it away to guys were Loose, and Cheap.) Although one time Jody confided in me If my old lady ever found I had an honest-to-God lover, she'd probably have a heart attack, and die of amazement! The bitch! she added, giggling, what a terrific idea, maybe I *will* tell her!

If I ever thought about marriage, and I did (aha, Buddy, a little of your own middle-class background sneaking in there?) it certainly wasn't anything serious, it was unspoken between us, how was it possible? I took care so she couldn't become pregnant, right now that was all that mattered, both of us were so close to being a couple of The Hundred Neediest Cases. *Marriage?* Insanity. (Thank God)

For by the time we did become solvent, we were instantly too busy ever to contemplate the marital state. Buck Dawes' secretary called (just before the New York Telephone Company was about to disconnect me for financial shortfall) to inform us her boss had us scheduled for an audition at one of the local TV stations; we were to give it our best shot, please, this was not for somebody as dumb and tasteless as Frank Fogarty, nor a Mr. Nite-Nite, no indeed, this was important stuff, this was The Network!

Came the day of our audition, we went up, nervous as hell, and gave it our best shot, in a small airless conference room up on the fourteenth floor of the network building, with Buck Dawes ushering us in to a small phalanx of stone-faced executives, the one in the front row was Al Crane, of whom we would see much more later, soft-spoken, impeccably tailored, the *capo di tutti capo* up there (this year, at least) and when we finished, they thanked us, said goodbye, Buck led us out, past a waiting room of other hopeful souls, left us at the elevators, assuring us we'd be hearing soon, not to worry, the situation was under control.

We went back to my place, by the time we got there Jody was in terrible shape, she never could handle rejection, now she was working herself up into a real state, we stank! she kept yelling, I know we stank, but so did they, those silent bastards! she stamped up and down my apartment, oh, did you see the hate oozing out of every jerk in that room? she yelled, who needs them? We work out our guts, and they give us a polite nod? Nothing I could say or do could convince her auditions are always like that, they're a barbaric ritual, the worst kind of obstacle course, by now she was near tears, what was the only tried and true method a guy could use to shut Jody's mouth? My own, I kissed her, petted her, soon I had her on my bed, she still complaining as I unbuttoned, unzipped, and tugged away at whatever collection of exotic thrift shop clothing she had on that day, it wasn't the easiest seduction I'd ever worked on, but eventually she began to respond, well, you can guess the rest, can't you, cliché-fans, just as we were about to make it, the phone rang, Buck Dawes calling, who else? to say we had the job!

Hysteria reigned, we were almost too jubilant to finish screwing. Almost.

How could we know or care it was to be a brutal killer of a schedule, a fifteen-minute three-times-weekly summer replacement, a musical show with original material, done for absolutely no budget, we got scale, or very little more, we were unsponsored, a time-filler. The music was provided by a talented little guy named Norman Paris, and his trio. Norman was one third of the group, conducted, wrote arrangements, helped me score the material I had to turn out each day, and sweated all summer with us in that non-air conditioned studio, what a treadmill, Mondays a show, Tuesday rehearse, Wednesday, show, Thursday rehearse, it went on like that, Sundays we could sleep. Were you taught in school that slavery had been abolished? Not in live TV, on we went (sans audience, so we never had a clue who was watching when we pranced out there three times a week) to sing "Summertime, U.S.A!/Everyone on a holiday/With Jody and Buddy, Norman too/Pack your duds and come along/To the ocean or the zoo" (On this budget you were expecting Cole Porter?)

Ten weeks we staggered on, all you historians, would you like to know how we lasted on that treadmill? Simple, we were too stupid to know such a show couldn't be done.

But by the end of August we were running downhill fast, exhuasted, the frustration was building up nicely, with each humid day Jody was louder in her daily litany of complaint, nobody up at the damn network was paying any attention to us, what the hell was Buck Dawes doing to earn his ten percent? wasn't unemployment staring us in the kisser, what now, would we have to go back to doing those idiot benefits for dear old Benny? Maybe it was time for her to throw in the towel and go back to being a secretary, who the hell needed this endless grind, she was beginning to develop insistent sinus headaches, she hated the material we were doing and kept picking away at it. It was my first experience with a manic depressive, frankly she was becoming a pain in the ass, the sex between us was no help, we were beginning to get on each other's nerves, we even had a couple of round-house arguments, we were seeing too much of each other, it wasn't like marriage, we were like two cell-mates.

Then it happened. We were summoned to a luncheon by Buck's secretary, could we meet at Louis & Armand's, on 52nd Street, that gathering place of the network greats and near-greats, it was all very unexpected, when we arrived we were led to a very good table, a banquette where Buck sat, smiling away like the Cheshire cat, we were shortly joined by none other than Mr. Al Crane himself, the waiter brought a telephone to the table so he could keep in touch with his office, and between the sporadic calls, Mr. Crane made nice with us, how were things with Summertime U.S.A? Before anybody could stop her, Jody proceeded to tell him, about the lack of air conditioning, the weight she'd lost on the daily grind he'd put us on, where was the audience, who knew we were alive?

No harm done, Al Crane beamed fondly at her, treating her like some brash naughty kid, something good was obviously going to happen if he wasn't upset by Miss Mighty Mouth, he ordered us champagne from the headwaiter, totally ignoring her complaints, he got right to the point, how would we feel about sitting down and preparing a half-hour show, starring Cassel & Grimes, a comedy pilot for the network's prime-time schedule? mmm?

An hour before, Jody had been threatening to quit the business forever, right? By the time the waiter brought the ice bucket with the champagne, my partner was hugging Al Crane, chucking Buck Dawes under the chin, doing funny bits with the breadsticks, using her napkin as a prop, bubbling over with suggestions, how about this for an idea? She could be a lady private eye, working for me, such a premise would give her all sorts of opportunities to do comedy, she could use crazy disguises, or long gowns, she could do Mata Hari, oh, wouldn't that be wild? Wait a minute, maybe we could be running an employment agency, that had possibilities, no wait, here was another idea, Buddy and she could be a down-in-their luck show business couple who hired out to be cook and butler in some fancy Long Island home, working for a stuffy rich couple, hey, that *really* had possibilities—

By the time the eggs benedict arrived Jody was flying, high above the table, sailing, we were all happy with her, she'd infected us, we were laughing, Al Crane was our leader, we loved him for his shrewd insights and judgment in having chosen us, he would be the one to make us into stars, good old Buck Dawes kept on smiling, properly modest, sure, he'd been the one who'd engineered it all, hadn't he, but only because we'd justified his faith in us, as he said Nobody can make stars out of no-talents, I'm merely the midwife, and we were all momentarily humble, for he was correct, was he not? Oh we were the golden kiddies that day, we'd clambered up the rungs of the ladder, up the greased pole, were we not going to be right up there with Benny, or Joan Davis, or Gleason and Carney, we would show the world, television was the place where new talent flowered!

So we were launched on expense-account Moet & Chandon that memorable day, and it was after I'd put down several glasses of that lovely bubbly while Jody kept on making kissy-face with everybody, and proposing all sorts of insanities of Al Crane, leaving her food untouched as she raved on doing her bits, why did I have a sudden wine-induced insight,

that if our boat was sailing at last, our captain was going to be a woman?

. . . No, I did *not* say lady.

. . . Bright sunlight woke me up. Morning? Yes, and not years ago, but 1984, it was past 7, and the door to my study was being pushed open by Cristina, who came in softly, her hair tied in a knot, wearing her jogging outfit, bearing a therapeutic tray on which was the *Times,* a pot of coffee, and a couple of croissants.

What a thoughtful creature, my wife.

"My," she said, "you look as if you've been up for hours . . ." She carefully put the tray down on my cluttered desk, leaned over to kiss me on the forehead.

"All night," I said, "or most of it." I poured myself some steaming coffee.

"Working?" she asked.

". . . Trying to, but not getting anywhere," I said.

"Problems?" she asked, perching herself on the sofa.

"I guess so," I said. "Somebody's about to get in touch with me about something I'm not sure I want to discuss . . . and I'm not sure I know how to handle it."

"Want to talk about it?" she asked.

I took a bite of the croissant. Delicious. "I don't think so," I said, ". . . See, I guess I'm really trying to lay an old ghost."

"What an interesting turn of phrase," she said. "Well now, it if's something really ugly, wouldn't it be better to let sleeping dogs lie?"

"Absolutely," I told her. ". . . if it were a dog."

". . . I'm certain you'll work it out," she said, patting me fondly as if I were her favorite spaniel. "Can't stay here watching you eat, not before I've done my morning run." She got up to go. "You know, I really do hate this daily jogging . . . it's so mindless."

"Give it up, then," I said. "A lady with your shape really does not need any more muscle . . ."

"Can't," she said. "It's *good* for me."

Ah, that wonderful, sturdy Protestant ethic. As she went out the door, headed for her good workout, I called "Run well, little one. Run one for the Gipper!"

But she was gone, her Walkman already turned on, she never heard my exit line, and it lay there, unheard, unlaughed at. Useless.

A bit like my past, maybe?

*   *   *   *

Eileen Tighe:

Sid Budlong had become bicoastal again, darting in and out, occupied with his usual run of meetings, rarely in the office, but when he did show up, a few days later, he stopped me in the hall to inquire what sort of headway I was making on Our Project, did we have anything tangible to discuss?

"Not quite yet," I told him. "Give me a couple of weeks and then I may be ready for you."

"Don't wait too long," he warned. "Somebody else may get there ahead of us, we don't want that, do we?"

. . . How could I tell him we were spinning wheels? Coming up dry. No reply to my letters to Grimes, or to Hatch, and while Tess Davidson was still dutifully researching, assembling whatever file material she could unearth at various libraries, so far she's turned up nothing tangible about Jody.

The more I looked at the pieces of TV history she brought in, the more depressed I became. So damned amorphous—this new medium, which had sprouted, grown like some giant mushroom until it dominated every hour of our lives, and all there was to show for it were clips from TV Guide, an occasional "think-piece" from Jack Gould in New York, or Cecil Smith here in L.A., and the usual run of press-agent boilerplate.

Jody Cassel was far from the only TV star who'd burst on the scene, found an audience, and then vanished. There were dozens of others, overnight hits, and just as overnight, gone, departed into limbo. But I wasn't interested in playing Whatever Happened To with *them*. Right now, I was only looking for her . . . and I'd damned well better find her, and soon.

Then came a breakthrough, from Bernie, bless him. He called me on the weekend. "I didn't forget you, luv," he said, "but The Source has been playing hard to get. He says there are probably more items on her, probably in the same place where he dug up that kine I showed you, but right now, he's busy on a major project, would you believe a retrospective tribute to Dinah Shore, *that* woman is positively indestructible—"

"Tell The Source I'm willing to pay for his time!" I said.

"Calm down, dear, so is everyone else," he soothed. "But so you won't consider it a total loss, he has come up with one fascinating piece of information. Brace youself—believe it or not, it seems The Spider Lady got herself married *and* had a kid. . . . Or have I got that in reverse order?"

. . . Ah! *Certainly*—that would account for her sudden disappearance from the public eye. "She retired to do the wife-and-mother bit?"

"I can't believe that," said Bernie. "Can you picture her puttering around the kitchen, or schlepping their kid to day nursery? Not her."

"When would this have been?"

"Somewhere around 1958—the guy she hooked was a musician, name of Ellis, Jimmy Ellis . . . ring any bell? He had some kind of a jazz trio for a while, here in town."

"If I located him, he'd probably know where she is now, right?" I asked, making a note.

"I wouldn't count on that," said Bernie. "Nobody, not even the most dedicated masochist, would stay married to Jody. And as for their kid, the Spawn of Wowoweeweewoh! How would you like to go through life with that heritage? Ugh . . . I truly hope the poor thing has found a good therapist by now."

"I can check the Musicians Union, and maybe there's something in *Variety*," I said. "Thanks, and thank The Source—"

"You're really determined about this, aren't you?" sighed Bernie. "Why don't you give it up, Eileen? Face it—nobody really gives a shit about the early days of television."

I did know one person who cared, besides myself.

Sid Budlong . . .

Dick Hatch:

. . . Dark night, flickering campfire, soft ominous silence . . . whirring of tree toads, jungle noises, is something lurking out there? No, we are safe here in the light, a sentry paces up and down, his rifle in hand, three of us seated around the campfire, nearby the horses, snorting softly, occasionally stamping their hooves, we have been here some time now, we are awaiting Pablo, the messenger, who will bring us the news from the capitol, has it been fired upon yet, has General San Tomas been able to breach the defenses? rouse the people to our cause? when will we have the signal that the revolution has finally begun, *amigos,* the time passes so slowly, *where is Pablo?* How can we continue with this godamned stupid scene until he shows up? The bastard, where is he?

soft voice, urgently hissing, *Pablo, where the hell are you?*

Another voice, hoarsely now, *cue Pablo, cue Pablo!*

Who is Pablo?

I am Pablo, but why is it I cannot move my legs, I don't know how to get to my horse, I am somehow paralyzed, ropes that bind me, no-some sort of weights, while the voices continue insistently

Cue Pablo, cue the messenger!

I sweat, I heave and tug at the ropes, I cannot move, the other men out there by the campfire are restless, now I hear a bell ringing, urgently, *ringringring.*

. . . Ah, thank God, another messenger? calling on the telephone, yes, at that pay phone which stands beneath that tree over there, here in the Central American jungles, a telephone booth, insane? what it's doing here God knows, why doesn't somebody answer the phone?

Cue the messenger! the angry voice says, Bastard will never work for *me* again, that's for damn sure!

Now dogs barking, hark hark, the dogs do bark, the beggars are coming to town, no, not beggars, you idiot, *messenger! Pablo!*

Dogs are barking, the ringing isn't from a pay phone.

It's from the telephone here beside my couch, no jungle, no I am here in my studio, why the phone is ringing here? I always turn the damn thing off, must have forgotten.

Dreaming? But why a scene from one of my old television shows,—Royal Playhouse—yes—a true nightmare! The night when the actor playing Pablo never showed up, the idiot had fallen asleep from exhaustion in his dressing room, nobody had checked on him, and there we were, on the air, maybe millions of people (hopefully) watching us out there, the ragged band of revolutionaries in Studio 8-H in front of the cameras, this was *live,* no tape, we were in the climactic third act scene where Pablo comes with the news, rouses the troops to tell them to join General San Tomas, and the sonofabitch is snoring away in his dressing room, and me, up in the booth, cursing and yelling to the floor manager, I could be heard all over America because some idiot had hit the wrong switch and the line was plugged in, and I'm saying *cue the fucking messenger!*

ringringringring!

Barking dogs. Bedlam.

"Shut up, dogs!" I yelled at my two Cairns, not their fault, they're terriers, who react to doorbells, knocking, loud voices, telephones, even heavy breathing. I reached out and picked up the phone.

"Who is it?" I demanded.

". . . My name is Grimes," said the voice on the other end, "and I'm looking for Mr. Dick Hatch?"

Grimes.

"Grimes?" I said. "The name sounds vaguely familiar—"

"Damned well should," he said.

". . . Seems to me I once knew a writer by that name, a talented fella, I often wondered what became of him." I said.

"This *is* Dick Hatch, isn't it?" he asked.

"It's possible," I said, yawning.

". . . Wake up, it's *me*—Buddy," he said. "You were responsible for me being in this miserable racket, remember?"

"So long ago," I groaned. "In my time, which is over, I have employed so many different people, they all pass through my head like a vast blur, you must excuse me, I am getting old. How are you keeping, Buddy?"

"I'm fine, but I'm frustrated," he said. "This is the fourth time I've called you, Dick, don't you ever answer your phone?"

"Rarely," I said. "If it's anything important, it goes to my lawyers, and somehow they take care of it."

"Why are you living up in the New Hampshire woods?" he asked.

"Because they're there," I said. Beside my couch, on the table was what was left of my perfectly good noontime Old Forester, so I finished what was in the glass. "How did you locate me, Buddy?"

"It wasn't easy," he said. "Had a girl at Bidwell working on it for days, tracking you down—"

"Who is this Bidwell?" I asked. "Would that be the university, the museum, the foundation, or the corporation?"

"The whole ball of wax," he said, "plus a few subsidiaries you left out."

"My, you certainly do travel in auspicious circles, sonny," I said. "What might you be doing with those deep-pocket types?"

"I am their television consultant," he said, "and let's not knock it—"

"Oh, don't be defensive," I told him. "You've done well. Certainly come a far piece from your old days. I can remember the time when young massah Grimes would never be permitted in the Bidwell lobby, probably not even past the main gate . . . and now you're working for them?''

"*With* them,'' he said.

"America is truly a great country, with opportunity for all,'' I said.

". . . What are you doing, Dick?'' he asked.

"I am semiretired,'' I told him. "And after I hang up on you, I will return to the hermit business.''

"You're not cooking up some mammoth new project?''

. . . Tell him I'd been working for three years now on my Master Plan, so long and complex that when it was produced, we'd need ten, no, at least twelve hours of time to tell the story properly, that to dramatize the history of the pioneer American plane-makers would call for months of production, no, years, a major sponsor, or a consortium of sponsors, it was the most challenging idea I'd ever tackled . . . sure, I could tell Buddy, but could I trust him? Yes, I'd known him, worked with him, but people change, you can't guarantee anybody's honesty, can you?—

"For whom?'' I said. "Those pinheads who're running the business these days? Why, they wouldn't know a decent script—''

". . . if it leaped up and bit them in the balls!'' he said, finishing my sentence. "You really have remained the same old Dick, haven't you''

". . . And on that note, what else did you wish from me before I return to the rest of my afternoon nap?'' I asked.

". . . It's six-*thirty,*'' he said. "What kind of a gentleman of leisure are you?''

". . . Time doesn't matter when you're having fun,'' I said. "Cut to the chase—or did you merely wish to reminisce with the old man?''

"Dick,'' he asked, "did you ever get a letter from some lady producer in California?''

"Possibly,'' I said, "but I rarely read mail, it only serves to aggravate the corpuscles . . .''

"What about important letters?''

". . . Oh, what's important does not come here, it goes to my shysters in New York, who get paid an obscene amount each year to read it and cope. What would this important female in California want from me?" I asked. "Certainly not my experitse. Lately I have become a drug on the market, haven't you heard?"

"Actually, I haven't," he said. "But Teresa Contini called me a couple of days back, and she'd been in touch with this lady—"

My! . . . Teresa Contini. Her I could remember, without any effort. Teresa, The Earth Mother, Teresa The Good, Teresa The Trustworthy (Up to A Point). What might she be up to these days?

Buddy filled me in. It seemed Teresa had returned to New York, a refugee who'd fled California, and true to her compulsive workaholic nature, she'd assumed a job as producer of a daytime soap, one hour daily, five times a week. Which should be sufficient workload even for her. The money would be enormous, security for her sunset years, and when she dropped from overwork, she would certainly depart this life in fine financial shape. "Which show is it?" I asked. "I couldn't care less, but my housekeeper, Mrs. Danvers, watches them daily—"

"Mrs. Danvers?" he asked. "That's a familiar name."

"True," I said. "Actually, she is a piece of granite, out of Henny Youngman, by Grant Wood, goes around the house snapping rustic one-liners at me. So why does any of this have to do with me?"

"I gather this California lady wants to talk to both of us," he said. "Since we both seem to be pioneers, survivors from the days of live television."

"An arcane subject if I ever heard of one," I said, and began kicking one of my Cairns away from the telephone wires, which he had begun to gnaw on, idly, out of boredom. He snapped at my foot, snarled, his sister nipped my toe, and when I finally had them both cowed, I returned to Buddy on the phone, who now seemed to be talking about another lady. *Who?*

"Jody Cassel," he said. "Believe it or not, *she*'s the one the lady is specifically interested in.''

Jody Cassel? My, my, the names from the past were swarming past like some cloud of bees, today . . . Drones, mostly, but Jody had been a queen, there, at least, for a while back there.

''She's looking for Jody,'' he explained.

''Well, tell her to start turning over rocks, and sooner or later, Jody will crawl out from under one. But wouldn't she be more part of your scrapbook of memories, Buddy?'' I inquired. ''She and I crossed swords only momentarily. You—she really hosed.''

There was silence from his end of the line. ''Ancient history,'' he said, finally. ''I think I can deal with the subject now, but I'm not sure I want to. What the hell, Dick, why would anybody want to know about Jody?''

''Fair question,'' I said. ''Strange times. People go wandering through the elephants' graveyards, turning up what they think are ivory tusks, inducing reverence for what turns out to be discarded plastic. You deal with the outside world more than I do, pal, so *you* tell me.''

''Dick, how about the two of us getting together, we could talk?'' he suggested. ''I'm only a few hours' drive away, I could come over to you—''

''Like a couple of old farts down in Florida, basking in the sun?'' I said. ''No thank you.''

''. . . Dick, do you really hate it all?'' he asked.

''Most of it,'' I told him. ''I have seen the future, and in the colorful argot of the young, it sucks.''

''You hate the future, you hate the past, what's left?''

The dog was back chewing at the telephone wire. ''You call me up out a sound sleep, expecting metaphysical answers to dumb questions? I thought you were smarter than that!'' I said, and launched into another duel with the dogs, my foot against their sharp teeth, and for a while the yapping was deafening, until they'd retreated beneath the couch, to growl at me. When I got back to Buddy, he was saying ''—and don't take your hostilities out on *me*, pal.''

He sounded like some small boy who'd just been put down

in front of the class by his teacher. Damn, why the hell *was* I picking on him for? I don't know why, sometimes it comes out like that, unexpectedly nasty, sharp, irritated, I lapse into one of those crusty cliché characters from a British play, waving a cane, stamping my foot— "I'm sorry, Buddy," I told him. "Didn't mean to be curt. You just got some of my daily bile, call me again sometime when I'm feeling friendlier . . ."

"You could call *me,*" he said. "Take my phone number."

He recited it. "Got that?" he asked.

"Sure," I told him. But I hadn't written it down.

What would be the point? Some more reminiscing?

Don't be foolish, said Voice Over, if he's working for Bidwell, they've got mounds of corporate-guilt money waiting to endow Worthy Projects, how do you know they might not be tempted by yours?

"Give it to me again, Buddy," I said. "I couldn't find my pencil."

After I hung up, one of the Cairns peered warily out from beneath the couch, then snarled accusingly at me.

"Okay, I apologize," I told him. "I don't take too many phone calls, so when I do, is it too much to ask you to behave? The rest of the time you can be your own rotten self."

For an answer, he darted out, lifted his leg, and sprayed me briefly on the foot.

Reliable, unswerving, these two. Perverse, bitchy, deaf to criticism, perfect people-substitutes. Having them around constantly reminds me of the assholes Out There I avoid by staying indoors.

I flicked the intercom to the kitchen. "They're coming down, let them out," I told Mrs. Danvers.

"Ayuh," she said.

When the dogs were gone, I dropped back on the couch, to try and finish my interrupted sleep.

Fame, indeed. Twenty, thirty years hard work in TV, old Captain Dick Hatch, The Trailblazer my crew used to call me, starting back in those frantic days when nobody, including me, knew which end of the camera to point at the waiting cast, struggling to get our shows on, in half-finished studios where the damned carpenters were installing soundproofing around us, banging away as we rehearsed, an incessant obligato to the dialogue—

Now some idiot lady in California is after me to pick my brains, not about what I remember, or what I accomplished, the playwrights I trained, the experiments I dared to tackle, no, she wants me only to tell her about a pathetic, noisy bitch—Jody Cassel? Whom I had to cope with for eight or nine—was it ten?—months—

For God's sake, it's like the old joke, the poor guy hauled into Night Court, the Judge asks him why did you do it? The guy replies "Judge, all my life I was a decent, hard-working fella, I never did anything out of line, but today I suck *one* lousy cock, and now I'm a cock-sucker!"

Hell, I'd never even have met Jody at all, had she not been Claire's roommate, in those early dim days when Jody was paired with Buddy, and I was cutting my teeth in the business as an A.D. for, (what was his name?) silly drunk, kept the bottle in his desk drawer, constantly whistled through his teeth as he talked, *pst! pst!* could drive you crazy—Lew something? *FOX.* who produced "Thriller," no, it was before, when I worked with that fat asshole "Koo Koo, The Clown," yes, that simpering old fool, has-been who'd found a new TV career playing to kids, used to dance up and down in front of the captive audience in the bleachers, chanting *Hello, Helloo, Say Hi to Koo Koo Koo! I'm here to dance and play with you.*

The two girls living in their small railroad flat, oh Lord, Claire was so godamned beautiful the first time I saw her, I kept on staring at her, hypnotized by that blonde hair falling down around her shoulders, incredible shape, down home she'd've been Prom Queen or something, amazing, wasn't it, she was attracted to me, we'd walk down the streets arm in arm and guys would lean out of trucks to stare, construction workers would whistle, it would never bother her. There I was, simple Dick Hatch, country boy up from the piney backwoods, living off the GI Bill, pulling down a fast $76 a week from my TV job, and I'd landed myself this girl, this hopeful actress—

Enough, said Voice Over. Claire has been gone from your life for twenty-five years—

Make that thirty. And she's still beautiful, isn't she?

Oh yes, the female Circe-symbol, so organized, so success-ful, running that lush high-profit Baroness Inc. business she inherited from her Mr. Wachtel, now *she's* the Baroness, you can read about Claire in *Forbes,* or *Barron's,* she is one of those success story that drives and impels every little female M.B.A. who's careening through the corporate world dragging her attaché case behind her—Claire, the boss-lady (hey, Teresa, you could use her as a character in your soap, couldn't you? . . . except let's face it's she's been done.)

. . . My simple, beautiful, blonde Claire, once you burst out of your coccoon, you certainly did take off.

. . . Remember what she whispered, we'd made love one morning, in the half darkness of our bedroom in Stuyvesant Town, a quickie snatched when our separate schedules meshed for a few minutes, and in my ear she sighed "Oh, Dick, I wish you got half as much satisfaction out of me as you do out of your show."

I said "Ah, honey, doing a TV show is work, screwing with you is pure pleasure."

Which was one hell of a lie.

How could one brief climactic peak, enjoyed between her thighs, ever even come close (please, enough cheap puns, scolded Voice Over) to the sessions sitting up in the control booth, watch-ing all the pieces of a show I'd labored over for days shimmering up into black-and-white life on those screens in front of me—I was like the conductor of an intricate symphony, totally in charge, the cameras moving in, pulling back, panning, at my command, the actors (with sweat trickling out from beneath their Max Factor Pancake) remembering their lines, giving me a performance even though they were exhausted, running on sheer nerve after five days of rehearsal on this treadmill—the performance moving forward, correct tempo, the rhythms, the tensions, all the subtleties I've fought to get are showing—*it's working, damnit!* The booth crew softly repeating my orders, Teresa, my third arm, fastened to me by an invisible chain—the clock up there keeps moving, so do we, how wonderful it could be when it all came together, and miraculously up there something good was happening, cut to Camera One, Camera Two, hold it right there please, nice, nice—

And sixty minutes whipped past, *Live, from New York,* we have brought you another star-filled performance of the best in television drama—

. . . Oh, Christ, dear Claire, why couldn't you ever understand the difference between the two orgasms? That I could possibly enjoy both of them, the minor one in our double bed (with the baby wailing outside in her crib) the other major one, in the control booth—why not accept that they were different, but just as necessary to me?

Ah, but not to her.

Hell, who needs a shrink to explain that, go home, Gloria Steinem, I can figure it out by myself, haven't I spent most of my years studying human motivations so I could provide my actors with solid insights? Up in that control booth, or down in the rehearsal hall, Claire was nothing to me, neither my handmaiden nor my partner. She had to settle for having me to herself for perhaps an hour or two on nonshow days, when her function was to become my Florence Nightingale, climbing into the hospital bed with an exhausted soldier and restoring him so he could go back to battle.

But the rest of me? That belonged to my cast, my crew, ten percent to Buck Dawes, my agent, and to faithful Teresa Contini. And no matter how I lied to Claire, and told her how much she meant to me, in the end she was assigned to be at home, watching my show as it took place up there on our set, absorbing it along with Mr. and Mrs. America.

Poor kid, she couldn't even have a stab at an acting career, even that was denied her, once she became Mrs. Dick Hatch, the producer's wife, she refused even the smallest bit part of my show, because she said (and she was so right) all the bystanders would sneer and mutter ". . . Sure, you know how she got the job . . . she's Dick's wife, get it?" And if she'd had to audition for some other show, the same wiseasses would be saying ". . . Hell, if she's any good, how come she's never gotten a job from him."

Poor, patient Florence Nightingale Hatch, it became tougher and tougher, didn't it? So who can blame you for eventually packing it in, walking, leaving to go off on your own to find someone, or some*thing* where you, too, might perhaps get to feel the tingle, the mounting surge, the burning excitement, and the same shuddering climax, not in a bed, but in front of a camera— in some major accomplishment of your own!

No, dear Claire, I have long since stopped blaming you, not even for taking our kids with you when you went . . . and God knows, everything you've got today, you earned.

How virtuous, sneered Voice Over, how noble, how tolerant you have become in your later years, Mr. Hatch. Cut away all the rhetoric and the exposition, and why not admit to the fact, once and for all, that when it comes to women, you like dogs better?

Dogs? I flipped the intercom. "Dogs back yet?"

"Nope," said Mrs. Danvers. "When you gonna be ready for suppa?"

"In a while," I said. "Whistle them in."

"Why bother? They're like you, they'll come when they've a mind to, not a minute soona."

Hey, Voice Over, I *did* like Claire.

Matter of fact, now that I think about it, she owes me.

Owes you? How do you figure that, Mr. Hatch?

. . . Because I was the irritation factor, the grain of sand within her shapely shell, which induced the pearl she became—

Could you try for a slightly more deft simile? That one stinks.

Screw the simile, it's the thought that counts. If it hadn't been for me shutting her out of my creative life, dear Claire would certainly have lapsed into a beautiful middle-aged bored rich, what the society columns call a *matron,* going to fashion openings, or Main Chance, sitting on charity committees, staying out of the sun in the Hamptons, having her face done every few years and watching her veins harden . . . instead of which, she is a Power.

That's why she owes me.

And she's not the only one. There's quite a list, including Buddy Grimes—if he's a good writer, it was me nagging at him got him started, and kept him going (who else would have taken the trouble?) and Buck Dawes, who got rich out of the shows I produced, *and* Teresa, who learned how to assert herself—

Hold it, said Voice Over. By the same process of logic, Mr. Hatch, *you* owe Jody Cassel.

How do you figure that, Voice Over?

Well now, if it hadn't been for her, that crazy dumpy girl with her funny faces, and the cross-eyed leers, the noisy braying laughter—where would you be today?

She was the grain of sand in *your* shell.

Or have you forgotten, Mr. Hatch?

No, I haven't.

"Dew Drop Inn." A trouble show, a mess, everybody in the production office knew what a pain in the ass Jody had become, but they had a problem. She was getting audiences—the people liked her.

And now she had the bit in her teeth, she was moving in, taking over, telling everybody within earshot how her show should be done, she'd already had a series of daily battles with Lew Fox, her director, the turnover on her show was constant, if you were on staff in those days, you worked on a different show each day. Sure, I knew Jody from when she'd been Claire's roommate, but I'd never worked with her until somehow the production office assigned me to be Lew Fox's Associate Director.

Which is where I also met Teresa Contini, the pride of Newark, Teresa the Good, Teresa the Reliable, Saint Teresa The Strong, who would become my earth mother, who came with a permanent clipboard attached to her arm.

"Dew Drop Inn" was a mindless little long-forgotten piece of fluff, but it had been on for a couple of months, and it was holding an audience with Premise 6B (*fish out of water*)—city couple transported to quaint New England locale, with a batch of second bananas doing hey-rube jokes, a song or two, some (hopefully) hilarious complications, get it up, get it on, get it off in twenty-seven-minutes-thirty-seconds, with two commercial spots and end titles.

Teresa the Wise clued me in on my first day ". . . The problem is our leading lady comes attached to Buddy Grimes, who's talented, but he won't push, and she does. So she's the one the audience goes for, he's getting less and less to do, she's greedy for laughs, Buddy's stuff is very elegant and tried to be smart. I'm afraid this team won't stay hitched very long."

My Italian Cassandra was perceptive. Around "Dew Drop Inn" life was one long guerrilla war, Lew Fox sucking his teeth as he staged the show, trying harder to contain Jody, Jody nagging at Buddy for more jokes, big ones, bombers! none of that classy stuff, Buddy losing his temper and stamping out of the rehearsal hall, and then Crane coming in personally to try and settle the problems. Buck Dawes hovering around, his arm on Jody, whispering assurances in her ear, then leaving her to go outside to pace Buddy up and down the hall, everyone trying to keep the peace, avoid hostility, get the show on. *"Keep her happy,"* was the message. *"We need her.* The audience likes her, give her what she wants, *keep her happy."*

Keep her happy they did, they'd brought in other writers, to "help out," Fat Freddy and the Typist, a pair from the Coast. Freddy was an idiot-savant of humor who remembered every joke and/or bit he'd ever seen or heard, and the Typist, a big laugher at old punch lines, could give it the switch before it was committed to paper. Lines like "For my next song I would like to sing 'I gave her the mine—she gave me the shaft'," would render the Typist helpless with joy . . .

. . . How we ever got that show on the air Tuesday nights is beyond me.

But we did—

—amid the arguments, the pushing and backbiting, the last minute changes Jody insisted upon, stopping the dress rehearsal to argue with Lew up in the booth, nagging Buddy about his material, somehow "Dew Drop Inn" went out on the mighty nine-inch screen, in glorious black and white, and when it was over, the audience loved Jody even more, she waved at them, it was a love feast, while up in the booth, Lew Fox turned to me and snarled wearily (more prophetic than he imagined) "Another victory for the Madwoman of 54th Street. Well, the idiots may love her, but you can have her, *I*'m going out to get sauced."

Before she could grab him with ideas for next week's show, he had disappeared into a nearby bar, to suck his teeth and get away from her with the help of Dr. Johnny Walker. Crane and the network people, Buck Dawes? Delighted. Jody was building every week, *TV Guide* was talking about a cover story, Earl Wilson was mentioning her, so was Leonard Lyons, even Jack O'Brian had taken note of her, and liked her, praise from Caesar. There were dollar signs dancing in Buck Dawes' eyes.

Finally, inevitably, Fort Sumter was fired upon.

The hostility built up to a new high when Buddy brought in a new piece of material for Jody, a delicate little number about spring cleaning, its humor gentle but charming. When he played it for her in the rehearsal hall, Jody listened to one chorus and promptly told him it stank, too soft, no laughs, where were the big bombers? The two of them went at each other like the *Monitor* and the *Merrimac*—and then Lew Fox barged in, to announce that he was the producer-director, and he was the judge of material on this show. "You're the judge?" yelled Jody. "Okay, *you* go out and do this crap in front of the cameras, and I'll stay home and watch!"

The gauntlet was lying on the rehearsal floor, Buddy walked. When he came back two days later, he brought a new piece of material, but by that time it was too late; Jody had insisted on changing the entire spot. Now it would involve physical comedy, juggling plates with an old vaudevilian whom Fat Freddy remembered as being a real wowser. So Buddy sat around for an hour or two, watching this, and then he walked again. By the time he came back, we were doing the dress rehearsal and he walked through what few lines he had with no enthusiasm; obviously he'd thrown in the towel.

It was during the dress, that gruelling stretch, just hours away from air time, that the shit hit the fan. Jody had moved in on the juggler's spot, stopping him as he worked with the plates, why couldn't she do this trick? Hey, here's a funny bit, *I'*ll catch the cups, okay?

We were fighting the clock, Lew finally exploded, out of control. "Miss Cassel," he said, softly , over the talk-back, "Do you want to direct this show? Because if you do, you're welcome. One more interruption, and it's yours."

"Stop giving me such a hard time," Jody bawled back. "I'm trying to make this bit work!"

"Okay!" yelled Lew, suddenly out of control. "Forget it! You want to take over this dog-and-pony show you call a comedy—it's all yours, toots! Be my guest!"

He slammed out of the control booth.

We took a ten-minute break, but when it was over, we couldn't find Lew. If he'd disappeared into a bar, we didn't know which one. There we were, hours away from air-time, sans a director, Jody down on the set yelling "Okay, when do we start, let's get this show on the road!"

I don't know how or why I did it, it was a battlefield promotion, I moved over into Lew's chair, told Camera One to get set up, Camera Two to move in, and gave Jody her cue. She looked up and yelled "Hey, who's calling the shots?" "I am," I told her. "Since when?" she asked. "Since you've got to do a show two hours from now, Jody,'' I told her, ''so shall we get moving?''

Sweating, almost wetting my pants up there, I sat up there with Teresa The Reliable, and God bless those boys on the crew, they helped me through the dress, and by that time it was airtime, I was too numb to realize there was an open line upstairs to the network offices, and everyone up there was aware of the crisis taking place down here, but it was too late to do anything but to allow me to stumble on across no mans land through the show.

What happened? I can't remember much except that the show got on, another fun-filled episode of ''Dew Drop Inn,'' the audience never knew the difference, that Buddy was now doing a small part, almost a walk-on (it was already Jody's show), the people were too busy laughing at Jody's corny gags (courtesy of Fat Freddy) and when it came to the juggler's bit, she was right, damn her, when *she* caught the plates, it got screams of joy.

Somehow, we got to the end, closing number, we rolled the credits, put up the end-titles, and I could say ''. . . Okay, guys, thank you,'' to the control booth and the guys on the floor, and went out to vomit in the nearest men's room.

When I got back to the booth, Teresa was holding out one of the phones for me, and while the crew clustered around, patting my back, I heard Crane on the other end, saying ''Congratulations, Dick, you just inherited Jody Cassel!''

Easy it wasn't, even after my first into-the-breech triumph. Sure, maybe I'd pulled it off once and gotten a battlefield promotion, but from then on I had to do it each and every week for the rest of the season, because Jody, once having found me, never let me go. I was exactly what she needed in a director, somebody proficient enough in TV technology to get her show on the air, but also to do it *her* way. Face it, I didn't have status yet, nor did I have enough balls to argue back when she suggested comedy bits for herself (which usually involved taking laughs away from other performers, who could either agree, or if they didn't, wouldn't return next week), I wasn't much of a comedy man, my training was theatrical, so who was I to sneer at the latest bad joke supplied by Fat Freddy and the Typist, or at the outrageous piece of mugging Jody devised? But I learned quickly enough, it was a crash course, totally immersion in survival. I let Jody run around and mug at rehearsals, having herself a good time, dominating every minute, and then, as we got to Show Day, I'd start my editing, cunningly suggesting cuts. (First vital piece of strategy I devised—Don't blame me, Jody, of course it's funny, but it's the clock, we're running too long, something has to go.)

Second piece of self-protection. I never got into the battles between her and Buddy. The two of them were bitching and arguing constantly, trying to mediate their personal conflict was a job for a shrink, not for a director. When Buddy sulked and stamped his way out of a rehearsal (so regularly now that it had almost become a stock joke around the show), I'd send Teresa out after him, to pacify him, soothe his ruffled feelings and bring him back. That way I could concentrate on the problems of getting "Dew Drop Inn" on the air each week, and still remain sane.

Oh, Jody was on a roll, and she was loving it, overnight she'd become an applause-junkie. The network press department was hard at work, that meant more space—Walter Winchell picked up on her and made love to her in his column, Lenny Lyons would quote (or misquote) what was supposed to be her latest quip (written by Fat Freddy) and then Jack O'Brian, who had a TV column, decided Jody was in the great tradition of Fanny Brice, Bea Lillie, and Martha Raye, and instructed his readers to pay attention.

Then there were interview spots with Faye Emerson, on her talk show, and personal appearances, items in the papers that Leland Hayward was considering her for a new musical, that film producers were nosing around, and a guest shot on Ed Sullivan's "Toast Of The Town." Each week, there were more fans clustered outside the studio stage door to get her to sign her name, to grab and clutch at her, she could sense how much they loved,

loved, loved her!—they threw kisses and screamed, and followed her all the way to Lindy's where they could snap her picture with their $9 flash-cameras so they would be immortalized with their Jody!

By then, my future was assured. It was Buck Dawes who took me by the hand and led me into the upper echelons of Success. First, I should sign the four copies of this representation contract (which he just happened to have tucked here in the inside pocket of his J. Press gabardine suit) and my future would be assured. How? Very simple—he would negotiate for me a new network contract, my status would change from that of lowly hired hand to upper-echelon producer-director, with a hefty raise in pay.

What would be my first assignment? Relax, that, too, would all be settled. This fall they had it set for me to take on (would I please keep this under my hat?) the *new* Jody Cassell Show, to replace "Dew Drop Inn," which was about to drop out.

The weekly salary Buck dangled in front of me sounded lovely, especially since I'd married Claire, and we had our first child on the way. I took out my pen and started to sign Buck's contracts; then I had second thoughts. Did this mean I would spend the rest of my life calling for close-ups of Jody Cassel yelling "Wowo-weeeweewoh?"

Oh no, not at all, Buck assured me. Once Jody's new show was well and truly launched, there were other plans for my future. Live TV comedy, even when the show was a hit, was much too iffy. The future of this new medium lay in good drama, and there were plenty of talented new writers around to be discovered and brought into the public's eye. Crane's network had plans for dramatic shows, and that meant opportunities for me and Teresa to move into one of our own. One more season with Jody, and we'd be up, up and away.

I signed.

The Buddy-Jody weekly battles continued, but now they were ironic, an empty ritual. I knew his presence on the show was superfluous, he'd become the stranger at the feast, but how could

I tell him what I knew? One warm May day we were rehearsing the show, and the customary argument between Buddy and Jody exploded, she insisting a piece of material he'd written was useless, what she wanted was big belly laughs, and Buddy for the nth time grabbed his briefcase, stuffed everything inside, and walked out of the rehearsal hall.

Silence. We were all embarrassed for him, she didn't have to carry on like that in front of all of us, did she? We were under pressure, so what? Buddy was a human being, deserving of better. So, as always, I sent Teresa out to bring him back. But Jody didn't miss anything; she hailed Teresa as she started out—where was she going? "Out to get Mr. Grimes, Mr. Hatch told me—" "Forget it, both of you," said Jody. "Buddy's a big boy, if he wants to sulk, let him. We have a show to do here, does anybody else want to argue with me?"

Neither of us picked up the gauntlet. Not that we didn't feel guilty about it . . . Buddy did not come back, not that day, nor for the rest of the season. Jody's fans didn't seem aware of the fact, Fat Freddy and the Typist were able to write him out without any trouble at all, and the Boss Lady seemed to have proved her point.

Yes, that's what she became, after *TV Guide* ran a cover picture of her, with a caption NEW BOSS LADY OF COMEDY, and by the time the show folded, Jody had decided to take a cottage out on Fire Island, what was the point of working so hard if you couldn't enjoy yourself with the trappings of your success? And since she needed somebody to enjoy it with her, she asked Claire to bring me out and spend as much time as we wanted during the July and August hiatus, when we would need a beach the most.

By now Claire and I had moved into that tiny apartment down in Stuyvesant Town. Oh, it must have been tough for Claire, watching her ex-roommate Jody making it big, while all Claire was making was our baby number one, staying home and puttering around the house, waiting for me to come home from my eleven-hour days attending to the Boss Lady. Even when Jody would embrace Claire and chortle "Oh, hon*ee,* how I envy you doing the mother bit!" Claire would smile placidly, but it must have annoyed the hell out of her.

I never realized how much until we got out to the Island. It wasn't really a vacation, it was a social treadmill, Jody was the newest celebrity on the beach, that meant a steady series of parties, all the best people out there, the Broadway producers and the writers and the agents; she was a prime catch, she'd liven any group, she'd perform her numbers, oh they loved her, and so Claire and I dragged along after her, feeling as if we were her retinue (which we damned well were) to be introduced as "my director" and "Claire, his wife, and one of my oldest friends."

Claire began to hate it, all the drinking and the pairing, the couples wandering off into the summer night to get it off somewhere out on the dunes, it must have been torture for her watching all the available women come on to me while she dragged around behind that awkwardly swollen bulge that would become our first. And what was supposed to be our vacation shortly turned into a series of work sessions, because sporadically the gag writers who'd been assigned to work with Fat Freddy and the Typist for Jody's new show would appear, bringing out comedy concepts and sketch material, which meant conferences. Then the two new songwriters we'd hired to do Jody's special material came out to audition their songs, Teresa came out with technical stuff for me to go over, Jody had to get into that; she wasn't letting anything go by now, even the technical stuff, without putting her oar in. Buck Dawes came for one weekend, that meant more preshow conferences, endless arguments and discussion, and while all this went on, Claire, more and more frozen out of the process, would spend her time cooking, or puttering around the rented cottage kitchen, serving sandwiches and getting drinks for everybody, and then cleaning up afterward. Then, while we sat around arguing, she'd silently put on a large floppy hat and a voluminous robe and disappear down the cement sidewalk, carrying her bag full of paperbacks and suntan oil, to end up very much alone, out there in the bright sunlight, by the ocean.

She went to bed early; we stayed up talking on about the show. One night I came to bed very late, Jody had kept me up arguing over a sketch, and I finally climbed in beside Claire. She stirred, rolled over to me and whispered, quite clearly in the darkness, above the sound of the waves out on the beach, *"Have you screwed Jody yet?"* I was so stunned by her question I didn't answer, and she went on, saying Oh, I wouldn't blame you if you did, Dick, the way things are with me right now.

Finally I protested, why in God's name would I want to do that?

Oh, it's not you wanting *her,* she said. It's the other way around, she has got to control you completely, and what's a better way?

I never answered that, I figured Claire was pregnant and that always gets women a little crazy, hormonal imbalances, right? I put my arms around her and we finally went to sleep.

When we finally left, to go back to the city, Jody saw us off at the ferry, threw her arms around Claire and said "Oh, God, what will I do without you here—listen, I'm buying that house, we'll come out here every year, right?"We agreed, pledged oh so firmly we would, then got on the ferry and went back to Manhattan. But the following year, after our baby had been born, and Claire was back to her old svelte shape, came spring, and Jody had the cottage again, when I mentioned to Claire we might plan to go out and spend a couple of weeks with her again, Claire shook her head and said ". . . Anywhere *but."*

As things turned out, it was an academic question, because by that time, Jody would not be on the best of terms with me. All during the fall and winter I'd served out my time on her new show. Whatever salary the network paid me, I earned; the show was a success and Jody was holding up as a star. The new format called for more of a variety format, with lots of guests, singers, dancers, actors from Broadway shows coming on for sketches, it was a lot like what Berle and Gleason were doing, and it worked.

Massa Buck Dawes was as good as his word, mid-March I got my reprieve. He'd been conferring with Crane on next season's scheduling, and I was called upstairs for a meeting, very hush-hush, where they told me to begin developing an hour dramatic show for this fall, something like Kraft, or Philco, I had all summer to prepare, and if I need staff, Teresa and I would be in charge of forming a proper cadre.

That afternoon I went back home and swore Claire to secrecy, we got a babysitter in and went out to celebrate, nobody else could know why, but damnit, we were entitled to enjoy a night out, dinner at Sardi's, I paid a fortune for a pair of seats to *Kismet* afterward we ended up in our own apartment, still euphoric and splitting a bottle of champagne in our bedroom, making love quietly so as not to awaken the baby, it was indeed a lovely night.

Early next morning I had a call from Jody, would I please come up to meet her at her apartment, she realized it was my day off, but she had to see me.

Unsuspectingly, I took a cab up to Central Park West, where she now lived in an old building, a large layout with high ceilings, furnished with all sorts of crazy pieces of furniture she'd been picking up all year long with the help of our set designer. The total effect was that of being in a theatrical warehouse. Jody met me at the door, a cup of coffee in her hand, she was wearing a bright orange robe trimmed with maribou, silently she led me down the hall and into the living room, which was now hung with drapes and filled with low cushions, so that it resembled the interior of a tent in which Rudolph Valentino might have seduced one of his leading ladies.

Before I knew what was happening, I found myself on the receiving end of a barrage of accusations, she let me have it right between the eyes, Okay, you traitor, she told me, I gave you your shot at success, and you took it, and the first thing you do is turn around and shaft me? Me, the one who got you started? Is this how you show your loyalty, by walking off my show?

My God, how had she learned already?

She obviously had been working up to this scene, and was playing it for all the drama it was worth, but for once, she wasn't hamming it up, she was underplaying, not raising her voice. Did

I think she didn't have sources who kept her informed of what was going on at the network? Hell, part of survival in this business was to know what was happening behind her, and if I'd been planning to walk off her show and take that bitch Teresa Contini with me, wasn't she owed at least the courtesy, the simple honesty of being told directly?

By now she was only a few inches away from me, still without raising her voice, but I could see the hand which held the coffee cup was trembling, so she really was holding herself in, not screaming like the Jody we all knew and loved from rehearsals. So, what did I say on my behalf? Go ahead, Mr. Hatch, *speak up*.

Oh, Lord, at that moment I needed some clever writer to feed me lines more than I ever imagined I would, somebody to supply the answers—

My old grandmother, down South, always said—When in doubt, tell the truth. Make it short and snappy, and get ready to duck.

So I did. I told her I'd enjoyed working for her, that it had been a terrific education, I'd learned a lot, but she knew and I knew the truth, that I wasn't a comedy man, no matter how I'd managed to direct her comedy show, it wasn't my future, what I really wanted was drama, I'd trained for it in school, came here to New York to have my shot at it, so if the network wanted me to do a drama show, hell, I was under contract to them, to do what *they* paid me to do, and not anybody else, and that was it, period, end of paragraph, and thanks for the year's training.

She continued to glare at me, breathing heavily, her lush bosom rising and falling beneath the sea of moving maribou, and then she finally said "Godamn you, Dick, if you wanted to be begged, okay, I'll do it once, and that's it. Stay with me, and screw drama." Then she leaned even closer and suddenly added "And if you want to screw *me,* that's okay too!"

The two of us stood there for a long moment.

I figured what she'd just said had to be a reflex, a comedic ad-lib, so I chose to ignore it, and began to explain why I thought developing new young writing talents for drama offered more of a challenge.

Did you hear me, buddy? I just offered to screw you, she said. Do you think that's something happens every day?

Before I could say No, it certainly wasn't, she had her arms around me, she was pulling me toward her, then her mouth had found mine and she was kissing me, hard, urgently, her tongue forcing its way into my mouth, now she was tugging me toward the low couch behind us, we toppled over onto a pile of those huge, overstuffed pillows, I was engulfed in maribou as she wrestled me down, the orange robe was coming open and now there wasn't anything between her ample shape and me, the whole thing was like a moment out of a burlesque sketch, except for the fact that she damn well wasn't playing it for comedy, her face was close to mine and she whispered So you'll stay with Jody, right? She nipped at one of my ears, then ran her tongue into it, humming softly. You'll fuck me, and then you'll fuck drama, right? She began to pull at my shirt buttons, crooning some tone-less little song over and over as she continued nibbling at me, wherever I moved I found one of her hands there ahead of me, just relax, relax and enjoy, she ordered.

I had to put a stop to this, but how? Nobody had to remind me hell hath no fury like a woman scorned. My throat was dry but finally I managed to say Jody, I can't do this.

You don't know how? she crooned. Okay, so you're a quick study, I'll teach you! and now she was back, tearing away at my clothes, all over me. It took considerable effort to disengage myself, even while I was doing it, I knew for certain that to refuse to screw Jody this morning was the end, finito, she would have to take it as a personal affront . . . but I also remembered what Claire had told me, that night in the cottage on Fire Island, another piece of true gospel, that once I screwed Jody, she would consider she controlled me completely.

What a Hobson's choice!

Somehow I managed to wrestle myself free of her, got up from those damned bulky cushions, looked down at her, then I said to Jody, I think you're absolutely great, many thinks for the suggestion, but I'm married to your friend Claire, and you wouldn't want me cheating on her, would you?

She stared up at me, the dressing gown wide open, that marabou waving back and forth, like marsh grass, framing those Titian-style breasts, and then she said, very softly, Hey pal, the Boss Lady does not have to beg. Yes or no, this is an offer which will not be repeated.

I nodded. Okay, I do appreciate it, I'm an ingrate, but no thank you, ma'am.

You're walking out on me? she demanded.

No, merely going home, I told her.

By now she was up, pulling her robe tight around herself. I started toward the door.

Remember Buddy? I heard her say. He figured he was indispensible, too—have you heard from *him* since he walked out on me?

By now I'd made it to the hall.

. . . So *go do drama!* she yelled.

When I got home, Claire wanted to know what Jody had called me all the way uptown for, and I told her it was the usual routine hassle, script changes for next week's show, and that was that.

We finished out the season with no replay of that ugly scene. Jody had obviously decided she still needed me, so she did her job, I did mine. Crane had auditioned a couple of hopefuls to replace me as Jody's director-producer, and eventually she decided on one of them, a seasoned Broadway veteran named Jess something-or-other, who'd had a lot of experience with revues and summer stock. He spent the last few weeks sitting in on our rehearsals and the actual show, so by the time we finished in early June, he had a pretty good idea of how she wanted it done.

The last night, the show ended, we rolled the credits, Jody stood there yelling and blowing kisses to her audience, and we went to black. I stood up and thanked everybody, cast and crew, there was a lot of sentiment, suddenly, everybody embracing and hugging, then, without warning, a bar had been set up backstage, caterers were bringing in food (the fine Italian hand of Buck Dawes, I later found out) and we were in the midst of an impromptu farewell party for me and Teresa. Claire appeared, as did other wives and girl friends, everybody seemed to have known about it except me, we all stood around swapping anecdotes and basking in the remarkable fact that we'd completed an entire season's run on live network television! (Remember, that was in a primitive era when hopeful new show concepts could be born on a Tuesday night at 8, cough into life for thirty minutes, and be scrapped by 8:32!)

Jody emerged from her dressing room in some remarkable outfit of bright blue, had a drink, exchanged laughs with the crew, chatted with Earl Wilson, the columnist, who'd dropped by to get some anecdotes for tomorrow's paper, giggled with our cadre of gypsy dancers, and then suddenly her dresser appeared, bringing out a Tiffany & Co. bag, filled with packages. Presents! She was passing them out, well, what they hey! Jody chortled, she was the Boss Lady, the network had picked up her option for the Fall, she could afford to be lavish, right? There were tiny elegant boxes for each of us on the show, right on down to the humblest stage-hand, when we opened mine, we found, amid the tissue paper, a cigarette lighter made in some Hong Kong factory, of finest gold-toned plastic, with a caricature of Jody grinning at us from one side, on the other, an inscription, LOVE AND LOTSA LAFFS FROM YOUR BOSS LADY!

A gag? Yes, it had to be—there had to be other presents. No, that was it, 50-cent lighters for all . . . And the sheer chutzpah of it, amazing, but well she knew that everybody on her show depended on her success, right at this moment, she was hot enough to get away with it.

I stood there staring at mine, and Jody came over. That's so you won't forget me, buddy, even while you're off doing that high-class drama shit! she said defiantly.

I thanked her.

Very thoughtful, Jody, said Claire, sweetly, but Dick doesn't smoke, or haven't you noticed?

Why yes, dear, I have noticed, said Jody, suddenly the smile was gone, her voice had developed an edge to it, oh Claire, she said, let us both face it, this man Dick Hatch here is absolutely perfect. He doesn't smoke, he barely touches booze, he certainly never screws around—he's very talented, and now he is going to bring live drama to the waiting TV audience—oh, you are so lucky he married you, Claire, because *you* are perfect, too, and since the both of you are meant for each other, *enjoy yourselves!*

Then she was gone, disappeared into the mob.

I went around and said goodbyes to the rest of the crew, waved at Buck Dawes and Teresa, and escorted Claire out of that theater studio on 54th Street for the last time.

On the way home, Claire said Well, she's really got it in for you, doesn't she? All because you had the nerve to leave her show?

Yes, I guess that must be it, I said, and changed the subject.

That was the summer we went far away from Fire Island, came up here to New Hampshire, and rented this house, which we finally bought. Where I sit now, up here in my attic-studio, thinking about other times, other place—

Enough reminiscing, said Voice Over. Ancient history, save it for your memoirs—

There were delicious odors filtering up the stairway from the kitchen below. As I went down the stairs from my studio, they became even more tempting; I was suddenly reminded I hadn't eaten since breakfast.

Downstairs, Mrs. Danvers was standing over her stove, doing things to her various pots. I came up behind her, put my arms around her waist and gave her an affectionate version of the Heimlich Maneuver.

"Quit it, you old goat," she said. "Ready to eat? I'm not plannin' on keeping this hot all night."

"I'll get the dogs in first," I told her.

"You and them nasty little dogs, what a trio I'm stuck with," she said.

"We love you, too," I told her, as I found my coat and a flashlight.

Her real name is Kozowski, she's been working for me ever since her husband came home from 'Nam. She's here five days a week, and on the weekend she goes to visit him. Sundays she rests up here from seeing him; he's a mental case. I blew her a kiss and went out the kitchen door.

Fresh air hit me, caused me to reel. I hadn't been out all day, out here tonight it was pitch black, not a trace of moonlight, cold, oh so sharp and clear, typical deep-freeze New England night. . . . Where were those damned dogs? I whistled, then called for them.

Far off in the distance, I thought I heard the answering sound of barking, but it was a sharp yapping, insistent, continuous, my two? Yes sure, I recognized it, I whistled again, the barking went on, irritating, stubborn little bastards, why wouldn't they come when they were called? Using the yellow glare of my flashlight to light my way, I stumbled through the underbrush in the direction of the sound. Gradually it was closer, on I went, stumbling through these damned woods, my domain, a random branch slapped at my cheek, I ducked, no stars above me by which to reckon, so dark and wintry, very foreboding out here, well now, said Voice Over, you're the one who wanted isolation, solitude, okay, you got it!

I crashed through another stand of spiny underbrush, and now the barking was louder, right at hand, I shone the flash in that direction, there they were! anxious, eager, the two little bastards, dancing on their hind legs, yapping madly at the base of a thick old oak, they were trying to reach something they'd obvious treed—"You miserable creeps!" I yelled, exasperated, "not up there—you're supposed to go after rats *under rocks!*" They ignored me, still jumping and leaping indefatigably, what the hell could be up there that was so attractive? I shot my flash upward, the beam picked out a pair of unwinking eyes, peering down at us below, ah, a raccoon, stretched out on that sturdy branch, perfectly safe from my two anxious Cairns, seemed like a female, she'd obviously been up there for some time now, she was prepared to stay as long as it took until these two noisy interlopers finally gave up and departed *her* domain, she'd outlast them, let them exhaust themselves, damned fools—". . . Come on, leave the poor bitch alone!'' I commanded, and grabbed at them, but they dodged away from me, still mad for the kill.

I wasn't going to play this dumb game, I'd had it, I went at them with my foot, kicked one, then the other, they yipped in pain, then ducked away. *"Home!"* I commanded the two miserable creatures, and gave them another boot to get them started, a brief yowl indicated I'd made my point, they both turned and snarled at me, "Okay, report me to the A.S.P.C.A.!" I said. "Home!" They went scampering off into the dark.

"Okay, baby," I told the raccoon, "they're gone, you can come down, it's safe—"

She didn't move, sat there, warily watching me.

As if she knew me. Survivor, in the tree up there, hey, was I going mad, or didn't she look like someone I'd once known, with those two big black circles around her eyes, that clown face, sure *that could be Jody*

Up above me, queen of the hill, sneering down at me, "Hey, Dick, I'm up here and I'm fine, screw you, who needed you, your dogs didn't scare me, wowoweeweewoh, these are the laughs!

. . . Jody, poor driven creature, out here in the cold?

I was hallucinating.

I started back toward my house.

. . . which way? After stumbling a few feet into the nearby brush, I suddenly realized I wasn't seeing any light, no sound, I was alone out here, surrounded by the dark, nothingness, only the sighing of the wind in the branches above me, now I couldn't even backtrack to where the damn raccoon sat—

Christ, it was cold out here a real bone-chiller, I hadn't brought out a hat, or gloves, who'd figured to be out here this long, damn those miserable Cairns for the mess they'd gotten me into

where the hell was I?

Hey dogs, where are you?

Was I going to end up a headline? TV PRODUCER FREEZES TO DEATH ON OWN NEW ENGLAND FARM

Well, at least the *Times* would have a decent obituary, researched with all my credits, going back thirty years or so, I'd probably get a good column or two in *Variety,* both the West Coast trades would pick up the story, on the Late News they'd run clips from some of the shows we'd one in the Golden Age, right? All my contemporaries would be sitting by their pools, or down at the Springs, shaking their heads sadly, Poor Dick, Jesus, how could he manage to be so sloppy, out in the woods, freezing, on his own place? Must have been sauced, or on something, it couldn't have been an accident, Claire's phone ringing, people asking her how it had happened, our kids bewildered, Teresa being called out of a script conference to make a statement, Buddy Grimes writing a sober but heartfelt paragraph or two on his mentor, Dick Hatch, and that damn in L.A. who wanted to know all about Jody Cassel would have to go elsewhere for her information, she'd never really know the truth.

Oh, Christ, said Voice Over. Stop dramatizing your exit—you haven't died yet!

Right. Screw it—too ironic, nobody would buy it as a plot twist, a man could not become lost, not even half a mile away from hiw own damned house—*where were the dogs?* "Hey—you bastards!" I bellowed, *"I need you!"*

". . . Here, *here!"* I croaked, my hands were getting numb, no feeling in my face, but yes, thank God, they were suddenly crashing back toward me, now they were whimpering and jumping at my feet, thankfully, they didn't remember just a few minutes before, the same feet with which I'd kicked them—they'd come to help me, save my life, if we were going to freeze to death, they were willing to stick with me . . . that kind of dumb loyalty is hard to come by from people, dogs are more reliable—

". . . Come on, take me home!" I commanded, now my lips were numb, so was my nose, they started off, I followed them, fighting the numbness, pounding my hands together to keep the circulation, when branches slapped at my face, I hardly felt it.

Then suddenly, thank God, there it was, behind a stand of bare tree branches, the faint light of our kitchen windows winking at me, as if to say "Get your ass in here, idiot."

When I stumbled through the kitchen door, the heat hit me but I could barely feel it, I stood there breathing hard, the flashlight practically frozen to my hand, my fingers too numb to release it, Mrs. Danvers stared at me and the Cairns. ". . . Well look what the cat dragged in," she said.

"Almost didn't," I told her, my mouth barely worked, as if I'd been to the dentist and was full of Procaine. I collapsed into a chair.

She reached for a bottle in the nearby liquor cabinet, poured me two fingers of straight Scotch, then held it to my lips. ". . . What in blazes was you doin' out there?" she asked. "You ain't no woodsman!"

I got the booze down, while she gently helped me off with my boots; faint life began to tingle back into my toes, then my fingers.

You see? taunted Voice Over. Your big death scene was premature, and now you're involved in an even bigger cliché situation, Dick—a beam of light appears, we hear celestial choirs, and just like in that old Frank Capra movie, you, Dick Hatch, have been given a second chance! . . . and what do you plan to do with it?

. . . The two Cairns were watching me warily from beside Mrs. Danvers' stove. Well, I should start with them, for saving me. "Okay, you're forgiven," I told them.

One of them growled at me, showing fangs.

"I love you, too," I said, and poured some more Scotch.

I had just about recovered enough to eat my supper when the damn telephone rang inside. "Don't want to talk to anybody," I told Mrs. Danvers.

She came back after a moment. "Lady in California," she reported. "Name's Tighe. Says she'd like to talk to you about somebody named Judy? Judy . . . Kissel?''

"The hell with her," I began, on reflex, but then Voice Over began crooning, warningly, Ah, ah, remember, you cannot blow your second chance, this Dick-baby, is the New You, *re-born!*

". . . Take her number," I told Mrs. Danvers. "I promise to call her back."

"You serious?" she asked, skeptically.

"For at least another reel or two," I told her.

*   *   *   *

Eileen Tighe:

You can find dozens of places like Radclyffe's, one of those medium-priced singles-bar watering holes that thrive, usually in shopping centers, all done up with comfortable booths drowned in seductive darkness, the decor plastic Tiffany-type lighting fixtures, the gloom penetrated by the sound of softly beeping video games. The ceiling is hung with the inevitable hanging baskets filled with plants a bit withered from exposure to cigarette smoke. The whole place is an efficient piece of profit-making machinery, set up for the lunchtime crowd who need enough time for two or three quick belts before they bolt down the daily Chef's Special (from the blackboard), after which they duck out into the daylight, either back to the office to close the deal, or perhaps off to the nearest hot-bed motel for another form of instant consummation.

When I got there, it was 2:30, and the place had begun to empty out. Soon the bar would be abandoned to the few steady afternoon drinkers, silence would reign until 5 (The Happy Hour) when the whole process would begin again. Meanwhile, I had an appointment here to talk with Jimmy Ellis, who'd been married to Jody, long years ago. He worked here at Radclyffe's, in the bar, playing piano for the lunchtime and evening crowds.

It had taken persistence to get this meeting arranged. When I'd first called him, to ask if we might chat about his ex-wife, there's been a long silence from his end of the line, then finally he'd remarked ". . . Hey, lady, what're you, some kind of archaeologist? That's *ancient* history."

I'd kept after him, explaining what I was about, no, I wasn't some crank fan, or a kook dealer in memorabilia, I was a fairly sane movie executive with Interfico, legitimately trying to assemble a possible film project about Jody, played against the background of early live TV, I could assure him I'd ask the right questions, and could we please have a talk about her?

(I didn't mention the legalities, drummed into my head by the firm's lawyers, i.e., whomever I interviewed about Jody should sign a formal release, protecting Interfico against any possible future claims of invasion of privacy. If this turned out to be an interview, I'd bring the release forms with me.)

". . . I don't have a helluva lot to tell you about the Bird Girl," he'd said, dubiously. "We married, she had Pretty Baby, then we split, she took the kid with her. Period, end of chorus. I don't think there's a movie in that . . . at least not for *my* four bucks."

"We could both be wrong," I said. "Could we at least talk?"

"Hey, that's not a bad first line," he said. ". . . *We could both be wrong* . . . but why not try it?" He began improvising.

Finally I got us back on the subject of Jody, and he'd agreed to meet me today, after his lunchtime gig here at Radclyffe's. ". . . But you gotta be barking up the wrong tree, sugar," he warned me. "It's been years since I saw or heard from either of them—the Bird Girl, or Pretty Baby Cassel . . ." Then he began crooning again, softly, ". . . *We could both be wrong* . . . I'll have to see where that goes."

. . . I'd seen some photos, unearthed from newspaper files, of the then Mr. and Mrs. Jimmy Ellis, snapped at some Manhattan boîte of the 50's. There was Jody, smartly togged out for the evening, wearing a chic turban, leaning adoringly on his shoulder, sticking her tongue out at the camera for a laugh, while Jimmy Ellis grinned lovingly at his wife. He seemed to be quite attractive, a tall, slender chap with a shock of blonde hair.

So I wasn't prepared for the sight of the middle-aged man with the ruddy cheeks and the large white mustache, who sat at the leather-padded grand piano here in the gloom of Radclyffe's bar, a cigarette dangling from his lips, moodily running through the strains of "Satin Doll," which served as an obligato for the chatter of the thinning crowd.

". . . So you're the lady doing the *Citizen Kane* bit on Jody?" he asked, after I'd introduced myself. He eyed me, grinned, and said ". . . Funny, you don't *look* like an archaeologist."

Then he launched into a bright, upbeat jazzy tune, one I'd never heard before. "Recognize this?" he asked. I shook my head. He began to sing, in his somewhat hoarse baritone:

". . . Here's the girl
We all adore.
Here's the pixy
We've waited for!
Laughing and singing—
She shows the way.
She's the kid who'll always play!
So raise your glass and drink a toast
To the lovely loony character we love the most—
Jody, Jody, Jody—Jodee, *it's you!*"

"You don't remember the theme song from her TV show? I wrote that," he said. "Sold at least fourteen copies!" He hit a few closing chords, then got up from the piano. "Not exactly Hit Parade material, but it got the Bird Girl on with a big flash, which is how she liked it." He led me over to a table by the window and we sat down. I ordered coffee from the waitress, who wore jeans and a tank top on which was emblazoned the slogan I DID IT AT RADCLYFFE'S! Jimmy Ellis ordered a daiquiri.

"You look like a sensible lady," he said. "Who ought to have a lot more to do than to go chasing around after survivors of the Bird Girl. Whatever made you think there's a movie in her story?"

"I think she's a very colorful character," I told him.

"Today?" he asked. "You think any of the customers still gives a damn about her?"

"If we dramatized her story . . . maybe," I said. Although I was far from sure . . . yet.

"Does the Bird Girl know you're doing this?" he asked.

I shook my hand. "Matter of fact, I don't know where she is. Do you?"

He stared at me over the rim of his daiquiri, finished it, and then waved the waitress over for another. "No, I thought maybe you'd tell me," he said. "Have you talked to Lenore?"

". . . Your daughter?"

"Was when I last looked," said Jimmy Ellis. "She'd be about 27 now, wouldn't she? No, 28." He sighed. "Christ, how tempus does fugit, right? I got a Christmas card from her a few years back, but that was when I was working in New York." He shrugged. "She probably lost my address, too."

He might have been talking about a female friend he'd once met on a cruise ship, certainly not his daughter.

". . . So you have an idea Jody could make a movie, do you? Well, what the hell," he sighed. "You get yourself some funny broad who can play her—it might work . . ."

"Who would you suggest to play you?" I asked him.

"Me?" he asked. "Ha. I come in for about forty seconds in the first part, strictly a walk-on. Sorry, lady, I couldn't be much help to you on this project. Jody and I weren't married very long." He glanced at his watch. "Time for you to play again?" I asked.

He shook his head. "No, I'm finished until tonight, but there's a soap I watch every day at 4—so I'd like to get home before then. Come on—we'll talk on the way . . ."

We walked a short distance down to a nearby apartment building, and went upstairs to his place, a small, impersonal bachelor layout. From his living room there was an adjoining terrace that offered something of a view of the boats anchored down below. The furnishings were totally impersonal; except for the small piano in the corner, the place had all the ambiance of a Holiday Inn suite.

While he made himself a can of soup in the small kitchen area, I kept him talking. Yes, of course I had the facts about Jody's career, her early triumphs, then her depature for films, but I had very little "handle" on her as a person. (I certainly wasn't about to tell him of Bernie's hostility, or Teresa Contini's open hatred.) But might he please help me with some point of view about Jody herself?

"On stage funny, offstage, she tried too hard," he said, sipping his soup. "But then, what's new about that?"

. . . Where and when—and how—had she and Jimmy met?

". . . Around," he told me. "I was gigging in New York, somebody asked me out to Fire Island one weekend, to play a party, I think it was at some producer's house, a Broadway guy named Levin? Harry, is that right? No. Herman. I think. Who can remember . . . it was all so long back, anyway, this was a mob scene, and I was playing piano, and people got up and did their schtick—and the first thing I know, this girl comes over to me at the piano and asks do I know 'Stormy Weather,' so I played it for her, she sang, and you know it was crazy, but we fitted— she made me sound great, and she was one damn good singer, did you know that? Jody could belt out a torch as good as any of them . . . Dinah, or Rosie Clooney, Peggy Lee, Maggie Whiting—she was in their class, you know we even made an album, I did the arrangements? 'Jody Sings At Midnight,' somebody ought to reissue that, you know? Now that all the old hits are back, thanks to Linda Ronstadt—anyway, that's how we met. . . and we went on from there . . ."

"To marriage?" I asked.

Jimmy Ellis grinned. "Well, we did rehearse a while, *first* . . ."

. . . They'd gotten married in late summer, it was after they'd palled around for a couple of weeks. "We found out we could have laughs together," he said," "and about then, that was all that mattered . . . good times. See, I wasn't out to get a job on her show, or to steal her money, or sell her some phony bill of goods . . . and God knows there were plenty of those creeps hanging around, you know, all those shitheels that come out from under rocks whenever there's a new hot star they can fasten on to, like moss . . ." He grimaced. "So I guess she must've liked me for myself, and it was mutual."

He'd moved uptown into Jody's Central Park West apartment, and then they'd gotten married, a private ceremony, just a couple of friends. "That's when I met her mother," he remarked. "Cold broad, very tight-assed—lived up in Westchester somewhere . . . sure as hell didn't approve of *me,* you know?"

There had been a brief honeymoon up at Grossinger's—" A couple of days was all the time we could steal. We had a ball, they gave us a big suite, treated us beautifully, why not? It was great publicity for the place, Jenny Grossinger saw to it that all the columns picked it up, but she was an okay lady, never asked for anything in return. Of course, Saturday night, show time, *if* Jody got up and took a bow, and ended up doing half an hour in one, for the people, up there on the stage, well, nobody put a gun in her back, did they? Besides, Jody was a real hambo—she couldn't say no to a crowd of people in love with her, she was crazy for all the applause, and the laughs . . ." He shrugged. "So why not? What else are we in this business for?"

He got up and went to the refrigerator, found a can of beer, and returned with it. "Her show was back on the air, she was working ten, eleven hours a day, busting her hump—me, I was playing with a group up at the Rainbow Grill, was that it? Yeah . . . so that left us Sundays to be together, turn off the godamn phone and be a married couple . . ."

He stared out the window at the rows of boats parked at slips below. ". . . Christ, that was some layout we had up there, she'd had the place decorated by a designer, Carl—he did her show, too, one morning I come in and find the two of them going over fabric colors, some bright blue, others pink, and I'm so dumb, I haven't a clue what's going on, I ask her why she has to redecorate one of the bedrooms pink or blue, and she says 'Well, doll, it's customary for when you do the nursery bit.'' And I ask 'Who's having a baby?' And Carl says 'Well, lover, it certainly isn't *me*—not unless I skip over to Denmark for an operation!' ''

That's how he'd discovered Jody was pregnant? Yes, and there seemed to have been a lot of problems after that; after all, she was the star of her own network show, and in those early days of the medium, somehow pregnancy didn't fit in with the image of rowdy comedy Jody typified.

Crane up at the network objected, her sponsors weren't too happy, but Jody persisted—she wanted the baby, damnit! "She argued with them, she said if Lucille Ball could have her baby on television, and all the fans loved it, then *her* fans would accept it—what the hell, she wasn't doing anything terrible, was she? She was married, perfectly respectable . . .''

". . . How did *you* feel about it?'' I asked.

Jimmy downed the rest of his beer. "Oh, what the hell,'' he said, softly. "If she wanted a kid, what was I supposed to be, the heavy who said no?''

Jody had been right, her fans and the TV audience seemed to have accepted her pregnancy with love and admiration. "Oh, that winter we had all sorts of wierdos hanging around,'' he recalled. "Fruitcakes from everywhere, ladies who knitted the baby special booties or sent in recipes, people who wanted to make tie-ups for their products, everybody had a suggestion for a name, I tell you, that Pretty Baby Cassel was a celebrity before she even opened her mouth for the first yell . . .''

Pretty Baby Cassel? . . . Strange, one would have thought if Jody had married him, it would be Pretty Baby *Ellis?*

. . . but I said nothing.

"Well, that's about it,'' he said. "She was born, a perfectly okay baby, in May, right after the show where Jody had Dr. Spock himself on for a guest shot—perfect timing . . . big kid, almost nine pounds . . .''

He rummaged around his bureau and returned with a framed photograph, taken long ago, Jody holding an attractive little girl in her lap, the two of them squinting into bright sunlight on what was obviously a California patio. "That's her," he said. "I don't have any recent ones. She's married, has her own life . . ."

Did he mind my asking, what happened to the marriage after that?

". . . Absolutely nothing," he said. ". . . I guess we stopped having laughs, that's most of it. Came out here the year after, Jody was making a picture during her hiatus, big deal, they'd started making a movie star out of her . . . We did the whole bit, the big house in Beverly, the nurse, the sports cars, you know? It was Jody's idea I do the music scoring for her pictures—she even got her agent, Buck Dawes, he came out here, too, to go to bat for me with the producer. But once I landed the job, Christ, I got to hate it . . . I mean, damnit, it was being *Mr.* Jody Cassel, her lover-man, that was it, nothing else, and things are tough enough in this racket without something like that going against you! . . ."

For the first time since we'd met, Jimmy Ellis had lost his cool, was grimacing at the echo of an old misery. ". . . Shit, it wasn't that I couldn't cut it!" he told me. "I mean, maybe I wasn't André Previn, or Dave Brubeck, but when I was going good, I could turn out the music as good as anybody working out here, so why did I need to prove myself every day? Ah, it wasn't Jody's fault, she was busy with her own problems, it got so whenever we sat down by ourselves, all we wanted to do is dump on each other, hell what kind of a basis is that for a marriage?" He sighed. "And it didn't get better from there, believe me. One day we had a real battle, next morning we both realized we were at the end of the line . . ."

He shrugged. "Always quit while you're ahead, cut your losses, that's how she felt, I guess . . . I moved out. No big deal. The divorce was handled in New York—that was her tax-man's idea—if it had been California, it would have meant community property, get it?"

He got up and stretched. ". . . So I got married again, a couple of years later, stewardess I met, Swedish, great broad . . . That didn't last, either. What the hell, maybe I'm just not the marrying kind, huh? Hey, not a bad title . . ." He moved over to his small piano, sat down and began to run through a few chords. ". . . Maybe I'm not the marrying kind," he sang, in his baritone, ". . . and maybe that's why you don't care . . ."

It was a pleasant enough strain, nothing brilliant, but certainly good cocktail lounge music.

"Where does it go after that?" I asked.

He paused. "Ah, that's the hard part, finishing them," he said. "Okay, enough about me . . . what about you? You married, sweetheart?"

"Once," I told him. "Not any more."

"Great looking lady like you?" he asked. "What a waste of talent." He began to play a familiar melody, after a bit I recognized it—an old Cole Porter tune, "You'd Be So Nice To Come Home To."

". . . Thanks," I told him.

"Oh, you recognized it?" he asked. "Okay, here's my next message." He segued into another Porter melody, this one was "Let's Do It." He watched me, grinning.

I shook my head. "Have to get back to my office," I told him. "Nonsense," he said, and segued into another song, this time I didn't recognize the melody at all.

I shook my head again . . . "What was that?"

"The song from *Love In The Afternoon,*" he told me, and winked.

"But I thought you wanted to watch a soap about now," I said.

"Ah, why watch them when we could make one up for ourselves, baby?" he suggested. He beckoned me over to the piano, to sit beside him, and began to segue again, to yet another song. This time it was "Come Fly With Me."

"Very flattering," I said, "but I really have got to get back to the office."

"Ah, come *on*," he said, "nobody's so busy they can't stop what they're doing for a nice half hour of relaxation . . . or even an hour, maybe?"

He had a point there, especially when weighed against the joyless, frenetic treadmill I travel on each day. So why was I so disinterested in staying on here, to make it with him?

It wasn't simply that I'm too old and sedate for matinees, but these days, when it comes to sex, I guess I'm a snob. I'd have preferred the surroundings to be a bit more exciting than this impersonal bachelor pad; it was depressing here, and so was he, this middle-aged man, going to fat, who exuded loneliness, wreckage, and the aroma of failed probabilities . . . who would lead me into his bedroom and have me by the sound of his FM, and once done, would get up to fetch himself another cold can of beer from his refrigerator.

Romeo, he wasn't.

But, then, who said I was still Juliet?

Jimmy Ellis winked at me again, and began to play another song, singing

". . . Don't run away little girl,
Can't you *fershtay,* little girl?
. . . I'm a great lay, little girl . . ."

How romantic. A lyric worthy of any of a Larry Hart, certainly.

No thanks. I stood up, gathered my notes, stuffed them into my bag. "Sorry," I told him, "I'll have to take a rain check . . . My loss. Thanks for the interview."

"Okay," he said, lightly, "so I'll watch my soap." He got up from the piano and came over to the door. For a moment, I thought he was about to grab me, to persuade me to stay, but he made no move in my direction. "Can't win 'em all," he said. Somehow, the fact that he wasn't interested in proceeding any further with the seduction wasn't insulting, merely proof I was doing right in leaving.

"Say, listen," he said, "if you ever do run into the Bird Girl anywhere, tell her I think about her. Not often, but—'' he began to sing again, ''. . . Once in a while . . .''

I promised I would. ''But so far,'' I told him, ''She's been very hard to locate.''

''The same goes for Lenore,'' he said. ''Pretty Baby Cassel.''

I went down the stairs from his apartment, and then I heard the sound of his piano again. Now he was running through a familiar melody, one I'd heard a long time back . . . what was it? Damn—I couldn't place the title.

It ran through my mind all the way back to Westwood, and it wasn't until I was on my way up in the elevator that I remembered what Jimmy Ellis had been playing . . . Such an irony. Was it intentional—or his subconscious calling the tune—that his exit music was a piece called ''Lucky To Be Me''?

It was when I got into my office that I realized I'd never asked Jimmy Ellis to sign one of these damned legal form releases.

. . . Well, what the hell, there hadn't been much usable in his story, so it could wait.

My secretary had left notes on my blotter. Mr. Budlong wished to speak to me instantly, *important*. And she also had dutifully recorded a message from the East; she'd called Mr. Richard Hatch—Mr. Richard Hatch had promised to call back later.

Beautiful—finally, a breakthrough!

''Go on in, he's expecting you,'' said his secretary.

I went on in, but did not see any visible Budlong.

''Where've you been all day?'' asked Budlong, his voice soft and gentle. It seemed to be rising from the floor, and in fact, it was. He was lying flat on his back, shoes off, feet bare, his arms extended wide, and he was staring at a small electronic device next to his face that was attached by tiny wires to his ankles and his forearms. On its miniscreen there were numbers and flashing signals; the device beeped, buzzed, and flashed steadily, like some minivideo game.

"This is to measure stress," he explained. "The meter keeps constant track of my blood pressure, measures the flow from the arteries, keeps a record of my pulse, while I do these modified yoga exercises, see? Got it in Hong Kong last week."

The entire scene resembled not so much science-fiction as it did a sequence from an early Boris Karloff thriller.

"Definitely worth the trip," I murmured.

"So," he asked. "How are we doing with the Jody Cassel?"

I launched into a brief rundown of my progress (which so far hadn't been too substantial, but I exuded clouds of optimism.) I had my lines out everywhere, and just today I'd had a meeting with Jimmy Ellis, her ex-husband, but the big news was—

"Get much from this Ellis?" he asked.

I shook my head. "Strictly a minor character," I said, "*But*— I've finally tapped into somebody mainstream. I'm about to speak with Dick Hatch—in New Hampshire."

Budlong stared at his medical jukebox.

"Who he?" he asked, finally. "Remind me."

. . . My God, talk about age-gap! Did I really have to explain to Budlong that Dick Hatch was one of the genuine trailblazers from those earliest days of live TV? Right up there along with Tony Miner, Fred Coe, Ralph Nelson, Del Mann—the innovators? That his contributions to TV drama and its programming would always be counted by his peers as truly primary . . . that he was a mover, a shaker, perhaps even one of our few authentic geniuses—

Ah, ah, Eileen, don't get carried away, remember, your boss Budlong was watching "Howdy Doody" over his TV dinner when all of this took place—"Okay, let me tell you about Dick Hatch," I began. "One of the very few people who were there when it all happened—he *made* it happen. He worked with Jody Cassel— that's how he got started, so he has to be loaded with firsthand information and history, anecdotes—and that's the best kind of dramatic in-put for this project—"

"Must be real old by now, eh?" mused Budlong. ". . . And if he's back East . . . that means travel bills." He grimaced.

"Worth it!" I insisted.

". . . Maybe," said Budlong. "Meanwhile, I've got some news for you. I think I've located somebody a lot closer to talk to—very lucky for us—and I'm meeting the guy tomorrow . . ."

Take a deep breath, Eileen—the secret in this business is not to have stress, but to induce it in others . . . "Which guy might that be?" I asked.

"Well, this is another one of those pioneer types," said Budlong. "Maybe even more of a pioneer than your guy. Came out of early TV, then made it to pictures, went to Europe for a long time, very big cult-figure over there, *Cahiers du Cinema* and all that crap, he's back here in town for a few days, so I though his brains could be picked a bit, no commitments, of course, nothing tangible, lunch tomorrow, just a little cheerful chit-chat . . ." He winked.

". . . and you'll want me there," I said.

". . . Mmm, not just yet," said Budlong, checking his pulse. "See, it was his idea—we're going to have a simple, low-caloric schmoos—plenty of time for a group-style getting-to-know-you and all that later, so please, Eileen—*please,* don't get paranoid, you are not getting sidetracked."

Damn him, how did he sense so well my instant Pavlovian responses?

"May your parallel trackperson ask, who is this wonder-man?"

". . . I'll tell you tomorrow afternoon," grinned Budlong, ". . . *if* he's a wonder-man."

On my way out, by some fortuitous circumstance, there was no guard on duty; Budlong's secretary had stepped away from her desk. I took advantage of her absence to glance at the appointment calendar she kept for Budlong.

Under LUNCH, for the next day, there'd been printed the name *S. Fischer, 12:30, The Friars.*

. . . The name rang no bell.

. . . Low-caloric lunch, at The Friars? A contradiction in terms. That was a watering-hole whose kitchen specialized in cholesterol.

I was determined to stay on our parallel tracks. Even if he was straying.

I went back to my office and checked through the Directors Guild yearbook. Finally I located him. *Selwood (Sully) Fischer, Director-Producer, member since 1954. TV Credits: (Live and Tape) Philco. Studio One. Climax! Perry Mason. The Fugitive. Arrest and Trial. Cimmaron Trail. (Films) Riders West. Cherokee Scout. Jamison, Federal Marshal. Four Rifles for Father Ryan. Manhattan Set-Up. I Love Louisa. The Cutting Edge. Give My Regards to Broadway* . . . on and on went Mr. Fischer's credits, he'd obviously worked steadily all through the '60s, crossed over to London in middecade (to take advantage of the lush tax-break to be gained by living and working out of the U.S.?). There he'd made Arms For the Queen, The Chalk Farm Gang, Assault On The Bank of England, Slattery, M.I.5, then he'd crossed the Channel to give us The Return of Arsene Lupin, Meet Me At Cap Ferrat, Beyond The Alps, then he'd gone south to Italy, for such further epics as Dr. Jekyll and Mrs. Hyde, Ciao Signora, Alpine Quest, in Yugoslavia there'd been Dalmatian Adventure, in the Near East he'd given us The Beirut Story, Hawk of the Dunes, Caravan to Djerba—on and on they went, this man's credits were certainly a cinematic grab-bag, he specialized in the sort of film you see through weary eyes when you turn on your TV at 3 A.M. . . . and what were Mr. Fischer's latest credits? For the past year or so, he seemed to have been Mexico-based, and from there he'd been responsible for Treasure of the Incas (1981) and something called La Turista (1982).

I couldn't get a fix on him at all. What could Sully Fischer contribute to a project based on Jody Cassel's career in live TV of the '50s? . . . and why was Sid Budlong playing him so close to the vest?

I needed Ozzie. Perhaps he could give me a clue, some sort of hint about the latest discovery of Sid Budlong's.

. . . But when I called Ozzie's office, he was out at a meeting in the Valley, and his secretary had no idea when he'd return.

Back to business. I put in a call to the New Hampshire number Dick Hatch had left with my secretary.

The phone rang several times, and then on come one of those damned message machines, I heard a voice from far-off, frozen New Hampshire, saying ". . . Sorry, ah've gone to sleep," with still more than a trace of that down-home Southern accent, ". . . but you leave me a name and a numbah, and ah promise to call t'morra . . . and that's especially for you, California lady . . ."

Click, beep, and silence.

. . . Damn, that meant I'd have to wait till tomorrow on *him,* too—

"This is a very frustrated California lady," I told his machine, "name of Eileen Tighe, wants to talk to you, waiting not-so-patiently—"

There was a click on the other end, and then that same Southern accented voice with its mellow timbre spoke again—"California lady? Don't hang up, it's me—"

"I thought you were asleep," I said.

". . . So did I, but I'm not," he said. "Let's talk. What's all this about Jody Cassel? You honest to God think there's some kind of movie in her life story?"

"I hope so," I said.

"Why?" he asked. "Who remembers *her?* Nobody even remembers me, and I got me a lot more credits . . . hell, to this generation, I'm like the dinosaur—"

"It's that whole period," I told him. "I grew up watching it evolve, I was one of your fans, and I think it could be fascinating and very exciting—especially if you told the story from the point of view of a young girl fighting to be a female comedienne in what was essentially a male world—comedy . . ."

"Close up, Jody wasn't precisely a barrel of laughs," remarked Dick Hatch. "So, how does *she* feel about this project?"

". . . I wouldn't know," I admitted. "Matter of fact, I don't even know how to locate her—that's been one of my real frustrations—"

"She don't even know about this?" asked Dick Hatch, then chuckled. "Hoo-eeh, that's a real switch! Usually, Jody'd be right up there in the pilot's seat, givin' the orders to everybody—you tellin' me nobody's heard from her big mouth lately?''

I filled him in on my latest strikeout with Jimmy Ellis, her ex, how I'd gotten precisely nowhere with Buddy Grimes and Teresa Contini—

". . . Ah, they wouldn't know where she was," said Dick Hatch. "But it ain't like Jody, disappearin' like that . . . Say, what about Buck Dawes? Certainly he'd ought to know where she is now . . . Did you check with him?''

No, I hadn't. Buck Dawes? The shadowy Cardinal Richelieu string-puller behind the ever-spreading conglomerate, EMC (Entertainment Management Corp)—not the easiest person to reach, especially on the phone—

"Don't know him," I said.

". . . Call him and say ah said to call," Dick Hatch instructed. "Anybody knows where the bodies are buried, it's old Buck, believe me, and why don't you try callin' Claire?''

Claire? Claire who?

". . . The Baroness. Leastways, that's the name of the business she runs. Her new last name's Wach-tel. You mean to tell me you go to bed at night without coverin' your sensitive kisser with Love's Mask? You don't rise and shine and rinse through every single pore with BeNeath? Why, Good Lord, California Lady, do you realize you are positively starvin' your derma?''

"I apologize!" I told him. . . . Certainly I'd heard of the Baroness, one of the most aggressive and shrewdly marketed cosmetic lines to survive in that cutthroat scene, but as for Claire Wachtel, its boss-lady—"Excuse my ignorance, but what's *she* got to do with Jody Cassel?''

". . . Talk to her, you'll find out," promised Dick Hatch. "For a while there, the way I heard it, she kept Jody out of the unemployment office, so get in touch with Claire, and if she plays hard to get with her, just tell her old Dick was the one put you on to her—''

"Old Dick?''

". . . That's me. Was a time when her name was Claire

Hatch,'' he explained. ''Small world, ain't it?''

''. . . I didn't know that—''

''Ancient history, California Lady. You call Claire in her executive office, don't deal with the hired hands, talk directly to her . . . use my name, try and locate Jody,'' he yawned, ''You'n'me'll talk again, soon—''

''Please,'' I said. ''I've got so many questions to ask about those early days, and your involvement—all the things that were happening then— We've got to sit down, get it all straightened out, if I don't get it from you, who's going to give me the history?''

''. . . Talk that way, you make me feel like some lame old Civil War vet, on display in the park,'' he observed, and yawned again. ''Sorry, I had me a long hard day, the booze is beginnin' to do its job, now I'm goin' to sleep, stay in touch, California Lady . . .''

There was a click, and my New Hampshire connection had signed off, before I could shoot my first question at him—had he ever heard of S. Fischer?

Let that wait.

. . . Claire Wachtel, the Baroness, and Buck Dawes—Cardinal Richelieu! Oh, indeed, I had big game to go after. Fianally I could move out from behind the goalposts, with, thanks to Dick Hatch, a solid entree to help open doors.

I picked up my phone to ring Sid Budlong, and tell him the good news.

Then, before I put through the call, I hung up.

Let him go his own way, taking his blood pressure and inhaling cholesterol with his new-found thrill, Sully Fischer. *I*'d go after the others.

. . . This was still *my* project.

*   *   *   *

Teresa Contini:

. . . Quarter to three, there's no one in my expensive pad here
except me . . . and *me*—with my new six-hundred red grand view
of Central Park, that wild downtown skyline twinkling at me, *hey
Teresa*, you got yourself some kind of a place here, wow, you
better believe it, nobody gets to live 24 hours a day with this kind
of a view who hasn't made it big, hey—you'll probably end up
having the place photographed by *New York* magazine—

—Sure, six and a half rooms, smack on Fifth, high-class
building, fully staffed, with that genuine wraparound terrace so
you can go out on nice days and soak up the soot—if and when
you get itchy in the summer, hell, you can always plunk down
another bundle and rent yourself some elegant pad in the Hamptons, where you and Patient Griselda can get away . . .

—Patient G., who's snoring away in the bedroom, she can
sleep even when you can't, simple kid, dreaming her dreams,
why not? what's she got to worry about? I work a six-day week
handling all the production problems, I bring home more than
enough to support this lifestyle, I'll take care of her, pay her bills,
her tuition in art school, she knows that, and why do I do it?
Because I need her and I want her around, so is that such a lousy
trade-off?

. . . *Hey, Teresa Contini*, you sure came a helluva ways from

New Jersey, know what I mean? Sitting here, in this expensive piece of real estate that's all yours (not even mortgaged, this is an all-cash building, thank you), with your corporation and your pension plans and your trusts and your tax-shelters, well, one thing for sure, Teresa, you ain't never gonna starve, right? No—lady, nobody's ever going to run a benefit for you!

Oh, Mama, I really made a liar out of you, didn't I? All the nice plans you had for your Teresa. I was supposed to grow up nice and clean and straight, learn to cook and sew, wear a girdle, go to church regularly, and save my precious body until I found the right boy (Italian, preferably, maybe, in a pinch, they'd accept an Irish), and then we'd be married, in church, of course, go on our honeymoon to the Poconos, we'd come home and start housekeeping, me cooking, him working, nine or ten months later, right on schedule, I'd pop the first bambino, then keep on turning them out, like a pasta machine rolling out ziti noodles, until after five or six kids I'd end up looking like my own mother, short, squat, and wide, and nagging my own daughters . . .

I didn't buy any of that. Drove my poor folks crazy in the process. How come I wouldn't? It was good for all my friends, they all were happy to become earth mothers . . . So what was it turned me instead into Ms. Teresa Contini, the big shot lady producer, living here in this expensive Fifth Avenue pad?

Who knows? Something inside me wanted something else, that's all, look at a flock of baby ducks swimming around the pond following their parents, you always see one playing tail-end, going off to explore, right? Okay, that was me. And oh boy, when I think of the yelling when I first tried to break loose from the family ties, to evade their clutches, how I argued and fought and wept until I was able to persuade them to let me go to Katharine Gibbs. What kind of a thing was that for A Teresa Contini? *Shame!*

And worse, I ended up getting my first job, not in Jersey, but in Manhattan—Sin City *itself!* Ay! Miss Contini, in the typing pool at Masterson-Whitfield, the advertising agency, there she started, a nervous little girl in her dark blue two-piece suit, with the simple white blouse, commuting every day, bringing home a fast $42.50 a week.

Ay! You should have heard the screaming at home in Jersey when I told them I was moving into my own two-room place in Chelsea, because commuting home each night on the Tubes was getting too complicated—that was after the agency had assigned me to be girl-Friday to that crazy bastard Lew Fox, who was doing their live half-hour show. I wanted to live *in New York?* . . . Where it was well known to all that girls could be attacked on the street by various gents of the ethnic persuasions. How cars could pull up to the curb and you could be grabbed by hairy hands and dragged into the back seat, to disappear into a life of endless white slavery. Or where good Catholic girls could be subjected to all sorts of humiliation by men with Only One Thing On Their Minds, and what about all those lustful married executives who lured you into their offices, where they'd lock the door, throw you on the couch and you'd have to submit, Or Else? . . . oh, yes, and those suave Park Avenue playboys in their tuxedos, who would invite you up to their penthouses where, after you'd been drugged with wine (laced with Spanish Fly, natch), off came your clothes, and they did unspeakable things to your defenseless, cringing body.

. . . So okay, Mama, I was ready. Did any of it happen?

Forget it.

Mama, how wrong could you be? When I remember all those nights when I lay awake in my narrow bed, down in that Chelsea cheese-box (the rent a fast $97.50 a month, nowadays that wouldn't even pay my telephone bill here in this pad), tossing in my virginal bower, exhausted from my twelve-hour secretarial days running around after Lew Fox, worrying about all the chores for tomorrow's rehearsal—had I forgotten any detail?, if I had, Lew Fox would chew me out in front of everybody—and finally dropping off to sleep, to fantasize what it would be with somebody here beside me, maybe one of the actors we'd hired that week, young Jack Lemmon, or George C. Scott, we had Paul Newman in to read but Lew Fox didn't like him so we turned him down, and instead we hired would you believe Jimmy Dean, sitting on the set scratching and snuffling, just a kid, and I couldn't take my eyes off him for the three days' rehearsal . . .

None of those bastards ever laid a hand on me, Mama . . . . Certainly not Lew Fox (later on I found out the bastard was queer, but how was a naive kid from Jersey supposed to know that?)— and he talked a good game, that was all.

So I went from show to show, and made more money each time, and pretty soon the family in Jersey was proud of their Teresa—look, *there's her name* on the credits at the end!

Sure, I was good at my work, damn good, they could rely on Teresa Contini, all through the rehearsal and the show, we were all pals, after the show, I'd go out with the crew to Hurley's, on Sixth Avenue, and have a couple of drinks, then we'd sag, exhausted, all everybody wanted to do was to go home and collapse on a bed. They had wives . . . Me? I had me.

Then I got hooked up with Dick Hatch, my Old Pappy . . . and for a while there, I thought, well, what the hell, Teresa, he's a Southerner, he's a Protestant, but you're not getting any younger, are you? If you're ever going to lose it, why couldn't it be with this tall, soft-spoken guy? So what if he was married, hell, the two of us had become pretty damned close up there, all day in our office, hour after hour down in the rehearsal halls, in the control booth, he spent more time with me than he did with his own wife, that beautiful blonde he kept stashed away at home . . . who probably figured he was fooling around somewhere . . . so why not *me?*

It just never happened. Not Dick, he wasn't gay, he was worse, he was driven. Old Pappy's first love was, first, last, and always, the audience, theirs was the only high he enjoyed, reaching them, stirring them up, getting them to respond to his creation each week . . . that was how *he* got *his* rocks off.

Oh, he did give me my first anatomy lesson, God how he drummed it into me . . . "Teresa, honey, when you pick up a script and read it, you got to look for the *spine*, see, then you find yourself the *heart* . . . and finally, the best part, is when you feel it touch a *nerve*.''

Okay, okay, Pappy, solid advice, when you're dealing with some blocked playwright who's got a half-baked script that needs work—so you lay those rules on him (and it usually works) . . . but not much comfort when the lights go off in a girl's bedroom, and she's there all by herself. . . . Where the hell was the somebody, the anybody, who'd reach his paws out from the car and lure me into a life of white slavery?

. . . Who could figure out I'd pick on Buddy Grimes?

Buddy, you mixed-up, talented sonofabitch, why did *you* have to be the one?

You got to me in the studio. It was while I watched you, Buddy, for so long you'd been letting that loud-mouth Jody trample all over you. Mr. Nice, standing there, allowing her all those childish ego-tantrums, her petulance, her demands, in front of us. You never faced up to her, oh no, the lead in *High Noon* wasn't your style, instead of fighting back, what did you do? You did your walk-away bit, stamped out of rehearsals, like some angry teen-ager, to sulk. You were as big a baby as she was . . . only she was *tougher*. Damnit, where would she have been without you? Still taking dance lessons somewhere in Westchester, sure. You'd spoon-fed the girl, done your best to show off her talents . . . and for what? So Buck Dawes could take her and blast off with her to the Land of Big Bucks? Ah, what was wrong with you, Buddy? You were the one with the talent. Why were you such a shrinking violet? Anybody else would have decked Mighty Mouth Jody right there in the studio. Not you.

(Teresa, you really know how to pick them, you *stupido!*)

So, did you ever stop to wonder what would have happened to you if I hadn't dragged you, kicking and screaming, into writing your own scripts, which was the beginning of the brilliant career you've had (and *now* who remembers Jody?).

Yes, Buddy, *me*. You think it was Buck Dawes, your loyal agent? Forget it. Or did you believe Dick Hatch did it all, without me to nag at him? And it certainly wasn't one of those smart-assed Broadway fringe types you were hanging around with, after you'd finally split with Jody, while you wrote your oh-so-cutesy special material for that so-called bright and contemporary Broadway musical revue—the one that was due to go into rehearsal soon, very soon. (As soon as the producer could raise some backing, which, with his track record, believe me, would be the 12th of Never!)

Oh yes, sweetheart, remember the night I ran into you again, down in somebody's Greenwich Village floor-through, at an audition of your revue, the place jammed with so-called backers, *ha!*—most of them freeloaders, in for free sandwiches and booze. Me—I'd come all the way over to sit in and listen that night because Dick Hatch had sent me to cover the audition, to look for new talent. Crane, at the network, had just presented us with our own one-hour drama slot and assigned Dick and me to fill it with original scripts . . . written by whom? "To be provided for our audiences by the most exciting of the new talents on the television scene!"—that's how the publicity boys had announced it. Translation: *Go Find Bright Kids Who'll Work Cheap.*

So there you were, at the piano, playing and singing your stuff, what was that song, oh yes, about a New York tourist in Jamaica, a comedy calypso number (why do I remember after all this time?)

". . . Man brought a bagel to Jamaica,
Now we all eat bagel in Jamaica
Man brought a bagel to Jamaica
And we plant him a bagel fruit tree!
Yellow bagel, don't sing up in any tree.
Yellow bagel, it drop like a rock on me!"

Lord knows, I had to get you off that kick. That night I decided you were the one I wanted to lure me into a life of white slavery, but when I came on to you, I was Teresa Contini, Girl Executive, all brisk and business. "Come up to the office and talk to Dick Hatch and me about maybe writing us a script, okay?" I wheedled. You played hard to get for a while, but finally you agreed, you'd call when you found some spare time . . .

You never did call back.

I was a determined girl, you couldn't brush me, so *I* called *you*, by that time I knew damned well it wasn't just your latent talent that interested me.

I'd told Dick about you, and *he* was interested; he'd already begun to trust my judgment about writers and scripts. Meanwhile, I'd done some checking around; Buck Dawes' office said you *might* be available . . . Might? Hell, you hadn't done anything decent since you'd left Jody Cassel, it had been downhill all the way, you'd worked on a couple of one-shot hour revues at NBC, tried your hand at a pilot script for some borscht circuit comic (who was being given a shot at the mighty nine-inch screen— and had missed). There'd been a few weeks writing special comedy material for Peter Lind Hayes and Mary Healy, then a stint with Faye Emerson, nothing permanent, so now you'd finally ended up writing intro-material for some band show, very smart stuff like ". . . and now, in a gayer mood, we go South of the Border, while the band plays 'Tico-Tico!' "

. . . No, not exactly the Big Time, was it? Not with Jody being rubbed in your kisser each week, in her own prime time slot, taking bows and yelling "Wowoweeweewoh!" to her cheering fans.

Dick and I finally dragged you up for the meeting, you paced around putting on your best stiff-upper-lip act, telling us all about the prospects for your new revue, and how busy you were. Then Dick put a fatherly arm around you and asked you if you'd like to handle an adaptation for us, a story right up your alley, it might make a good one-hour TV script. Which one was it? Now I remember . . . sure, it was "The Uppers and The Lowers," all about an old jazz musician from New Orleans who needs a new set of teeth before he can make a comeback playing his horn in some New York club . . . and the young New York girl who tries to raise money for him by betting on the horses with her neighborhood bookie, and then she and the bookie fall in love, it was all very Damon Runyon, but not a bad idea, hell, in those days we could get a playable one-hour script out of much less . . . and often did.

You were still being hard-to-get, you had so many other commitments . . . and how did you know it was your kind of a story? "I'd have to read it first," you said.

"Fine and dandy, pappy," said Dick. He was running around doing three jobs back-to-back as usual, editing scripts, getting a cast together for next week's script, this was Friday and rehearsals began Monday, with us it was always frantic-time. ". . . If you don't mind giving me an answer in half an hour," he said.

You read the story and came back, shrugging and shaking your head. Okay, you thought you might just give it a try . . . so when would we want a first draft?

"Yesterday, pappy," said Dick. He wasn't kidding, we had other writers coming in every day with scripts that were maybe only a day, sometimes mere hours away from actual production . . . talk about being under the gun? Hell, we were *in* it!

We laid out the ground rules for you, told you how many sets wer could handle, how big a cast to write for, the various restrictions involved in our weekly one-hour dramas . . . we'd settle the money (a respectable fee, maybe $750, well it sounded pretty respectable back then) and could you please get started pronto?

I walked you down the hall and out to the elevators, and you asked "Listen, what makes you so sure I'm right for this?"

"You're not?" I said. "Well, this is a hell of a time to confess that."

You stared at me, and I knew what it was, sure, for all your bluff in the office, you'd been having it rough ever since Jody had dumped on you, maybe you'd begun to doubt your own talents after all the various disasters, now you were safe in your little weekly cocoon, writing stuff like ". . . Ah, yes, there may be a hundred different ways to say 'I love you,' but has anybody phrased it better than Messrs Rodgers and Hammerstein, whose next simple statement will be . . ."

"Listen," I said, "we're here to help, remember, it's not a written exam, it's a script."

"That's what they all say," you said. "In the beginning."

"You'll write, and it'll be good," I said.

". . . and if it isn't, you'll put out a contract on me, correct," you said, and then, you caught yourself. "Sorry, bad ethnic joke, Teresa, *scusi.*" You learned over and bussed me on the cheek. "I really do thank you."

"You're welcome," I told you. "And could we see some pages by, like . . . Monday night?"

"For a nice Italian girl," you said, "you're developing into a real Jewish mother."

That was my function, to keep calling him every couple of days, to nag politely. Dick had his meetings, rehearsals, script conferences, so I had to explain how anxious we were to see what you'd done. "Maybe after you read this, you won't be so anxious," you told me. That was after my third call. "Sorry," I said. "I forgot you're a comedy writer. How about tomorrow afternoon?"

"Listen, Miss Contini," you said, "in the immortal words of George Bernard Shaw, don't call us, we'll call you!"

Finally your first draft came in, and I grabbed it. When I finished reading it, I felt like throwing up. I didn't need Dick Hatch to tell me it wasn't right at all, maybe I'd pressured you too hard, whatever it was, you'd obviously written it with your left hand. Glib and flashy, it was all incident, hardly any characterization to the characters. (See, I was already a graduate student of the Dick Hatch School of The Script, with his anatomy lesson firmly drummed into my head.) Okay, maybe you had a spine here, so what, that was what you'd started with, but heart? None. And as for nerves? No tingle anywhere.

Dick got to read it, but he wasn't discouraged. "Ain't got there yet," he drawled, "but if we keep naggin' at old Buddy, maybe he'll come through for us.'' He was so busy getting ready for next week's dress rehearsal that he scribbled off a batch of his notes and delegated me to get in touch with you to go over them right away.

You finally showed up, later that day, during the dress, and I took you over to a quiet corner of the studio, behind a flat, and we sat there and I went over the notes. That was a real fun session. As you listened to the various changes we were suggesting, I could see the hostility steaming up out of your ears into a dark grey cloud.

You didn't say much, you just sat there, nodding and listening to the notes . . . I could have been talking to the piece of scenery behind you. During a break, Dick stopped by. ''How we doin'?'' he asked.

''We're telling me how I flunked the exam,'' you said. ''Okay, so the script stinks, but if you wanted drama, you should have called in Arthur Miller. I am a comedy man, remember?''

''. . . Take it easy, pal,'' Dick said. ''It ain't so dire . . . Take the notes one by one, we'll work with you—ain't the first time we did rewrites—''

''Nope. Forget it,'' you said. ''I make you a present of the script, you can have it all back—*you* make it into a silk purse. *I* abdicate.''

You grabbed your briefcase and started to walk off the set, while Dick rubbed his eyes and shook his head. ''Hey, does he think he invented tension?'' he asked, wearily.

I knew what you were up to, it was the same old bit!—the walk-away-from-it, I'm-taking-my-marbles-and-going-home number you'd done so often with Jody, but this time I was godamned if I was going to allow you to be so self-destructive—besides, I was the one responsible for bringing you in, it was up to me to clean up the mess! . . .

So Teresa the Good went running after you . . . (which was, of course, what you'd wanted all along, right, you complicated bastard!)

Caught up with you down the hall, just before you could get

into an elevator, "You and I have got to talk," I said, "It's not the end of the world—every script needs work, what are you afraid of?"

I practically grabbed your arm, took away your briefcase, made you follow me to the tiny coffee shop on the downstairs floor, in Grand Central. It was late in the day, they wanted to close up soon, in the back they were mopping up the floor, but the Greeks knew me, so they let us sit in a booth, and there we sat, glaring at each other over cold coffee, and finally you said ". . . I've been turned down a lot lately, and I just don't need any more of it, thank you . . ."

"Understood," I said. "So you blew your stack, and now you feel better, right?"

"Nope," you said. "Not a bit."

"Why can't we get a few simple rewrites out of you?" I asked.

You shook your head and made a face. ". . . I don't know—I guess I just can't handle rejection," you said. ". . . My old man could . . . he was a master at it. Not me."

. . . And you started to tell me about him. Rudy Grimes . . . once the star of "Laffs & Company," a vaudeville comedian, according to you a pretty big name on the circuit, right up to the end of vaudeville, when talking pictures came in and killed it dead. The '30s were pretty tough for him, Rudy had scratched around, taking what he could, bits in two-reelers out in Brooklyn, a few night clubs, maybe a summer stock job here and there . . . The more you told me about him, the more I realized how much you loved the old man, suffered for him, a lot of his contemporaries, Fred Allen, Jack Benny, Phil Baker, and the others, Burns & Allen, his cronies, from vaudeville, had made it big in radio, but not him . . . and it must have hurt, but he never showed it. Then you told me how once, you were still a teen-ager, you'd gone along with your father to an audition somewhere in midtown Manhattan, went inside with him to meet with the bookers, two dapper guys sitting in their office, behind desks, one of them eating a sandwich, the other cleaning his fingernails, your old man giving them a big smile, then going into his *shtick*, knocking himself out to be good, busting his chops to be good. ". . . And when he finished," you said, shaking your head at the memory, "the first booker belched, took a swig of his coffee, and said 'Sorry, we really can't use that kind of stuff, Rudy, the public won't buy it, send in the next one, on your way out, okay?' " And your old man had smiled, and shrugged, and went over and shook hands with them before he left. "Shook hands with them!" you said. "I wanted him to kick those two guys in the ass! On the way out, I told him so, and he said 'Oh, come on, Buddy, you can't win 'em all. Who knows—tomorrow they could use me, right?' "

You looked at me and said "Maybe he could handle rejection, how, I'll never know . . . but not me. I can't."

So now I'd begun to understand something about why you'd had so much difficulty coping with Jody's big mouth, and how she'd put you down. But it was time for you to get rid of these adolescent hang-ups, damnit!

My clipboard had a sheaf of notes for the rewrite on your script. Underneath was a fresh yellow pad. I took it out and slid it across to you. "Here, this is for you," I said.

"What for?" you asked.

"Your next script," I said. "The one you're going to after you've done the rewrites for us. It'll be all about your father— he's a great character, and you'll do him and his story—but first, you take these home and go to work." And I handed him the pages of our notes.

You stared at me, and then you shook your head. "Wrong twice, Teresa," you said. "No rewrites, no more cockamamie TV drama for Buddy Grimes. I know better than to try and write what I don't know how to write."

"Oh come on!" I said, and I was beginning to lose patience with him. "You don't know—*nobody* knows! How many people do you think were born knowing how to write one-hour television dramas? This is the first grade—we're all learning—stop fighting and join the rest of the class—"

You shook your head. "Sorry, I'm busy," you said.

"Remember, I've got a show that's being prepared for *Broad-way*—I don't need these distractions—'' Oh God, how you could equivocate!

"Fine, agreed, but in the meantime, would you please go home and do these rewrites?'' I said. "You know you don't get paid *until* you deliver them.''

That shook you.

"I already did a first draft,'' you said, angrily. "I'll send Buck Dawes after you—''

"Read your contract,'' I said. "I'll explain it to *him,* too. No rewrites, no check.''

I passed the pages with the notes over to you. "By tomorrow night, for sure?''

You glared at me, then you took your thumbnail, bit it between your teeth, and aimed it at me, the old Italian symbol of fuck you.

"Hey,'' I said, "I thought we were finished with the ethnic jokes . . .''

"Ah, Teresa, get off my back, will you?'' you snarled.

But I wouldn't. I kept on, nagging and wheedling, never let you off the hook. Once, in the midst of the nth set of third-act changes, you stared at me and asked "Hey—were you always such a godamned perfectionist? Why are you doing this?''

". . . To get a good show for Dick,'' I lied.

What was I supposed to say? Blurt out that I'd been spending my nights lying on my virginal bed, not thinking over your script, but fantasizing what it would be like were you there, over / under / anydamnedways with me, acting out a complete catalogue of forbidden erotic fantasies, starring Teresa and Buddy (Held Over By Popular Demand), in scenes my subconscious hadn't supplied me since my high school years, when the star of my midnight pornos had been some bull of a fullback named Pinky LoPresto.

Okay, so finally your script was finished, and Dick found time to read it, and he was happy, *amazing!* pleased with your work (*your* work, ha!) he patted me on the back, then called to congratulate you, the script went off to mimeo, and we began talking to agents about casting, as usual we were on our tight treadmill of a schedule, we needed "The Uppers and The Lowers" for two weeks from now . . .

—And that's when the shit hit the fan.

Who expected it? Crane called Dick upstairs to his office and they discussed all the future projects, Crane was very approving until he got to your script. Was Dick serious about this one, about the old musician?

Now remember, this was in the early '50s, these were the Eisenhower years, the time of the crewcuts and the straight-arrows, with Joe McCarthy ranting and raving about Commie infiltration, sponsors running very scared, Big Brother was always looking over your shoulder, oh boy, was it an uptight world, do you remember what a flap it created when, was it Harry Belafonte? casually put his arm around, was it Dinah Shore? in the midst of one of her shows? So figure out how Crane welcomed a show that starred a sixty-seven-year-old coal black jazzman, needing false teeth and getting help from a nice WASP New York girl? "It simply doesn't seem to fit right into our current audience patterns," went his double talk. "There are a lot of *non*-New Yorkers out there, remember? Frankly, its appeal is very limited, do you follow me?"

That rocked Dick. Now it was his turn to yell and fight, "Ah'm from the South," he reminded Crane. "Ah know all about that mentality you're hiding behind, don't give me that shit about limited appeal, we've got a character who isn't Stepin Fetchit, he's for real, he's a universal, the audience will understand him, the network will make a lot of points with the F.C.C.—"

No use. Crane smiled and patted him on the back and agreed with him, but . . . Couldn't Dick table this one for a while until our show was a little more solid in the ratings? This wasn't a turndown, not at all, nobody was against the script, everybody merely felt Dick should put it on later, okay?

It's the process known as beating a project to death with a sofa cushion.

And we were too busy doing our show seven days a week to go out on strike against Crane—over one script, right?

So how do you tell this to Buddy Grimes, who's broken his hump to turn out a script better than anything he's ever written before? And what about Teresa Contini, who's gone to bat for him, making herself into the all-American nag, pushing and shoving him through endless hours of rewrites?

. . . Because she has the hots for him?

I asked Dick what we should do, and as usual, got it dumped right into my lap. "Send him a check for the balance of his fee," he said, "Then call him and tell him his script is on hold for a while. And tell him I personally guarantee we'll find him another assignment, soon's I can . . ."

Oh, that was a fun call.

You, on the other end, yelling at me—where was the urgency, the deadline? Why were we postponing your script—what was the problem? After all your godamned work?

The script was beautiful. How could I tell you we'd run into executive-suite bias? After all, I worked for the network, didn't I? All I had to do was to open my mouth and let Crane's decision leak out, and I could end up out of a job, on the street, oh yes, that was the climate back then, keep your trap shut and go about your business, protect your own back at all times, in those Madison Avenue halls—we were sloshing through paranoia up to our hips

"Listen, we'll have another assignment for you very soon," I insisted. "Meanwhile, why don't you try your hand at an original drama . . . something of your own?"

Silence. Then you said "For instance?"

". . . Your father," I said. "A marvelous character. He's stayed with me ever since you told me about him—so write *him*."

This time you didn't even tell me to get off your back. You merely hung up.

I felt lousy.

. . . Thank God I had a job that kept me so busy I didn't have time to brood about what had happened.

Then, one morning, some guy from *Variety* was on the phone, doing a piece about original TV dramas, and how Dick was one of the leading producers around town, along with Tony Miner and Fred Coe, over at "Philco Playhouse," and Marc Daniels and Marty Manulis, and Dick was locked in rehearsal, so I had to field the questions, and when he asked us about all the projects we had in the hopper for the future, I named a few titles. Then— don't ask me what made me do it—I added ". . . We've got a very exciting original coming in from Buddy Grimes, he's one of our writers, it's a show-business kind of a story—"

Did it have a title?

Why did I say "Sure, it's called 'Get Off My Back.' "?

Then, a week later, you finally called.

"What the hell are you doing?" you yelled. "Announcing mythical scripts by me?"

"As long as they spell your name right," I told you. "When do we get to read the first draft?"

"I am very busy writing revue material," you said. "Lay off me, will you?"

"Okay, sure," I aid, "but you wouldn't want to disappoint your old friend Jody Cassel, would you?"

"How the hell did *she* get into this discussion?" you asked, and your tone was even more hostile.

"Well, she reads *Variety,* too," I said, "and she'd want to know why your original script for us never got on, wouldn't she?"

You didn't answer.

I figured I'd opened my big Italian mouth too wide this time, but before I could apologize, there was a click, and you'd hung up on me.

And I went back to feeling rotten.

Until one afternoon, very late, a few weeks later, while Dick and I were going over the changes in the script for tomorrow's rehearsal—Lord, did we ever stop doing that?—there was a knock on his office door. Before Dick could answer, it opened, a hand snaked through, holding a manila envelope, and then tossed it, so it soared across the room, and landed, *crash!*—in the middle of Dick's desk.

. . . Scaring the hell out of us both.

(How was I to know your old man had taught you a few juggling tricks?)

"And now," you announced, peering through the door, "I'll thank you both to quit bothering me about a script. There it is, and if you' don't like it, tough titty, *I'm not rewriting*—is that understood?"

"Of course not, pappy," said Dick, who by this time knew about the *Variety* story. "Sit yourself down and I'll read it right away quick . . ."

"No!" you said. "Screw that! You call *me!*"

. . . God, you must have been nervous after you left.

Right then, we both grabbed "Get Off My Back," that's what it was, and began to read it, Dick handing me the pages as he finished them, and oh Lord, what an exciting feeling it is, what a high when you start reading a script that's good. How did we know? Oh come on, after you've read enough second- and third-rate scripts, you somehow learn to spot the gold. I remember once discussing it with Audrey Wood, the play-agent, and she, who must have read thousands of scripts over the years, remarked ". . . It's in the first ten or eleven pages, dear, when a little light goes on somewhere in your head, and you know you're reading a winner."

You'd written from somewhere deep down inside your guts, you'd told your father's story, but turned it into a real piece of theater (how tough it must have been for you!). How your old man in his middle years had been rejected all over the place, but finally he gets suggested for a straight character part in a play, something entirely new and strange for him, no comedy bits to rely on, no makeup, no funny hats, no shtick, he would have to get out there and simply do it—could he make himself do it?

Damn good dramatic premise—it always was, and always will be. Maybe I was emotional about you, sure, but as I read I had the feeling I was watching a pitcher out on the mound, striking out the batters, on his way to a no-hitter, maybe? and I was praying for him, go, boy, go—see if you can do it—*please*—

Did the old man make it? Could he get out on the stage and conquer the audience? Well, what do you think happened? Of course he did—and he was a hit! Sure, it was corn, but then, what the hell sells tickets if it isn't good, old-fashioned corn?

. . . and as Dick was always fond of telling me, ". . . Honey, the reason a cliché is a cliché is because it's *true!*"

We finished your script and both of us were grinning at each other like a pair of happy idiot kids. "He's done it!" Dick said. "Gave us the spine, the heart, and as for nerves, he's played on half a dozen of 'em! Like a damn harp?"

He got up and stretched. "*Call* him," he said. "Keep callin' till you get him. We want him to come in for a meeting, so we can get started on this little darlin' . . ."

Then he looked at me and said ". . . How the hell you think he wrote us such a good script?"

"Beats me," I lied.

. . . Wow. Once a nice honest Italian girl. Lately, Teresa Contini had certainly become very adept at lying.

All that evening your damn phone didn't answer (later I found out you'd taken it off the hook, something your analyst could explain, fear of rejection, *natürlich?*), so about ten I jumped into a cab and had myself driven over to your Greenwich Village place. The least I could do was to leave a note under your doorway, or in your mailbox, so you'd know our reaction, but when I rang your downstairs bell, you answered on the intercom. ". . . It's *me*, Teresa," I said. "Your script is terrific!"

"No shit!" you said, finally, and buzzed your door open.

Up the stairs I trotted, until I found you standing in your doorway, a big drink in your hand, a stubble of beard on your chin, greyish pouches under your eyes, you were tired, but now you were grinning at me like some slap-happy kid. ". . . You really liked it?" you asked. *"Both* of you?"

"Ah, come on, like is not the word!" I said. "We're crazy about it! Why the devil do you think I'd come around here to tell you, oh, Buddy, you are a genius—you did it!"

"Hey, great!" you said, "Wowee!" as if you'd just realized your horse had won, you'd hit the Daily Double, or the Irish Sweepstakes, you threw your arms around me, hugged me, hard, your damned drink sloshed all over my good coat, but so what? you shoved the glass at me, I took a drink, a loving cup, right? now I was enjoying this moment almost as much as you were, and then—was it gratitude, friendship, excitement, whatever?— you kissed me.

Later we were inside your apartment, the door had swung shut behind us, the two of us still hugging each other, oh, such a great high for me to share it all with you, somehow we'd emptied your glass, we giggled, we had another loving cup, we hugged again, you turned on music, some late-night radio program, you swung me around the floor, well we didn't so much swing, that place was so crowded we were stumbling . . . "Really good, eh?" you asked. "Great!" I said. I can't remember when things suddenly switched, changed from us being good buddies enjoying your triumph . . . to a serious embrace, with your hands beginning to explore me, and our mouths opening against each other's . . . Maybe you were sloshed by now, maybe I was, too, so what, we were entitled! ". . . Little Teresa, my teacher," you crooned into my ear, "such a messenger of good news, oh toots, I do thank you kindly . . ."

You began to unwind yourself from me, but I wouldn't let you leave me now, suddenly I had no inhibitions, I'd waited too damned long for this! I held you against me, and kissed you again, harder now, letting loose all my bottled-up desires, wow, had you opened up a can of peas! I remember thinking Is this what it's like for nuns when they take vows of chastity, and they have to keep it all locked up tight for the rest of their lives? No wonder they get their jollies slapping little kids' hands in school, instead of having this, with a man, poor ladies, it isn't worth it, girls-foregoing these sensations I was beginning to respond to, oh the warmth, the glowing, these waves . . . Why had we waited so long?

And now I was sprawled on the couch with you, you must have been astonished by the Vesuvius you'd tapped, this creature who was writhing in your arms, moving against you like some octopus, no stopping Teresa now, embraces, fumbling, she was after you, your body, we broke free for a moment to pant, I stared at you and I realized if you hadn't thought of taking me to bed, I'd have to take over (my God, was this Teresa, the demure Katharine Gibbs graduate?) . . . and so now I began whispering in your ear "Please, please, Buddy, make love to me,"

. . . amazing what you can do when you have to.

. . . And now it was time for you to become as aroused as I was, you reached up and snapped off the light, and now, finally, it was no longer my midnight fantasy world, this was It.

For the first time on any bed, here in a personal appearance, ladies and gentlemen, presenting, on this side, Mr. Buddy Grimes (appropriately tumescent), shrugging off his trousers, taking off his shirt, he returns to the center stage, to be approached, and greeted, on this side, by a somewhat dishevelled Teresa Contini, revealed, for the first time in a stranger's bedroom, in her demurely chaste Plymouth Shop underwear. He (the ever decent middle-class lover) had taken The Proper Precautions, it is now safe for them to move toward each other in the shadowy darkness, he draws Miss C. toward him, four hands begin exploring various topographical features of our two stars, and

now he arranges her for a Round One, and she closes her eyes and awaits his next ploy,

the bell sounds and then

he

and then she

and then they,

and now she and he both

onward and upward
and the bell sounds.
End of Round One.

. . . so *that* was what was involved?

It seemed simple enough, almost too simple, and for that matter, not a whole hell of a lot seemed to have happened . . .

Maybe we should rewrite it? Try it another way?

. . . No, Teresa, that is the way it goes, the first time, whether you like it or not—

(And I must say, I didn't, not much.) Was that all?

Remember the old joke—*you wouldn't cheat a poor blind girl, would you?*

. . . I wanted to ask Buddy, but he had gotten up and left me in the bed, and there I was, covered by a sheet, thinking, God, if my mother could see me now, and what would my father say— he'd kill me, sure—or maybe, he'd settle for merely killing Buddy?

. . . who returned a few minutes later, this time he had a fresh drink in hand, slid into the bed beside me, kissed me gently, and offered me a sip.

Which I swallowed, what the hell, I was on the road to Perdition already, so in for a penny, in for a pound, right, you brazen scarlet tramp! . . .

. . . You yawned, and then you said, gruffly, ". . . I didn't really expect this to happen, Teresa."

From someone I knew was a good writer, hardly your most original line.

"Neither did I," I said. . . . almost as original, eh? "But I don't mind, Buddy, in fact I guess I wanted it to happen."

. . . which was certainly a midnight truth.

Then it became my turn to leave our bower of love for some cosmetic repairs of my own; when I returned, still wrapped in your top sheet, you were staring at me like some guilty schoolboy.

". . . Teresa," you sighed, "I'm sorry . . . I . . . I never figured you were a—"

You'd obviously discovered my Secret.

". . . a pure-as-the-driven-snow, honest-to-God Italian virgin?" I said. "And you're the wicked city boy?"

You nodded. ". . . Now they'll be after me, right?"

"Who?"

". . . Your family," you groaned. "You got brothers?"

"Three," I said. "All tall, strong, and vicious. But first they have to find out about it," I told you, "So try and keep your big mouth shut, will you?"

You laughed, and reached out for me, and then we kissed.

Which meant I got back into your bed.

No, believe it or not, I wasn't saying goodnight, and / or hurriedly climbing back into my clothes to get the hell out of here, oh no, I was happily climbing back into my seducer's arms, folks—

Maybe today, no big deal, but remember, these were the 1950s, believe you me, nice girls didn't behave this way, especially not chaste Teresa The Good, raised behind a steel fence of inhibitions, oh hell, maybe a girl could fool around a little, neck, sure, but S-x? Going the Limit? In my time that was strictly for the marriage bed, and Don't You Ever Forget It, You Hear?

. . So here I was downing another of your drinks, then dropping off into a friendly doze, your arms around me, your newly discovered male warmth against me—

the two of us, exhausted now, you from exorcising your paternal demon (your script), me from getting my parents off *my* back (two Italian demons for the price of one, I had much the better deal, eh?).

Amazing, it was as if I'd been doing this for years.

. . . oh, the time I'd wasted.

We were so tired, it was Fade Out—

and then we went to Black.

Until about seven in the morning, when light began to seep through your bedroom window and woke me up, startled, where was I? This wasn't my bed, oh yes, now I remembered, when I stretched and turned, there were muscles that were sore, places that ached from unaccustomed activity. Hey, Teresa, this is a new you, you are no longer Teresa The Good, Teresa the Pure, starting as of now you are Teresa the Bad, kiddo, when you walk down the office hallway this morning, everybody will know, they'll be able to see it, right? *Ya, ya, Teresa* does it—*with writers!*

So what if she does? You were wrapped against me, a tired boy, snoring slightly, your beard scratching against my back, as I tried to move to get away from it, there came an answering murmur from you, then your hand snaked around and began with a life of its own to explore me, hey, what was this? Not in the morning, enough is enough—

Oh, something else came on the dinner? I hadn't had the whole menu?

. . . so what happened now?

What happened was that you did, and then I did—

and this time was a lot better, now we were getting into the part, comfortable with our two roles, no pressure, no need to prove anything, it was slow and easy, and then we began to move in perfect tandem, collaborators now, going for the gold together, and then, and then, oh, nice, nice, *of course!*—*this* must be was what all the fuss was about!

Thank you, you talented, difficult . . . stubborn . . . gentle man . . .

Then it was time to go to work.

"Where you going?" you asked, as I got up.

"To the office," I said.

"So early?" you asked. "Why?"

"I'm not a writer, I'm a working girl," I said. "Got to get your beautiful script into mimeo. Oh, Buddy, you've got a busy couple of weeks ahead of you—"

"—*not* rewriting!" you said.

"Of course not," I said, as I got dressed. "Every word is pure gold."

When I was ready to leave, you got up and made an attempt at politeness, escorting me to the door, you gave me a chaste kiss on the forehead, and then your murmured ". . . Nice of you to come over here last night . . . It was . . . special."

"It sure turned out to be," I said. "Glad you feel that way."

". . . Will I be seeing you later?" you asked.

"Incessantly," I promised.

I went home, showered, and changed. In my bathroom mirror I seemed to be the same Teresa Contini, perhaps a little tired, bleary-eyed, but then, in my job, that was a constant.

Got to the office . . . and miraculously, nobody seemed to be looking at me with anything more than the customary early A.M. sullenness today.

I brought Dick his neatly typed-up notes for today's rehearsal. "Did you reach Buddy last night?" he asked.

"Oh yes, I spoke to him," I said. "He was very pleased."

"Pleased?" he said. ". . . That old boy should be thrilled . . . when he sees what I'm going' to do with his script . . ." He grinned. "Just hope he hangs around till we're done."

". . . why shouldn't he do that?"

"well, if I remember correctly," said Dick, "old Buddy has a habit of walking out the door when things aren't going good, remember?"

". . . We'll lock the rehearsal hall door," I promised.

Dick wasn't just whistling Dixie about the production, the minute your script came back from mimeo, we were in production, and from that morning on, there was no looking back.

If what you and I had begun was an Affair—there was a word nobody ever used in the Contini house, ah, Mama, did you ever imagine your daughter Teresa might be somebody's l---r?—well, from then on, we went into such a tight schedule, any repeat engagements up at your place were logistically impossible, at least until "Get Off My Back" went on the air.

Everything came together in a most remarkable way, even for those hectic days, when there were many weeks when we got our one-hour dramas (live, not tape or film, folks) on the air through sheer momentum.

The first problem was casting the lead, Charlie Duffy, the aging comic who gets a shot at a straight dramatic part, his last chance, and isn't sure he can cut the mustard. We needed somebody with real comedy training, a pro. We got lucky, there he was, recommended by his faithful agent, a crony from the Lambs Club, where they'd both hung out for years. Harry "Ham" Berger, droll, witty, the part fit him like a rubber glove, he'd grown up in vaudeville with his parents, toddled onstage at the age of four and got his first laugh, there wasn't a comedy bit he didn't know by heart, he was a computer bank of gags and shtick, lately he'd kept busy with guest shots on Ed Sullivan's "Toast of the Town," and luckily he would never starve, he'd invested his money in real estate. But he wanted to work, no pro likes to quit; he came up to the office, read your script, whistled softly and grinned, and said "Say, this is a little weird. The kid's written my autobiography."

Then there were meetings with you and Dick and Ham; Ham conquered his fears and agreed to do it, he respected good writing, he said to you "Listen, kid, if it's not on the page, it ain't on the stage, and with this script, it's all here. I only hope I can learn the damn words . . ."

Nobody paid too much attention to Ham's asides, so we sailed forward, Dick suggested a few changes, you complained, but by now you were infected with the same enthusiasm we had for the script, you wanted it to be good, we went down the hallway together, you squeezed my arm and said ". . . You know, it could really work with Ham doing Charlie, couldn't it?"

Your feeling good had the same effect on me—I'd never seen you so optimistic. "It'll be a smash!" I promised.

"Yeah, sure, well, wish me luck with the damned rewrites," you said, gave me a fraternal pat, blew me an asexual kiss, and ran off to the elevator.

Then we went into production, a twenty-four hour a day treadmill, rehearsal halls, late-night conferences in the office, everything seemed to be going fine. Too fine. Somewhere we had to hit trouble. (Shh, Teresa!) Bad luck, don't think about it . . .

Then the shit hit the fan.

. . . Ham Berger had gone through the first two days rehearsing sans problems. he sounded okay, he looked the part, he kept everybody happy with this wry comments and occasional gags . . . but by the second day, the rest of our cast, all of them veterans of live TV, had learned their lines. Not Ham . . . he was still working from his script.

. . . That night, when Dick mentioned it to him, Ham said "Don't worry, kiddo, I'll have it by tomorrow, remember, I'm the new boy on the block around this cockamamie business . . ."

Third day, he was back, he sailed through the first act letter perfect, and we all grinned happily at each other. We were rehearsing in an upstairs hall down on Second Avenue, near the famous old Ratner's, where we all went for hearty vegetarian lunches. At noon, Ham didn't sit with us, he retired to a quiet table by himself, no swapping jokes with the old waiters today, he stayed there intently studying his lines, sipping tea with honey and chewing on sweet roles.

On the way back upstairs to the rehearsal, he grabbed me by the arm, drew me into a dusty corner, whispered "Hey, Contini, can I tell you something? I love this part, it's going to be a great show, but you folks better get yourself another boy."

Was he serious? My lunch began to churn about in my stomach. *"Why?"*

He sighed. "Can't learn the words, toots," he said. "The old brain ain't what it was. Just thought I'd give you all fair warning, so now you got time to get somebody else to be Charlie."

"We *don't*—there is nobody else!" I said. "It's got to be *you!*" And I wasn't kidding, where the hell were we supposed to get somebody else to fill in a lead, two days before dress? And even if we brought in a standby, could *he* learn the part? *No*, we had to go with Ham Berger, and he had to know that.

"I won't tell anybody we had this conversation," I told him. "You're going to be fine, believe me . ."

"Yeah, sure I will," said Ham. "Please God."

He went through the second act much slower, stumbling over his speeches. When he came to the third, he picked up his script and began to read.

By that time I'd told Dick about Ham's insecurities. Dick shrugged. "He's a money-player," he said. "All these old pros are . . ." By now you, Buddy, had joined us, your face as grey as Ham's, you were as worried as he was. "You grew up with these guys, right, Buddy?" asked Dick. "They always come through when the chips are down, you'll see."

You shook your head. "I don't know," you mumbled. "I'm worried."

"Ah, pappy," said Dick, "you just worry about your next script—and leave me to worry about the actors."

You walked away. We both watched you.

You didn't walk out. Not yet.

Ham came in the fourth day, and by now he had shadows beneath his eyes, he was off in some dark corner every moment he could be spared from the rehearsal, mumbling his lines to himself, it was painful to watch, none of us went near him, except to pat him on the shoulder and tell him how good he was, which he denied. Now that I think back on it, the whole thing was eerie, something out of the "Twilight Zone" perhaps, there he was, playing with some part! side by side with himself, Ham Berger, ex-comic, doing his first straight part, and suffering from doubts, playing Charlie Duffy, doing *his* first straight part, and suffering from doubts . . .

. . . While you, Charlie's son, the comedy writer, who'd written your first drama—

—sat sweating it out in the corner, trying desperately not to run, to get the hell out of here, to flee back to the safety of ". . . and now, in a gayer mood, we go south of the border, etc. . . ."

. . . Poor Buddy, how I wanted to go up and put my arms around you, try to reassure you, *it was going to be all right, you'd see!* (I was a proficient liar by then.)

How could I? In front of the actors, the technicians, the crew, and Dick, prowling around on the outskirts of the sets, framing shots with his hands, unflappable, our strong father symbol, sheperding us all toward our fifth day . . .

Which was spent uptown in the actual studio, where they'd put up the sets for us, and we did camera blocking. All day long, stopping and starting, with the cameramen lining up each shot for tomorrow's performance. By now Ham looked exhausted, his voice was a rasping croak, he was sipping gallons of tea laced with honey (and please God, that was all it was). But he at least had most of his lines down pat, and he went through his scenes without hesitation, his performance was pretty shaky, sure, but he was out there, if he wasn't giving us anything much, he was least a warm body, we hadn't had to replace him. (How could we?)

". . . I do believe he's gonna make it," Dick murmured, as we finished that endless day.

"I believe you, captain-massah-boss-suh," I said.

". . . You have to believe him," you said, from behind us. "You work for him!"

"Well, genius, how do you feel about things?" Dick asked. "Got any ideas for rewrites?"

"Yeah," you said. "I'd like to start with the entire first act, which stinks. And then we could go on from there." You made a face. "God, it looks so awful," you said.

". . . You'll feel better in the morning, pappy," said Dick.

You still hadn't walked out . . .

When we finally finished, Dick and I stopped by Ham's dressing room. He was stretched out on the couch, a washcloth over his eyes.

"You're gonna be just fine tomorrow, pappy," Dick said.

". . . Don't shit me, pal," said Ham, his voice a soft rasping croak. "I'm lousy and you'd like to replace me, but we're both stuck with each other . . ." He groaned. "Christ, all my life I wanted a good straight part in something high-class, you know? And now I've got it, I'm too *old*, I can't cut it for us . . ."

"Okay, we're stuck with each other," sighed Dick. "So . . . let's just do the best we can, and then we'll go home, okay?"

"What kind of a business is it where you don't even get a couple of nights in New Haven before you open in New York?" complained Ham.

"Pappy," said Dick, "you go home and get a lot of sleep."

"Sleep? What the hell's that?" asked Ham.

I wanted to reassure you, too, but you'd already gone. And I couldn't go looking for you, Dick and I stayed there until ten, checking over all our notes with the crew, the last minute stuff with the scenery, the costumes, and script-timing (crucial because each performance ran at different speeds, depending on how the actors were doing it, either speeding up, or perhaps stumbling over lines and losing time . . . that was the hardest part of those live shows, the proper length.

Then both of us went home.

. . . Neither of us mentioned Ham Berger.

How could we dare ask each other the question—what happens if he blows his lines tomorrow night?

Show day. That was a long day's journey into night. Starting at about 8, we were hermetically sealed into that control booth and the stuffy studio, with its bright fluorescent lights, that was our miniworld for the next thirteen hours, there was a whole world going on outside, but we had no sense of its existence, we were focused on one project, this one-hour show. By 10 A.M. the actors had come in, we'd had danish and coffee, the shots were all lined up, the cast came out of makeup and costume, by 11 we were ready to go through our first run-through.

We all sat up in the booth, with Dick calling the shots, to his A.D. and me timing, and away we went. Ham? . . . went through the run-through without a stumble. Lines he had . . . *amazing!* But performance? Deader than yesterday's fish.

"He'll get better, you'll see," said Dick.

". . . He's playing the part like a sleepwalker!" you grumbled.

"Relax, pappy, he's a pro, he's gonna come through for us," said Dick. "Just stick around and you'll see I'm right."

You stuck . . . although you now really looked as if you'd like to bolt at any second.

I went down to Ham's dressing room to give him Dick's notes, and found him lying flat on his back, staring at the ceiling again. "Nobody ever told me this drama shit was such hard work," he grumbled. "I'm going back to dropping my pants for a laugh . . ."

"Tomorrow," I said. "Meanwhile, here are your notes . . ."

"Oy, notes!" he groaned. "I can hardly remember my lines, and she's got *more* for me to remember? Go Away!"

You met me as I came back up to the control booth, and I could tell you were even more uptight than Ham Berger. "Listen—how do we light a fire under him?" you asked. "The man's *dead!*"

"Relax," I told you. "If I knew how to make you a miracle, I'd do it . . . Just trust Dick, you're going to have a great show."

". . . I need more than that half-time pep-talk crap!" you said, and walked away.

We had lunch, and now it was time for the dress, and once again, Ham went through it letter perfect, but with all the vitality of a robot. ". . . I can't watch this any more," I heard you mutter, behind me, as we got to the third act climax. I glanced around, just in time to see you doing your disappearing act, out the control booth door.

. . . Oh well, you'd stuck it out longer than I'd expected you might.

We finished without you.

Dick turned to me, and it was a good thing you'd left, for the first time Dick was obviously at a loss for optimism. "Listen," he said, wearily, "maybe with old Uncle Ham what you see is what you get, mm? Maybe he ain't *got* any more to give . . ."

And what was I supposed to say to that?

The control booth clock pushed inexorably toward 8 P.M., Dick said "Good luck, everybody," on the talk-back, "Places, please, opening shot, and cue the theme music, and cue the announcer, and here we go—"

"*Live*, from New York!" said the announcer, "the first performance of a new play by Buddy Grimes, "Get Off My Back.""

. . . And for the third time, that long day, we saw the opening scene, Charlie Duffy being called into an agent's office and told his career as a comic was over, nobody wanted him with his funny hats and slap-shoes and bamboo cane, *but*, if he wanted to take a crack at something else, there was a part in a straight play . . .

This time, we saw something else.

On our monitors, we saw not Ham, but Charlie Duffy! a couple of inches taller, it seemed, his eyes open, alert, aggressive, his energy level suddenly raised, Charlie Duffy come to life. Angry, argumentative, masking his own deep insecurity with jokes and throwaway lines—he was alive—he *was* Charlie Duffy!

Oh sure, missing a couple of cues here and there, omitting words in some of your speeches, but what difference, the man was giving us a performance—*from where had it sprung?* Amazing.

No sense asking that question, we just sat there, Dick calling the shots, following Ham on the monitor as he acting out his fears, his nervousness, through Act One, through the commercial break . . .

"*Wow*," I heard behind us, a hand grabbed me by the shoulder, I turned around, you were back with us, shaking your head in amazement. "Where is he getting it?" you asked me.

"From *you*," I whispered. "On the page, on the stage!" and went back to my stopwatch, to Dick, and the second act, where Charlie finally summons up enough courage to try the new career, and on through the next commercial break, into the third act, which was our climactic scene, Charlie conquering his opening-night jitters, getting out there and doing it, his wife watching from the rear of the orchestra, her fingers crossed he'll make it, he finishes his scene, the audience applauds, Charlie takes his bow, then comes offstage. We see him make the long walk to his dressing room, dissolve to the final scene, his wife comes backstage, she finds him slumped in a chair, staring at his face in the mirror.

Even all these years later, I can still remember how you ended it.

". . . They loved you, Charlie!" she says.

"Sure," he replies. "Guess they've got good taste."

"So why are you sitting here brooding?" she asks.

"Just thinking," says Charlie. ". . . All that time I wasted getting laughs from the civilians, when I could've been playing Shakespeare, huh?"

". . . and starving to death?" she asks him, tears in her eyes, and they both laugh and embrace.

Then we went to black. Finished.

". . . *Cue the theme,* roll the end credits!" said Dick.

We went into the closing crawl, set to the theme music. It was over, my stop watch said 59 minutes 10 seconds, almost on the nose, not bad timing, in those days we didn't have a closing commercial at the end, it would have destroyed the mood of that final drama, all the tension we'd worked so hard to dramatize through that hour . . . (Today, your script would have been riddled with commercials, but what's the sense of inveighing against that? You want pure, go to PBS.)

The crawl finished. We were off the air.

"Thank you for a terrific show," Dick said, over the talkback. "You, too, gang," he said, to all of us in that hot airless booth.

We were all too tired to respond.

Suddenly you lunged forward and bear-hugged Dick. "You're a godamn genius, thank *you!*" you said.

"Hey, Buddy, you still around?" Dick asked. "That means it must've been better than I thought!"

That broke the tension, we whooped and laughed, kissed each other, shook hands, you turned and sneaked in another bear hug and kiss for me . . . while Dick flipped on the talk-back and called down "Ham? Ham Berger? Absolutely gorgeous! You are the greatest!"

Down on the floor, on Camera Two, we still had a close up of Ham, who stared up, grinned at us, did a little time step and yelled "Bet your ass I was!"

"Godamned money player," said Dick. "I told you, didn't I—"

Now the phones began to ring, one after another, people wanting to tell us how good the show was, that didn't usually happen, this was our audience, one after the other the calls came in, viewers responding to Charlie Duffy's story, how good the lead actor was, why didn't we do more inspirational stories like tonight's? Buck Dawes calling to congratulate his client, on the inside network line we suddenly had Crane himself calling, to tell all of us personally what a really dynamite piece of work we'd done, it got to be a mob scene, with visitors crowding in, slapping backs and shaking hands, it finally began to dawn on us that "Get Off My Back" *might* be as good as we'd thought it was . . .

Dick embraced Buddy again. "Well, B.G.," he said, grinning like a tall Cheshire cat, "looks like we had a hit on our hands . . ." Then he turned to me and said "C'mon, let's go out and celebrate for twenty minutes, before we start on next week's show."

We ended up at a front table in Lindy's, Dick's wife, Claire, came down to join us, she'd spent the whole day taking care of their kids but she still managed to look gorgeous that late at night. That's when we knew we'd done a good show, a hit! people started pushing up to tell us so, beaming at Ham Berger, who sat wolfing chicken soup and matzo balls, he was the king of the place that night, one of their own who'd come back from sitting on the bench to his stardom in this mammoth new medium, TV . . .

Ham, being properly modest, saying "Yeah, yeah, but it's a good script, see, where would I be without Buddy's words, and this guy Dick, he's beautiful, I love him," he was being properly grateful, tomorrow he'd be telling everybody at the Lambs how *he'd* saved the show, sure, but tonight he could afford the largesse of leaning over to Buddy and saying ". . . Kid, your old man would've been proud of you!"

"Listen to the man!" I told you.

You nodded and turned to me, and you said ". . . Thanks, I will," and a little later you whispered into my ear ". . . Tonight? Or are you too tired?"

Yes, I was, but I wouldn't admit it, so I nodded back, *yes*—we started to make goodbye noises, preparing to leave, but before we were able to settle up our check and go, there was a sudden commotion at the front of the restaurant, by the cash register, and I heard a familiar female voice, braying ". . . *There* you are, you godamned genius!"

Jody Cassel?

Blowing kisses, surrounded by a cadre of her writers, Fat Freddy and the Typist, a couple of other flunkies, tonight she wore a bulky raccoon coat, with a crazy wimple-like hat, she charged over and threw her arms around you, *"Buddy! Bud-dee!"* she screamed. "Oh, baby, I saw your show, you are absolutely something else, you know that? But who was the one who always said so, *who?"* By now she had you in a tight embrace, and with one arm she waved to us and pointed to herself. *"Me!"* she announced. "I found this boy! He's mine!" she kissed you. "Now listen, Genius," she went on, with everyone paying attention, "you're going to write *me* a show now, you hear? You're going to make Mama a dramatic actress, too, Dick Hatch will direct it, we'll win all the awards, but remember, Buddy, Jody has to have big love scenes, like this! Because Jody always gets her man, like this!" She kissed you again.

From a nearby table, somebody applauded.

"Wowoweeweewoh!" Jody chortled. "See, my fans demand it!"

". . . Sure, sure," you said, grinning, despite your embarrassment, she was still holding firmly to you, now she whispered something in your ear, you reddened. "Ah, come *on*, Jody," you told her. "No, it's *true*," she said. "Would I forget a thing like that? Come on, let's go home, Genius, and we'll talk."

You shook your head. "Sorry, I can't," you told her.

"Oh, turning down the star?" she asked. Still smiling, she said, "Okay, you had your chance, just remember, I'm a very busy lady, this offer will not be repeated." She let you go, she leaned down and kissed Dick. "Remember who got you guys started!" she brayed. *"Mama*, here!"

"Oh, is that the truth?" asked Dick, amiably. "Well ain't that somethin'."

"Bet your ass!" said Jody. "You guys hadn't been bounced off my show, you'd never have come up with this one, would you?"

. . . My God, what an ego. And why didn't either of you tell her to go screw?

No, Dick was too tired, and as for you, you let her carry on for another couple of minutes, now she was congratulating Ham, and then, from a nearby table somebody yelled "Go get 'em, Jody!" and then she'd left us. I saw you, watching her go, and suddenly I realized, you may have thought she was outrageous, sure, but you didn't hate her for the way she'd treated you, no, deep down inside you admired her, she fascinated you . . . and if I hadn't been there, could you have gone home with her?

In the car, you put your arms around me and we kissed, but it wasn't so much passion, from you this was gratitude. The two of us were so exhausted that we were like a pair of punch-drunk fighters, stumbling through the ninth or tenth rounds . . . I was almost asleep in your arms. When you said ". . . Maybe it's better if I take you home, mm?" I was too tired to argue, besides, some kind of crazy intuition kept telling me, had I gone to bed with you that night, there'd have been three of us under the blanket . . . and no girl enjoys having a ghost beside her as she's trying to make it, with that damn voice braying "Wowowwee-weewoh!" into her ear . . .

So I ended up in my own bed, alone, certain that it would all get straightened out between us later, you and I would be seeing each other and we'd pick up where we'd left off, that wonderful fine sexy morning, had it only been nine days ago?

. . . but we didn't.

Time passed, and we went in different directions. Friends, sure, but nothing more.

Strange how these things happen. It's a long time later, and there are nights when I still sit and ponder, as I am doing tonight . . . with my Patient G. snoring away in the expensive bedroom we share . . . what might have happened if I'd maybe fought a little harder to stay awake that night, coming back from Lindy's, and found the energy to go upstairs to your place with you? Had it out with Jody's ghost in your bedroom?

Would I have ended up differently . . . Mrs. Grimes, the well-known producer, wife of the talented writer, maybe?

Who knows?

. . . But when you come to think of it, it sure makes an interesting plot for a script, doesn't it?

(So why don't you write it, Buddy?)

*   *   *   *

Eileen Tighe:

It might have been easier locating the ace of spades in a sidewalk three-card monte game than it was to turn up Jody Cassel. Even with Dick Hatch's suggestions.

Buck Dawes? Seemed to be out of town, travelling, would you believe *Asia?* and not due back for several weeks, damnit, so he went on Hold.

As for Mrs. Claire Wachtel, the boss-lady at Baroness, getting through to the Ayatollah by phone might have been easier. Three straight days I called her offices in New York—(from my house, of course, if I'd made long-distance calls from the office, everyone at Interfico would buzz buzz buzz about what I was up to, Budlong would ask, and how could I answer without anything tangible to tell him?)—I'd managed to get through to her executive secretary, Miss Farmer, an efficient, British, female sergeant-major type, whose job was obviously to field such calls as mine. The first day, Mrs. Wachtel was In Conference, the following morning she was still In Meetings, and Miss Farmer, the keeper of the gates, wished to know might *she* help me?

I told her I needed information from Mrs. Wachtel, and she, in her best British put-down style, suggested I might speak with someone in the Baroness Inc. public relations department? No, thank you, I explained this was a personal matter, it had to do with an old friend of Mrs. Wachtel's from the early days of live television—ah, then, came back Miss Farmer, perhaps I should speak directly the the gentlemen who handled the television advertising for Baroness, at the agency—

No! Finally, in desperation, I shot my big gun off at her. "Would you tell Mrs. Wachtel it was Richard Hatch himself who suggested I call?"

She would transmit that message, but she hoped I would understand, these were the days of annual sales conferences, Mrs. Wachtel was extremely busy—

"All I need is two minutes of her valuable time," I said. "In a pinch, perhaps one?"

Miss Farmer promised to do what she could, but she offered no guarantees.

I was back to Square One.

. . . and at the office, more frustration. Sid Budlong, back from a quick trip to Mexico, where Interfico had a cadre of partners shooting a low-budget runaway Western, had brought with him a severe case of La Turista, but that did not keep him from offering me a suggestion, i. e., he wanted me to have a talk-session about Sully Fischer, whom he felt would be helpful to our TV project.

"On what level?" I asked.

". . . I'm certain he'll have valuable input for the story," he told me, between sips of Kaopectate. "You and he should interface. When it comes to that era, remember, the man was There, so what he could fill us in on is valuable Background. No offense meant, Eileen, I've scanned the material you've assembled so far, excellent research, but it's only facts. Where's the concept? The Thrust? The Shape?"

I couldn't argue with his analysis.

"Give us a little more time, we'll get there, I promise—" I told him.

"Don't be defensive," said Budlong, "but remember, one man's a lousy team. Now, we're not ready to run up preliminary script costs by hiring a writer, but is there any reason why we can't pick Sully Fischer's brain? Especially when he's standing around, waiting to be picked?''

"With no commitments to the future of this project?" I asked.

Budlong shrugged. "He's offering, without strings. How can we say no?"

Beware of out-of-work directors bearing gifts, I wanted to say, but it was obvious Mr. Fischer had already sold Mr. Budlong a bill of goods, and for the moment, my best offense would be to put on a happy face and agree to meet with S. F. Budlong promised he'd arrange the time. "By the way," he asked, belching slightly, "have you located that Jody whatever-her-name-is, yet?"

"No," I said, "but I've got a few lines open to her . . ."

He grimaced. "Waste of time," he said. "If we have to, we can always do without her. Use a prototype, know what I mean, create our own character, someone Like—"

"No, Sid," I protested. "She's a unique—there's nobody Like her—"

"Ah, come on," he said, rising from behind his desk. "Don't say that. The world is full of aggressive female types, fighting for space—"

"Thanks a lot," I said.

"Don't get paranoid," he replied, and with hands on his stomach, he hurried out of the office.

Thanks to Ozzie Kaufman, who knows everyone, I was briefed on Sully Fischer, over an informational lunch.

". . . My old pal Sully?" he said, when I brought up the subject. "Oh, he's a real cute one, a charmer. Watch yourself around him, at all times."

Might he please expand on that?

"While you're not looking, he might just lift your eye teeth," said Ozzie. ". . . and I wouldn't want that to happen to a nice girl like you, not with the current price of Beverly Hills dentistry."

Then Ozzie knew Sully Fischer well?

". . . From Day One, my dear," said Ozzie, proudly. "We hit this town together, just before World War II. Sully's always fascinated me . . . He was a preppy type before anybody out here had ever heard of J. Press jackets and white buckskin shoes. He started out as a kid actor . . . Universal musicals, you know, the college kids singing and dancing and putting on shows in the old barn, remember? Then, during the war, he was 4-F, so he got a lot of leading man parts in B pictures—that's what they used to call Victory Casting . . . In the forties, he did a lot of those Bikini Beach pictures, then he figured that there wasn't much future in acting, and he was right, now that the heavy hitters were back from the Army, who needed him? All he had was his hair and good looks and around this town, they give that away with your morning coffee . . . so Sully looked around and saw television . . . it was just getting started, he took a running jump and *ootzed* his way right in."

". . . *Ootzed?*" I asked.

"Sorry, I keep forgetting you're not ethnic," said Ozzie. "An *ootzer* is a twister, a pusher, he's the guy who starts through the revolving door behind you, then comes out the other side ahead of you, get it? That's Sully—a championship class ootzer."

Of course, he might also have been talking about non-ethnics such as Sid Budlong, or any number of others with whom one deals out here . . . including perhaps, me?

"Well, he ootzed his way into the right living rooms around town," continued Ozzie, "He played tennis with the A people, got to the good parties, found himself a girl with good social connections, she wasn't beautiful, but she was crazy about him and ambitious as hell. So the two of them got married, but it was more of a partnership, she went into the interior decorating business, he got jobs through the people he knew, so did she, twice a year they'd give a party and pay everybody off, oh they were a very special pair, Mr. and Mrs. Ootzer . . ." Ozzie chuckled. "Know how they operated? They'd get the word that somebody really double AA was giving a party—Sam and Frances Goldwyn, maybe Danny and Sylvia Kaye, or Bill and Edie Goetz—

and if they hadn't been asked, no hesitation, no shame, Sully or his wife would call up and say 'We know you're giving this wonderful do, and your secretary obviously made a mistake—we haven't ever gotten our invitation, maybe it's lost in the mail?' And you know something, they'd end up being there!''

". . . Then he went to Europe and did a lot of pictures out of Hollywood," I said.

"Why not?" said Ozzie. "Courtesy of the I.R.S., and its regulations on working overseas, so wherever the A crowd went, Sully went along, it was a club, they took care of each other, London, Paris, wherever, he kept on *ootzing* himself into something else, like Eliza, crossing the ice, you know?"

"Is he still married?" I asked.

"Not to Number One," said Ozzie. "This one is Number Four, now, or is she Five? Hard to keep track . . ."

Before he left, to return to his office, I said "Oz, tell me one thing, it's important. Has this guy any talent?"

". . . You tell *me,*" said Ozzie. "Is that important?"

"Cynical, aren't you?" I said.

"It goes with the territory," he smiled. "But today, I'm feeling very paternal toward you, sweetie, so when Sully shows up, keep your legs crossed—unless, of course, you enjoy being *ootzed* . . ."

"That goes with the territory, too," I said. "But it's comforting to know you care."

"A lot," he said, patting me. ". . . and hey—when you see Sully, be sure and tell him Ozzie sent his best wishes."

Sully had negotiated with me and agreed on a date for 11 A.M., in our office conference room, but he arrived three minutes early and barged directly into my office, beamed at me, and said "Your time is more valuable than mine, so here I am, the Mountain, come to *you.*"

He was a charmer, no doubt, the best preserved and sharp sixty-one-year-old (I'd looked him up) aging juvenile I'd ever met. Good color, no double chin, that sandy hair was either his own or the best piece I'd ever seen, no false teeth, he didn't need glasses, unless those were contacts he wore over those bright blue eyes, beneath those doeskin slacks his waist was trim and flat, and that was obviously muscle that filled out his expensive dark blue cashmere blazer . . . (All those years of tennis and laps in the pool.)

He accepted some office coffee—black, no sugar—beamed at my secretary, who beamed back, then he sat down, put up his feet in those expensive British suedes with the gold buckles, sipped coffee and proceeded to *ootz* his way into my heart.

"According to Sid, you are one dynamite lady," he began, "and I've checked around; you're even sharper than that. I mean, the proof is this project you've come up with. Sensational idea—and I've seen a lot of them in my time. So do me a favor, where did the genius notion come from?"

Neat ploy. It meant I would tell him all about Jody's old kines, and the excitement they'd generated, how the idea had developed and what we'd been doing (or trying to do) in researching Jody's career. He let me ramble on, oh such a good listener, he nodded, nodded, smiled, affirmed everything I was telling him, subtly, he'd already made me his associate, he wasn't being paternal, he was being my partner. And of course, I ended up telling him much more than I'd ever expected to, so I stopped. Now it was his turn. Damnit, let him sell *me!*

If I wanted words of wisdom, what I was to get was twenty-odd minutes of anecdotage. Well told, he was a damned good raconteur was our Sully; one story involved a live comedy TV show he'd done, with dear Janey (Powell) and good old David (Niven), where they'd had trouble with one of the doors on the set, it continually stuck, causing great distress, there was another anecdote about good old Jack (Lemmon) doing a show with Dick (Powell) in which the corpse, supposedly dead, had miscued his exit, gotten up and walked off the set in full view of the cameras! ". . . We were truly pioneers," beamed Sully. "Isn't it wonderful to think we've all ended up, preserved on old kines, exhibits in a museum on East 53rd Street, Mr. Paley's Waxworks?"

More names kept dropping, like autumn leaves, dear Fayesie (Emerson) and old Bob (Montgomery). Lord, this man had obviously been on a first-name basis with the whole of live TV!

At last we got down to business, i.e., how he, Sully Fischer, the veteran, could help in developing this project. Did I still expect specifics? *Forget it, Mrs. Tighe*—pure generalities replaced the name drops. What we needed was to capture that fine frenzy, that excitement, that sense of pioneering, the pressure-cooker atmosphere under which TV had developed, thirty years ago—we had to do it, it was vital to recreate history—

By now, Sully was selling *me* on my own vision. Capture the 50's, create a smash piece of entertainment, and the glory part of it? ". . . it's about youngsters, making their mark in a new world— so—that's how we will connect with today's teen-agers, the ones with the cash to spend. Perfect!'' he beamed.

"Glad you agree,'' I said. "Now, how do we get a fix on Jody Cassel herself?''

Sully beamed. "Simple. Her we know already. A mixed-up, spoiled bitch, out to make the world pay attention to her. What's new?''

I didn't know her at all. How did *he?* ". . . You worked with her?''

". . . No, but I heard about her from Sammy, and Shirley, and Frank,'' said Sully. "Everybody around town knew about Jody—Miss Trouble. Strictly a six-months wonder, bitched herself out of the A group, then she ended up scratching. You know, there are some people who simply cannot handle success—''

My phone buzzed, interrupting Sully's philosophic dissertation.

I picked it up. "Hel-l*o,*'' came a British accent. "Miss Tighe— Mrs. Claire Wachtel returning your call.''

Damn! —what lousy timing.

I didn't want Sully Fischer listening in on this call.

"Excuse me, I want to take this in another office,'' I said, smiling at Sully. Let him stay here—if he wanted to read what was on my desk, so be it—then I went outside and waved to my secretary to get up from her desk, I'd take this call here. "Go take a coffee break," I hissed, and took her seat.

". . . Eileen Tighe?" said Mrs. Wachtel. Her voice was careful, reserved, somewhat remote. "Dick Hatch told you to call me?"

I explained the circumstances, and how he was being helpful on the subject of early TV—

"But why should he suggest you talk to *me?*" she asked. "I have had nothing to do with that scene for years and years—"

"But I'm specifically trying to locate Jody Cassel," I told her. "And Mr. Hatch says you'd know how to find her."

". . . Does he, now?" she said.

"Do you?" I asked.

". . . and tell me, why are you specifically looking for her, Miss Tighe?" she asked me.

"It's *Mrs.*" I corrected, and explained—Jody's story as the focus of a possible film dealing with a woman, trying to make in a male world. I figured that aspect should appeal, certainly, to her.

". . . and you say Dick Hatch is involved with you in this?"

"No, he's merely trying to be helpful," I said. "By long distance."

"He's still hiding up in New Hampshire?" she asked. ". . . Was he sober?"

"He sounded sober to me," I said.

"Is he working?" she asked.

"I wouldn't know," I said. "Please, could you tell me one thing up front, is Jody Cassel still alive?"

There was a moment's silence, and then she said ". . . When last heard from, yes."

Good! At least we'd nailed down one positive fact. Now, if this very busy powerhouse executive lady could provide me with an address, or a number, where I could reach Jody—

"Hold it," she told me. "I'd have to think this over. I'm not at all certain she would want to talk to you—or for that matter, to anybody else, about her past career. She's gone through quite a lot, and I believe she's left all that behind her. Have you spoken with her daughter?''

"No, I had no idea where she is, either," I said. "But I'd certainly like to, if you'd put me on to her—"

Again, silence. Damn—please don't tantalize me, Mrs. W., I was praying, I've waited so long, looked so hard, gotten nowhere, and now I've come in sight of Jody, don't wave me off—

"What makes you think this is a viable project?" she asked. Something today's audiences would find interesting? My market surveys indicate these kids today are totally unresponsive to things that happened thirty years ago—to them, that is the Stone Age. How would they possibly relate to some young female's struggles for identity, way back when?''

I wanted to ask her—wasn't she at all sentimental about her own past, her own struggles? . . . But I thought better of it. "We're willing to take a chance on the subject," I said. "But I'd want it absolutely authentic—and since our main line would revolve around someone like Jody, I need to talk to her. I can't offer you guarantees about how the script will end up, but I can promise you this would be done by the very best talents—"

"Please don't sell me," said Mrs. Wachtel. "It's been done by experts. The person you'll have to sell is Jody herself. If she wants you prying around in her past life, that's strictly up to her. Unless, of course, you choose to do it *without* her approval, which is how you people always seem to do *me*. Oh yes, I'm a battle-scarred veteran of that ploy, dear. I crop up in all sorts of hack novels and miniseries, haven't you noticed? The female executive, head of a cosmetics conglomerate, da-da-da-da, I've been done so often, I've become a cliché.''

Now she had *me* on the defensive . . . Very slick. "That's not what I had in mind about Jody Cassel," I said. "Please, Mrs. Wachtel, might I at least discuss it with her directly? She's certainly a grown-up person, she can make up her own mind."

She thought it over. Then she said "Fair enough. I'll try to reach her. If she wants to let you speak with her, I'll be back to you. *If.*''

". . . Just a minute, Mrs. Wachtel, if you want to reach me, it's better at home—" I said. But the phone had disconnected. She was over and out.

I hung up. Well, at least we'd gone a few steps further than—

". . . Was that *Claire* Wachtel?" asked Sully Fischer.

Who was standing beside me, beaming down at me here at my secretary's desk.

He'd been here a while, how much had he overheard?

(Championship class *ootzer,* Ozzie had warned.)

"Oh no," I said, carelessly. "That was an old friend of mine, Muffy Wachtel, from Boston—"

"Oh, too bad," said Sully, obviously disinterested. "We met dear Claire last winter, down in Palm Beach, at the charity benefit she always runs. Marvelous lady." He glanced at his watch. "Tennis date. We'll pick it up again soon, and meantime, you and I and dear Sid will stay in close touch, won't we?"

"Oh, absolutely," I said. Damn, I was beginning to sound like him.

He bussed me briefly on both cheeks. "You're a wonder, Eileen, my pet." (Already we were on a first-name basis. Would I ever graduate and become one of the names he dropped to others?) "Our project is going to be a definite winner!"

The moving *ootzer* having become my partner, ootzed on, out of my office.

Leaving me to wait, not so patiently, for Claire Wachtel's next call.

. . . Or maybe I'd get lucky, and it would be Jody herself?

*   *   *   *

Claire Wachtel:

Outside, through the deck windows, the Atlantic was a thin grey-blue, almost an eye-shadow blue? Sun pouring down on the beach, nobody much out here yet. Too early. All the smart ones would arrive after Memorial Day, but meanwhile, I could safely hide out here at the summer house, alone for the first time in days, and enjoying the silence.

At 4, I had a massage scheduled; after this past week of meetings, planning sessions, and various arguments, I needed Inga's Swedish-steel hands on my frame, to let it all run out, to restore me.

I'd left it to Farmer to try and reach Jody on the phone. Sometimes getting through to that Godforsaken spot in Mexico where she's been hiding out—El Lindo? El Whatever?—can take hours.

What would Jody's reaction be to this proposal?

I knew mine.

. . . Nostalgia. Last year. Over. Put it away. . . . Who needs it?

All these people, trotting around, painting rosy pictures of the past, packaging the good old days into something salable. Marketing another time, another place. This Mrs. Tighe, out in Los Angeles, who's so desperate to speak to Jody, to offer her instant renaissance, to glorify Jody's "struggle" . . . she's got to be one of that mob.

Everything that happened before is better than now, that's their rallying cry. Crazy. Here we are, mid-1984, stress-ridden, high on coke, boozed out, crime everywhere, inflation, we're teetering on the edge of some nuclear disaster, down in Washington is there anybody minding the store? most of us dropping like flies from cancer and heart disease and herpes and AIDS? And ten years or so from now (if we're here) somebody like Mrs. Tighe will be planning a big retrospective on these days. ". . . The Mid-Eighties—That Wonderful Era When We All Lived Life to The Ultimate!"

. . . Set to the music of the Sex Pistols.

Sam always said ". . . Not last year, Claire. Tell me about *next.*"

He was always Mr. Next.

Reminisce? Forget it. Why should he? Brag to people how he'd grown up a desperately poor Newark boy, born in a tenement, how he'd got his first job working in a cheap cologne factory when he was thirteen, how ten-odd years later he was already out on his own, pushing the first item in a line of high-profit margin cosmetics he decided to call *Baroness*. ("It had the proper class image," he explained to me. "And I went for the most expensive packaging I could.") Which took him from being a very new small fish in a big pond to tilting with the sharks, and winning out—until he finally achieved piranhahood?

He never looked back. For Sam, that story was strictly Last Year.

. . . So now the proposal on the table is to restore Jody Cassel to stardom?

Also Last Year.

Mrs. Tighe out there in L.A. has worked up some vision of a young girl, the struggling Saint Joan of the 1950s, who came charging through an obstacle course operated by lustful males, trying to carve out a niche for herself in history by making the people laugh. A pioneer Pagliacci (Pagliacc*a?*) who fought the good fight, but when she finally lost, lost nobly.

Bullshit, Mrs. Tighe. How wrong can you be?

From the first day I met her, I knew Jody was a driven lady, a classic case of the obsessive personality.

What was the itch? The drive? Easy. Her darling mother, that dominant bitch out in Westchester, piss-elegant Doris, the middle-class consumer, who thrived on her charity benefits and her golf game, who gave birth to Jody in between tournaments at Sunningdale, then, three years later, took a look at her toddling daughter Jody and decided that small piece of female humanity wasn't beautiful enough.

. . . and let Jody know it.

From this mother's stupidity, the world would acquire a comedienne. The years whipped past, and our Jody, who had to achieve approval from Somebody, if it weren't her own mother, would become the class cut-up, the playground funster, the recess clown, the lunchroom face-maker, doing jokes about how the boys wouldn't try to put their hands down her blouse, (for fear of barbed-wire scratches!) using self-mockery as her only defense, hiding her hurt, inducing love.

. . . Sorry, Mrs. Tighe. It really had nothing to do with Women's Lib, or Saint Joan.

In fact, it's an interesting speculation. If one—only one—of those elementary schoolkids *had* tried to feel Jody up, who knows, she might *never* have ended up a star.

But they didn't try. So she went on to kick, claw, and knock down everybody who got between her and that audience.

Then, the people became tired of her, and moved down the playground to begin laughing at some other fresher-faced cut-up.

Where did that leave Jody? Nowhere. With nobody to laugh at her . . .

But she could still mock herself.

I remember that day she came up to see me, at the Baroness

building, Sam's headquarters, on Fifth.

Dark glasses, heavy coat, her hair done up in a babushka, she looked as if she were in hiding—and perhaps she was. "Okay, Claire," she said, "say hello Madame Bombo, the Great Egg-Layer, Flora Flop!"

That season she had gone through a disaster, a ninety-minute prime-time TV show, all her own, negotiated by Buck Dawes, "Jody and her Friends." What she'd always wanted, the ulti-mate—a one-woman showcase.

Watching it had been painful. Nobody likes to see anyone go that wrong, and when it's a friend . . . wow. Our Jody had pranced out with a cadre of boys, wearing a collection of glitzy Bob Mackie costumes, grinned and mugged her way through painful dialogue with a couple of guest stars; then on it went, too much Jody, she was into everything, special material sketches, mocking herself in the elegant clothes, kidding when the scenery didn't work, and finally, launching into an interminable medley—solo—of bal-lads, rhythm numbers, torch songs, à la Al Jolson, climaxing with her, in a spotlight, having the chutzpah to essay the "Solil-oquy" from Rodgers and Hammerstein's *Carousel*.

That one even *I* knew wasn't right for her.

Whose idea had *that* been? . . . as if I didn't already know.

("I figured if Sinatra could get away with it, why shouldn't I?" she said. "So okay, I made a mistake!")

The critics had been brutal, so had the ratings. Jody was bloody but unbowed. "Gleason bombed on *his* solo show—Jerry Lewis laid a terrific egg. At least I'm in good company!"

Later, when we'd nibbled on some dietetic lunch, she broke down and gave me the bottom line, which was dire. Since her public shaming, things were rotten. Nobody was calling her agents for anything except bookings in the Catskills or summer music tents. She was in debt (who knew where the money had gone? who kept track?) She was supporting her eleven-year-old-daugh-ter, Pretty Baby, whose father, the musician, never came up with a dime, and Pretty Baby was coming to that age where she'd need orthodontia, private schools, and maybe college—

"Don't lay on me!" she warned. "I know—I've been a schmuck, I let other people handle my money, and run my life, and they've screwed me, I don't have Buck Dawes to handle things any more, he's a big producer, and I've never been able to replace him, damnit, I've been out there knocking my brains out for the audience . . . now they hate me! Why?"

Slouched down in one of my office chairs, she wasn't the old Jody, no this was a beaten lady, worn, her energy level obviously below her ankles, and there was also desperation in her. "I have got to get going again, build up some momentum, in this business, if you don't go forward, you're finished, they forget you," she told me, moodily. "It isn't only the dough, Claire, don't you see, I've been at this for so long, I don't *know* from anything else! I'm not like you. You threw it away, gave up your acting career—"

I stopped her. *"What* career?"

"Oh, come *on,"* she said. "You were the most delicious broad I'd ever met. I wanted to be you so damn badly—I mean, you were easily as beautiful as any of these—" She waved a hand at my office wall, on which were large color photos of this year's Baroness, done by Dick Avedon. "And you could act—certainly as well as any of those other bimbos we ran around with. But instead, you went for Dick, you got married, and gave up your career to raise your kids . . . *His* kids. *How?* I wouldn't have done that . . ."

How? Who can answer that? Could I pinpoint the morning I looked in the bathroom mirror and told myself "Claire, you're beautiful, no question about it, you look very good in a strapless evening gown, nice legs, good boobs, you can read lines well, but so can approximately six hundred and twenty-nine other girls who're staring into their mirrors here in Manhattan, or out in L.A. *They* are not going to become Katharine Hepburn, sweetie-pie, and the odds are *you* aren't, either." That's the day you realize it's all a steeplechase, and you've been running for a long while with very little forward motion, so what's terrible about getting married to a nice talented man like Dick Hatch? . . .

. . . and when you make a baby with him, there's nobody around to say "Thanks very much, but you're not quite what we had in mind . . . *Next?*"

I knew that afternoon, up in my office, I'd have to be Jody's life preserver. Pull her up and out of that pit she'd dug for herself, get her back on her feet, somehow find her a way to go. Who else was there to do it? (For helping her, I got plenty of flak, before and during. *Jody Cassel?* Bad news, a troublemaker, a big mouth, an impossible bitch—oh, in this business, when you're marked lousy, it's with a capital L, and it sticks.)

I never bothered to explain to anybody why I put up with Jody, with her tantrums and her paranoia and endless demands. But, if I'd had to, I would merely said I owed her one. Maybe two.

For Sam and me, she'd been our inadvertent Yentl, the matchmaker.

. . . She hadn't meant to be, she was only being my friend.

When Dick and I split, and he walked away from me, Jody was the only one who comforted me. Held my hand, kidded me out of my self-pity, chucked me under the chin, insisted ". . . Hey, Claire, this is *not* the end of the world, he is replaceable. (Listen to me—the woods are full of swordsmen who'll want what he's turned down . . . These guys adore divorced women, get your beautiful ass out there and start mingling! Oh, God— how I wish I had half of your equipment!"

She did more than cheer me up, much more. In order for me to regain my self-confidence, she insisted I should get back into the public eye and be seen. Work was good for me—"and the money wouldn't hurt, either!" she said.

I ended up with that ridiculous job on a TV quiz show— "Baroness Presents—*Bet A Million!*" Courtesy of Jody's connections up at Buck Dawes' agency, there I was, no longer the *hausfrau* Mrs. Hatch, but overnight I was Miss Claire, your lovely Paying Teller, who glided onstage in a long white Larry Aldrich,

smiling and showing the teeth, awarding the check-filled envelope to that lucky contestant who'd just answered a batch of tough
questions (carefully chosen by the staff so that his winnings were
under control at all times) and who was now on his way to financial Nirvana, courtesy of the owner of Baroness, Samuel Wachtel.

. . . who sat each week in the wings, at a desk, and personally filled in the amount of said check, right then and there (very
shrewd publicity, guaranteed to get space in the next day's paper)
signed it, put it into the envelope, and personally handed it to
me, his Paying Teller.

Yes, that is how Sam and I began, he holding up the envelope
for me, me leaning over to pick it up from him . . .

Sam, my Sam, who made no bones about eyeing the view I
afforded him when I leaned over. Sharp-eyed Sam. Nervous, wiry.
Shrewd Sam. Affable, sure, but a killer if you tried to play games.
"Cross me once and that's it," was his credo. Rarely did anyone
go for a second shot at Sam.

Sam, who said to me, one night, casually, ". . . Know something? I've decided you're not another broad I should romance
for a quick *shtup.*"

"That's good," I told him. "Because I don't know what *shtup*
means, but I can guess, and I'm not interested, either."

"In *shtupping?*" he asked, "Or in me?"

I didn't know about him, yet, so I let that pass. The next
week, he asked me to dinner.

"Can I ask what you have in mind this week?" I said.

"I don't know yet for sure," he said, "but hang around me,
Claire, and you could be anything you wanted to be."

An interesting sales pitch. I wasn't sure what he meant, that
night. Later on, I found out.

. . . He was a widower, whose kids were grown up and didn't
want to be in his business. He had no hobbies excepting that
business. Where were the two of us going? What was the percentage—for a widower and a divorced lady with two teen-aged
kids?

We spent some time together, no *shtupping* (that came later, and when it did, it was fine), but mostly talking.

". . . *Bubele,* you've got all the necessary equipment," he told me, one night. "How come you've never used it for yourself? Always for other people's benefit. Don't you want to be different from all those other beautiful, brainless ones?"

Sure, another sales pitch, he was a fantastic salesman. But it was also based on truth, and I realized it. With Dick I'd always been an ornament, a handmaiden, something decorative, good-natured and comfortable, who kept the home fires burning.

With Sam I expanded. I learned. He was a hell of a teacher, but I was a terrific student. That's why he'd chosen me. Damn, he was sharp . . . In and out of bed, up in his duplex, or out here at the beach house, he had me enrolled in his cram course. Why was he filling me in on the daily happenings at Baroness? "You have a good head for business," he said. "Listen. Learn." All day, all night? ". . . Neither of us is exactly a teen-ager," he said. "We don't have an endless supply of time."

Soon he had me following him around, down at the Baroness offices. In a year I went from Marketing Consultant to Executive, and soon after that, I went from Claire Hatch to Mrs. Sam Wachtel. That meant I had Sam's relatives to contend with, glaring at me in stolid silence, I was the blonde *shiksa* who'd been their middle-aged father's *shtup,* and who'd managed to seduce him into marriage. What difference? Sam had laid down the law to them (and his lawyers had added iron to it) and they all knew better than to cross Sam. I was Mrs. Wachtel, a fact of life.

They didn't know what I'd found out by then, that Sam's elegant silver pillbox was filled, not with saccharin, but with nitro capsules for his angina. He'd chosen Claire, the Paying Teller, to be his Galatea, he'd trained me carefully, and by the time my lovely Sam died, in my arms, in the middle of the ghastly night in Palm Springs, while we waited for the godamned ambulance to respond to the 911 call, I was ready to become his surrogate.

. . . all due to Jody.

So, that day, up in my office (once Sam's) staring at my

defeated friend Jody (what an unlikely fairy godmother!) I had an idea. A possible way to pay back this poor, mixed-up creature . . .

Impulsive, sure, but I'm good at using my intuition. Sam knew that, he encouraged me to speak up and not be afraid of venturing an opinion. ("You have to be wrong before you're right," he'd say. "Deliver me from those salaried *schmuckos* who always play it safe.")

Jody's purse contained a photo of Pretty Baby, her daughter, now an amazingly attractive eleven-year old, on the verge of puberty. Grinning happily up at her mother, the two of them on some California beach, Jody mugging back. Clowning, having laughs, mother and daughter obviously enjoying the hell out of each other.

I thought—*that's* a salable commodity.

Could Pretty Baby possibly be a model?

"Screw that!" Jody told me, firmly. "I don't want her going through all the crap I took, no way!"

Translation; her daughter was far more beautiful than she and she did not need the competition.

So I thought fast, and came up with an end-run, which turned out to be a real winner. Why couldn't it be a sister-act, using both of them? Equal billing—Jody, the perpetual mother-hen, hovering over her Pretty Baby, the two of them in the bathroom; dialogue? ". . . Oh, sweetheart, you have such bee-yootiful skin," (big, typical Jody Cassel laugh) ". . . but you got it from me, right? So listen close, the important thing for you to remember is to take good care of it—with this BeNeath Face Cream of mine!"

Pretty Baby (laughs cheerfully) ". . . Oh, mo-thurr, haven't you even noticed? I've been using *yours* for weeks, now."

Double take, and then they both laugh. We move in on their faces, side by side, in the mirror, and Jody says "Yep—we're both definitely BeNeath girls! Wowoweewewoh!"

Simple? You bet. Direct, persuasive, and it also hit both age groups, mothers and daughters. The TV audiences laughed, but they remembered it the next day, and when they got to the drugstore, they bought BeNeath. So much of it that we kept on doing those commercials with Jody and Pretty Baby for the next few years. We even used the two of them in print and display ads, and we sold a hell of a lot of BeNeath.

Whatever they made doing the job for us, and it was plenty, as old John Houseman says ". . . They *earned* it!"

. . . As did I, putting up with Jody's constant suggestions for rewrites in the ad copy, her arguments with the director on how he should set up his cameras, her midnight calls from anywhere she might be with her spur-of-the-moment ideas for the next campaign.

The BeNeath commericals also gave Jody a considerable boost back from her last flops. She began to do dinner theaters, or music tents, and occasional guest shots on whichever TV variety shows would have her. There were also sitcom pilots for various producers, but none of them clicked with the networks.

The income from BeNeath tided her over the slow spots, and I suggested she put a lot of it away for her golden years. "I've got a better idea," she said. "Find me a rich guy and get me a job as *his* Paying Teller. That'll take care of my old age pretty good!"

She invested a good chunk into a chain of fast-food places, to be called Jody's Chicken Shack, a franchise deal that would induce instant riches. I should get in on it with her, we'd both make a bundle. Tactfully as possible, I turned her down, and suggested she invest in AT&T bonds instead.

When the scheme collapsed, and the bankruptcy proceedings began, her partners had flown the chicken coop. "I ended up with enough frozen birds to last me until I lose my teeth!" Jody grumbled. *Now* would she consider investing in U.S. Treasury Notes? ". . . *So* boring!" she complained.

She married again, this time to a dance director whom she insisted was the most reliable man in her life. "Which isn't saying a lot!" she chortled. She became the financial backer of a new dinner theater to be established in Arizona, with her husband as director. Didn't I agree that the Sun Belt needed such an enterprise? Yes, I did, provided the management was capable. When I suggested Jody's capital would be safer in Arizona real estate, she wouldn't listen. "Who needs to own cactus?" she said.

The restaurant started out well enough, but after two losing seasons, it failed. "My God, in Arizona they wouldn't even come out to see *Oklahoma!*" Jody complained. "Tell me, what is it about me? Why do I always go for the wrong men? *You,* I could fix up—*me,* I can't do a thing for!"

Having lost her equity in the dinner theater, and her husband as well, Jody went back to work, wherever she could find it. "I have to!" she told an interviewer. "I'm not rich, like my darling daughter."

She was referring to Pretty Baby's trust funds, in which reposed her considerable income from those BeNeath commercials (by order of the courts, since she'd been a minor at the time). Administered by lawyers and bankers, those funds paid for Pretty Baby's schooling, her orthdontia, her upkeep, and then her college tuition.

. . . Jody would never have to worry about Pretty Baby following her into show business. Our little teen-aged BeNeath salesperson grew up disinterested in comedy bits and *shtick.* What began to interest her was English Poetry of the Eighteenth Century, and what interested her even more was the bearded young assistant professor who taught the course in her college.

Now they're married, and living in England, while he teaches at Cambridge. "What did I do?" Jody asked me, after the wedding. "Where did I go wrong? Who knew I was raising an intellectual?"

Swathed in Harris tweed, Pretty Baby may be unrecognizeable as the BeNeath girl . . . but for years now, those trust fund checks have dropped out of her British mailbox, every three months. (*Her* trustees didn't need to be told about IBM and AT&T.)

. . . I remember when Jody called to tell me Pretty Baby had just presented the world with her first child, a baby girl. Wasn't she delighted? ". . . Hell no!" she groaned. "Who wants to be a grandmother? From now on I have to dye my hair blue and play benefits at Sun City!''

I wasn't outraged; I knew the feeling. By that time, I, too, was a grandmother, and my own life had become littered with family stresses and strains; the older I became, the more complex were my relationships with the succeeding generations.

Over the next years, Jody and I didn't see much of each other. At one point I saw her picture in a gossip magazine, the kind you read at a supermarket checkout; she had her arm around a young blonde man. IS THIS IT FOR JODY AT LAST? read the headline. ''HE IS ABSOLUTELY THE GREATEST!'' SHE SAYS.

In the photograph, her face had that lustrous, waxy sheen that often results from cosmetic surgery.

That Christmas, I received a card from her; on it was a handwritten note. ''He's gone,'' said her note. ''But at least this time I didn't invest any money in him!''

One night, very late, when I was down there in Florida, resting, I got a long-distance call. It was Jody; she tracked me down through my secretary; it was vitally important she talk to me! . . . How was she? Exhausted. ''I'm touring with this half-assed bunch of no-talents,'' she said. ''We play one-nighters and travel by bus, would you believe? *The Hit Parade of 1950!* What the hell, it's a living . . . Now listen, Claire, I have got the brainstorm of the century!'' she said. ''Do you remember how great Pretty Baby and I were—how we sold product for you? Well, are you ready for this—how's about *three generations!* Aha? Aha?''

. . . Melissa, her granddaughter, now aged eight, Pretty Baby . . . *and* Mo-thurr—all of them—pitching our product?

It might work . . .

I promised to think it over, and to get back to her.

''Don't give me any of that executive-type shit, Claire,'' Jody said. ''You're the boss of the outfit, what *you* say goes— so let's decide right now, yes or no, do we go to work for Baroness again, or do we take this fantastic idea somewhere else?''

I was beginning to sense a frenzy in her; in the middle of the night one didn't come to such decisions, she knew that—

I asked her ''How does Pretty Baby feel about this?''

''Screw her;'' said Jody. ''Stubborn bitch, she'll do what's needed for her kid, just the way I did, and she's an idiot if she doesn't see what a terrific idea this is, I mean, it's fucking *genius,* Claire, we meet with your ad people as soon as possible, tomorrow, maybe, set it up, right?''

Tomorrow? . . . was she on something?

Where was she?

''What the hell difference does that make? Wait, I'll look— Hey,'' she yelled, to someone nearby. ''Where are we, Irving? I've got this important executive on the horn wants to know where I am, all these godamn towns look alike . . . *Where?* He says Woonsocket, Rhode Island. Would you believe, I'm in Rhode Island? Hey, one guy says 'Did you know my Rhode Island Red laid a square egg,' and the other says 'An act of Providence!' Wowoweeweewoh!'' she chortled. ''Okay, Claire, do we have a deal, shit or get off the pot, honey, the three girls won't wait forever . . . *yes or no?''*

Even at this distance, I could tell there was something very wrong with my old friend.

''Give me a number where I can reach you tomorrow,'' I said.

''. . . Nobody can reach me tomorrow,'' Jody said, wearily.

Silence. The long distance lines hummed in my ear.

''Jody,'' I said, ''I *will* call you, but I have to know where—''

''Listen, Mrs. Wachtel,'' she said, ''I do *not* need your godamned shitty condescending charity. Understood?''

When she'd hung up, all I could think of was Sam's favorite saying, something he'd read in Mark Twain, I think it went ''If you feed a dog, he will not bite your finger. That is the essential difference between a dog and a man.''

Nothing ever happened with that idea of hers, nor did I hear from her until a couple of years later. This time the call came from Mexico, where Jody informed me she'd been in residence there for some time. My midnight analysis had been correct; she'd been under treatment down there with a Dr. Katzen. "For what?" I asked. "Name it," said Jody. "Oh yes, grandma tried everything, the sauce, the uppers, the downers, anything she could get her hands on . . . Have you ever played around with that stuff?"

No, I hadn't. "Luckily I've been too busy," I said.

"Well, don't bother," she said. "Suicide is easier."

Her voice was calmer, less frenetic. She made no reference to her proposal for the TV commercials; show business seemed past history. "I have found this wonderful guru, Dr. Katzen, and he has changed my entire life, rearranged my head, helped me to *see*," she said.

"I'm glad," I said, and I meant it.

"Come down here and meet him, he is something else, Claire," she assured me. "I'm here full time, we can talk, it's great, you'll love it."

Was it a retirement home, or a spa?

"Some of that, but it's much more," she assured me. "It's really a healing environment for people who need help . . . and Dr. Katzen has me around to help."

Then she had gone into business with him?

"It's beyond anything so mundane," said Jody. "He has remade me, Claire," she continued. "I feel so different, dear . . . and so will you."

"I think that's absolutely marvelous for you, Jody," I said, and I meant it. "But what do *I* need from your doctor and his environment?"

"Peace. Serenity . . . Balance," Jody intoned.

". . . I think I'm fine in those departments," I said.

"Don't be defensive, dear," said Jody. "All those years and years you've spent peddling artificial beauty aids for peoples' externals must have given you some sense of how hypocritical it is. We know it's the *internals* which matter."

"Listen, Jody," I said, now I was trying hard not to lose my temper, "those artificial beauty aids for the externals have done pretty well by both of us, *and* by Pretty Baby, and—"

"You're getting angry," she said, "and that's good. It means you're responding on a valid level, and venting your hostilities—"

"Hostilities to what?" I demanded.

". . . That whole business you've been saddled with," crooned Jody. "Isn't it time you unloaded some of those responsibilities Sam saddled you with, and began to *find yourself?* You know, you really do owe that much to yourself, Claire."

She sounded exactly as if she were doing a comedy bit, a takeoff of one of those early morning gospel preachers in a dark blue suit, on Sunday TV . . . except she wasn't taking anyone off, she was serious.

"Oh, come off it, Jody," I said, "what is this inspirational message you're delivering to me? For years you've been running around the landscape doing just exactly what you damned please— somebody else has always minded the store, and in this case, it's *me*—"

"Darling Claire," she said, "I can see I'm finally reaching you. If you're a slave to the process, you're *not* alone. Oh, I made the same mistake—I thought making people laugh was all I needed—but it's *not*. Honestly, dear, if you'll only come down here for a few weeks and sit with me and Dr. Katzen, you'll find out where we make the mistakes—the wrong turns—"

"How much does this process cost?" I asked.

"Now you're being defensive," she said. "What does the cost matter, when we're talking about internal *truth?*"

"I'm a business person," I said. "I like to get these things settled up front so there's no misunderstanding afterward. Now, does your Dr. Katzen give a written guarantee when I sign in?"

"Oh, Claire, dear," she said, softly, "I've spent my whole life doing the jokes . . . which enabled me to avoid facing the truth. But honestly, jokes are no real support when you're in trouble, believe me—"

"I am not in trouble, Jody, believe *me,*" I said, and I was having trouble controlling my temper now. "I think maybe—"

"When you're ready, call me," said Jody, sweetly. "I'll be right here, waiting to help you."

Which explains why I haven't called her before this.
I wasn't ready.

. . . Now I was in the rented car, driving across the desert, headed toward Jody's Mexican retreat, for our meeting, the bright sun beating down (why was there no air-conditioning in this damned rental?) outside, the low dusty landscape dotted with ugly, barrel-shaped cacti, bleak, somewhat forbidding, no place to break down . . .

That spot on the road ahead, could that be a hitchhiker? All the way to hell and gone out here? Never stop out here, who knows what somebody could be doing—

—As I came closer, I could make him out now, wearing a broad sombrero, floppy white clothing, a silver belt gleaming in the sunlight, dark glasses on his eyes, a man, puffing on a large Havana cigar, waving to me to stop.

My God, it was Sam.

Out here?

Why? How?

. . . I braked the car and stopped—

He peered in through the open window.

"Hi, Mrs. Paying Teller, you going to Jody Cassel's place?" he asked. "I have a date there, take me with you?"

"It's me, Sam," I said. "Don't you remember me?"

"Sure I do," he said, and pulled a small ugly dog from beneath his floating white shirt. "Now, do you know what kind of a dog this is, lady? This is a genuine Mexican Spitz."

Before I could tell him there is no such breed, the dog leaned over through the car window and said ". . . Señora—" and then spat at me. *Ptoo!*

"Thank you, and now, moving right along . . ." said Sam—

Since when had Sam become a stand-up comedian, in a Mexican outfit?

He shrugged. "It's a rotten job, but somebody's got to do it, Claire," he said. ". . . Speaking of my mother-in-law, she's down in Florida last week, see, staying at a fancy hotel, and she's getting dressed to go to breakfast, having trouble picking out the right jewelry, and her husband says 'Why don't I go for a quick swim?' and she says "You don't know *how* to swim,' and *he* says—"

Somewhere a bell began to ring, *ringringring*. Sam grinned and said "I know you're out there, I can hear you ringing—get that, Belle darling, (get it?) will you? Tell 'em I'm out on the desert—*dry*. He coughed, gasped, stuck out a tongue, and said ". . . Seltzer, seltzer!"

Phone? Where?

. . . here in the car? Yes, beside me. In Mexico? *No*—

Sam had vanished, the desert as well, the phone was beside me here on the table by my bed, where I'd been lying down after the massage. It was late in the afternoon, the sun going down out there, over the ocean the phone ringing—

Who knew I was here?—

. . .Oh yes, *Jody*.

"Señora Wach-tel?" asked the operator, over the long-distance humming and hissing. "I have Señora Cassel for you—"

"Claire!" she said. "Wonderful! You've finally decided to come down. You won't regret it, I promise—"

"How are you, Jody?" I asked.

"Perfectly content," she said. "You will be, too, after you've put yourself in his hands. Now, when are you coming? I have to make all the arrangements, you'll need to be met and driven here—"

"That's not what I called you about, dear," I said.

". . . Then what is it?"

I told her about Mrs. Tighe, out in California, and her proposal for a film project. ". . . She wants to talk to you about being immortalized, and I told her I'd have to speak to you before I'd let her have your number . . .''

''. . . Why did she call you?'' Jody asked.

I explained about Dick Hatch and his connection.

''Is he involved in this? It was his idea?'' she asked.

''I don't know what Dick is involved in any more,'' I said. ''He's a hermit.''

''Is this some sort of a historical documentary, with research, and interviews?'' she asked. ''I get letters every so often about early TV, you know, graduate students doing their theses, who want to talk with the survivors of the past . . .'' She chuckled. ''In a way, I guess they're right—I *am* a survivor.''

''We all are, honey,'' I said. ''It's really up to you. Do you want to discuss your television career making people laugh with Eileen Tighe?''

Jody sighed. ''. . . I don't know. All of that seems so long ago. Why should anybody be interested in that Jody? I'm not. It took me so long to purge myself of her, and her ego-factor. Whenever I think about those times, it's so strange . . . I mean, it's as if some other person lived them, you know? Not me.''

I waited for her to make up her mind.

''What about you, dear?'' she asked. ''Are you content with yourself?''

What a question.

''Listen, dear,'' I said, ''I'm alive, I'm standing erect, with my eyes open, I have all my faculties, I have three grandchildren and my own teeth, and I don't need my face lifted. Isn't that enough?''

''. . . Externally,'' she said. ''But what about *inside?* Please—come down here. We'll peel away the trivia, and get to what really matters. Please . . . *come?*''

''. . . Absolutely,'' I said. ''As soon as I can clear the time. Meanwhile, what do I tell this lady in L.A.? To forget it?''

''That's not for me to decide,'' said Jody. ''The woman has to do what she wants to do, whether I'm interested or not—''

''But she's specifically looking for *you*,'' I told her. ''You know, you've been hiding out a long time, Jody—''

''. . . I am not hiding,'' said Jody. ''I have merely metamorphosed. What this lady wants is some other Jody Cassel, not me.''

Even at MCI rates, this metaphysical discussion was becoming expensive . . .

''Fine, then,'' I said. ''I'll tell her to forget it.''

''Good,'' said Jody. Then. ''. . . No, *wait,*'' she said. ''I'd better think about it.''

''. . . Please, do that,'' I told her. ''Meanwhile, take this lady's telephone number, then you can think about it, and if and when you decide you want to talk to her, you can call her up.''

''No,'' said Jody. Then ''. . . *wait,*'' she said. ''Give it to me, I'll take it down.''

The sooner I got off this merry-go-round, the better.

I gave her the California telephone number; when she'd taken it down, I said ''. . . You know, I suddenly feel like your agent . . . remember? Buck Dawes?''

She didn't answer.

''You remember *him,* don't you?'' I said.

Then she broke the silence. ''. . . In your wildest nightmare, Claire, dear,'' she said, softly, ''you could never feel that ugly. That man is a lost human soul, externally *and* internally. There is absolutely no hope for him, he's willed himself into this state, believe me, *I* know.''

Buck Dawes was now a demon? Since when?

. . . What had brought on this messianic paranoia? *Deliver me,* I thought, my old friend Jody has indeed metamorphosed, she is now a full-time card-carrying resident of Dr. Whateverhisname's Cloud Cuckooland, down there south of the border . . .

''Okay, I do not feel like Buck,'' I said. ''Meanwhile, I'll get back to that lady in California and tell her that after you've thought it all over, you *might* call her . . .''

''Fine,'' said Jody.

Then, *''Wait.''* she said. ''Give her this number. Let *her* call *me.''*

And as the sun sank over the Atlantic, I said goodbye to the new Jody.

Then I laughed. Let *her* call *me?*

Well, that guru of hers might have metamorphosed the old Jody . . . but he hadn't completely purged from her all the original I-am-a-star-and-don't-you-forget-it . . . had he?

Tomorrow I'd have my secretary call Mrs. Tighe and give her the number, from now on, let her cope with Jody . . . the new Jody, the old Jody, I didn't much care which any more, I suddenly realized, I'd given up the franchise.

If it's tough being a lady comic in a male-dominated world, it's even tougher being said lady comic's friend.

. . . and good luck to you, Mrs. Tighe.

*   *   *   *

Eileen Tighe:

A late-model air-conditioned car met me at Mexico City airport, and the driver, a quiet young man named Enrique, who smoked acrid black cigarillos, silently steered us, at speeds never below eighty-five, down the busy main highway, whipping past trucks and buses with nonchalant aplomb. Eventually we arrived safely, he silent and relaxed, me dizzy from that roller-coaster ride, into a sleepy town, out of its quiet shuttered store fronts, and then up a winding road, which led to Dr. Katzen's Casa Lindo.

I don't know exactly what I'd imagined I'd find, here where Jody Cassel had been "in residence" for these past years.

. . . Some walled hacienda, patrolled by watchmen with guard dogs, a remote rest home for affluent guests with "problems"? Or a discreet drying-out tank, perhaps, a high-priced Silver Hill established south of the border, away from the prying eyes and ears of the press? Or might this be a sophisticated medical mill, an expensive private clinic, devoted to desperately sick people, willing to pay high non-Medicare fees for some dubious new medical "treatment," provided them by the paternal Dr. Katzen?

The Casa Lindo turned out to be a very confusing place.

The main house resembled some prosperous city merchant's country *estancia*. Casual, relaxed, a large rambling two-story building, no sentries, no Dobermanns, in fact, not even gates. The grounds were dotted with twisted old trees; as we came up the road, nondescript dogs barked fiercely, we were waved to by some cheerful kids playing with farm animals in the fields. To the rear of the house I could make out glimpses of gardens, stables, and beyond that, a broad rolling valley where there were several horses, feeding quietly in the late afternoon shade.

Enrique, who hadn't said a word throughout the drive, carried my bag to the front door and escorted me inside. I offered him a tip; he smiled, waved it away, and disappeared.

Whom did I expect to welcome me to the Casa Lindo? Vincent Price, perhaps, in a white coat? . . . or a George Zucco type, beaming at me through thick glasses, ushering me into his remote and vaguely ominous lair?

No, instead there arrived a cocoa-colored lady, of indeterminate age, in a red skirt and blue blouse, who waddled up to me, smiled, and said softly ". . . You Miz Tighe? I'm Kitty. Great to have you here at the Casa, hope you enjoy the amb-iance, Miz Jody's out stuffing some cabbage, and the Doc is busy doin' I don't know what, so lemme sign you in . . ."

She led me to a low reception desk, casually made note of my passport number, and had me inscribe the register. Who else was here? I couldn't tell; my name was on the top of the page.

"You in Room Nine," she told me. ". . . Up those stairs and down the hall a ways, you too tired to handle that bag? We a little short-handed today, you know?"

I could handle it. When would Jody be free?

". . . Who knows when?" shrugged Kitty. "She's occupied. I mean, that lady is like some buzz saw, she's always into something, you know? You go freshen up now, we'll give you a call when it's supper-time . . ."

I got myself and my bag upstairs and down a long quiet hall that led to Room Nine. It was extremely silent, almost as if it were deserted, no sounds from behind any of the doors. . . . But what was I expecting? Moans? Screams . . . Sighs?

The room itself was small, but clean, the furniture decent, the bed broad and inviting. Through the window there was a view of the mountains beyond. As I looked down, a young blonde girl came riding past, she glanced up and waved at me, and then was gone. . . . She didn't seem to be a patient, or was horseback riding some form of Dr. Katzen's therapy?

On a table by my bed I found a bowl of fruit and a bottle of mineral water. Also, a small stack of paperbacks, mysteries, mostly, and one well-thumbed copy of *Eastward Ha!* by S.J. Perelman. . . . What a strange choice for bedside reading, here in Mexico, at Dr. Katzen's clinic / private hospital / clinic? Dry-out tank? This was certainly the most relaxed setup I'd ever encountered; being here was like spending the weekend in northern Connecticut, say, or Virginia, at some friends' home. Except that I was definitely a paying guest. The sign on Kitty's reception desk had read: WE ACCEPT MAJOR CREDIT CARDS, but beneath it was another hand-printed one, which added BUT WE DON'T ENCOURAGE THEM.

I showered and changed. The bathroom plumbing was not new, but efficient, and there was ample hot water. Then I lay down on the bed for a brief siesta. I was tired from my trip down here, and also from the past few frenetic days at Interfico.

. . . but I couldn't do anything now save doze, intermittently.

I was too hopped up at the prospect of meeting Jody Cassel, after all this time. The one and only, live and in the flesh—

. . . what would she be like?

Could I get her to go along with this project of ours?

. . . When I'd reached her on the phone, Jody wasn't the noisy aggressive character I'd grown to accept from all those old shows . . . no, she was pleasant enough, but vague, reserved, somehow remote. Oh yes, she knew about me, she'd discussed me with Claire Wachtel. She hoped I would realize I was far from the first person to suggest some sort of historic callback of her early days in live TV. There'd been others, researchers—

But I wasn't a student, I was a story executive, very much

interested in *dramatizing* her own story—

. . . well, there'd been those, too, and even an author, who'd wanted to collaborate with her on some sort of an autobiography, in which she'd Tell All . . .

Mine was a different approach, I continued to persuade her of that, and I needed to have her own participation, if I were going to use her story as the core of a film—

". . . Why me?" she asked. She didn't sound as if she were being coy, but was truly asking for information.

"Because you're unique," I told her.

For the first time, she'd laughed. "Come on now, that's not enough." she said. "Everyone who's on this planet is unique."

Conceded, but ". . . Some people are a hell of a lot more unique than others," I countered, "and you're one of them. I've seen enough of the work you did back then to recognize the talent—*real* talent—"

"Ah, ah, now you're selling me," she said. "On *me*. I'm not really interested in the process. Having to sell myself to others is something I stopped doing a long while back . . . once I'd managed to purge myself of the need."

Purge? Well, I could understand that. I'd never used the word, but I understood the process, that mysterious passage which causes one to fall out of love, with a piece of furniture, say, or a particular song . . . or even a man. Hadn't it happened to me, not with a sofa, but with my own husband? Yes, I knew about purge.

"But that earlier Jody Cassel—that's still talent," I insisted. "Worth showing to the world . . . even if you don't wish to do it . . . so why not let *us?*"

". . . Now you're selling again, Mrs. Tighe," she said, softly.

We continued like that, a gentle ping-pong game, back and forth, for a while, and our first call ended up nowhere. The second call was just as inconclusive, but at least we had a dialogue going; by the third call, I took a shot at suggesting a face-to-face meeting.

. . . no, she had no plans for coming up to California.

Then might I come down to visit her?

. . . I held my breath while I waited for her answer.

". . . We always enjoy having visitors here," she said, "so if you'd like to, by all means, come ahead."

I hung up, suddenly exhilarated. My God—a breakthrough—she was willing to meet!

Then I thought, how do I sell this to Sid Budlong?

I could already hear him. Be realistic, Eileen, a trip to *Mexico,* some wild-goose chase after a has-been, retired comedienne, some nut recluse who's so far not terribly receptive to anything about this half-assed proposition you've been trying to get off the ground, and which so far is nowhere?

Oh, damnit, Sid, *why not?*

I bit the bullet, went in, and told him about Jody and how I'd located her in Mexico.

He sat at his desk, nodding, and playing with a tiny model train, his latest executive-type toy—which buzzed back and forth on a tiny track, laid out on his blotter. Its function? To bring paper clips from one end of the blotter to the other, a distance of perhaps thirty-six inches.

Sid had surprised me.

He heard me out on my proposed trip, to see Jody, face to face, and to try and win her over to the project. When I'd finished, he nodded, and said ". . . I don't think we want her involved. She'll get in the way, honey, they always do."

After my calls to Jody, I didn't think she'd have the slightest desire to be involved.

"Don't be naïve," he told me. "She's a performer. They all give you that pious crap up front, but later on, they stop being virtuous, they turn egotistic, and believe me, we will never get this woman out of our hair. On the other hand, *if* she's willing to let us take her life story, use it as source material, to run with it . . . *then* we can talk . . ."

I couldn't believe it. He was *agreeing* that I should go see her?

He held up a cautionary hand. ". . . Yes, *but*—you'd better keep me posted on what's happening down there, every time you talk. Keep notes, call me," he instructed, "and do I have to remind you are not to get into any discussion of money, or legal rights—that's what we have a business affairs department for, remember?"

But I could get her to Agree in Principle, couldn't I?

"If you can," said Sid. When was I leaving?

. . . As soon as I could make travel arrangements, I'd use the weekend, I didn't want to have this fire go out, to have Jody turn cold on me . . .

"Good, the sooner the better," he said. "This project has been spinning its wheels for much too long." Oh yes, before I left for Mexico, would I see to it that copies of all my research material on early TV was brought in to him? He wanted to look it over . . . ". . . So I'll know what we're discussing when you're down in Old Mexico . . . and oh yes, you better get a couple of release forms, you know, that legal stuff that protects us—to make sure we're protected *before* she starts talking, know what I mean?"

Certainly, that made sense.

As I got up to leave, elated that he was going along with this, he peered at me from behind his buzzbuzzbuzzing train set. "Tell me, do you think this crazy person *will* talk?"

"That's a good question," I said. "And if there's anything I like, it's a good question. Next question?"

". . . You know, you've been around this lady comic long enough, you're beginning to sound like one," he'd said. And actually grinned.

. . . It was getting dark outside, and then the phone beside my bed was ringing. I heard Kitty's soft voice on the other end. "You hungry?" she asked. "Come on down to the dining room, and we'll tie on the old feed bag . . ."

She led me down the hall to the Casa Lindo dining room, a modest-sized place, with tables set here and there at random, lit by candles. On the walls were hung lots of paintings, done in a gaudy, bold style, heavily painted oils, Mexican landscapes with churches, peasant men and women, burros, kids, motel-lobby style art.

There were no other diners in sight yet, save for the main table, to which Kitty led me. There sat a small, wizened gentleman in a brightly checked sportshirt, wearing a jaunty beret. He waved me to a seat beside himself. "Hi there, Missus Tighe," he said. "I'm Doc Katzen, Ben to you—welcome to our happy home away from home. You're the lady figures it's time to remind the world about Jody, correct?"

His age was indeterminate, but his accent was unmistakeably purest Manhattan . . . or could it be Brooklyn?

Yes, I was Mrs. Tighe, and this was certainly a most interesting place he had here. Were there other . . . guests . . . in residence, besides me?

"Oh sure!" said Katzen. "Most of the time we got nine, ten around. Some stay, some go. They'll be here pretty soon, tonight they wait on table, and clean up after. And tomorrow, you can help. That's how we do it here, everybody has a slot, a job—see, cleaning the rooms, making beds, gardening, all that stuff. Everybody pitches in. We're a sort of a family . . . very *hamische,* you know?"

This was Jody's guru? He seemed more like the operator of some Catskill mountain adult camp, transferred down here to Mexico for the winter months. . . . And where was Jody, herself?

"Don't worry, she'll be here. She's busy. Aha—here they come!" he said. "And about time! I'm starved."

From the kitchen there began to emerge a procession of people, bearing trays of food. The first was the attractive young blonde I'd seen this afternoon on horseback. ". . . That's my little baby, Diana," said Dr. Katzen. "Hiya toots," he smiled, as she began to serve us bowls of soup. "Looking good!" She smiled back, leaned over, and kissed Dr. Katzen on the forehead, without spilling soup on him. no mean feat.

When she'd moved on, he confided in me ". . . Refugee from

Silicon Valley. Spent years designing a new-type computer, finally finished, made a potfull of dough, couldn't take the pressure, cracked up. Now she makes the best damn leek-and-potato soup you ever tasted. *Eat!*''

It wasn't Mexican food, but it certainly was delicious.

Around us, other people were bringing in side dishes of vegetables, salads, and then serving each other at the tables around the room. Conversations were beginning; the room was filling with sound.

Was this some sort of a rest home, then?

"If you want it to be," said Dr. Katzen. "Have some salad—everything is washed, believe me, no *turista* around here. Trust me. *Eat,* eat! Jody's speciality comes next."

Jody was one of the cooks?

"You better believe it," said Dr. Katzen. "Tonight she's *the* cook—made her famous stuffed cabbage, with plenty of kasha on the side!"

Our plates were removed by a thin young man, in his mid-twenties. "Hiya Artie," said Dr. Katzen. "Remember—only wash 'em *once!*'' Artie nodded and disappeared into the kitchen. "Compulsive dishwasher," explained Dr. Katzen. "Had his own restaurant up in Seattle, but had to give it up because he was so busy washing dishes, over and over, he could never get around to feeding his customers!"

The salad was delicious. "So," he said, "as long as you're down here, you'll pitch in and do a little work for old Doc Katzen, right? What do you like, gardening? How're you on making beds? Or maybe you want to go do a little laundry? They tell me that's as good as water therapy any day . . .''

I told him I'd think it over.

". . . Maybe you'd like to help Kitty." he suggested. "You look like you've got a business head on you, *bubele*—''

What exactly did Kitty do?

". . . Well, whatever the doc needs, honey," said Kitty. "Now me, I handle the front desk and the phone, and the bills and all that paper jazz . . . Which keeps me here."

. . . Could I ask why she was here?

"Sure," she told me. "Because I *need* to be here. Times I gets out and goes somewhere else, I run into all sorts of bad feelings, and they make me feel ugly . . . and I start belting away at the tequila to wash it all away. But if I stick around here with this beautiful old cat, I don't have to worry about all that ugly stuff. *Fershtay?*"

"Then this is a drying-out place, too," I said.

"Only if somebody wants it to be," said Dr. Katzen. "I just try to do what Kitty wants me to do for her . . . *Ah ha*—finally— the cabbage!"

Fragrant tureens of stuffed cabbage had emerged from the kitchen. Ours was brought by a middle-aged gentleman with a bushy mustache. *"Bonsoir, et bon appetit!"* he said, as he served us. "Hiya, Pierre, say hello to Missus Tighe, she's in from L.A." said Dr. Katzen.

"Bonsoir, madame," he said. Bowed and went on serving. *"Reste tranquil avec mon ami, le docteur . . ."*

"Et vous, aussi, merci," I said.

Pierre moved on to another table.

"He's from Duluth, Minnesota," said Dr. Katzen, softly. "A Buick dealer. But he always wanted to be French . . . so he comes down here and we let him be French all over the place . . ."

"That seems only fair," I said, even though I didn't quite understand why anybody would go to Mexico, instead of Paris, to become French . . .

On the other hand, why not? Maximilian had, with Carlotta. Why not Pierre? I was beginning to get into the spirit of this place, which was certainly nothing like any establishment I'd ever heard of. Or been to . . . Casa Lindo? No, Casa Laissez-faire.

Where the stuffed cabbage, and the kasha, was superb.

"Didn't I tell you, the greatest?" said Dr. Katzen, his mouth full. ". . . and it's all from our own gardens. I tell you, if I wanted to turn this place into a motel, we could make a fortune."

Jody had done all of this?

"Except for the desserts," said Kitty. "That's Harry's speciality."

After we'd finished the main course and the "guests" had cleared the dishes away, Harry emerged from the kitchen, a tall, beefy chap with an amiable grin, bearing a huge tray on which was an assortment of fragrant pastries and small cakes.

"Here's your baker," said Dr. Katzen. "So for one night, you'll forget calories, why not? If Harry wanted to go into the pastry business, he'd drive Famous Amos up the wall, right, Harry?"

"With my hands tied behind my back," said Harry, and moved on to the next tables with his calorie-laden bounty.

". . . Would you believe he's an advertising genius?" confided Dr. Katzen. "Runs his own shop, bills millions a year, big bucks. One of the hottest in the whole business . . . One day, last year, he climbed up the fire escape to the roof and started repainting an outdoor billboard . . . by hand." He tapped his forehead. "Now he's with us."

". . . So you're really giving psychiatric treatment here?" I asked.

Dr. Katzen shrugged. "Me, I do what's needed," he said. "I try to help people who want me to try to help them, that's all." He stuffed another cream-filled horn into his mouth. "Oy, boy—what a piece of pastry!" he said. "Let's hear it for Harry!"

There was scattered applause from the rest of the diners. Including me. It was absolutely superb pastry.

Suddenly the door to the kitchen was pushed open, and a middle-aged lady peered out. She wore a bright blouse and a native skirt, on her head was a chef's cap, perched at a jaunty angle, her greying hair was pulled back in a demure bun . . . Was she—could she be—*yes*—

. . . going a bit to fat, perhaps, but even after these past decades, the broad grin was recognizeable, so was the familiar voice that called ". . . Was that hand for *me*—or was it for my stuffed cabbage?"

Jody Cassel.

". . . Both, honey!" called Kitty.

. . . A few scattered cries of "Ole!" came from around the room, as Jody beamed, walked through, acknowledging the praise from her fellow diners. When she arrived at our table, she leaned down to kiss Dr. Katzen on the top of his head. "Had enough to eat, angel?" she asked.

"Overstuffed as a sofa," he said, "thanks to your magic hands, honey."

"Got to keep you going," she told him, and sat down. "Ohhh, that's better. Off the old tootsies. Stuffed cabbage is very tough on the feet, you know?" she said to me. "You're Mrs. Tighe, the executive?"

"Also Mrs. Tighe, your fan," I said.

"You must be—to come all this distance," she said.

". . . and not merely for an autographed photo."

She nodded. "No, you're after my whole life, right? All the various ups and downs, the heartaches, the laughter, the hits and the flops, the emotions . . . which make a career in the show biz so fascinating." She grimaced. ". . . Mainly to those fantasists who don't have anything else to do but to read about it, correct?"

She had a point. "Don't you think it's the old greener pastures syndrome?" I said. "Most people need a vicarious second life . . . even me."

"This *is* my second life," said Jody. "The first one wasn't all that fascinating . . . Right, Doc?"

Dr. Katzen shrugged. "I don't know," he said, belching slightly. "Some of the people you told me about, I could have done without . . . But the *jokes?* Not bad. You know, when old Doc Freud wrote them all down, back in Vienna, he bored the hell out of everybody. But when *you* tell 'em, it's different. I crack up. Like, remember the one about the two Jews on the train to Minsk—It has the whole philosophy of existence in it—"

"Come on, Doc, you're an easy laugher," said Jody, with obvious affection.

"He's not the only one," I said. "So am I. So were your audiences."

"Ha. Now you're selling me . . . on *me?*" she said. "Hey, lady, my audiences are gone with the wind. We're not in Vegas now, or Atlantic City, we're here at the Casa Lindo, haven't you noticed? Where it's not exactly show time."

"But the food's better," I said. "Where did you learn to cook like this?"

"Some people have Jane Fonda tapes," she said. "Me, I have Julia Child." She turned to Dr. Katzen. "Doc, I think we got us here a real *schmeichler*-lady, you know? She figures she'll flatter me into instant stardom. What do I tell her?"

Dr. Katzen stood up and stretched. "Never say no," he remarked. "Tell her you'll think about it. Sleep on it. That's what I'm gonna do, everybody." He yawned noisily. "Old Doc Katzen is headed for the feathers."

Jody blew her diminutive guru a kiss. ". . . Good night, you beautiful person."

Katzen beamed at her. "Takes one to know one," he said.

Jody watched him leave. She shook her head. "Look at the aura he sends out," she mumured. "Love, pure love."

I hadn't noticed any particular aura, but I took her word for it. ". . . What *is* his medical speciality?" I asked.

"What the hell difference does it make what it says on his diploma?" Jody said. "I don't even know if he has one. All I know is that marvelous human creature saved my life. Isn't that a fact, Kitty?"

"Oh, you'd better believe that," said Kitty. "I'm here as a *witness* to it!"

I couldn't restrain myself. "Can we talk about that?" I asked.

"Can we talk? Can we talk?" echoed Jody. "You sound like that new lady comic up in the States, the thin one—"

"Joan Rivers?" I said. "She's not as good as you—"

"Don't be silly," Jody told me. "She has to be good. You don't get to be where that one is without giving the people something they want—believe me, *I* know."

"Okay, fine," I said. "Conceded. Educate me on what it's

like to be a female comedian—''

"I was not a comedian," Jody said, as if to a small child. "I was a *comic*. A comedian is someone who says funny things. A comic is someone who says things funny."

She pulled off a shoe and rubbed her foot.

"Tell me more," I said.

"*Mañana*, honey," she said. "I spent the whole day stuffing cabbage. The old Jody never had such problems, believe me."

"No," I said, "the old Jody would have done six or seven minutes playing around with the stuffed cabbage, and she'd have had the people howling."

"You can always get a laugh by stuffing something," said Jody. "Find an opening, start the pushing, you're home free." She stood up. "Of course, I'm referring strictly to *props*. *Mañana*, maybe we'll find some time to talk. Meanwhile, why don't you give Kitty a hand clearing off the table? Good night, Mrs. Number One Fan."

She waved and left us.

Just before I dropped off to sleep, upstairs in my new quarters, I suddenly remembered my instructions from Sid Budlong— that I was to keep him posted on my daily progress.

What to do? Get on long distance downstairs in the office, call L.A. and fill him in on the Casa Lindo? On Doc Katzen and his various "guests," and that Mad Hatter's tea party of a dinner, complete with Jody's stuffed cabbage? (Luckily I'd brought some Titralac along with me; tonight I'd needed it.)

Then Sid could ask me how had my first session gone with the newly discovered Queen of 1950s Live TV, and I'd report how, instead of selling Jody to agree with our proposed film project for Interfico, I'd spent another hour or so helping a compulsive dishwasher named Artie Something to dry the dinner dishes?

Which had not been easy—because as fast as I finished drying a batch of his china, he'd grabbed back the pieces, and washed them all over again. And again!

No, I knew Sid Budlong, and I was certain he would not consider my bulletin a satisfactory progress report.

Sid can wait, Eileen. You can sleep.

You have at least made contact with Jody Cassel, here in the heart of Mañanaland, at the Casa Lindo.

So *mañana,* we'll talk. Right?

*   *   *   *

Jody Cassel, A.K.A. New Jody (NJ):

Can we talk? she asks.

Yes, we can talk.

But the question, folks, is—why should we?

New Jody is perfectly happy *not* to reminisce ever again, Mrs. Tighe. You think she hasn't done her share? Sat and spilled her guts out for hours and hours with Doc Katzen, telling him the details of everything that happened to Old Jody, since Year One? Got it out of her system, finally. "Good, that is now another person, *bubele,*" said Katzen. "Her show closed out of town. Herewith, Old Jody's career is a statistic, strictly for the record. Forget her, fold her up, put her away, the same way I once put away Old Ben."

"Say," I asked "don't tell me you're the Uncle Ben from the rice business?"

For a minute I thought he might tell me something about *his* who / what / when / where, his ancient history from back in the States. But he ducked away from my question. "No, I am Ben from the people business," was his answer.

"Agreed," I told him. "You are everybody's Coast Guard," I told him. "You stand on shore and throw out life preservers, and pull us drowners out of the sea."

"By you I'm in the Coast Guard," he said. "By me, I'm in

the Coast Guard. The question is, by the *Coast Guard* am I in the Coast Guard?''

''Old joke, Doc,'' I said. ''You should have been a stand-up comic.''

''Teach me how,'' he said.

''No, you'd look lousy in a dark blue suit, Doc,'' I said.

So now we have Mrs. Eileen Tighe actually here with us, doesn't seem like such a bad sort of a dame, a little too anxious, maybe, very sincere about this half-assed idea she's dreamed up in her air-conditioned L.A. office, right away she wants action / movement / forward thrust. Press the INSTANT FLASHBACK / REPLAY button, to get New Jody spilling all sorts of events that happened to Old Jody, years ago.

. . . Rehashing all those people who dumped on OJ, and were dumped on? about OJ's stupidness and dumbness, and her loud-mouthedness? The infighting, and the clawing and the back-stabbing, and the desperation-type screwing, boozing and pills, the crash diets—

Chew that cud all over again?

Reminisce about poor OJ, locked into her love affair with those desperate crazies in her audience, who laughed (on cue) and applauded and cheered (on cue) and stood outside the studio stage door, screaming (Pavlovian-style) OVERHEREJODY! OHGOD, we love you JODY JODY you're gawdgeous, you're so funnee, OHGOD *there she is!* Blow us a kiss JODY JODY, I wanna a pichure of you with me, JODY, stand over here, doll! OHGOD I'm standing with her! touching her! MYGOD how we love you JODY! Okay, there she goes, let's hurry over to the Mark Hellinger and catch Rex Harrison when he comes out, *quick!*''

''. . . Can you believe I once believed that pack of loonies, those flakes, actually loved me, Doc?'' I said. ''That I was happy about it, fed on it, felt I needed them?''

''*She* thought, *she* felt.'' he said. ''OJ had lots of dumb ideas, so what? Everybody makes mistakes. That's why we have divorce laws, right?''

''. . . Were you ever married, Doc?'' I asked.

''I gave it some thought,'' he said. ''Once or twice I came close, but no cigar.''

''You'd have made a hell of a good father,'' I said.

He chuckled. ''You mean I'm *not?*''

Such a tricky fella, my Doc. No wife, no relatives (that I ever saw) but one hell of an extended family down here. *''Now* I know your billing,'' I told him. ''The Jewish Spencer Tracy. Father Katzen of Boys Town.''

''Sexist,'' he said. ''You'll get me in trouble with Gloria Steinem.''

''Okay, then, Rabbi Katzen of Person Town? Listen, Doc— I have a terrific idea for you. We hang a billboard outside the gates, a big picture of you, standing there, with your arms outstretched, and the sign says 'Give me your tired, your lonely, your nut characters freaking out, and I will give them a list of chores to do here all day long at my Casa Lindo, which will completely take their minds off how rotten the world is, *outside—* at least, temporarily!' How's that?''

''Catchy, but it could use a little trimming,'' commented Doc.

. . . I'd expected this Mrs. Tighe would be calling, long before she actually got in touch, ever since the first bulletin from Claire, the Dowager Duchess of Wachtel. So I'd gone and dumped my problem on Doc.

''What should I do about this lady?'' I asked him.

I needed his guidance. He's kept me on the right track for a long time now. ''Why should I want anybody making some dumb cheapo movie about me?''

''Correction,'' he said, gently. ''Not *you.* OJ would be the star.''

Fine, but that would still mean *I'd* have to sit and tell this dame all about OJ, a smart-ass ugly kid, and her miserable teens in Westchester, with the Viola Wolfe dancing class where she was sent by her pushy mother, and then how she stumbled her way into that summer camp job, and Buddy Grimes, who walked out on her (which wasn't such a bad thing, was it?) ". . . and from then on, how she reached the lofty heights of stardom, *ta da!* And from then on, and from then on, and so what's new, Doc? It's all been done. Strictly yesterday's news. You heard it all from me, you went arm in arm with OJ down the Yellow Brick Road . . ."

"Certainly did," said Doc. "A lot of it was pretty interesting, too. I loved those old songs you sang for me—"

"*OJ* sang for you!" I reminded him.

"—Okay, and all that stuff about the vaudeville people she had on her show," he said. "Jimmy Durante, that hoofer, Hal LeRoy, oh yeah, and Bert Wheeler and Hank Ladd, and the story about the guy who wanted a piece of Bulgarian Cream Pie—"

"My God, you never forget anything, do you?" I said.

"I may look as if I'm sleeping sometimes, but I'm not." he assured me.

". . . Did *you* ever want to go into show business?" I asked.

"Who doesn't?" he said. "Those people up there, talented, with the spotlight making them look so great, doing everything we wished *we* could do. Of course I wanted to be one of them."

"So you haven't got the spotlight, but you're a great doctor instead. What kind of an act would you have wanted to do, Doc?"

Doc sat back on his old leather armchair and puffed away on one of those fragrant little Cuban cigars he loves. ". . . Saw a guy once," he told me. "Never forgot him. Big fat guy, very black, name of Brown? Yes, that was it. Very graceful, light on his feet, comes out and sings a song, something about balling the jack, does that ring a bell?"

"Ah yes, know it well," I said.

". . . Anyway, when he's finished, he suddenly pulls a pair of spoons out of his pocket, no, it must've been four, because all of a sudden he's got a pair in each hand, see, and now he starts tap dancing, tap, tap, tappety-tap, with the feet, and now he's playing the spoons, tick, tick, tickety-tick, he's accompanying himself, he's doing a duet, the feet and the spoons all going together, oh so graceful you could die—up and down the stage . . . and oh boy, did I ever want to be him.'' Doc sighed.

Funny. All little ugly Westchester girls wanted to be OJ.

. . . And here's little thin Benny Katzen, wanting to be fat, black and graceful.

. . . And what had that spoon-player-dancer from long ago wanted to be?

Perhaps he was happy, being what he was?

"I'll bet you Mr. Brown didn't end up chasing around in some flea-bitten bullring,'' I said. ''Being almost killed by some angry toro.''

"Ah, ah, come on, now, honey,'' said Doc. ''That was OJ, *fershtay?*''

"You expect *me* to forget her last public appearance?'' I asked.

. . . bright hot sunlight, dry, dry, so damned hot that day, dust in the throat, you could choke. In the distance, the Mexican cheapo music, Herb Alpert-type brass section, playing, over and over again that damned *GranadaGranada*GRANADA! . . . didn't those bastards know any other song?

OJ's been sitting here under the bright lights, angry, nervous, edgy, the frustration boiling out of her, down here in Mexico all these weeks, stuck on this miserable project, making a movie she'd been conned into by that producer, Paul whatshisname, in L.A., he'd promised her the A-treatment, her agent had gone along with it, what did either of them care? Up in L.A. it was always OH SURE, Jody, absolutely, you'll get added scenes, you'll have your own spots where you can score, the cameraman will make you look sensational, we'll bring in writers for you, you can't turn it down, it's a helluva chance for you, Jody, your fans are waiting for you, all those people who love you, everything's settled, right, three boff sequences for you, a real change of pace, you'll score big with them, you always have—

—Poor deluded, driven OJ, suckered (at her age, yet!) by all that shit, falling for the con, should have known from Day One this whole thing was a bummer, doomed, an exercise in mediocrity, not good enough even for cable TV, the director, Jerry something, a smart-ass from sit-coms, all he knew was slam-bang, shoot it, print it, and let's move to the next set-up, the rest of the cast down here to pick up a fast check and run back to L.A., but OJ stuck, holed up in her hotel suite bored out of her mind waiting for her sequences to be shot, and *no* extra scenes being written for her, *no* writers brought down from L.A., *nothing* promised her coming through, her agent in L.A. not answering her calls, Paul whatshisname the producer off somewhere else making deals, and the godamned Jerry paying no attention to her problems, telling her he'd deal with it when the time came, he was busy, couldn't she see he hadn't time to deal with her temperament?

Temperament? She'd show him temperament!

Cool it, Jody, it's just a movie. What are you so mad at?

(Mad at *herself,* natch!)

So finally, they'd scheduled her big scene—here in the bull-ring, under these hot damned lights, OJ in costume and makeup, she's not prepared, what is she supposed to do? She's supposed to be the duenna to the leading lady . . . Midmorning, who can be funny?

The night before she'd been out gargling margueritas in some bar in the fleabag town, with a couple of guys from the crew, this morning she was hung over when they'd rousted her out of bed abruptly, change of schedule, we're doing your scenes *today,* Miss Cassel, car's waiting downstairs.

WHERE'S MY FUNNY STUFF? WHERE ARE THE JOKES?

. . . The makeup girl could see she was in trouble, she'd slipped her a couple of absolutely harmless but wonderful pink numbers, here Miss Cassel, these will fix you up, you'll be sharp as a tack.

But she's still feeling rotten, sitting up here, those damned bright lights never off while the director is running around behind the cameras, fussing with the angle so it's absolutely right on the leading lady, Veronica, the blonde idiot who must have gotten the part by screwing Paul, what other excuse is there for hiring a no-talent like this one—

Okay, says Jerry-baby, now in the next scene, I want some funny business between you and Veronica, okay—

For instance what?

That's up to you, Miss Cassel. You're hired to be funny, BE FUNNY.

That's it? Oh shit, sure, turn it on, be funny, 11:30 in the morning, her head throbbing, the script with nothing in it, there aren't any writers around, her head can't come up with anything, the pounding in her ears is like a couple of Cuban drummers.

You want funny? I'll give you funny

Turn on the cameras, Jerry-baby, PAY ATTENTION—

She's standing up, waving at the crowd, the crowd is staring and now they're yelling at her *"Olé! Olé!"* they're yelling for OJ, right?

(Who knows what was in those pink pills? she's suddenly flying.) Running down the aisle, past the cameras and Jerry, all the way down to the bottom of the aisle, here's a wall, hey, a bunch of Mexican bullfighters standing around—

Here's funny! FUNNY!

Before these bums knew what was happening, she'd grabbed the cape from one, the sword from another, and the funny hat off the third one's head (whew, his breath reeked from his breakfast garlic as he yelled at her) Ducked away from them

through some kind of a door in the wall
and now out to this broad space
Arena? Now on goes the funny hat
get into the cape, and wave the sword
Hey, up there, a real mob of people all staring at her.
Howdy there, ladies and germs! It's ME, JODY!

Olé, olé, gringo! somebody up in the stands is yelling, OJ waves back, wait a minute, I haven't done my opening jokes yet, wait for the laugh. But they're still yelling

Why, she doesn't understand. *I*'m out here, *I*'m funny

. . . What they're trying to make her understand is she's not alone out here—

—Over there, on the opposite side of the arena, half-hidden in the shadows, pawing at the dry dusty earth, snorting—

a bull

Toro, toro, *toro!*   Waiting for somebody to come after him.

She sees him now, aha—hey! Wow, this is a real wowser of a funny spot. FUNNY—the bullfight bit, it always works, just the way Eddie Cantor would have done it, or Milton Berle, Danny Kaye, Chaplin, surefire, but never before with a *lady* comic, right? This is Jody's big spot, come on Jerry up there, turn on the cameras, here she goes—

Stick out your tongue at the bull, and hey, you know what would be FUNNY? the bull is chasing her, see? and she's running, she ducks and comes back, then she starts sticking it to him, and she *sings*, something like "You Always Hurt The One You Love," yeah, oh good—FUNNY, LAUGH YOU JERKS—

she runs—hey, what's this? Couple of stooges here?

funny uniforms   blowing whistles   waving clubs?

Police?

Hey, not a bad idea, sure, *use them* like Keystone Kops, right? they're in the act, chasing OJ! See, over on that side, they're chasing her, she ducks away

oops! Here comes the bull, on the other side!

oh, Lucille Ball would kill for a bit like this!

Up above, in the stands, the crowd is screaming. Bet your ass—*now* they know it's Jody Cassel down here, doing her well-known FUNNY

Are you getting all this on film, Jerry? Keep those cameras rolling, you wanted FUNNY, you'll get FUNNY—

You've got to love Jody, folks, she is the wildest, LOVE HER

Gimme an L, gimme an O

Gimme a V and an E—

All together now,
WOWOWEEWEEWOH—

Arms yanking at her
   Lego!
   Pulling her away She stumbles on something
   Sword?
   Hey, good, keep that in, it works—
   Where's the hat?
   Dropped?
   They're still laughing, keep that in!
   Fall.   *Oof!*   Hurt
   dirt in the mouth, dry sandy dirt, Mexican dirt   Yuch . . .
   Dizzy . . . but they're screaming, right?
   KEEP THE CAMERAS ROLLING JERRY
   Lift her up? Okay, where's the bull? Got an idea for a new
shtick, she's flat and stiff, rigid, the people will think she's dead,
see?
   (Dead in the business, at least.)
   Oh yeah? Not after today!
   Sorry, Jerry, I can't do it again
   Hey, whoever is pulling at my legs, careful of the merchan-
dise
   It belongs to Jody Cassel. Remember, they *love* her
   They love Jody Cassel. She is *not* dead in the business
   (Bullshit!)
   hey, that's funny bull*shit* bull*ring*
   joke somewhere in there, need another word, jokes work in
threes, bullshit, bullring bullwhat?
   too hard
   getting laughs is such hard work

   Blacked out then?
   She woke up later, much later.
   Nurse leaning over her, pretty girl, too much hair on her upper
lip, saying something in Spanish
   OJ couldn't understand what she was saying, simple enough—
someone was here to see her *Doctor?*

Somebody named Katzen. Dr. Katzen. Little short guy, brown as a nut, wrinkled face, loud checked shirt.

"You're the doctor?"

"Yes, I'm Doc Katzen." he said.

". . . I'm dubious."

He stared at her. "Why?"

"Not *why*," she said. "You're supposed to say 'Pleased to meet you, Mr. Dubious.' That's how the joke works . . . dummy."

He shrugged. "Okay. Pleased to meet you, Mr. Dubious."

". . . Maybe, it should be *Señora* Dubious?" she asked.

"Aha," he said. "You're feeling better."

"How can you tell?"

"You just made a funny," he said.

"I'm not feeling very funny," she said. "It was a reflex."

". . . Whatever gets you the laugh," he said.

Which is where we began.

. . . I should tell Mrs. Tighe all that, Doc?

How you sat and talked to OJ, held her hand, listened to her babble on about how the world had dumped on her?

How, after a while, she looked at you, sitting there, and realized you were the only person who'd come to see her in this miserable quiet room, where she'd been stuck, in this hospital?

Which wasn't a local hospital (this town didn't have one) but some place near the town where they'd been shooting that rotten picture (don't ask what happened to it, let it rest in peace on the Late Late Show)

Yes, this was the Casa Lindo.

Which was what?

"Down here, they call it a casa. By us, it's a house," you said.

"A house? You a white slaver?" OJ asked him. "My mother always warned me about you guys. But I have to warn you, middle-aged lady comics don't appeal much to horny high rollers . . ."

You grinned.

". . . Unless it's *you* got the hots for me," OJ said.

"Listen, kiddo," you said. "At my age, believe me, the most satisfying thing you can look forward to is a high colonic."

". . . *Now* who's doing the jokes?"

"You're the professional, don't worry," you said. "Me, I'm just a talented amateur."

"Who does what?" OJ asked.

"Anything he can to help out people who've got problems," you said. "If you want, you can stick around here, you and I can *schmoos* sometimes, and maybe something good will come from it, what do you say?"

Ah, a shrink, then?

"No, not really."

A doctor—of what?

"A little of this, a little of that," you said. "Call me Ben of all trades."

OJ was getting tired of fencing around with this sun-burned midget. "Listen," she said, "enough of this cross talk."

"Sorry," you said, "I don't get you."

"That's when the comic comes out and does five or six minutes with the straight man," OJ said. "Now tell me, without any more of the jokes, just what the hell are you, Doc?"

"You said it," you told me, and smiled. "I'm a straight man."

"For *who?*" OJ demanded.

". . . For you, Jody," you said. "If you want me."

". . . How did you come to appoint yourself to the job?" OJ asked, irritated at this little guy's chutzpah. "I mean—who asked you?"

You shrugged. "Tell me," you commented, softly, "you got yourself a better offer at the moment?"

OJ thought about that. "No," she said. "And that isn't funny."

"Aha," said Doc Katzen, softly, "*Now* we can maybe talk to each other?"

Which is how we started, Doc, and me—OJ, who became NJ.

"And ever since, we've had ourselves a pretty good run down here at the famous ever-popular Casa Lindo, right Doc?" I said.

"Just keep those stuffed cabbages coming," he said, "and we'll manage."

He still hadn't given me his word on what to do with this Mrs. Eileen Tighe, from L.A. "Doc," I said, "to get back to the original two slices of bread—" (His favorite joke, the guy in the restaurant who sits down and complains about why only two slices of bread, the owner keeps adding bread each day, but it's never enough, finally, in desperation, the owner takes a loaf of bread, slices it in half, puts it on the table, the guy comes in, sits down, takes a look and says 'The food is fine, but how come you're back to the original two slices of bread?')— ". . . what do I do about the L.A. lady?"

"What's the problem?" he asked.

"I'll give it to you straight," I said. "I'm NJ—sure, all day long I can be her, and I've put OJ away. That took a while, as you well remember. Now, all of a sudden, I'm supposed to drag OJ out into the daylight for Mrs. Tighe to see, to let her start prancing and dancing around, doing her Wowoweeweewoh, yelling at people, creating problems, doing her I-am-funny-love-me-love-me number—tell me, do we really need a movie about Old Jody, Doc? I mean, is she your idea of a role model for the next generation?"

"You know what?" he asked. "From where I sit, you sound like you're afraid of OJ."

"Not afraid," I said. "What I feel is sorry for her, not much else."

"Good. But you mean you wouldn't like to see a movie about her story?" he asked. "If it was a *good* movie? Come on, of course you would, Jody. Who wouldn't want to see herself—OJ or NJ—up there in wide-screen?"

I stared at him. "You know, I don't believe I'm hearing this from you. You're selling me, as if you were an *agent*—"

"*I*'d like it," he said. "Just think—*The Doc Katzen Story,* starring Robert Redford. Why not?''

"*You* want it, you can have it," I said. "But don't be so sure you know what *I* want."

He pointed a bony finger at me. "Who was it told this California lady to come down here?"

"I wanted to hear her out, is all," I said.

"Ah, ah, Jody," said Doc. "Who was it said to her friend Claire—have *her* call *me?* I was there—I heard it. Now—who was that talking—you, or OJ?"

He was right, as usual. Sly bastard!

"Oh my God, I see what you mean," I said. ". . . I've already let OJ out of the attic, and she's calling the shots. Again. This is like something out of an old horror movie, you know, I'm the ventriloquist—she's the dummy who takes over—"

Doc lit another one of those Cubans and puffed happily. "Eric Von Stroheim in *The Great Gabbo*," he said. "Always a good story, that one. Don't worry about it, sweetie. You can listen to Mrs. Tighe tell you what she has in mind to immortalize OJ, and you can make up your own mind. But remember, if you're really worried about what kind of a movie it's going to be—which may or may not be why you're hesitating—isn't there something that can be written into contracts by those high-priced lawyers, called 'artistic control'? Which remains with *you*—all the way?"

I stared at Doc.

. . . Sly? Oh, he was better than sly.

He was brilliant.

But why was I surprised? In all the time I'd been down here at the Casa with him, this darling little Coast Guardsman had never failed to come up with the answers for me. Diplomas, degrees, what the hell did he need them for?

"Doc, tell me something," I said. "You originally came from Brooklyn, then Manhattan—"

"Among other places," he said.

"—but I still haven't a clue about what you did for a living . . ."

"You call that a living?" he said, and grinned.

"Okay, you're not a psychiatrist, but were you once maybe a lawyer?" I asked.

He shook his head. "No, but I had an uncle who was an ambulance-chaser."

". . . Then were you ever a producer, maybe?"

Doc blew a smoke ring. "I may be cuckoo," he said, watching it float lazily off into the bright Mexican sunlight. "But I'm not nuts."

"Then I give up," I said. "What is the secret of your vast education?"

"Big ears," said Doc. "I use them to listen a lot."

"Which you taught me how to do as well?"

He nodded. "I certainly hope so, my dear."

Amazing. Who else could do Oliver Hardy and W.C. Fields in one line?

I kissed him on the forehead. "Thank you, Doc," I said.

"You're entirely welcome," he said. "So what are you going to do with Mrs. Tighe?"

"Listen to her," I said.

"You sure NJ can handle OJ, if she plays a return engagement?" he asked.

"With one hand tied behind my back, Doc," I said.

Can we talk? Mrs. Tighe had asked.

Oh yes, *now* we could talk!

*   *   *   *

Doc Katzen:

I remember our Civics teacher, 4B, Mrs. Goldfarb (how do I remember *her* name when I can't remember what I had this morning for breakfast?). Tough little lady. Always used to tell us "America is a great country. In order to succeed here, all it takes is hard work. Just remember, children, in the glorious U.S.A. you can be *anything* you want to be."

Some smart ass stuck up his hand and asked her "You mean I can be President?"

"Certainly you can," she said. "Why not?"

"My father says Al Smith can't because he's Catlick," said the kid.

"Cath-o-lic," said Mrs. Goldfarb. "And that's not true. Someday we will have a Catholic president, perhaps someday a Jewish one, even a female. Someday, even *you* may be president."

Which got her a big laugh. Augie Pisani, *president?* Mrs. Goldfarb must be nuts!

She wasn't nuts.

Hey, Mrs. G., wherever you are. You were absolutely right. Look at me. Your little ex-pupil, Benjamin (Fast Benny at Recess, on the playground) Katzen, has been anything he wanted to be.

Lots of different things, some good, others (about which maybe the less said the better) he wasn't so proud of.

And I had a lot of names along the way. Little Benny Twinkle Toes, that's what somebody called me once. Who was it? Some girl? Maybe. There've been so many different handles I've gone under. B.K. Hey-you-Katzen. Also numbers, provided me by some machine down at the Social Security office, or by my draft board. Or the I.R.S. which is still sending me nasty letters every so often, and good luck to them, the statute of limitations has run out, and they can't hang a glove on me down here.

I know who called me Twinkle Toes . . . That dark-haired lady in California, from the days when I was plain B. Katzen, and I would travel out to peddle paintings and drawings donated by artists back East with a social conscience. We would hold an auction in some hotel room, and raise money from the fat cats out there, who also had a fat social conscience along with their fat paychecks, and we'd use the money to send ambulances to the gallant fighting men in Spain. (My God, is it that long ago?) She was the one who bought a couple of Reginald Marsh pictures from me (oh boy, what they would be worth today) and she had me deliver them personally out to her big place in Malibu, a big empty house.

Her husband was away on location in Canada, directing a picture; she was home alone, gorgeous girl, frustrated actress, frustrated everything. We spent most of the day together, her telling me how miserable her life was, her husband making all that dough, her feeling useless, unworthy. After we'd *shtupped,* she broke down and wept. Then she wept some more, and we *shtupped* some more, we took time out to charcoal-grill a couple of his fine sirloins, and it went on like that, her weeping and grabbing me for another go-round. In the morning she grabbed me and said "Benny, you have such a talent, you know why? You make people feel better. You are a healer. Why weren't you a doctor?"

"In our family, who had money for medical school?"

"It's still not too late," she insisted. You have such a gift!"

She managed to get one more *shtup* out of me before I staggered out of there. But it was all in a good cause; it was for those gallant fighting men in Spain!

When I left, I wasn't feeling like a doctor; I felt more like I needed one. But eventually I recovered. I never saw her again, but she was the first one who recognized what Little Benny Twinkle Toes could do for people.

Doc Katzen. When did they start calling me that?

It certainly wasn't while I was in the Army, all those long months I was stuck in the Z.I. (Zone of Interior) which was how the Army took care of such characters as Private Benjamin Katzen, Religious Preference: None. ASN 32430215, P.A.F. (Stands for Premature Anti-Fascist) When the guy in Classification got through with me, I had that attached to my name, never got rid of it, and where did I end up? Would you believe Grand Island, Nebraska, where I froze off my ass as a clerk-typist in a Quartermaster Corps warehouse? That's how the Army took care of guys like me, keeping us stuck away inventorying shoes and long underwear, where (according to some paranoid brain in the Pentagon) we couldn't do anything to sabotage the war effort. Private Katzen? *Yo!*

Got back to being *Mr. K.* Hooked up with that crazy Swede who had the plastics business up in Nyack. He needed Mr. K.-in-the-front-office; he stayed in the back making things. Swenson? Swanson? Who can remember? All I remember is the money, my God, how much. Remember ball point pens? He had a way to make the housings, by the thousands they were stamped out each hour, in one of the factories went the stuff for the molds, out the other end came money. Me. Mr. K.-in-the-front-office, signed my name so many times a day, checks, bank accounts, contracts, money is easy to make, once you learn how. Also so boring.

But still, not Doc. Not yet. Sure, I had another name, later, from the wife I married. By her I was *Benny-Baby*. She was the one got me into that hotel deal down in Florida. Prime real estate. Sun and Surf. Come on down!

If you think plastics is boring, try living in the Sunshine State. God's Waiting Room. She—what's her name?—is still down there, working on her fourth, maybe her fifth facelift. Anybody wants to make a movie out of my life story, I know who could play *her*, get that British actress, what's her name? Elsa Lanchester. No, correction, she has talent, too classy. Call Shelly Winters.

Moshe. How did I get to be that? Well, it had nothing to do with medicine, either, it was a name went with driving down to the Hoboken docks at night and unloading stuff off a truck, into some dark ship tied up there, wooden crates marked "Restaurant Supplies," headed for Athens, but they never got to Athens, hell no, that stuff went further along until it got to Tel Aviv. We never asked what was inside, or what it was for, we knew we just loaded it on, somebody said "Good work, Moshe" and we left.

More names, more numbers, who can remember?

When did I become *Doc?*

. . . Later.

Does it matter where, or when? You need facts, you call up the New York Public Library, mention my name, see how far it gets you. Besides, it's not *my* life story this lady from California is after, she wants Jody Cassel, my star boarder, the cabbage-stuffer.

And by Jody, I have always been Doc. She never knew any of the earlier Benny Katzens.

One day she looked at me and she said "Doc, I'm trying to figure you out. Can I ask you a personal question?"

"Shoot," I said. "But don't expect too much of an answer."

"Just between you and me," she said, "why *me?*"

"Why *not* you?" I asked.

"Please, don't give me any of that Zen stuff," she said. "Let's take it from the top. I go off my rocker, in some flea-bitten Mexican bullring—"

"That I remember," I said.

"—I wake up in some strange room, and there's this guy with

a little beret on his head, he's staring down at me, and he grins and says 'I'm the doctor.' ''

"Taking a little poetic license there, I'm afraid," I said.

"All right, so you have no diploma and you're not paying dues to the A.M.A.," she said. "But why were you there? How did you find me?"

"I took the afternoon off, and there I was at the bullfights," I told her. "Maybe I'd been reading too much Hemingway the night before. Anyway, after I saw your act, I figured you might use a little help."

"Everybody in the whole damned arena knew that," she said. "But you're the one who came around."

"Nothing mystic about it," I told her. "I like to help. What was I supposed to do, stand around and wait for one of your relatives to take over?"

Why *me*, Doc?

Couldn't answer her question, why her? Why *any* of them? Kansas City Kitty, who keeps the books straight while she's trying to keep herself likewise? Diana, the beautiful refugee from Silicon Valley, who wants a heart instead of a microchip? Pierre, the pride of Duluth, Artie the demon dishwasher? Harry the baker, or Arturo and his partner Desmond, who bounce in here each year like a double yo-yo, after their annual winter freak-out in Vancouver. We have ourselves some kind of a guest list here, it's never dull. Much more interesting than running some Florida hotel, and we're not listed in any tour-guide. I give them a place where they can unwind, or crank up, whatever, talk if they want to, or not if they don't. Where they can work and feel useful, and in return, I keep the joint open. Correction, we all keep it open.

Sure, the Casa is a high-class kibbutz, with cactus. In the old days, before the hippies got into the act, we'd call it a commune. Like those places up in the Catskills where all us Premature Anti-Fascists used to go for the fresh air and the free *shtupping* under the trees.

We never need to advertise, we don't need travel agents to recommend new guests. We rely on our own private word of mouth. Like the old motto used to say, A satisfied customer is our best advertisement.

"I don't like to think what it would have been like for me if you hadn't shown up that day." Jody said.

"I'd've been there, don't worry. Doc goes where he's needed."

It's a fact. I like helping. Way back when, when that unhappy married lady out in Malibu looked up from between my legs and said "Oh God, you have such a talent. You make people feel better." ("Please, don't stop now, you flatterer!" I said.)

She was right.

Not that everybody agreed with her. Which one of the women was it, somebody I married? No, it was Alice . . . Alice something, very tall, liked short men. Called me *Igor*. Later, I saw a Bela Lugosi movie and then I found out why . . . Anyway, I remember her getting sore at me once and she said "You know what your problem is?"

"I only have one?" I asked.

"You like to play God, Igor," she said. "And one of these days, God is liable to get sore at you."

"For what?" I asked. "For trying to clean up after some of His messes? Why should he get angry at me for that? Forget it. He should write me a fan letter."

"Igor, darling, you are not only totally demented, you are blasphemous." she said.

I tried to explain to her that I was only realistic. "Look, some guys have a talent for golf, or poker, others go snorkeling, or play the commodities market, but those are strictly hobbies. With me, helping people is serious stuff. If I have the knack, I have to use it."

"You think you're some kind of a faith healer?" she asked me. "Wrong, Igor. What you need is to go see a shrink."

"A shrink?" I said. "Forget it. Who'd listen to whom? And who'd be paying the $60 an hour?"

That argument didn't last very long.

Neither did Alice and her Igor.

She went on, looking for some other short fellow to go up on her, and as for Igor? . . . Well, that would be about the time when certain parties around the landscape were running down to Washington to spill names to their Uncle Sammy.

One of those stool-pigeons certainly could have mentioned Little Benny Twinkle Toes, or Mr. K., or Moshe, even Doc, so I didn't hang around waiting for somebody from the House Un-American Activities Committee to hand me a subpoena, under whatever name it came. In the immortal words of old Karl Marx, ". . . When in doubt, punt."

I bought myself a ticket on Aeronaves de Mexico, packed a bag, and ever since then, I've been down here, in the God business.

Well, not actually that. Let's say, Doc Katzen is an innkeeper who listens.

For a while after I brought her here, Jody treated me as if I were her own private God. Then she finally began to get things straightened out. Which was fine by me. Truth is, I never wanted that job. Better I should be demoted to being her surrogate father, the one she never had when she was OJ, the angry kid in Westchester.

The one who could never bring herself to believe a man could want her.

She's over that, too.

. . . I remember, a couple of years back, when she got the hots for that young Mexican who came out from town to repair one of our water pumps. The one who was working all morning outside in a pair of tight jeans and nothing else.

After lunch, she found me and asked me what I thought, was it okay for her at her age, it had been so long since she'd been turned on, it was a whole new thing for her. "I can't help it, he's so . . . beautiful," she said.

"You need my permission?" I asked.

"No, Doc," she said, almost shyly. "Your opinion."

"Go ahead," I told her. "Just don't stay out too late. Remember, we have a big day tomorrow."

Next day I didn't get to see her until lunch time, and she looked positively radiant, she was giving off that tired-but-happy glow. Before I could say anything, she grinned and said "Had a big day last night."

And did I approve?

"Me?" I said. "As long as he does the job, why should I mind?"

"Take it from me, Doc," said Jody. "The guy's a wizard with a pump. Both of them."

I guess, in a way, that was her Graduation Night. Mine, too.

When they come to make the movie of her life, let them hire that good looking Mexican who restored her plumbing. He can play himself in the love scenes, that sequence ought to get an X rating, and it will certainly goose up the grosses.

Make a note, Doc, Jody should have a percentage of the gross, *not* the net. From the first dollar, thank-you—I know what bandits those film distributors are, didn't I once have an uncle in the business? (He was known as The Beast With Twelve Fingers, that guy knew more ways to make a dollar disappear—*your* dollar—than Harry Blackstone, the magician!) I wish the bum were still around; it might be a good idea to hire him for Jody, so he can check up on how much they're stealing from her. If he's a thief, at least let him be a thief for *us*.

Meanwhile, Kitty can see to it whatever money Jody's picture earns should go direct to that bank we use on the Island of Jersey. (A Mexican bank? Señor, are you loco?) And let it sit there so it can help take care of Jody, in her sunset years. Also Kitty.

Also the Casa Lindo.

After I check out.

Which can't be so long from now. Old Doc is held together with rubber bands and staples. What's the secret of my old age? Smoking, *shtupping*, and stuffed cabbage, in regular doses. Works like magic. But that Mexican doctor in town (he's got a diploma so down here he's legit) gave me the *emmis*, a couple of months ago, after he checked me out for those funny pains I've been getting. "Señor Doc," he said, "you are a medical marvel. For a man of seventy-four, you have a great constitution." He didn't need to tell me the rest of the line. ". . . but don't go investing in any green bananas."

Beautiful. Here I've been looking for a piece of long-term insurance for the Casa Lindo's future, and it drops into Jody's lap. If it works, Doc Katzen's Casa Lindo will keep on functioning. As far as my regular guests are concerned, when they need a replacement Doc, well, Jody can take over that job. By now she's certainly had enough training; she knows her part.

Later, everybody will say what a shrewd bastard I was. Had everything planned for the future, right?

Certainly I did. After all, what's a father symbol for?

I was thinking, the other night, lying awake upstairs waiting for the old stomach to quiet down from Jody's stuffed cabbage . . . what will happen when I cash in my chips, and I end going upstairs? To be met at the pearly gates by God?

He's a little sun-tanned shrimp in a checked cap, looks a lot like me, in fact. Smoking a pre-Castro Cuban. (Nice to know a person can get a decent smoke up there.)

Anyway, He takes a look at my identification, checks through his card file, comes up with one of my names, then another, then the entire batch I've had. He shakes his head and he sighs and He says "Katzen. *Doc* Katzen. I have a whole folder here on you. Boy oh boy-, have you ever been in and out of the red, Benny. I've been waiting for you to show up, so I could finally put it to you. What've you been doing down there, trying to make like Me? Huh? Whatever made you think *you*'re equipped to be God?"

"Well," I'll tell him, "this all goes back to the fourth grade, Civics, see? We had this Mrs. Goldfarb, terrific teacher, stood up in front of the class, and she told us we kids could be anything we wanted to be. Now, just between the two of us, are You suggesting You want to make a liar out of Mrs. Goldfarb?"

*   *   *   *

Eileen Tighe:

Next morning I found a scribbled note from Jody stuffed beneath my bedroom door. It read; "We *can* talk. See you later this A.M."

Finally!

It was a bright, beautiful, triumphant morning. I hurried down for breakfast. No sign of Jody in the dining room, nor were there any other guests in sight; Doc Katzen's guests either were early risers or room-service-diners. A small buffet of fruits, pastries, and coffee was laid out. I helped myself to some delicious croissants (Harry the Baker's latest triumphs?) and sat by a window, enjoying the view.

Outside there was some activity. A couple of people seemed to be painting the swimming pool. Further off, I could see where horses were being exercised. For anyone seeking an oasis of peace and serenity, this Casa Lindo seemed the best kept secret in old Mexico.

I carried my dishes into the kitchen. No sign of Artie, the demon dishwasher, so I washed my own at the sink. Firmly closed the tap. It leaked. I closed it tighter. No use, it still leaked.

Did I expect total perfection?

The halls were quiet as I went back upstairs to my room. Feeling somewhat like the new girl at summer camp, I made my bed and did a little light cleaning. I wondered . . . would there be Inspection later?

I went to the office to see Kitty about putting in a call to Budlong, in L.A. She helped me negotiate with the Mexican long-distance operators, and while we waited for the complex bilingual machinery to expedite my call to the States, I asked her where Jody might be found.

"Her? She could be anywhere, honey," said Kitty. "She's one busy lady."

"Where's the Doc?" I asked.

"He could be out, he could be in, he's a busy man," she said.

Could she give me a little history of the Casa Lindo?

Kitty shrugged. "All I know is, it was here before I got here, and it'll be here when I'm gone." She kept tapping away at her electronic adding machine.

The Doc and Jody—they were obviously a very happy couple, fond of each other. Where had they met?

"They met at a bullfight," she said. "You want to know any more, ask Jody."

"That's what I'm trying to do—if I ever get to see her," I said.

"She said she'll talk to you, she'll talk to you, *fershtay?*" said Kitty. "You know, honey, you got a bad case of the L.A. Jumps. Slow down. Let everything inside of you sort of *unlax.* You'll live longer . . ."

"Do I really seem that impatient?" I asked her.

"The precise word is tense," said Kitty. "We get a lot of that here at the Casa. Some places are for drying out, or cold turkey—this here is for cooling down. You stick around the Doc here for a while, Eileen, you'll improve—"

The switchboard buzzed; she took the call, then motioned me to the desk phone. "You're on."

Over the crackling and hissing of long-distance, I heard the

Interfico operator up in the air-conditioned, hermetically sealed Wilshire Boulevard tower, so far away from this quiet one-burro Mexican retreat; she accepted the charges, whom did I want? Mr. Budlong? she'd switch me—

Budlong's secretary came on, ah yes, Mrs. Tighe—he'd been expecting to hear from me before this, but he was away right now, wouldn't be back until tomorrow, out of town, might she give him a number where I could be reached? I gave it to her, and then had her switch me to my own office.

My secretary gave me a brief rundown on my calls since I'd left. Agents, mostly, inquiring about the status of various projects, there'd been two calls from Ozzie Kaufman. *Two?* That meant he was being more than social. I instructed her to give Ozzie my number down here. Anything else? ". . . Mr. Fischer was in most of yesterday," she informed me. "I let him use your office, he needed a place to make calls . . ." Mr. Fischer? Mr. Sully Fischer? What had he been doing in our offices? In *my* office?

She didn't really know; did I wish to speak to him if and when he came back today?

No, not necessarily. She already had my number down here, she was not to give it out, but she should keep me posted.

. . . (A) Budlong unavailable. (B) Two calls from Ozzie Kaufman. (C) Sully Fischer, uninvited, using my office? A + B + C = . . . *what?*

Damn, I wished I were there, so I could find out.

"You look unhappy, honey," said Kitty.

". . . Did you ever had the feeling something was going on somewhere, and it was behind your back?" I said.

"Honey, you are looking at somebody who used to be Mother Paranoia," said Kitty.

". . . So what do you do about it?" I asked.

"Doc always says relax and let it happen. It's never as bad as you expected it to be."

"Passive resistance, à la Gandhi?"

Kitty grinned. "*He* lived longer for it. And the Doc ain't no chicken, exactly."

. . . I guessed she was right. Forget cabals, imaginary or otherwise, in L.A. Concentrate on Jody.

Wherever she might be.

Lunch was a simple meal, presided over by Pierre from Duluth, who proffered a simple wine list and/or excellent Mexican beer. I took a salad and iced tea. Outside the opened doors was a small terrace. I carried my lunch outside to a cool table with an awning over it, sat down and ate.

In the distance, the mountains shimmered in the bright Mexican sunlight. From a nearby table, Diana from Silicon Valley waved to me. She and Artie the dishwasher were eating and simultaneously playing a game of Scrabble on a pocket board.

Still no sign of Jody.

"Oh boy," sighed Doc Katzen, sitting down beside me. "What a perfect day, so what's new? Every day here is perfect; you've been here long enough, you start wishing maybe you could order up a hailstorm or something. You and Jody have your *schmoos* yet?"

No, we hadn't.

"Mm," said Doc, spooning up some yogurt and cottage cheese from his plate. "She's busy, but she'll get around to you. Tell me, did you do anything constructive this ayem? You really shouldn't sit around waiting. Fill the time, you know?"

"I made my bed and cleaned my room," I told him, once again feeling like the newest girl at the summer camp, now being quizzed by the head counselor.

"Okay," he said. "Say, how do you feel about carpentry? I've got a little idea for some shelves we could use, in the main building—"

"You've got the wrong girl, Doc," I said. "I'm here to try and research a possible picture, remember?"

"Just a suggestion," he said, amicably. "If you don't ask, you don't get."

"All right, I'm asking . . . How did this place get started, will you tell me that?"

"Sure, I'll tell you that," said Doc. "But not now. This is my rest period."

He pulled out a small pair of earphones from his pocket, put them on his head, switched on the Walkman he set out on the table, sat back in his chair, and began humming softly to himself. "Excuse me," he said. "It's siesta time, and I like to relax with a little music." His eyes closed, and he began singing, softly, to himself, accompanied by the tape in his ear . . .

". . . Oh, go back and get it where you got it last night,
'Cause you ain't gonna get it here . . ."

I tiptoed away from the table so I would not disturb this Hebraic Bessie Smith and brought my dishes back into the kitchen. Where I found Pierre standing at the sink, staring balefully at a rising cloud of suds. The leaking faucet I had struggled with earlier this morning was now gushing steadily into the white Niagara below.

"*Oh, la la!*" he said. "*C'est un dommage, veritablement, n'est-ce-pas?*"

"*C'est un stopped-up sink,*" I said. "*Ou est le plumber?*"

"*Il faut telephoner! C'est un crise!*"

I left him trying to mop up around the sink. "Leave it to *moi,*" I said, and went looking for Kitty.

"*Pas encore,*" she groaned. "That plumbing's been backed up three times this month. Damn plumber comes, fools around, then goes home. I'll call him again . . . By the way, Jody's here. She's been looking all over for you, girl."

The Jody who sat down with me in the lounge was not the gregarious, jovial lady of the night before. No, this was more a purposeful, executive type, with definite points to make with me.

"Before we start talking about my life," she said, "we had

better get a couple of things straight. I don't have a lawyer here, or an agent, it's just you and me—so the two of us will have to draw up some kind of paper, sign it and have it notarized in town—''

"A paper which says what?" I asked.

"A memorandum," she said. "Your people will want to work out some kind of financial deal, option on the rights to my life story, fees for my participation, percentages, you understand all that, so we have to agree to agree, in effect."

So far, so good.

"That's point A," said Jody. "But point B is more important, we have to be straight on this right off. If you want to do Old Jody as a movie, then New Jody will have to retain creative control over the script."

Creative control? I didn't think Budlong would agree to that, no way. It's not something that is granted lightly in any deal situation. Money, percentages, equity, ancillary rights, sure, those can be negotiated for . . . but creative control of the script and/or the production made from it? Wow—before we'd even started, she'd thrown a deal-breaker at me.

"You don't want much, do you?" I asked her.

She smiled. "You're the one came down here to ask," she said.

"I'll have to discuss this with my people," I said.

"Of course you will," she said. "Then you can get back to me with their response, yes or no."

. . . And it would take time, with Budlong away.

"Couldn't we talk beforehand?" I asked. "Broad strokes— not business, but generally, what's to be included in your story, background material, characters—"

"Why not?" said Jody. "Just as long as you're in a position to guarantee that nothing gets used without my approval. If you want to do tape recordings, they're my property . . ."

Sharp lady.

She was putting me into a very frustrating position. I wasn't empowered to negotiate . . . so where did we go from here?

"I'll have to call my office and lay out for them what you're asking for," I said. "But I have to tell you, we won't be getting any answers by the end of today, or even tomorrow—you know it doesn't work that way—decisions take time—"

That didn't seem to bother her a bit. She shrugged. "I'll be around," she said. "I can wait. Believe me, I have plenty of other stuff on my mind—"

"You sure aren't making things easy for me, are you?" I said.

"Listen," said Jody, "Every time OJ made it easy for somebody, she got screwed. You tell me, why should NJ make the same damn mistake?"

Before I could rebut, Kitty came charging into our conference. "Excuse me! Crisis time!" she announced. "Kitchen sink is flooding—local plumber is away for the day—what do we do?"

"Plumb, what else?" said Jody. "Go find the toolbox, Kitty, come on, Tighe, we can talk inside—"

Pierre, his clothing drenched, stood by, watching the sink, which was now a disaster area. Water seeped from both sides, a soapy mixture of suds cum garbage, and the tap above poured on.

Her skirt tucked around her waist, Jody waded in. "Hand me the plunger," she instructed. I reached into the toolbox and found it, passed it over. "I'm going to need a hand with this," she said, dropped it down into the sink, on top of the clogged drain. With me helping her, the two of us worked on it, up and down, up and down, like a pair of riders in an old railway handcar, where had I seen that? Oh yes, in *The General*, with Buster Keaton! No use, the water didn't recede, the sink was stopped up tight, and the tap was still running.

By now we were drenched. "Give me the Stilson wrench, we'll try to close up this tap from below," Jody said.

We both got down on our knees, searching for the shutoff valve, down in the grime and darkness beneath the dripping sink. Come south to a quiet, gay, fun-filled stay at the Casa Lindo! I thought, as we tried to attach the wrench, getting a grip on that slippery old piece of metal was next to impossible. But eventually, the two of us managed to get it turned a few times, considering its coating of rust, a miraculous feat—

But up above, the sink tap still went on leaking, leaking—even after we'd managed to give the second shutoff valve a couple of turns . . . Why?

"Who knows? Have to pull of that sink handle and check the seal inside," Jody said, puffing. "Damn plumber never really fixes anything—give me the wrench up here—"

We clambered back up, suds everywhere, we slipped and slid, she got the wrench attached to the faucet, we both bent our backs into it, to unscrew that damned handle—But the damned thing would not move—

"Brace yourself with your foot," Jody suggested.

I did so, and then we both pulled at it again—

The handle began to turn, slightly, at first, and then more—

Off came the damned handle—plop into the sink—

and *more water poured forth!*

"You think we tapped an underground spring?" Jody said.

The wall, adobe, behind the sink taps, weakened by so much moisture, began to crumble. Pieces of adobe dropping, plop, plop—into the water, down from the opened wall—water still spraying like Old Faithful, behind the sink, rusty old pipes revealed—

"Go turn off the main valve!" Jody bawled.

"Where is it, honey?" asked Kitty.

"Outside—by the pump, I guess—" said Jody.

"—wish me luck!" called Kitty. She and Pierre left us—

. . . There we were, a pair of middle-aged ladies, sopping wet, sloshing back and forth through this mess, fighting to tap the damned flow, that gaping hole in the wall growing larger by the minute—"We need help!" I groaned.

"What kind of help you got in mind?" Jody snarled.

"Plasterers, plumbers, carpenters—*anybody*—" I suggested.

"A terrific suggestion!" she told me. "Why the hell don't

you go find them? So far *you* haven't exactly been much of a help, honey—"

That did it. "Okay," I told her. "You're on your own."

I turned to go, tripped, fell, flat on my ass in the floating mess around us!

I couldn't help it. I began to laugh.

"What the hell's so funny?" Jody demanded.

". . . *We* are," I told her, gasping. ". . . We're the Mexican Willie, West, and McGinty!"

"Hilarious!" she said, turned away, still angry. Then, she stopped, blinked, pushed wet hair out of her eyes, and did a take. ". . . *Yeah,*" she said. "Of *course.*" She grinned. "Exactly!" She began to laugh along with me. ". . . *You* saw them?" she asked.

I nodded. ". . . I was a kid . . . 'The Ed Sullivan Show'?"

"Oh, God, so great!" said Jody. "What an act!"

. . . Ineptitude carried to the ultimate. Three old men who emerged onto the set that was a construction site, carrying planks, buckets, shovels, blowtorches, tools—all sorts of assorted paraphanelia. In the ensuing eleven or twelve minutes they would proceed to crash into, topple onto, or burn with blowtorch, hit smash and fall onto each other, until their audience was helpless with laughter.

"—I had them on my show once," Jody said. "God, the way they made an audience laugh, strictly deadpan, they moved like some crazy ballet. I wanted to be them. They were the kind of comics made *me* go into the business—" She shook her head. "They were *artists.*"

". . . So that's what got OJ started in the comedy business?" I asked.

Jody nodded. "Yeah, I guess so." Then she grinned. "As a comic, she was famous. As a plumber, she was unknown. Hey," she asked me, "how come you're such a perceptive smart ass?"

Without warning, she cupped her hands and splashed filthy suds all over me.

On reflex, I splashed her back. "It's my job!" I told her.

"Well, you're *fired!*" yelled Jody, "Wowoweeweewoh!" and let me have a huge handful of suds right in the face—which I gave her right back, in equal measure—splash! splash! we were suddenly no longer hard-working lady plumbers, we were a pair of demented kids, releasing all our frustrations and hostilities in some messy Mexican wading pool. Splash! Splash—on we went—then—

"Hey! *Look!*" she said, pointing.

Behind us, the kitchen tap had stopped flowing. The gusher was capped.

. . . Miraculous.

Panting, we savored the sight. "Well, at least somebody knew what she was doing around here," said Jody. "It certainly wasn't me."

Exhausted, like a pair of large crabs, we crawled away from that tidal wave of dirty suds, then stood up. "C'mon," suggested Jody. "Let's go take a bath."

"I thought that's what we were doing," I said.

"You get one laugh, and right away, you're a comic," Jody said. "Forget it, lady. *I* do the jokes."

". . . Is that OJ, or NJ talking?" I asked her.

Jody peered at me, through her tangled mat of wet hair; her face resembled one of the gargoyles I once saw decorating Notre Dame Cathedral. But then her features relaxed; she did not lose her temper. She grinned; she was New Jody again. "Kiddo," she told me, and punched me lightly on the shoulder. "I like your style. Let's you and me go get cleaned up, and while we wait for the plumber, we can talk some more."

"Okay, but I can't give you any guarantees about a deal until I've talked to my people," I warned her. "Especially about creative control . . ."

"I know, I know," she said. "But what the hell, anybody who knows about Willie, West, and McGinty can't be all bad. You're a fan—we can talk about comedy."

"You just got yourself a deal," I told her.

We walked out of that filthy, wet Mexican kitchen.
Who'd ever believe we'd just held a meeting at the summit—
under the sink?

*   *   *   *

Eileen Tighe:

The plumber finally came roaring up to the rescue midafternoon in his battered truck, to apologize profusely, explaining he'd been out of town attending to some other major crisis, but now he would not leave the Casa Lindo until there was *agua* for El Doctor's precious friends, he would be here until all was well again, on the sacred soul of his dear departed mother, he would swear to it—

". . . Same exact oath he took the last three times he came," Kitty muttered, disgustedly.

Meanwhile, Jody and I had jumped into the pool, and got into dry clothes.

Then we found a quiet corner in the lounge, and began talking. And since she didn't object to it, this conversation went on tape.

Jody: But do we have to do an oral history type thing? My God, what is there about OJ that I haven't spilled out for years and years? . . . The ugly little kid from Scarsdale, who overcompensated for being unattractive by going out to force laughs from all the people. *Boring,* Eileen. Psychiatry 1B. It'll never sell, believe me.

Eileen: Okay, I'll change the subject. We won't talk about you at all.

Jody: The hell we won't. What did you come all the way down here for if it wasn't to talk about *me?*

Eileen: I don't know any more. I'd rather talk about Willie, West, and McGinty.

Jody: Anarchy. The greatest kind of comedy. Did you ever see Jimmy Durante?

Eileen: Once or twice—

Jody: You had to be there, belive me—sheer heaven! He'd come out on a stage and begin to sing some song, like "I Can Do Without Broadway, but Can Broadway Do Without Me," see—and then he'd get into a battle with the orchestra in the pit, he'd accuse them of double-crossing him by playing the wrong notes—he'd insist it was pure jealousy because he was too talented for them see? Then he'd yell something like *"I'm surrounded by assassins!* Ha cha cha!'' And he'd carry it on until he was ripping apart the piano he had up there on stage, and he'd actually throw pieces of it into the pit at them! And they'd throw them back! Anarchy! God, it was so beautiful, you'd be sitting there absolutely helpless with laughter with that angry man going bananas up there—you think there are still any kinescopes around where you could see Jimmy?

Eileen: I'd have to check. Was he your favorite?

Jody: Comic? Lord, I don't know. There were so many. That's like asking me who was the greatest lay I ever had.

Eileen: You were so lucky you have a choice?

Jody: Turn off the tape recorder and I'll answer you, smart-ass.

Eileen: You serious?

Jody: . . . No. I've changed my mind. I'd rather discuss comics. Did you ever see a guy called Bert Wheeler? I had him on once, he used to work with a guy named Hank Ladd . . . Bert would stand there holding a big piece of cake, munching away on it, and talking to Ladd, Bert was little and Hank was tall, sharp dresser with a little mustache. Wheeler would keep looking at him, and then he'd finally say, "You know, you look like a guy who once sold me an Essex." . . . Is that a great line? After that, Ladd would heckle him, he'd be saying to him "Okay, you're supposed to be funny, why don't you go ahead and make the people laugh?" And while Wheeler started to tell his joke, behind him, Ladd would open up his coat, and there he'd stand, with his shirt showing, and he had collar points about two feet long, see— a real wild visual gag—and they'd be roaring at him, and poor Bert is still trying to tell his joke—now that's a whole different kind of comedy—the guy that's pathetic and gets laughs out of sympathy—. Am I boring you with this?

Eileen: Hell no, I'm having a wonderful time.

Jody: It's just that I suddenly felt like I was doing a lecture— you know, COMEDY THROUGH THE AGES—I never want to be like one of those people who gets up and tries to analyze what makes an audience laugh. I mean, it's there. It's either funny, or it isn't, and who the hell knows why? Did you ever hear the story about Bert Lahr?

Eileen: Which one? I read a whole book about him—

Jody: This wasn't in it. I think. Anyway, Bert was the original worrier, you know that, I had him on a guest shot on the show once, and he spent four days worrying the hell out of everybody over whether the comedy sketch he was going to do with me, it was about a cop and a showgirl he's arresting, he'd done it for years, would still hold up! But he taught me how to do it, how to time the laugh, how to hold still, absolutely still—not to crack a smile when I was doing the punch line of a joke, he held my arm and kept saying "Don't move around, you'll kill the laugh, toots, *trust* me—" He was right, it was like having a great teacher— but I had bruises where he'd held my arm—

Eileen: What was the story?

Jody: What? Oh yeah. Seems Bert was doing a musical revue years back, and he had special material written for him by a couple of sketch writers, very good ones, and they brought Bert a scene they'd written, and they read it to him, and while they read him the jokes, they kept cracking up at their own material, roar-

ing with laughter, you know? Bert sat there and never cracked a
smile all the way through, and when they were finished, he finally
said "Listen, fellas, you may laugh, but this stuff is *funny!*"
Now do you understand why you can't analyze comedy? It's like
explaining to somebody why Hank Henry was funny doing
"Slowly I Turn."

Eileen: Excuse me, but who's Hank Henry?

Jody: That's what I mean. Only one of the greatest. Out of
burlesque, which I hasten to admit I was too young for. I caught
up with him in Vegas, when I was working there, God help me,
and Hank was across the Strip at a place called The Silver Slip-
per, they'd put on a burlesque show there twice a night. He was
a big burly guy, with a face only his mother could love, a nose
like a banana, and a voice like a bass frog croaking on a lily pad,
but oh my God, was Hank funny . . . *Funnee—*

Eileen: What did he do?

Jody: It wasn't what he did—it was the way he did it. He'd
come shambling out on that stage, funny hat on his head, he'd
glare at the audience, make a face, he knew every trick in the
book, a skull, a double skull—

Eileen: What's a skull?

Jody: Oh God, you are a civilian, aren't you? It's a *take—*
like—wait a minute, you come up behind me and say "Hi there,
Jody—"

Eileen: Okay. Hi there, Jody.

Jody: What? W-what? What the hey? *Ang-gang-gang! Ptoo,
ptoo!* That's a spit-take, see? Now, I just did three takes in a row,
how's that?

Eileen (Laughing): Very funny . . . Wow.

Jody: I learned from Hank. He taught me sketches. Did you
ever see "The Fart Doctor"?

Eileen: No, and I'd've remembered something like that.

Jody: How about "Go Down To The River and Take A Ship
For Yourself?"

Eileen: Wasn't that the one which got the Pulitzer Prize last
year?

Jody: No, smart-ass, that was another one. "Slowly, I Turn."
Now, would you like to see me recreate my role in that classic?
You be the straight man, and you stand there—and I'll be the
comic—and whenever I say "Niagara Falls," you grab me and
start beating me on the head—do you think you can handle that?

Eileen: I'll try—

Jody: Okay, here we go—

Kitty: Excuse me, ladies—

Jody: What, what? How dare you interrupt us—we are about
to perform a classic piece of theater! What do you want, crazy
lady?

Kitty: I want to tell you the plumber hasn't finished, but we're
gonna have dinner anyway.

Jody: Without water? How're we going to manage that?

Kitty: Well, now, why don't you and Miz Tighe just come on
in and find out. Unless you're too busy doing this important dramatic scene here—

Jody: You're right. Screw drama—I'm hungry. How about
you, Eileen, want some food?

Eileen: Food? What the hey! Gnang-gnang-gnang! Ptoo—
ptoo! When do we eat?

Jody: Do you believe this? Half an hour with me, and she's
stolen all my skulls!

Eileen: How was I?

Jody: Leave your name with the girl, don't call us, we'll call
you!—Bring the tape recorder along, maybe we can talk some
more—let's go.

Eileen: Listen, I just remembered an act I once saw, down in
Florida, I think it was—I was there with my husband—

Jody: And he was funny?

Eileen: He thought so.

Jody: What did he do to get laughs?

Eileen: He asked me for a divorce.

Jody: Hilarious. But it's been done.

Eileen: Anyway, there was this guy, he was tall and lanky—
sort of crazy, came out and played "Begin the Beguine" on a

table set with all kinds of china dishes, he hammered on them with xylophone mallets, and when he got to the release, he would get carried away, and he'd hammer on the dishes with so much enthusiasm that he'd break the plates, and send pieces of china flying in all directions!

Jody: Funnier than your ex-husband. What was his name?

Eileen: Who, my husband?

Jody: Oh, please. Listen, who's this? "My name is Jonee. How are you today? Not so close, please?"

Eileen: I know—Señor Wences!

Jody: Very good. Was he the greatest? How about him and his box, he'd open it up and there'd be an old man's head inside, that *spoke?* The man is a genius—

Coming down the hallway that led to the dining room, we could hear the faint sound of the invisible plumber, still hammering away at the kitchen pipes, inside.

Diana, the beautiful blonde refugee from Silicon Valley, was standing by the dining room doors, obviously tonight's hostess.

"Listen, honey," said Jody, "I know you're some kind of a genius, but tell me, how are you going to do supper without any kind of *agua?*"

Diana tapped her forehead. "Yankee ingenuity," she said, and opened the door.

By the buffet table was a small, hand-printed sign. EMERGENCY RATIONS, it said. BROUGHT TO YOU BY THE MYSTERY CHEF, *SANS AGUA.*

Spread out on the table was a series of very dissimilar dishes. Deep-dish chicken pie, next to franks and beans. Lasagna, a casserole of Tex-Mex refritos, a three-bean salad, beside a steaming pot of lobster newburgh, a bowl of hot sauerkraut, some sliced and toasted English muffins? Yes, and finally, for dessert, strawberry-topped cheese cake, to be washed down with iced tea.

Doc Katzen had joined us as we made our way down the buffet. "Amazing," he said. "Heartburn, international style."

"I feel like I'm on a ship of fools, and this is the midnight buffet," said Jody. "What demented dietician came up with this?"

"We cannot lie," confessed Diana. "We emptied out the frozen food locker. Just be grateful the oven is still working."

Napkins and plastic utensils were being handed out by Artie, my dishwashing friend. Brisk little chap with a pointed beard, tonight he wore a T-shirt that bore the slogan GOD WANTS YOU TO BE CLEAN. He sighed as he handed me my necessities. "Isn't this depressing?" he remarked. "No *agua,* nothing to wash."

"It'll be repaired soon," I said. "Then you can go back to your suds."

He brightened. "You really think so?" he said. "I can't tell you how much I hate anything *disposable* . . ."

"Artie's obviously crazy about you," said Jody, as we sat down with our food. "You must give good wash."

"He may be crazy, but it's not necessarily about me," I said.

"Ah, come on now," said Jody, digging into her deep-dish chicken pie. ". . . Everybody gets his jollies a different way. You two could rinse and wipe, arm and arm, into the sunset . . ."

Eileen: Hilarious, but listen, I just thought of something. How come all the comics you and I have been discussing are male? Why is it so tough for a woman to be funny?

Jody: Wasn't tough for OJ. She was funny.

Eileen: Accepted. I've seen you, I *know.* But what I meant—

Jody: I know what you meant. Some guy wrote an article about it—the usual psychological crap about comedy. According to him, the reason women have trouble making it as comics is because they have to distort themselves—you know, with the mugging and the faces, and the gnang-gnang stuff—and that makes them some sort of a threat to the women in the audience.

Eileen: Do you agree with that?

Jody: Sort of. Yeah. Now that I think of it, you know, it's very tough for a women to get out there and be a comic without giving up some of her femininity, whereas, a guy—well, maybe it's because he didn't start out by being a sexual object, see, so what's he got to lose by making a fool of himself? Here's Doc. What do you think?

Doc Katzen: I don't think. I'm on my rest period. What do you want to know?

Jody: Eileen is asking me about lady comics, and why there aren't so many of them, compared to men.

Doc: I don't know. Maybe they don't have as much talent.

Jody: I'm going to turn you in to Gloria Steinem!

Doc: I wish you would. While you're at it, give her my phone number.

Eileen: But seriously—

Jody: Listen to her! Now she's doing monologues. "But seriously, folks—" . . . I'm sorry, Eileen, I couldn't help it. Easy joke . . . Ask your question—

Eileen: How many big lady comics can you name? Lucille Ball—Fanny Brice, sure—and Barbara Streisand—

Jody: She's only funny doing Brice, so that's only two.

Eileen: Bette Midler? Joan Rivers. Phyllis Diller.

Doc: What about Martha Raye?

Jody: Very funny. What about Nancy Walker? I don't mean doing those commercials, selling paper towels, I'm glad she's so rich, but when she was on a stage she was great—I remember seeing her do a sketch with Bert Lahr, the two of them both worked in pantomime, a married couple, they hated each other, see, and it went on for ten minutes, the two of them slamming drawers, glaring at each other—and they *never spoke—*

Eileen: Sounds like my marriage—

Jody: That's why it was great—it was *everybody's* marriage!

Doc: Listen, what about Bea Lillie? Did you ever see her? She would do a thing with a rope of pearls, she swung it around herself like a hula-hoop—

Jody: Oh yes, I remember that bit! I had her come on with me once, just so I could steal it from her.

Eileen: But we're still talking about a minority. So far, it's a very short list.

Doc: I know one you left out. Very funny lady.

Eileen: Who?

Doc: Guess.

Jody: Oh God, he's being so coy, aren't you, Doc? He means little old OJ, don't you, *bubele?*

Doc: OJ? In my book that stands for Orange Juice.

Jody: Har har de har! What the hey! *Gnang, gnang!*

When we'd finished that extraordinary meal, we brought our paper dishes and cups back to the end of the buffet where Artie stood, accepting the refuse and moodily stowing it into a large plastic sack.

When I'd finished dumping mine, he winked, and offered me a small piece of folded napkin. "Read it later," he said.

I tucked it into my blouse pocket.

Out in the hallway, I opened it. Printed on it was written "Dear lady, you are the greatest dishwasher I ever had the pleasure of rinsing with. Your fervent admirer, A. Benson."

I passed it over to Jody. "Somebody's playing jokes, right?"

She read the note, then she shook her head. "No . . . this looks like serious stuff," she said. "I think you may have turned Artie on . . ."

Sex, among the suds? What kind of a conquest could that be? ". . . It *is* a gag, isn't it?"

Jody shrugged. "Hell no," she said. "This is a first, believe me. You'll have to treat it seriously."

". . . *How?*" I demanded.

"Well, a little water play never hurt anybody," she said, grinning.

"I wish he turned me on," I told her, "but I have a feeling making it with Artie would be like acting in an Ivory soap commercial."

Jody snickered. "You could always try a water bed."

"No—a soap and water bed," I amended.

"Fun*nee*," she said.

"What does Artie do in real life?" I asked.

"Real life?" she replied. "This *is* his real life. The outside world—that's fantasy. Haven't you figured out our secret motto? Doc provides us with a home away from the mess outside."

Eileen: Can we talk a little more about that?

Jody: We talked a lot already. More than I figured on. But . . . we had laughs. So what else?

Eileen: A couple of questions. Is OJ completely out of the business?

Jody: Which business?

Eileen: The comedy business.

Jody: Listen, did you ever hear about that old English actor, Edmund Gwenn, who was very sick, and they asked him how he felt, and he said "Dying is easy. *Comedy* is hard."

Eileen: Okay, I get it, but what does that have to do with OJ?

Jody: She didn't retire, she *grew*. She's an adult now. She doesn't need to be on, twenty-four hours a day. That's why she's NJ.

Eileen: Either one of them still knows how to get laughs—

Jody: Anybody can learn to do that—and you don't forget it, either.

Eileen: I don't believe that for a minute, and neither do you. If it were true, the world would be full of comics, and Lord knows, it's not.

Jody: I don't know—*you*'re getting there pretty fast.

Eileen: I'm funny?

Jody: In the old days, OJ would have considered you a threat.

Eileen: Thanks! . . . Was this . . . change in you . . . due to Doc Katzen?

Jody: Is this an interview?

Eileen: No, I'm really trying to find out. I mean, I've been here a while now, and I've seen how this place operates, but I don't know a damn thing about the *why* of it.

Jody: What's the question?

Eileen: You say Doc Katzen gives everybody with a home away from the mess outside—but he's not really an innkeeper—

Jody: No, he's more of a host. But that's not all.

Eileen: He's not running a sanitarium here. Is he?

Jody: Look. It's whatever you want it to be, get it?

Eileen: No. Not really.

Jody: You're trying to complicate things, honey. Go with the flow.

Eileen: That's Artie's department, isn't it?

Jody: Not bad. Remind me to use that.

Eileen: Seriously, Jody—damn, I've got to stop saying that— I don't figure you and Doc for a pair of mystics, but why is it, whenever I ask a question, all I get for an answer is—if you'll excuse the expression, some kind of a pseudo-Zen line?

Jody: Maybe because if you ask a silly question, you're entitled to a silly answer.

Eileen: All right. You mean, what happens here at the Casa Lindo is that . . . people show up and stay here, and do things, or don't . . . and leave when they want, or stay, or come back—

Jody: —and sleep late if they want to, or get up, if they don't—

Eileen: And help out with the work—and that is the entire ball game? That's the treatment? How they're helped?

Jody: If you want it, that's it.

Eileen: Okay. How were *you* helped?

Jody: You mean, how did I ever get to be NJ?

Eileen: Exactly.

Jody: I wish I could give you a magic formula, but I can't. Doc helped me by listening, sure. But most of all, he kept me busy. So busy I found out I didn't to get laughs all day long. You hang around here a while, and maybe you'll be helped, too.

Eileen: Me? I need help?

Jody: You don't? You think you haven't got room for improvement?

Eileen: . . .There's an Old Eileen, and he could help me develop into New Eileen? My sister Eileen?

Jody: See, now you're doing jokes again. That's fine, it's a normal defense mechanism. God knows I know that—OJ used them for a hell of a long time, but she never knew why.

Eileen: Why? Why did she?

Jody: You're looking for motives?

Eileen: Yep.

Jody: For the movie, or for real?

Eileen: I figure for both. Because that's the kind of movie I want to make.

Jody: Good. Because I wouldn't let you make anything else about OJ and NJ—that's for sure, toots.

Eileen: I'll ask you again—she used jokes for a hell of a long time, but she never knew why. Now she does. *Why?*

Jody: Because for a long time, it was the only thing she had going for her. To be able to get them to laugh—it was the same as love.

Eileen: Then she found other ways to induce love?

Jody: Hey, that's a good word—induce. Classy.

Eileen: Not seduce.

Jody: Okay, okay, I got it. Yeah. I guess so. Other ways.

Eileen: Such as . . .?

Jody: ". . . How do I induce thee, let me count the ways." That's Browning. We learned that in high school.

Eileen: I know. So did I. So . . .?

Jody: I'm thinking, I'm thinking! You know something, you're turning into an after-dinner nag—

Eileen: Sorry—I—

Jody: Forget I said that. It's late, and I'm tired, what a hell of a day we had . . . I'm not sure of what I'm saying any more. What other ways? Doing things with people. For them. About them . . . and getting affection back when you don't expect it— does this sound a lot like the *Reader's Digest?* Well, what the hell, it's fact—

Eileen: . . . and that's why you stay here?

Jody: Sure.

Eileen: For keeps?

Jody: Who knows how long that is? All I know is, it's a better place than some stage at Vegas or doing guest shots on "Love Boat," after you've had your face lifted—

Kitty: —Excuse me, ladies, but I thought you'd want to know— the plumber has finally restored the *agua* in the kitchen.

We heard a burst of scattered applause from inside, and then a muted ragged cheer.

Jody yawned. *"Now* I can go to bed," she said.

"Thanks for talking," I said, as I packed up the recorder. "To be continued, in our next?"

". . . First, I have to sleep," she said, and went up the stairs.

Before I went up to my bed, I suddenly realized I'd better try to call L.A. Damn—I hadn't heard from Budlong, or from anyone else all day—

"After what we went through here today, you serious about trying all that long-distance crap again?" asked Kitty.

She was right. "I guess not," I said. ". . . *Mañana.*"

"Glad to see this place is beginning to get to you," she said.

Upstairs, I put the tapes safely away in my attaché case.

. . . Began to get ready for bed. A long day. But rewarding. To have finally broken through to Jody . . . Good thing I'd brought along a lot of blank cassettes. So much more I needed to get from Jody; reminiscences of the early days, when OJ had first begun working in live TV, in New York . . . Buddy Grimes. Dick Hatch. Oh, I had lots of questions.

As far as NJ, and the Casa Lindo, I wasn't at all certain I understood what the hell she was talking about . . . Her life here, among all of Doc Katzen's people, but . . .

Maybe tomorrow I should find a few minutes alone with Doc himself, and see if he could explain more about how things functioned, at least it was worth a try—

—and tomorrow I'd call Budlong again—

I got into bed.

Snapped off the light.

Outside, the Mexican night was soft, and luminous. Off in

the distance, dogs barked . . . or was that a coyote?

Somebody began to knock softly on my bedroom door.

Who? I sat up. "Who is it?"

Instead of an answer, the door was pushed open—Lord, I'd never thought to check if it self-locked, had I?—and a shadowy figure peered in.

"Hope I'm not disturbing you," said the voice, softly, "but I just thought, if you hadn't fallen asleep, you might like to come downstairs with me. Me, *Artie* . . ."

The dishwasher?

At this hour? "To do what?" I asked.

He stepped inside and closed the door behind him.

"Well, now that the plumber has the water turned on again, I'm ready for action," he said. "We have all those unwashed dishes stacked up there, just crying out to be washed, and you're so good at it, Miss Tighe—may I call you Eileen?"

I didn't believe this scene.

. . . But perhaps I'd better. Jody had warned me—*serious stuff*—

"It's very thoughtful of you," I told him, "but really, not tonight—"

"I can't tell you how impressed I've been with your style," he said, coming closer. "Obviously, you're somebody who *cares* . . . The way you take such pains with the china, the way you handle it—it's been years since I had such a partner . . ."

By now he was seated on the end of my bed, waiting expectantly for me to . . . to do what?

"Please believe me," I said. "I am flattered. But I've had a long and busy day—"

"Of course you have," Artie said. "That's because you care. That's what makes you different, Eileen, I can tell. I can always tell. I had a girlfriend once, I thought she was like you . . . at first. Lovely girl, very nice hands. Named Margo . . . oh, she was so sympatico. I thought. We had a marvelous relationship, Margo and I. We washed and dried, washed and dried for hours . . . We had so much going for us. I thought . . . We'd talked about moving in together, and sharing the plumbing . . . so I decided to prepare for her. I went to a plumber, and I had him order the finest kitchen sink available, top of the line . . . a Kohler. Oh, it was the Cadillac of kitchen sinks. Why not? Nothing was too good for my Margo. Well, when it was finally installed, I called her up, it was supposed to be an engagement present for her. Wouldn't you have been tickled to have your own Kohler, Eileen?''

When one is dealing with Artie, I told myself, one must go with the flow. "I would have been astonished," I said.

Artie's face had hardened. *"She* wasn't,'' he said. "She walked out on me. Left me a note. Written on a paper towel. Yuch . . . You know what she said? 'I am not going to sacrifice my only two hands to this obsessive water-play.' Gone, just like that. But now,'' he said, smiling, "I think I've found somebody to replace her at the Kohler . . .''

"Listen, Artie,'' I told him, "I can understand how shattered you felt, and I'm flattered you feel this way about me, but would you mind excusing me tonight? I really must get some rest—''

"I know just the thing,'' said Artie. "Why don't we wash *you?*''

Things were not improving here.

"I've already had a bath, thank you,'' I said. "Now, would you please—''

". . . Maybe just the feet?'' He suggested. "Foot-washing is very good therapy, and I'm expert at it—''

This conversation is not taking place, I thought. I have already fallen asleep, and this is an early nightmare brought on by that confused dinner they served us—

No, it wasn't a nightmare. Artie was still perched on my bed, he'd moved closer now and was waiting for my answer—

"No, *no,*'' I told him. "I already did my feet. I did everything—''

"I figured you might have,'' he said, admiringly. "You're such a clean person. That's what attracted me to you in the first place . . .''

"Thank you, Artie," I said. "Now if you don't mind—"

"Since you're completely clean," he said, "we could forget the washing for tonight and get right down to fucking . . ."

Trapped with the Don Juan of the Detergents, our heroine struggles to break free . . .

"Listen, Artie," I told him, "if you don't get out of here and let me have this bed to myself, I'm going to yell for help . . ."

Perplexed, he stared at me.

"Help?" he said, aggrieved. "What sort of help would we need? I'm here, you're here, we're a *team.*"

"Yes, sure we are," I said. "But not tonight, partner. Let's meet for breakfast," I suggested, "and then we can do all the dishes together, before anybody else gets a crack at them . . ."

"In the morning?" he said. "Just the two of us?"

"Suds coming out of our ears," I promised. "So now, beat it, partner, I need all the sleep I can get, so I'll be ready for you at the sink . . ."

". . . I can't wait," said Artie. He leaned over, and gave me a brief kiss on the cheek. His face, redolent of Tide, loomed above me. "Night, now," he whispered. ". . . Mmm—you smell so damn *clean* . . ."

The door finally closed behind him.

". . . what the hey, what the hey," I said. And fell asleep.

*　　*　　*　　*

Eileen Tighe:

Mañana came and went at the Casa Lindo, and so did another, and I still hadn't connected with Sid Budlong, up in L.A.

I suppose by then I should have been actively paranoid enough to suspect something might be rotten up in that air-conditioned Wilshire Boulevard tower, but my guard was down, I rationalized I was so busy on his behalf, making such progress. (Wrong!)

When I did give thought to Interfico, and our fearless leader's silence, I excused it with another naive rationale, he was a very busy onthego executive, in and out of his office, meeting/meeting/meeting, either at the Polo Lounge/Ma Maison or somewhere, or on a Concorde/deal-making in London/Paris/visiting money in Switzerland/Nassau/Texas, or wherever? No need to worry, we were on parallel tracks, weren't we? My existence was as complex as his . . .

Besides, my Casa Lindo schedule would be so difficult to describe. You had to have been there . . .

How could anybody understand that each day I would be spending long and complex sessions with Artie and those endless dirty dishes? Absolutely no one but me could satisfy my new admirer. "Lady, what *is* your secret?" Kitty asked me. "The man refuses to allow anybody else near his suds . . ."

We started taping, but not before Jody and I signed a letter, copies for both of us. "Friendship is one thing, business is something else," Jody told me, the morning after our plumbing adventure. "Yesterday we talked, we enjoyed, fine. Today, when we start to talk, it's business. So first, we have to make ourselves a piece of paper. You got a lawyer to do it?"

No, I didn't. "Neither do I," she said. "So we'll do it ourselves. Go write."

I came out of Kitty's office a few hours later with a couple of paragraphs that laid it out as clearly as I could state it.

"Dear Ms. Cassel. This is to confirm that you and I are currently engaged in a series of interviews, recorded on tape, which deal with the life and career of Jody Cassel. Said interviews are contemplated by us to be used as the basis of a screen treatment, and/or a film script.

"We agree that a/my current employer, Interfico, will, as promptly as possible, enter into negotiation with you and your representatives, to agree up on financial terms for the rights to said life story, and will attempt in good faith to reach a contract binding on both parties. We are also agreed that b/said life story of Jody Cassel, whether it eventually becomes a commercial film, or a film designed for TV use, commercial or cable, cannot be released for sale or lease by Interfico, or its licensees, without your express written approval of the contents of the screenplay, and the finished film . . ."

"Is this legal?" asked Jody.

"How should I know?" I said.

"It sounds very impressive," she said. "Who taught you how to throw around all these clauses?"

"Lawyers," I said. "Who charge a whole lot more than I do, believe me."

"I believe you," said Jody, and signed. "Remind me to hire you for my next lawsuit."

. . . But finding time for regular taping sessions wasn't as simple as all that. In fact, it was damned frustrating. The complexities of the Casa Lindo and its "guests" kept intruding.

We'd begun by talking about the earliest days of her career, when she and Buddy Grimes were struggling to get a spot in a Greenwich Village nightclub. ". . . When I think of the act we used to do, how little OJ *knew*—and yet, she could go out there every night and perform, in front of the people—you want a definition for *chutzpah?* That, believe me, is it."

—And then we'd be interrupted by some current event, here in 1984. Either one of Diana's mares down at the stable was about to foal, and Jody was responsible for making certain that the vet was on call, or it could be Pierre, who had taken it upon himself to redecorate some of the upstairs bedrooms, and wasn't sure which *couleur* to use for paint, Madame Cassel must decide . . . All day long it went on like that; after lunch we had to run into town for some special supplies for Kitty, later there was a tape session where we almost got up to the night when a TV producer came down to the Village to watch Jody and Buddy Grimes do their act before it was supper time, and after that I had to go off for my regular evening date with Artie, at his Niagara Falls of suds . . .

When I finally got out of his squeakyclean clutches, it was late, and Jody was nowhere to be found.

Wearily, I went out to the terrace and flopped down on one of the lounge chairs.

From nearby came the fragrant, familiar odor of a Cuban cigar.

". . . So, how goes the Jody Cassel Story?" asked Doc Katzen.

"Like the Army," I told him. "Hurry up and wait."

"That's all right," said Doc. "It's the pace down here. Much slower. Much healthier. You'll live longer, believe me."

He blew a beautiful smoke ring which floated lazily over towards me. Where was Jody?

"Somewhere," he said. "She'll be back. Relax."

. . . From somewhere inside the Casa, I heard music, the sound of a trumpet playing? Yes, lazy and mournful, a pure tone, echoing through the soft darkness, now I could recognize the ballad the trumpeter was playing, it was a song I remembered from my prom-going days . . . "But Beautiful." Lovely, one of Bing Crosby's best . . .

"That's Harry," said Doc. "Started out in life playing in his own college band. Then he met some girl and got married, and had to earn a living, so he gave up music and went into advertising instead. Big man in advertising. One of the biggest . . . Comes down here every once in a while, makes pastry. Some nights, he gives us a little concert . . ."

Lovely, that pure Bobby Hackett tone coming from Harry's trumpet.

"Harry should have stayed with the horn. He would have been terrific."

"I know that," said Doc. "He does, too."

. . . That was the shortest biography I'd ever heard.

Also the saddest.

"Doc," I said, "what exactly have you got going here, is it some sort of a Port of Missing Persons? Is that what you run the Casa for—to provide aid and comfort?"

"I don't have any purpose that specific, doll," said Doc. "This place stays open for people who like to come here. They like it, we like them."

When it came to fielding questions, he and Jody were experts.

"*They* all come and go," I observed, "but Jody seems to stick around."

"I guess she likes the place," he said.

"Why?" I asked.

". . . Ask her," said Doc. "She's the one you're supposed to interview."

"I have asked her," I said. "And all I get are as vague a bunch of answers about you and the Casa as you give me."

"What are you, from the A.M.A.?" he asked. "Or the Federal Trade Commission, or the I.R.S.? There's nothing to tell. What goes on here isn't all that important. Stick with Jody's life story, keep asking her about OJ. It'll make a terrific movie, be a big hit, and the profits should keep NJ very nicely in her old age."

"Oh, Doc, you make it sound so simple," I sighed. "Do you have any idea what a miserable job it is to get a movie made in 1984?"

"No, I don't," he said. "Why should I? It's not my business—it's yours."

"Doc, what *is* your business?" I asked.

"Me? I'm retired, sweetheart," he said. "Don't change the subject. You know all about the movies, so you're going to take OJ's story and get it made, *right*—I know you will, Eileen . . ."

"What makes you so sure?" I asked.

He reached out a bony hand and patted mine. His fingertips were cold, even in this warm Mexican night. "Because you're a real pistol, Eileen," he said. "Some exciting piece of woman, believe me," he said, and now his hand was running carelessly across my thigh. "Definitely my type," he said. "Oh, if I was twenty years younger, believe you me . . ."

"Don't stop there," I told him. "Pretend it's 1964. What then?"

". . . Artie wouldn't have a chance, that's for sure," he told me.

I laughed. Where had this remarkable old man acquired such a consumnate gift of flattery?

His hand remained on my thigh. "Oho, so you think it's funny?" he demanded.

"No, Doc, I don't," I said. "Honestly . . ." I put my hand on his. "I love what you said . . . But I also think you are one of the greatest *schmeichlers* I've ever met."

". . . What does that word mean?" he asked.

"It means flatterer—a kind of—" I laughed again. "Here I am explaining Yiddish to *you?*"

"Just wanted to make sure a nice *shiksa* like you knew what she was talking about," said Doc. "And you do, which is even more impressive. You're a woman of many parts, Eileen. You put them all together, they spell action. Success. You can do anything you want, sweetheart, just go to it . . . if that's what you want.''

. . . What a salesman.

Off in the distance, Harry's trumpet played on. Now he'd switched to a lovely old Gershwin tune . . .'' ''Embraceable You.''

Suddenly, it hit me.

All this *schmeichling* was not casual, of course it wasn't . . . with old Doc Katzen (doctor or not, or whatever) it was part of his technique, a basic tool of whatever therapy system he operated here. Ego massaging his ''guests,'' making them feel worthy—

—Exactly like that British lady, what was her name? The one who specialized in problem dogs, whose technique consisted of sitting beside the dog and staring directly into its eyes, telling him again and again how marvelous he was . . .

That was basic—

But then, to go along with the *schmeichling,* Doc went a step further, providing *his* dogs with useful tasks here at the Casa, jobs to make Him feel worthy, or some chore She had always thought she could do, basic things, daily things—

—All that was missing was a system of Merit Badges.

No wonder Jody stayed on permanently. She needed Doc's affirmation. She was hooked on it. Once it had been the whole big wide wonderful audience out there OJ needed, now she was NJ, and had narrowed down her need to only one lover . . . Doc Katzen, available on a no-strings-attached basis, this remarkable diminutive guru, father symbol, troop-leader, den father, whatever. Who, with his hand on your thigh, continues to praise you.

Paternal, whimsical . . . reliable. Truly a winning combination.

Did it work? Well, the Casa seemed inhabited by satisfied customers, didn't it?

''Doc,'' I said, ''I think I'm beginning to understand you, now. You're everybody's support-system. Twenty-four hour service, satisfaction guaranteed.''

". . . Whatever that means," he said, amiably. He flicked away the stub of his cigar. It soared off into the night, and landed, with a small shower of sparks, onto a clump of cactus.

"You know what?" he observed. "Life is like a cigar."

". . . Am I supposed to ask why?" I said.

"Yep," he said. "Everybody smokes one," he said. "But there are good cigars and bad cigars. In the end, no matter which one you've smoked, all you're left with is . . . a little piece of ash."

His hand was still on my thigh.

". . . Do you have something in mind, Doc . . . or is that just a general observation?" I asked.

He cleared his throat, but before he replied, the door to the terrace was pushed open and Kitty peered out. "Hey, Eileen, you got yourself a call from L.A." she announced.

Budlong? Finally.

"Excuse me, Doc," I said. "My master's voice."

"Just tell him you're gonna make a great movie," he said. "We're all counting on it." He chuckled. ". . . A little piece of ash . . . hey, not bad."

"What the hey, Doc, what the hey," I said, and followed Kitty to her office.

. . . But when the buzzing and the singing over the long distance wires subsided, and a human L.A. voice finally came over, it wasn't Budlong's, it was my old friend Ozzie Kaufman.

"Say, Mrs. Tighe, don't you ever return calls?" he asked.

"Sorry, Oz," I said, and explained how busy I'd been down here, but I was so glad to hear from him, I could tell him I'd actually found and been interviewing Jody Cassel! (amid all the other events taking place here) and the way it looked, the project was moving forward . . . finally. ". . . And it can be something really exciting, I hope—"

"It's moving forward up here, too," he told me. "I had a memo cross my desk, seems you people have hired one of our clients to work on the screen treatment."

Since when?

"What writer?" I asked, trying to keep the astonishment out of my voice.

"Reginald Rose," he said. "Very talented man—and an old live TV hand. Very shrewd of you people to go after him—wait a minute, didn't you know about him?"

"I've been down here, remember?" I said. "Who actually hired Rose?"

"Wait a minute, let me look—I thought you were in on the decision," said Ozzie. "Oh here it is, your producer, Sully Fischer."

. . . *My* producer?

"His name's on the booking slip," said Ozzie. "When did he go on the project?"

. . . What kind of an end run had Budlong just pulled on me?

"You didn't know about this deal?" Ozzie prodded.

"No," I confessed. "But that's between you and me—" I took a deep breath, trying to control my anger, talk about stress? At that moment, my blood pressure must have set a new, all-time high.

". . . Take it from your friend Ozzie, it might be a good idea if you got your attractive tush up here, and found out what's going on in your office, pronto."

As usual, he was making sense.

"As soon as I finish taping, I will," I promised.

"I wouldn't wait too long it I were you," he said. "If you do, you might not have an office to come back to."

". . . Whatever that means," I said.

"It means we live in a prehistoric society out here," he said. "Remember?"

"Yes—surrounded by assassins."

"Call me as soon as you get back," he said. "If I hear anything more, I'll keep you posted."

"Thanks, Oz," I said. "You are really a friend."

". . . Cherish me," he said. "I'm the last of a dying breed."

When I hung up, I became aware of Harry's trumpet, still playing. But he had switched to playing something else . . . a bugle-call. One I remembered from my summer camp days.

I could hear it, soft and sweet, echoing down the hall. Was it some kind of an omen?

He was playing "Taps."

Kitty was looking curiously at me. "Bad news, honey?"

"I guess it might be," I said. "Depends."

My heart was slowing down; hopefully the pressure was dropping.

". . . Don't get yourself riled," she said. "It'll pass, always does." She grinned. "Even for the poor folks."

So. I had a tape recorder and a couple of cassettes with Jody's reminiscences on them, I had a signed letter between her and Interfico—

—but did I still have a project?

Had Budlong decided to forego our parallel tracks, and to go on some other track, without me? That would certainly account for the silence from his end, he'd throw Sully Fischer and Reginald Rose at me when I got back.

Or would he? I could be up the creek . . . or out at sea, cut loose to drift. Or marooned down here at the Casa Limbo . . .

—I knew, I knew, Lindo—but right now, I was entitled to my Freudian slip!

No Doc on the terrace, but Jody was waiting for me.

Doc had gone to bed, wishing us both a good night, and after this day, she was beat, however, we would start taping again mañana morning? "First thing after breakfast," she promised. "No interruptions until noon, at least, guaranteed."

"Sure, why not?" I said.

". . . What's wrong?" she asked.

"How can you tell?"

"Honey, you're giving off very bad blips," she said. "I know them when I feel them, what is it?"

It could be bad, it could be good . . . I didn't yet know how to read the radar screen. Should I confide the Interfico situation to her? No, not now. No sense telling her it was bad news for our project until I was sure of it.

"Office politics," I said.

"Somebody's trying to shaft you?" she asked.

Sharp, wasn't she? "Might be that," I admitted.

"What do you plan to do about it?"

"Haven't decided yet," I told her.

". . . Feel like fighting?" she asked.

"I'm not certain about that, either," I said.

"Is it about OJ and her story?" she asked. "Don't be coy—we can handle it. We're used to handling problems here, haven't you noticed?"

". . . I don't know that yet, either," I said. Which was the truth. "I'll have to do some calling tomorrow, and I may even have to go back up there to L.A., I'm not sure—but I have to tell you one thing, I'm not about to let them screw me around."

My blood pressure was starting to go up again.

Jody nodded. "This is very important to you," she commented. "Sit there and cool down, and listen to the old lady. Before you start the infighting, ask yourself *why*. Once I learned to do that," she said, "I was able to write OJ's epitaph . . . *She Learned To Ask Why. Fershtay?*"

"I *know* why," I told her. "I'm convinced OJ's story would make a marvelous movie. And—"

"That's *her* why, not yours," said Jody. "NJ knows that."

She was waiting for me to reply.

I took the easy way out. I got up to go; I was too beat for any more self-analysis.

"Thanks for the afterdinner psychiatry," I said.

"Any time," said Jody. "First thing tomorrow, we can go back to wowoweeweewoh . . . if you still want to."

"Of course I want to," I said.

But I wasn't certain. On the way upstairs to my room, I kept turning it all over, trying to get a handle on that question she'd just thrown at me. . . . Why *did* I want to do this project with her so much that I'd been at it for so long? Was it for her . . . or for *me?* What was I out to prove?

. . . Was this Eileen Tighe, ex-married-lady-now-executive, who spent her days and nights prowling through that Pavlovian maze called The Business, any different from Jody's frenetic OJ? Wasn't Eileen driven by that same basic need for affirmation? *lovemelovemeloveme,* I'm Eileen, I'm good, *please! pay attention to me!*

. . . I needed more time to field that one.

More than that, I needed some sleep.

I pushed open my bedroom door.

To find, stretched out on my bed, in the shadows cast by my bedside lamp, a familiar nocturnal visitor.

Artie.

. . . Rising and coming over to close the door behind us.

Oh, for God's sake! "Enough—we've already done three sets of dishes today—"

"Shhh!" he said. "Poor Eileen, I was waiting for you." His arms went around me, his fingers, puckered from too much hot water, caressed my cheek. "You're tired and you're upset . . . Artie's here to help you out of your problems . . ."

"How do you know I'm upset?" I said. I tried to move away, but he held me firmly with all those muscles that were hardened by long hours of washing.

"Around here, we always know," he said, and with one hand he began to unbutton my blouse. "Tell me everything . . ."

"Could we talk tomorrow?" I asked, and now I was too tired to fight, he was crooning in my ear. "Leave it to Artie, just relax, Artie is here and he's going to wash away all your dirty problems . . ." My blouse was open, then it was off, and his fingers were working at the zipper of my jeans, he was obviously as expert with female clothing as he was with delicate chinaware. "I've drawn you a nice hot bath in there, and the tub is packed full of lovely bubbles," he promised, his voice was soft and hypnotic, I was drifting back to my early childhood when kind adults did this for me, they were usually women . . . but no matter. My clothes were dropping on the floor, and now he was undoing my brassiere. ". . . And when you're finished with all that lovely washing," he went on, "then we'll dry you off in a nice big soft towel, and we'll powder you . . ." . . . Off came my bikini pants, and now he was leading me into the bathroom, ". . . all your problems will disappear," promised Artie, testing the water with his wrist. "In you go," he instructed, and helped me into the tub.

"Wash first," he instructed, "and then, a nice, friendly fuck."

Oh, what the hey, *why not?* I thought, as I sank back into the warm suds. This is certainly the best room service available in Mexico.

. . . room-and-bath service.

. . . Mustn't let this get around, or Artie will be flooded with requests.

Ha . . . ha . . . ooh.

His fingers were beginning to do something lovely with the soap, down there . . . mmm . . . oh . . . oh *yes* . . .

. . . Oh Sid Budlong, if you could see me now . . .

(you and your parallel tracks—)

Forget it, it's too good for you! . . . It's for *me. Me!*

Ah! . .

*   *   *   *

Eileen Tighe:

Six days later, when the Aeronaves de Mexico plane brought me into L.A. International, I still hadn't been in communication with Mr. Sid Budlong, Esq.

He hadn't called, but what is more important, for the past week, I'd stopped trying to reach him. I'd spent my time at the Casa Lindo, doing what I'd come down there for in the first place.

In my attaché case, carefully numbered in sequence, were nine of Sony's best tape cassettes, containing roughly fourteen hours of OJ's life story, as related to me by Jody, ready to be transcribed.

The result of my newly acquired strategy. KYPS—Keep Your Priorities Straight.

. . . For a while there, after Ozzie had called with his bulletin, I'd panicked.

The morning after my love-in-the-suds with the Midnight Scrubber, I'd gotten up with the sun, long before breakfast, and gone for a walk in the desert. Turning over in my mind what to do next. Call the airline, get on the next flight to L.A., get ready for the inevitable infighting, the office struggle for territorial imperatives, (this-is-my-project-I-instituted-it, what the hell is going on here, etc., etc.?)

. . . or stay here, with Jody? Which meant not to know what the hell they were all doing behind my back?

I came back into the Casa dining room, still undecided.

But ravenous.

I brought my *huevos rancheros* in and sat down at a table with Kitty.

"Feeling okay?" she asked me.

". . . About what?" I asked.

She shrugged. "Nobody's referring to your social life," she said. "You going up to L.A.?"

I shook my head. "Can't make up my mind," I said.

We ate for a few minutes in silence.

Then, ". . . Mind me making a suggestion?" she asked.

". . . Why not?" I said. "Around here, it seems that's everybody's hobby."

"It's not a hobby, it's the way we operate," Kitty said. "Now. You got Jody talking with you. Believe me, you're about the first one she's opened up to . . . and you got to know there've been others, all those characters who come buzzing around, wanting to do their cheapo books, or something for the *National Enquirer,* you know? Or have her do a lecture at some Nostalgia Convention . . ." she grimaced. "Anyway, if she trusts you the way she does, I wouldn't want you to quit now . . . do you read me?"

Yes, I certainly did. But I also had problems. While I was away, who was minding the store? Assuming I still had one to mind.

"All well and good," I told her, "but while I'm down here taping, they could be dumping me."

"Girl, you got Unemployment Insurance?" she asked.

I nodded.

"You broke? Got you a little bread in the bank, put away for bad times?

". . . Some, not much," I conceded.

"Okay, then, so you won't starve," said Kitty. "If it was me, I'd get the rest of my interviews done, *first*—and then go back to your boss-man with them in my hot little hand. Then, if he starts playing dirty poker with you, you automatically got a better hand than he does, *fershtay?''*

Absolutely true. The lady made good sense.

". . . and if I'm out of a job when I get back, will you take me in down here?'' I asked.

"Sure, why not?'' grinned Kitty. "Seems to me you already got yourself a permanent spot in the kitchen . . . least while Artie's around.''

"You noticed that . . .'' I said.

"Who couldn't?'' she said. "This morning you look like a very clean and very happy lady.''

I nodded.

"So stick around,'' she said. "Doc loves you, too. Girl, what is it you've got they all want? If we could only bottle it, you and me could make as much as Paul Newman and his damn salad dressing!''

. . . so I'd stayed on, sitting with Jody, spending the time constructively, filling hours of tape. For my own R and R (Rest and Recreation) I could always join Artie, either at the sink in the kitchen, or after hours, upstairs in the bath.

On those cassettes, she'd given me all sorts of personal insights, valuable anecdotes about early live TV, firsthand discussion. . . . Buddy Grimes, her first partner? (". . . Ah, such a sweet, talented guy. Much too sweet to survive in such a miserable business. Buddy built a failure factor into everything he did, I realized that later, it was so he'd always have an escape hatch through which he could bail out. . . . But he's over that, and once he did, there was no looking back. He's a big, big talent . . . Where's he living? Cape Cod? Oh, fine, now he's got the entire Atlantic to brood over . . .'')

. . . the terrible treadmill daily grind of doing a weekly live show. ("You know, we'd finish on a show night, and I'd be plotzed down in my dressing room, and thinking to myself, how in hell did we ever get through that one? And then somebody like

Teresa Contini would come charging into my dressing room and toss me some pages and say, 'Here's the script for next week, don't worry about the second half, the boys haven't finished it yet, but they'll be ready for you by 9 tomorrow, see you then. By the way, good show.' Sensitive creature . . .'')

Dick Hatch? (". . . Another big talent. I knew I couldn't hang on to him, he was too good. His head was always full of show, show, show—he had no room for anything or anybody else up there . . . Not even his wife . . . The only time he was really happy was when he was directing. He actually got his jollies up there in the booth . . . if you ever see him, tell him Jody sends her best to the old bastard . . .'')

How did it feel to be a star? (". . . I'll tell you something. All those years of working in TV, making big money, all I remember is—coffee in paper cups. Everywhere, rehearsals, backstage, always coffee in paper cups. *And* heartburn . . .''

One moment she'd been talking about these contemporaries of her times who'd succeeded, . . . Sid Caesar and Imogene Coca and the crew from "Your Show of Shows," Carl Reiner and all the others (". . . a total gestalt, a piece of human machinery, all functioning beautifully each week to make a terrific show, nowadays everybody takes bows for it, but I remember there was a secret ingredient, a little guy named Max Liebman, very quiet, smoking a big cigar, but always up there on the bridge, steering that boat full of talent . . .'')

We discussed her other contemporaries. Gleason. (". . . Beautiful! I always wanted to work with him but he didn't need me, he came equipped with his own stock company of comedy people, mainly himself.") Berle. ("What can you say about Uncle Miltie that he hasn't already said about himself? I did a guest shot with him. Once. Got more laughs than he did. Are you going to ask me why I didn't get a return booking?")

. . . and other lady comediennes? Lucille Ball? (". . . Somebody asked me how come she'd lasted all these years, and I hadn't. The answer's easy. Maybe I was as funny as she was, maybe I wasn't—but—she's got the evidence, and I haven't. She never did anything that *wasn't on film*. So, she could retake until it was perfected . . . and once it was in the can, she could run it for the rest of her life, and her kids' lives, it's her annuity, baby. And don't ever knock that . . ."

Interesting point. Hadn't her own agent, Buck Dawes, that very shrewd and (by now) enormously successful executive, ever suggested that Jody go to filmed TV? And if not, why not?

Jody shook her head. "I don't know. Why don't you ask *him?*" she said. "Let's talk about something more interesting . . ."

Finally we got down to more philosophical matters. The problems induced by instant success. (". . . God, I feel so sorry for the youngsters today, these kids who hit it big overnight . . . In like fifteen minutes, they're stars making a million dollars a month, totally unreal—compared to what we earned, we look like poor relatives . . . But it's what all that does to them—no wonder they can't handle it . . . that poor Janis Joplin, or the fat boy, what was his name, Belushi? It's so overwhelming for them, overnight they take off, they fly, they think they're indestructable and it's forever, oh I know that feeling . . ." She sighed. ". . . So sad. Most of them never make it to their forties. What's the point?"

We sat there in the sunlight. Off in the distance we could see a couple of Diana's horses frolicking in the pasture.

After a while, Jody smiled at me. "You know, every morning I wake up, and I think, all right, you're not OJ any more, you're not a star, nobody remembers her. You're sitting on your ass on a pile of sand and cactus down here in sunny Mexico, watching your skin freckle, so what? You're alive, kiddo, and most of your equipment is still functioning . . . You don't need booze, or some Dr. Feelgood to shoot you up, or the local coke dealer to make a delivery so you can get through the next day . . . or even the next hour. So you're way ahead, kid . . . Consider the alternative." She shrugged. "Am I making any sense, or am I just running off at the mouth?"

"You're making sense," I told her. "For both of us."

". . . I don't want to sound like an article you read in the dentist's waiting room," she said.

"What if you do?" I said. "Maybe the *Reader's Digest* will end up buying your memoirs."

She tapped the tape recorder that sat on the table between us. "Forget memoirs, honey," she told me. "I'd hate that. Books about has-beens like me, Christ, it's like turning the pages of somebody's college scrapbook . . . no, this stuff here is only for a movie. And don't ask me how you plan to get one out of all my ramblings . . . that's *your* job."

And my job was also to get back to L.A. and fend off Sully Fischer and Sid Budlong and whatever palace plots they'd devised . . .

"Listen, Eileen," Jody said, "if the movie doesn't get made, so what? I'll still survive, you know? And so will *you,* Eileen. You've got to believe that, honey . . ."

"I guess I'm beginning to," I said. "Hanging around down here with you and the Doc, and the others—it's been quite an experience."

"It helped?" she asked.

". . . A lot," I said. "I'm amazed how much. I feel so . . . content."

"Aha," said Jody. "Watch it. You dould end up a permanent guest, like me or Kitty. But please, keep it to yourself. We don't need referrals. We're booked solid for the next couple of months. Let your friends keep going to La Costa . . . agreed?"

Dinner was my farewell meal. Nobody seemed to make much of it, but when it came time for dessert, Jody came out with a small cake and everybody applauded when she put it in front of me. One of Harry's creations, it was meticulously crafted in the shape of a large sink, its top covered with a sea of white suds. What kind of a cake? ". . . A sponge, of course!" said Harry.

Doc Katzen came over and held out his plate for a slab. "In your honor, I'm overcholesterizing." he said.

"You?" I said. "Listen, you're so thin, that—"

"Ah ha, there she goes, doing one-liners. Two weeks here, and everybody's a comedian." He put his arm around me, and kissed my cheek. ". . . No long goodbyes, cookie, but remember, if you need us, *call,* you got that?" I felt his hand give my breast a fond but gentle squeeze.

". . . What the hey, Doc, what the hey," I said. "Feel free."

I did my farewell set of dishes with Artie, then I settled my bill with Kitty, said my goodbyes to the rest of the guests, and went up to bed.

Artie was waiting there in my room. The bath was drawn, the towels were ready, the Vitabath poured. But he was staring sadly at my packed suitcase. ". . . Change your mind and stick around," he coaxed. "We've got a good thing going here. . ."

I kissed him fondly. ". . . Come on," I suggested, "let's get in the water and play ships that pass in the night . . ."

. . . As the light from the early morning sun began to filter in through the blinds, Artie stirred in the bed beside me.

Then he groaned. ". . . How'm I going to get along without you?"

". . . Ah, baby," I said. "You'll find somebody else to do your dishes," I said. "It's the suds that matter, not who's in them. . ."

". . . don't want to lose you," he said, and his hands began gently exploring me. ". . . you're good for me . . . and it's not just therapy. . ."

". . . I know, I know," I said, "but I have to go back to L.A. . . . maybe we could see each other again sometime . . ."

". . . Would you come visit me?" he asked, like a small boy requesting his weekly allowance. ". . . You'd like where I live . . . it's on the Jersey shore . . . kind of a nice old place, a house with nine rooms . . . and eight baths. . ."

". . . Only eight?" I giggled, as we moved into each other's arms, moving gently, we could have been a pair of swimmers,

stroke, stroke, stroke . . . against each other
   ". . . and a pool," he said
   stroke stroke
   ". . . a hot tub! . . ."
   stroke, stroke,
   ". . . a Jacuzzi! . . ." stroke, stroke—
   ". . . and a triple kitchen sink!"
   ". . . I'll come, I'll come!" I promised . . .
   and did.

Through the miracle of jet flight, late that same day, I was finally back at L.A. International, that man-made funnel through which endless masses of human bodies are daily jammed, a form of horrific punishment modern man has devised to torture those of his fellows; the obstacle course which begins when the jet's wheels touch down, and only ends when one has fought one's way through Customs, and through the moving hordes outside, fighting past the endless stream of coaches, stretch-limos, cabs, rental-car buses.

Welcome to Southern California, Mrs. Tighe.

My eyes tearing already from the smog, I fled that inferno and finally made it to my home.

Exhausted, I dropped my bags in the bedroom, turned on the air-conditioning, and went inside to take a shower.

Without Artie around, it suddenly seemed very empty in the stall. I was no longer used to bathing alone.

There was mail, stacks of it, to go through, and messages to take off my answering machine, but they could wait until tomorrow. I needed sleep.

I crawled into my solitary bed . . .

. . . the Casa Lindo and its guest list seemed to be so far away, another planet.

But the nine cassettes Jody had filled were there, safely on my bureau, and so was the letter we'd drawn, signed by both of us.

Tomorrow? Confrontation time.

I didn't yet imagine it would turn into The Shoot Out At Interfico.

*   *   *   *

Eileen Tighe:

The following morning, I was up with the birds, unpacking, skimming through my mail, making notes for today's phone calls—

Amazing. Back from the peace and quiet of the Casa Lindo for only a few hours, and already I'd completely reverted to my old compulsive California-type self.

First things first. These Jody Cassel tapes should be transcribed; since that process would take time, the sooner I got them into work, the better.

I got out the car, and headed over to Westwood, to the Interfico offices, dodging the early morning joggers as I went.

The office was dark. I let myself in the door with my key and went down the empty, quiet halls.

On my desk I found a pile of unanswered business mail, interoffice memos, progress reports, and the usual towering stack of screenplays submitted by hopeful agents in my absence. In order to make myself work space, I began moving the mass to one side; in the process, a manila interoffice envelope fluttered off the pile.

The label it bore was addressed to MR. S. FISCHER, % TIGHE.

Oh?

. . . my office was now his mail drop?

Bad sign.

Since there's no federal law against reading interoffice mail, I opened the envelope.

Inside, I found a neatly typed set of pages, with a routing memo clipped to the top.

FROM: S. Fischer
TO: S. Budlong
RE: Our project.

These are notes after our preliminary conversations.

While we wait for finalization of negotiations by Legal with our prospective writer, I'm setting them down. He can have these after we've signed him. I thought I'd run these past you for any further input.

A. We are completely agreed about our audience. We're targeting the 12–18s. If we get their parents, good, but we'll consider them a bonus.

B. We go for a major star, Travolta, or Stallone, that area. He's our *lead,* he's a writer-director in live TV, circa the 1950s, he's also a hoofer, sexy, hard-driving, ambitious, loaded with macho dynamism. He has his eye squarely on success in the Big Apple. Right now he has himself a small-time TV show to do, but he has big plans. Nobody will get in his way, he'll walk all over them to prove himself, but he's charming when he wants to be.

C. To play opposite him, we pick up on our *heroine*. She's about 18, young, attractive, personable (Kristy McNicol, Phoebe Cates, Diana De Mornay type) from a small town, lower-middle-class, blue-collar people. Loves to dance, probably was in the high-school play back home, now she's come here to N.Y., trying to break down doors, be seen, be recognized (à la *Fame*), she answers an audition, ends up being hired as one of a trio doing a commercial spot for the same small-time live show being done by our *lead*. Instant sparks between them, a love-hate relationship. He's out to make her, with him it's strictly physical; she is looking for something deeper and more lasting. They will be the spine we need for our story, against the background of live TV.

D. Another character we've discussed. *"Happy"*—an old-time comic (male, female? we're still fluid here). Wise-cracking, cynical, has been through the mill, seen it all. Will act as a sort of counterpoint to the two young leads. TV is a big break in his/her life; without this new medium he/she would have been a complete has-been. We're discussing whether or not Happy has some dread disease, is dying, but his/her agent keeps it a secret from the world. I can see us going for a brilliant death-bed Pagliacci scene here, all stops pulled. Whoever gets this part has a shot at the Academy Award.

E. Musical numbers. We'll recreate Broadway and Tin Pan Alley numbers of the period, *but,* since this project is aimed specifically at the youth market, we must intermingle the nostalgia stuff (songs of the '50s, be-bop, rock-and-roll, stuff like the Twist) with original material created directly for us by NOW songwriters, Manilow, Neil Diamond, Randy Newman, et al.

These are preliminary notes, but they seem to me to be pointed directly at a box-office smash. I'm putting down more notes as fast as they come to me. Meanwhile, I'll await any of your thoughts.

S. F.

. . . across the bottom of these immortal pages, was a brief hand-written scrawl. RIGHT! LET'S MEET AND TALK MORE. SID B.

Well now, the bees had really been busy while I'd been away.

. . . I could feel my heartbeat going, like the beat, beat, beat of the tom-tom—

And the jungle shadows had certainly fallen around me.

. . . Hey, Eileen, baby, not only are you surrounded by assassins, they are *untalented* assassins.

What a collection of garbage! He's a hoofer, the hard-driving director type, she's a starry-eyed kid from a small town who dreams of becoming a Broadway star . . . and then, there's Happy, the hermaphrodite clown with the dread disease. (I know what he/she has, doctor, she's/he's dying of a massive cliché, along with me!)

I felt the first faint twinges of nausea.

. . . and I hadn't even yet had my breakfast.

It was while I was making myself some medicinal coffee in the secretarial pantry that I had a dreadful thought. . . . Sully's vision of 1950s live TV was a dreadful piece of crap, a paint-by-the-numbers fake-out job, an assemblage of waste parts from old movies, sure . . .

. . . but so dreadful that it had every chance of being a big hit.

For those 12–18s with money in their jeans for tickets, this stuff wouldn't be recycled crap, not at all. Chances are, if the film were cast properly, they'd flock to this dreck—and find it all new and thrilling.

So I went back to my own office and began to improvise some sort of battle-plan.

"Well, Eileen, *baby*," said Budlong, rising from behind his immaculate desk. "I missed you."

"Me, too," I said, smiling. "How many countries have you visited since I went off to Mexico?"

"Only a few," he said. "What makes you think I was away?"

"You didn't answer my calls," I reminded him. "I figured you didn't love me any more."

"Of course I do," he said, jovially. "I was simply up to my ears here—and I figured you were, too. Listen, in this business, when you're on parallel tracks, you have to allow for a few mix-ups."

Mix-ups? That was his explanation? Not very ingenious, Sid—

He was waving me to a chair. "Sit. Coffee?"

I nodded.

"Milk?" he asked. Again I nodded. He pressed a button on his desk, opened a drawer and spoke softly into it. "One coffee, with milk." he repeated. "Now," he instructed me, *"watch."*

To one side of his desk, a panel slid open, and I saw something emerging. A small, bubble-headed . . . *what?* Humming and buzzing, a pair of tiny red lights flashing inside the plastic, this . . . thing moved directly across the room until it arrived beside my chair. Now, I saw two long metallic arms holding out a tray toward me. On the tray was a cup of steaming coffee.

"There you go," said Budlong, like a proud father.

I took the coffee off the tray; my hands were shaking.

"Where's the milk?" asked Budlong.

The . . . thing swivelled, and there shortly appeared a small container of half-and-half on the tray. I took it.

"Very efficient, eh?" asked Budlong, beaming. "He is an 88201 RB5X."

"Hi there," I said to the robot. There was no answer, just a gentle humming.

"Doesn't speak," said Budlong. "I haven't bought the Voice Synthesis Package. I'm not sure I want him talking. *Return,*" he instructed.

RB5X obediently slid back across the carpet, lights flashing, and went inside the waiting open panel. Then the panel slid shut, and Sid and I were once again alone.

"He's in there recharging himself," Sid said.

"Seems only fair," I said.

"You know anybody else who has one of those?" he asked.

"No," I said. "The most expensive coffee urn I've ever seen."

". . . Very funny," said Sid. "Okay, now, fill me in on Mexico. How are we doing?"

"Not too well at first," I said. "Took me quite a while to break Jody down. She's a very defensive lady, enjoys her privacy, isn't too interested in being given the immortalization treatment on film—"

"Screw her," said Budlong, as if on reflex.

"—*no,*" I said. "She's agreed to agree with Interfico—so now we can go ahead—"

I passed him over the letter Jody and I had signed.

He read through it quickly. When he looked up at me, his expression was obviously disapproving. *"Creative control?"* he repeated, spitting out the words as if they were bullets.

"An absolute must," I said. "The rest of the deal is negotiable, but that one is the deal-breaker. No tickee, no laundry."

Budlong nodded. "Don't you think it might have been wiser for you to consult with *me* before you went ahead and agreed to this clause?"

"Tried to," I said. "That is what I was calling you about."

". . . and without touching bases, you went ahead and signed this?"

"What choice did I have?" I asked.

"You could have said *no*," he said. "You aren't authorized to deal for Interfico, Eileen."

He reached down, flipped an unseen switch, and in a moment, I heard, from a speaker in the bookcase, the sound of voices—*our* voices.

". . . You'd better keep me posted on what's happening down there, every time you talk. Keep notes, call me, and do I have to remind you are not to get into any discussion of money, or legal rights? That's what we have a business affairs department for, remember?"

Jesus—he'd had us bugged?

Then I heard my own voice. ". . . But I could get her to agree in principle, couldn't I?"

". . . If you can," said Sid's voice.

"There," he said, turning off the tape. "I always tape conversations, specifically because of situations like this. You did get into a discussion of legal rights."

"Are you taping us now?" I asked.

My throat was dry, and even though the air-conditioning was on, I was perspiring.

"Yes, indeed." said Sid.

"Okay, then let's go on to the next question?" I asked him. "Whatever happened to our parallel tracks?"

"I don't think I understand your question?"

"I'll clarify it for you," I said, still smiling. "This live TV project was supposed to operate with us working together . . . you *and* me . . . correct?''

"Yes, while you've been down in Mexico contravening our game plan," he said.

". . . and you've been up here doing exactly the same thing," I said.

"I have?" he asked softly. "How would I be doing that, Eileen?"

I took a deep breath. I felt my pulse racing . . . and went ahead anyway. "By hiring Sully Fischer as producer on this project, authorizing him to hire a writer, conferring with him about the shape of the story . . . without ever once discussing any of it with me. Those are parallel tracks?"

Sid got up and went to the window, stared out at the landscape below. "Eileen," he said, his voice controlled, "it seems to me you've got a confused notion, or let's call it, an image of what you do around here."

"No, I haven't," I said. "Senior Production Executive is the title on my stationery—and that's my job—I'm not a bit confused—"

"Take a look at my stationery," said Sid, "and you'll see that I am President here, which means I make the decisions, and I do not have to consult with you, or anybody else, unless I decide I want to—"

"Parallel tracks?" I asked. "That's on the tape, too—"

"I'll wipe it," said Sid. "Sully Fischer is working on this project, so get used to the idea—"

"*Not* on the same project you and I discussed," I said, and my pulses were racing even faster now.

"Forget that," he said. "You've been in Mexico, making a deal you had no authority to make, with some old time has-been broken down whatever—What goes on *here*, believe me, *I* am totally aware of—"

"If it's going to end up being the kind of screenplay Sully Fischer wants—" I blurted, and then I stopped myself.

Quiet, Eileen. *She who fights and runs away,* et cetera, good motto, stick to it—

He wasn't going to let me live to fight another day. "Yes?" he asked. "What about Sully Fischer's screenplay? How do *you* know about what he wants?"

Oh, what the hell, why bother waiting to fight? Why not fight now?

"I read his notes," I told Sid. "Somebody left them on my desk, and under the circumstances, I felt it was all right to read them. I am still with this firm, aren't I?"

He stared at me. "I don't know, Eileen," he said, finally. "I'm worried about you . . . You seem quite different from the executive I sent down to Mexico, a while back . . . Have you changed so much?"

. . . Was it that obvious?

"I guess I have," I said.

"From where I sit," he said, "you're aggressive, you're hostile, suddenly you seen to be dragging around a giant-sized chip on your shoulder."

"Right," I said.

"Why?" he asked.

". . . Maybe," I said, thinking it out as I said it, ". . . it's because I very much resent you referring to Jody Cassel as an old-time, has-been, broken-down whatever . . . and—"

"I do wish you didn't," said Budlong. "Because that means to me you're definitely playing on *her* team, not ours."

"What am I, some kind of double-agent?" I asked. "You're not making any sense!"

"I'm not?" he said. "You'd certainly never have signed a piece of paper like this," he waved the letter I'd brought back from Casa Lindo, ". . . *if* you'd had Interfico's best interests at heart." He shook his head sadly. "No, I can only go by what I read here on this page, here you've not only handed the woman the moon, but what's worse, you did it on *your* own authority—"

Macchiavellian! He'd turned the tables completely around on me . . . now *I* was the villain—

". . . Something tells me," he said, "you're not going to be very happy working around here any longer, Eileen. . ."

"You'd much rather have a batch of little robots around, right?" I said. "All you want to do is to press the buttons, and have everybody slide in and out, on batteries—never talking back."

"Not funny," said Sid, glaring at me.

"Unfortunately, I do not fit your specs, do I?" I asked.

"Not lately," he said.

"So go with Sully the *Ootzer*," I said. "I hope the two of you get along beautifully—"

"Thank you, we do," he said.

"But I want to warn you, you may think you know how to manipulate people, but when it comes to screwing people you're only an amateur. Sully's a four-star professional—and he'll have your job before you can say Parallel Tracks—look out, he's going to get you, smart-ass—"

"Wait a minute!" said Sid. "Nobody talks to *me* that way! . . ."

"Are you firing me?" I asked, sweetly.

"No, damnit," he said, his voice rasping. "You have a contract—"

"Glad you remembered . . . See you later, Mr. President," I said, and I got up.

"Nobody said this meeting . . . was over . . ." rasped Sid, and now I noticed perspiration on his forehead.

"*I* did," I told him.

I started across the office.

As I reached the door, I heard a soft, choking sound behind me.

. . . the robot?

I turned. Saw Sid, slumping in his desk-chair . . . his face suddenly no longer ruddy, but somewhat greyish, his hands scrabbling toward his desk drawer. As I watched, horrified, he pulled the drawer open, found his electronic pulse machine, brought it out with hands that shook, and tried to attach it to his arm . . .

But couldn't manage it.

"What's the matter?" I asked.

". . . Pain . . . in my chest . . ." he croaked.

Angina?

How could Sid, the all-American executive, be having an attack? He, who kept himself so fit—

. . . heaven help me, I couldn't help thinking of the old Harry Cohn line—". . . I don't get ulcers—I *give* them."

And yet, here was Sid, slumped back in his chair, sweating, his color ashen, obviously in much pain.

I came back toward him. Never mind his pulse machine, I could see he needed air. I helped him pull open the buttons of his shirt, he was slumped back in his chair now, having trouble breathing—with one hand he was pointing at the telephone on his desk, his fingers shaking as if palsied—

Of course—*911!*—Call them, right away, there'd be a paramedic team up here to handle this.

I reached for the phone.

. . .then it hit me.

Evil question.

Did I want Budlong to be rescued?

. . . or did I want him to have a real blockbuster of an attack, effectively removing him from Interfico for a while, permitting me to handle the Jody Cassel project without him—

. . . God what a terrible decision to make.

All my years of Sunday School training, and philosophic ingraining, *do good! do good! do good!* took over.

. . . I punched 9 1 1.

. . . When the Police Department answered, I gave them explicit instructions as to how to get the paramedics up here, heart attack in progress, no it did not seem like cardiac arrest, no, I certainly would not touch the patient, nor do anything that might worsen his condition, thank you officer, we'll be waiting—

I hung up.

Our fearless leader was sprawled, arms akimbo, perspiring in his executive-style chair, his breathing shallow, definitely Cheyne-Stokes (I knew that from a medical show I'd once worked on).

He stared at me, suddenly helpless. In extremis? No, not yet . . .

He'd recover. People like Sid Budlong always recover . . .

"They'll be here soon," I soothed. "Relax, Sid. No stress—that's primary . . ."

He nodded. ". . . Don't . . . let . . . this get to . . . the trade papers . . . No publicity . . ." he instructed. ". . . Bad for the company's . . . image . . ."

"Oh, don't worry," I assured him. "I'll simply tell them you're out of town, as usual . . . *Relax.*"

". . . Eileen," he croaked, . . . I owe you."

My my, I should have gotten that down on recording tape, shouldn't I?

". . . Don't thank me, Sid," I told him. "I should thank *you*, for not going into cardiac arrest."

". . . Why?" he croaked, between wheezes.

"Because that would mean I'd have to give you mouth-to-mouth resuscitation," I said, ". . . and under the circumstances, I'm not sure I could bring myself to do that."

He blinked at me, perplexed.

". . . Wowoweeweewoh, Sid," I told him. "These are the jokes."

*   *   *   *

The paramedic team that arrived shortly was just as efficient as all those actors on medical-type series we've grown to love and cherish. They had Sid out of the office and down to Cedars-Sinai Hospital in very short order . . . by the rear elevators, so nobody could see his farewell exit.

By the end of that day, the reports from the hospital were that Sid would be in Intensive Cardiac Care for at least forty-eight more hours while they did the tests and decided whether (a) he had in fact a heart and (b) whether it needed surgery.

Meanwhile, the Interfico office staff functioned as usual. Since we were all accustomed to having our leader off on his various journeys, his absence wasn't too difficult to adjust to; in fact, a lot more got done in his absence.

Sully Fischer called in; Sid's secretary transferred the call to me. Sully let me know that he was in constant touch with Cedars-Sinai, and with Sid's various doctors, and although at first he, Sully, had been Disheartened and Dismayed by the terrible news, he was now Optimistic for Sid's immediate recovery.

I, in turn, let Sully know that I was prepared to Carry On, that was what Sid would want us to do, so I was ready to meet with him at any time to Move the TV project Forward.

Sully waffled about that.

. . . could we really proceed without Sid?

"You have a choice," I told him. "It's either me, alone, or we wait for a bedside conference at Cedars-Sinai. I think we'd better take on the responsibility ourselves, don't you?"

Sully changed his tune, and promised me he would certainly be in at ten, the following morning, how was that?

. . . Round One, to me.

I sent Jody's tapes out to be transcribed, and went about my business.

It wasn't until that evening that my elation began to ebb away . . .

. . . to be replaced by a fine, old-fashioned depression.

It was triggered by a bulletin I got from, who else? My old friend and source, Ozzie.

We were having a late Chinese dinner alone, just the two of us, in a cheapo place I fancy way out on Olympic, so completely unfashionable that nobody we know can ever overhear our conversations.

I'd filled Ozzie in on the last few hours in Budlong's bunker and my ensuing tilt with Sully. Wasn't he proud of me?

". . . Yes, *but,*" said Ozzie. "I can't put my finger exactly on what it is—yet—but the word is that Interfico is headed for some kind of a corporate metamorphosis . . ."

". . . A changing of the guard, if and when Sid is replaced?" I asked.

"Oh, I'm sure he's out," said Ozzie, nibbling on his moo-shoo pork. "But this is more basic. Maybe a merger, a buy-out, some sort of a financial fold-up. Some German conglomerate is sniffing around . . . haven't you heard the rumblings?"

Suddenly I'd lost my appetite. ". . . Why in heaven's name would they want to fold up Interfico?" I asked. "We're in very good shape, got deals going—and one of the pictures Sid bought points in—*Drive Me Home,* a real piece of junk, but it cost peanuts, and it's a surprise smash—"

". . . That," said Ozzie, "seems to be exactly the problem. Interfico was not supposed to be such a money-spinner, remember?"

"Since when?" I demanded.

"Oh, come on, baby, wake up. Your outfit was designed for *losses.* Nobody wants profits—it louses up all your various investors, ruins their tax-shelter situations—don't you understand the game plan, Eileen?" asked Ozzie. "Nobody wants the I.R.S. breathing down his neck. Why do you think your good pal Sid has been under such pressure lately?"

". . . For succeeding?" I asked.

Ozzie grinned. "Despite himself," he said. "Amazing, isn't it? The hotter he gets, the more trouble he's in!"

"Oz," I said, "you're a cynic."

"But a survivor," he reminded me. "Remember that."

". . . How do you know all this before I do?" I asked.

"Listen," he said, "I am a middle-aged, grey-haired radar screen. I collect ten percents for knowing what's happening, who's doing what to whom and how and where *and* when—before you do. Just be damned glad I read the screen and warn you when it's time to get out the life preserver and prepare to jump ship. You're a bright lady, you'll get another job—"

"Oz," I said, feeling a faint twinge of nausea. "You're making this up . . ."

"For your sake, I wish I were," he said. "If you don't believe me, go ask your financial boys what they plan to do with all the profits from *Drive Me Home.* That dough is a real threat . . . a time bomb. Bye-bye, Interfico . . .''

"Damn!" I said. "Here I am with a project going I'm really crazy about—what am I supposed to do with Jody Cassel?"

Ozzie finished the last of the Lake Tung Ting Shrimp. ". . . Both of you better find yourself a lifeboat," he said. "And start rowing."

. . . my fortune cookie was no help.

The motto inside read "All that glitters is not sweet and sour sauce."

That ancient Chinese philosopher and my faithful radar screen Ozzie knew much more about Interfico's future than I did.

Much more.

. . . but not more than the world's champion *ootzer,* Sully Fischer, with whom I had a date the following morning at ten.

I was sitting there, waiting for him, and for the knock-down-and-drag-out I knew we'd have to have about those terrible story-line notes of his, when there was a rap, rap, rap on my office door.

It was pushed open, and there stood, not Sully, but a thin, ramrod-straight young blond gentleman in a Bond Street suit, his hair crew-cut, beaming at me through thick glasses, exuding a cloud of expensive French cologne.

". . . Good morning," he said, with a slight accent. "I am Klaus Dieterhelm, from Berlin. *Münchenfilmverken.*" He bowed, clicked his heels, so help me, he could have been Eric Von Stroheim. "And you are Frau Tighe?"

"Oh yes, I am," I began, and then, before I could continue, I spied Sully Fischer, standing behind Herr Dieterhelm, doing his best tour-guide bit. "Ah, yes, Eileen here is one of our most productive brains," he said. "Later this morning, we're going to have a conference on a new project. Perhaps you'd like to join us, Klaus?"

"Perhaps," said Herr Dieterhelm. "I have much to do today."

"Of course you have," said Sully. "You want to take a good

look at what you and your people have taken over, that's only natural, eh? Let me show you the rest of the shop—''

"Yes, indeed!" said Klaus Dieterhelm, who was staring at my front with more than casual interest, obviously a tit man, he. ". . . We must continue soon, eh, Frau Tighe? *Auf Wiedersehen!*"

"Oh, definitely *auf*," I told him, as he disappeared down the hall, side by side with Sully, who would definitely be sitting next to him soon, pitching him various projects that were subtly shaped to work in the German market.

. . . How the hell had Sully gotten to him so quickly? He'd even beaten Ozzie Kaufman to the punch.

That was truly elegant *ootzing*.

. . . Attacked by Unterzeeboat 89 (Das Boot, Captain Klaus at the Dieterhelm), Interfico had already taken its first torpedo, and was in big trouble.

Time to man—no, *person*—the lifeboats, Mrs. Tighe.

SOS! Jody, what do I do next? SOS!

*　　*　　*　　*

Buck Dawes:

    . . . Ordinarily, you could not get me to come to one of those charity banquets unless you put a gun to my back.

    They're all so damned predictable. Only the prices change, always upward (tax deductible, so who cares?)—for which you get the same cocktail hour, with everybody clapping you on the back, comparing golf scores, or the profit on the latest deal, telling you how great you look, lying with a big smile, showing the bridgework. Their wives and girlfriends all making kiss-face with each other, comparing Adolfos, or the jewelry, the latest breast-lift or eye-job, checking out the musical chairs of who's gotten married, or who's split, or who's died since the last dinner . . .

    Then, after a couple of drinks (is anybody still drinking these day? I thought the whole world is getting its high from the white stuff) then the crowd moves on inside to the main ballroom, where everybody checks to see who's sitting with whom, at what table, and are the souvenir bottles of perfume at each place better than last week's—

    The food begins, always the same hotel food, so you can usually predict exactly what cut of beef the waiter will drop on your plate, while up on the dais, time for the invocation by Father/Rabbi/Reverend, the music plays, then on comes the emcee. Probably Bob or Johnny, on his night off, or Frank, who's flown in from New York just for tonight, but what the hell, when you're a pal, you do things like that—or maybe it's a senator (if it's a Serious Cause, it could be even a VeePee, but they save him for big fund-raisers). Then we go right into the entertainment, a singer, maybe Dino, up from the Springs, a comic, probably Milton, telling a few gags, getting in a gentle rib, or that new hot English Dudley Moore, who can play the piano while he's doing the jokes, or if it's a Southwest crowd, they always get in a country music singer, Willie, or that Dolly . . .

The dessert, the coffee, and now it starts—

We're here tonight to pay tribute to my good friend, ladies and gentlemen, that wonderful guy—

They clear away the tables and we get after-dinner drinks, and more rhetoric—

I'm here to say I'm thrilled to call him my good friend, yes, he's a great humanitarian, folks do you understand what a fine public-spirited citizen he is, I am proud tonight to pay tribute here to this sweet person, this great, great human being, this man here, this wonderful guy, I want to tell you a revealing little anecdote about this man, this beautiful human being, so selfless, so *caring*. I walked into his office one afternoon, he's a busy man, you all know how busy, but he's never too busy to take the time to help somebody in need, somebody's who's not as fortunate as he is, folks, and this man, this beautiful human being—

. . . About an hour of that, and the people are now looking at their Piagets and their Corums, furtively checking the time, because it's Sunday night, remember, and tomorrow they all have to be up at dawn for the jogging, or the Jane Fonda aerobics tape, then by seven they're dressed and off to whatever breakfast meeting they've got scheduled . . .

So, could the emcee, be he Johnny, Frank, or perhaps it's Hal Kanter up there (at least he does new jokes, and since they're original with him, they're funny) please get on with it? Give this humanitarian up there his award already, we've got to get home, hell, we've all paid our dues to this beautiful person, showed him our faces, now he owes *us*, right?

Do I really need another night like that? Hell, no.

But this one, I had to come to.

. . . the damned dinner was in *my* honor.

(*Your* honor, Buck?

Oh, I can hear Margaret's voice somewhere, saying "Hold it, let's get the billing absolutely straight, my sweet. That clinic building has my name on it, not yours.")

Right. So when it comes my turn, I will say—Ladies and gentlemen, tonight I am strictly a surrogate here, I came as a proxy, to accept this very prestigious award on behalf of someone no longer with us, a noble humanitarian lady, a very beautiful person, my wife, the late Margaret Sutphen Dawes.

(You wanted humble, Margaret? I'll give you humble.)

. . . But it does occur to me, my sweet, wherever you are, wouldn't you agree I should ask our accountants to take a bow?

After all, they're the crafty ones who designed the Dawes Clinic. Based it on the community property laws of the great state of California, which gave you, dear Mrs. Margaret Sutphen Dawes, fifty percent, down the middle, of whatever I've earned out here in the past twenty-five years. They were the ones who worried you might predecease me, and so they came up with the plan to minimize taxes on your fifty percent by leaving a very big hunk of capital (our capital?) to build and endow the Dawes Clinic. And since you did predecease me, angel (this being in the pre-Reagan era, before the I.R.S. revised the tax-code on inheritance between married couples), you could say that all those battered wives and children now in the Dawes Clinic should get up each morning and give thanks to Turtletaub & Weinstein, CPAs . . .

(Tell me, Margaret, why shouldn't we build an annex for Husbands, Battered by the I.R.S?)

Here sits Buck Dawes, up on this dais, under the lights, looking fairly well preserved by most standards for a man my age, in my well-cut Anderson & Shepherd dinner jacket, waiting for this program to run its course . . . and checking *my* watch, too, because

I'd like to get this over with as much as all those $500-a-plate guests spread out down there in the Main Ballroom.

Fairly soon now, it ought to be my turn to speak.

First they'll hand me the bronze plaque, then I will respond.

I will make it short, and very sweet.

. . . No, not because I have to be up at dawn tomorrow, but at 9 I do have an appointment out at U.C.L.A. Hospital with Dr. Donald Granger, a very busy specialist, who wants to tell me the results of all those "tests" they did on me this morning. Him, one does not keep waiting.

. . . I will finish my remarks, and people all over this room will stand up and applaud, they'll blow kisses, wipe away tears, pay me tribute because I am a beautiful, beautiful person.

(. . . Next month, they'll do it for some other beautiful person.)

Then I'll go back to Table One, my table, which is full of people close to me. All the dues payers. My lawyers, my secretary, Louisa, and her husband. Turtletaub and Weinstein, of course, the New York delegation, Sir James and Lady Beatrice, who flew in from London, Gene and Amy, from the investment bankers, and Jack, here from Washington . . .

Margaret's family? Well, certainly not her parents, they never wanted me to marry her in the first place. Brad, he with that Long Island lockjaw voice, and that inbred lineage, which goes back, if not to Plymouth Rock, at least to the third boat that made it in after the Mayflower, and Muffy, her mother, that mouse blonde who kept a sherry bottle hidden in her makeup table, and whose main claim to fame was she'd had her coming-out party with Eddy Duchin playing, in the very bottom of the Depression . . . They're not here, and neither are the in-laws. Although they might just have shown up if I'd sent airline tickets and guaranteed their room at the Beverly Wilshire.

. . . my family? Who's here from my side?

Not my father, Mike Dawes (né Myer Dackowitz, but if you want to sell haberdashery to Harvard undergraduates, it's better you change your name and assimilate yourself, *du herst?*). Well, he's no longer around to crack a couple of bad jokes and brag to his pals how proud he is of his son Buck, who went through Harvard on a scholarship and acquired himself a whole gang of *goyische* friends . . . Oh, a real go-getter, my boy Buck, you heard of him, he's a Big Man in the Business, believe you me, knew how to make a dollar into two right from the start . . . Knew how to dress (that he got from me, I told him it's how you look makes the best impression, always wear quiet colors, don't go for flash, it never lasts, when in doubt, wear a blazer) . . . he would have enjoyed tonight. Too bad he isn't here to do a little basking in my limelight . . .

. . . and my mother? Lee Dawes (nee Leah, the Belle of Brookline?). Well, she's in her nice little suite in that expensive retirement place down in Florida, with the nurse, on the veranda where she and her pals can play canasta, inside there's a video-tape machine, the finest I could send her, so she can play tapes each night for her friends. Next week she'll have a videotape of this whole thing here tonight (Look, it's my darling boy Ben— excuse me, *Buck*—oh, he's such a good son, he takes such good care of me, I wish I could travel to be there . . . I don't see him, or his kids as much as I'd like to . . .)

(Neither do I, mother. See, here in my pocket, I've got a congratulatory cable from my daughter, Della, far away in Brazil now, with her second husband . . . And my son Eric, who's settled down up near Vancouver. Says he'd like to be here, but he couldn't make it tonight, this week is planting time.)

(Never mind, darling, your mother is very proud of you, I couldn't ask for a better son. You run a big company, you're always busy, but maybe you could find a little time, come down here to Florida and sit with me, we could play cards? I know you're an important man . . . but . . .)

A very important man, yes, who at this moment, desperately needs to get up from his seat on this dais and excuse himself.

And disappear, headed for wherever the plumbing is.

Anxious to get on to the most humanitarian rite available to a beautiful person. To take himself a pee.

On my way back inside the ballroom, I go through what I think are the same doors I came out, but instead, I find myself headed toward Table 18.

Wrong. I'll go back. I work my way through the tables, headed for the dais.

A hand plucks at my arm, and a voice says ". . . *Buck . . . sweetheart.*"

I turn, and find a guy standing, beaming at me.

. . . Oh yes. Now I remember. Ozzie Kaufman.

Thin, tan, dapper. Always dressed in good taste . . . How long have I known him? Ever since I first got out here. Good agent. Honest. Solid. Never made the switch to producer—

"A very big night for you, Buck," he says. "What a pleasure to be here to pay homage to a beautiful person."

"Thanks, Oz," I say. "Now I've got to get back up there—"

But he has me firmly by the arm.

"Lady here I want you to meet, Buck," he says. "She's Eileen Tighe, very shrewd person, and she has a special reason for wanting to talk to you—"

Nice-looking lady, sitting next to Ozzie, brunette, she's got a few years on her, but nice shape, she's well preserved—very good dress, nothing flashy. She has a special reason? They've all got special reasons for cozying up to Buck Dawes, so what makes her different from the rest of the entire world?

"This isn't exactly the night to discuss it," she says, "but I've just come back from Mexico, and I spent a lot of time with a friend of yours—a very old friend—"

This is a new pitch. ". . . I have a very old friend in Mexico?" I say. "News to me."

"The two of you go a long, long way back, Mr. Dawes—"

I don't really need to play Trivial Pursuit with this lady.

"A lot of people do—or did," I say. "I've got to get back up there, excuse me—"

"Jody Cassel," she says.

What is this, some kind of a rib?

Not funny.

Jody? An old friend of mine?

Not for a hell of a long time.

". . . As a matter of fact," this Eileen is saying, "I called your office a couple of weeks ago, and they told me you were in Europe, you see, I have this project, and it involves Jody, and a lot of her friends—"

Christ, right here tonight, she's pitching a deal?

". . . and I didn't call you back," I say.

She nods. "But I wish you could talk to me about her—I do appreciate what a busy man you are—"

I nod. "Try my office," I tell her.

"Tomorrow?" she asks.

"Afternoon," I say.

And I leave them both and head for the dais.

Tomorrow I can tell Louisa not to put her through.

Jody Cassel . . .

. . . there's a ghost from the past. Who needs her?

But a real live ghost.

Living in Mexico? Married . . . or what? With some poor masochistic bastard she found for herself?

And the kid? What's the name she gave her? Oh yes, now I remember, Pretty Baby. Jody, being cute . . .

When was the last time I heard from her?

Why do I even want to remember?

Back to the dais.

Sit down, time for me pretty soon, meanwhile, it's the senator, introducing me, and making himself a few points (next year is an election year)

". . . and I have known this beautiful man ever since those days when he first began putting together that vast enterprise out in the Valley, that marvelous piece of American ingenuity and commerce, uniquely Californian, which touches us all in our daily lives . . ."

Translation: I'm Chairman of the Board now, and the business is in the hands of a cadre of hot-shot under-thirties killers, racing around making deals, deals, deals, cutting each other to ribbons—

(The way you did, Buck, remember?

Before you became such a Grand Old Man of the Industry, you beautiful person.)

. . . God, that night in New York, with Jody. Ugly scene . . .

Sure, I remember, she came up, barged into my office, it was late, I was still working, trying to put together pieces of a special, what they called a "Spectacular," it was for Leland Hayward, he was doing one of those big fancy spreads, two-hours, in those days that was something absolutely unheard of, awesome—two hours of prime time on *live* TV? But that was Leland's style, he always enjoyed taking a big leap ahead, doing something bolder and brassier than anybody else, he'd find some corporate sponsor and charm them into opening up the company bank account, then he'd start spending their money like there was no tomorrow. Hiring Jerry Robbins to direct, getting Lindsay and Crouse to write the script, Oscar Hammerstein and Ed Murrow as the hosts, Mary Martin and Ethel Merman to do spots, and then to work in a duet, God, he could come up with the damndest layouts . . .

There's nobody around like Leland any more, no showmen. All we have today are accountants, with pocket calculators . . .

. . . Jody came charging in, plunked herself down on my antique sofa, and started right in on me—why was I ducking her?

Ducking? I was busy. Well, screw that; she told me—She was my most important client and she was entitled to a lot more attention.

What did she want?

She wanted a spot on Leland's show. I should sell her to Leland, I should pick up the phone right now and call him, arrange for a meeting—

She certainly must have been on something, all hopped up that night, pacing up and down my office, never sitting, giving me orders, not listening to my answers—

How could I tell her Leland had already turned her down?

I knew Jody, I knew she couldn't stand any rejection, she'd take it personally, turn nasty—

He's already cast, I told her.

What the hell kind of an agent was I? I couldn't pitch her, my most important client?

". . . and never once have I known this man to be unavailable for any worthy cause, which needed his valuable input . . ."

I'm a good agent, I told her, the best, and you know it, but sometimes there are deals you can't cut, face it, Jody, you've got plenty to do with your own show.

Bullshit! she said, my show is a piece of crap, what I want is a class spot where they can see how great I really am . . . Oh, boy, was she loaded for bear tonight. Don't give me that bullshit doubletalk save it for the other clients, this is me, Jody Cassel, remember that, we go a long ways back, Buck, without me, you'd be in some cubicle down the hall, an office boy, booking seven-hundred and fifty a week stand-up comics in the Catskills—

The hell I would! I told her, I had never lost my temper with her before, and I was trying hard not to tonight, but damn her, she was pushing me too hard . . . I'd worked my ass off for her, took care of all her crazinesses—

So get me with Leland Hayward, big-shot, she said.

I can't, I told her.

You mean, you won't, you bastard, she said, now she was leaning over my desk, really giving it to me. You stone-face, she said, you never move a muscle in that damn face of yours, are you alive under your face, Buck, what goes on with you? Were you designed by Walt Disney, you android! Let me see—

She started pulling away at my shirt buttons, I slapped her hands away. You get your kicks out of being such a bastard, don't you? she said. Never showing your hand to anybody, again with her fingers clawing away at me, now she was moving onto me, taunting me, there wasn't any sex here, it was open hate, she crawled on me. This is going to be your opening night, kiddo, she said, you're going to react, you won't do it for Jody, okay, you want Jody to do it for you?

Damn her, she was really bugging me, and she knew it, she was enjoying it, she started biting me. Come on, Buckie, *react,* she said, sing Melancholy Baby . . . or show us your cock!

God, she was impossible to deal with, she was crawling all over me, her hands were fumbling with my zipper, damn this broad, I didn't need any of this—everybody has his limits—

". . . and in troubled times, his door is always open. Do I have to remind you, all of you, his friends assembled here, of the many, *many* times he has responded, wholeheartedly, to whomever, or whatever, is in need? . . ."

What the hell were we doing on the floor, on that expensive old Persian carpet, she was wrestling with me now, cursing me, sneering at me, damn it, this was one crazy lady, Go ahead, Buck, show me one emotion, she was yelling. Just one, you have to get your jollies somehow . . . Or are you some kind of a closet queen, *bubele?*

That did it, I couldn't help it, I whacked her across the face.

. . . and it didn't get any better after that, oh, it got much worse, because I'd discovered how much I wanted to hurt her, how long I'd been waiting to punish Jody, it had built up inside me all this time, I had her under me now, moaning, whimpering, and damn her, all I wanted to do was to humiliate this noisy bitch ripping and tearing at her clothes not even thinking if maybe there was somebody here in the offices still working late tonight God, it was insane taking such a chance and for what? To have this crazy egomaniac bitch on the floor? we were like a couple of angry animals   Hating it and wanting it   Me throwing her over onto her stomach and punishing punishing

". . . and so now, tonight, we have gathered here, from all the corners of this great land of ours, nay, from all over the world, come here to do him honor . . ."

When she'd come back from the ladies room, she'd fixed herself up, she had a bruise where I'd smacked her, but that was all. "Congratulations, Buck," she said . . . "You finally came out of the closet. So . . . when do I get to see Leland Hayward?"

Damn her! What did she think had happened here tonight? Was it simply some kind of a swap-meet, a barter? Herself for a spot on his show?

". . . What do *you* call it?" she asked me. "A scene out of *Romeo and Juliet?*"

She certainly had a point.

Hayward finally agreed to use her, it took a lot of selling on my part, he was a tough trader. She ended up with a spot of her own, not a big one, but with a piece of special material written by Comden and Green. As usual, she got what she wanted . . . a spot on a class show.

. . . Of course she didn't thank me.

We never discussed that evening in my office; what the hell would we have said about it? She got herself married, to that musician, I was at the wedding, Margaret and I, we even brought our kids, they were thrilled to be at a real-live TV star's wedding. That was before we moved out here to L.A. where they got to know everybody in the business on a first-name basis . . .

I stopped handling her after she had the baby . . . How long ago was that?

I lose track of time.

". . . and I know I speak for all of us here, when I ask him to stand, so I may present this award to him, to this man who so richly deserves the title engraved on this . . . Humanitarian Of The Year . . . *Mr. Buck Dawes.*"

Oh, yes. *Me.*

. . . Time to get up and say a few short words, you beautiful person.

*   *   *   *

Does that do it? I kept it short and sweet. Got a couple of good laughs there. Why not? I can afford the best writers.

Now they're all standing, applauding, waving, the music is playing softly . . .

I'm bowing. Am I being humble enough for you, Margaret? That's all, folks. Time to go home.

I'm on my way out, I'm looking for Dan, where is he? He usually finds me right away, but not tonight, there's a crowd and I'm trying to get through it

Here's Ozzie again, and his lady friend, Jody Cassel's friend, Eileen? Whatshername?

"Beautiful speech, Buck," he tells me.

"Thanks, pal," I tell him, I'm looking for Dan—

"I'll be calling tomorrow," says Jody's-friend-Eileen.

Yes. Suddenly I want to know about Jody Cassel, I don't know exactly why, but it's important—

"Really call me, don't forget," I tell her.

"Of course she's going to call you, she's been waiting to talk to you for months!" Ozzie says.

I get a sudden flash.

"Ozzie, you *brought* her here tonight to meet me, didn't you?" I ask.

". . . Why Buck," he says, "what makes you think that?"

". . . Suppose I hadn't had to go to the Mens room, and I hadn't run into you two?" I ask. "You'd never have talked to me—"

"Oh, come on now, Buck," says Ozzie. "You know better than *that* . . ."

Big laugh. Ha-ha. Smart-ass sonofabitch, he's been around a long time, knows all the tricks—

Somebody has my arm. *Dan—*

"Excuse me, Mr. Dawes, your car is waiting." Takes me gently by the arm, leads me through the crowd. I'm not worried, I'll be hearing from Eileen tomorrow, that's for sure.

He escorts me through the side entrance out to where he has the limo waiting.

Into the back seat. He closes the door.

Limo starts, and off we go. Tired now, I can undo my tie, kick off my McAfee pumps. Back to the house where I can dump this plaque, get out of this dinner jacket, sack out . . .

"A very nice night," says Dan, beside me. "I was proud of you, Buck."

"You should have sat at the table with the others," I tell him.

"No, too many people watching," he says. "Why give the bastards anything to talk about?"

"They'll talk anyway," I say.

". . . Besides, I knew your speech by heart, didn't I?" he says. "You rehearsed it for me last night . . . so there were no surprises tonight, lover."

In the last couple of years, since Margaret died, and he moved in, Dan has gotten to know a lot about me. But he can't know about one surprise I had tonight.

. . . Jody Cassel.

He pats me gently. ". . . Don't worry," he says. "This time tomorrow, it'll all be taken care of, and you're going to be fine . . ."

"Now you're a doctor, too?"

". . . I've been pretty good medicine for you, haven't I?" he asks, softly.

". . . You've been a beautiful person," I tell him.

*   *   *   *

Buck Dawes:

. . . I sit there in my office, sipping iced Earl Grey tea and I listen, while Mrs. Eileen Tighe goes into her pitch.

Bright lady. A little nervous when she starts, but she gets better as she goes along. Good pitch.

. . . Early days of live TV, New York, the 50s, young girl alone, wants to be a comic, fights her way through a man's world, has a boyfriend, they make it to the top, then they split. She goes on to be a solo star, fights to stay there. Conflict, action, emotion, plenty of color. Nostalgia.

(Was it that exciting while it was happening? Strange, today I can't remember. Mrs. Tighe could have been describing a whole other world, not the one I went through. To her, it's exciting, glamorous. It's history. How about that, Buck, did you know then you were making history?)

Question. Make it into a movie?
Will the 1985 audience buy it?
Dumb question. Who knows what they'll buy?
The only way you can win in this business is to play averages.
. . . and never fall in love with any one project.

She sits waiting for my answer.
". . . How come you need me for this?" I ask. "Why couldn't

you put it together at your place? Interfico?''

I want to hear if she's going to snow me, or level.

She levels.

"It's not *my* place any more,'' she says. "You've already seen the trades—you know Interfico is in bed with a German syndicate. Germans don't know much about American TV in the 50s. I could wake up tomorrow and find they've put me to work selling lederhosen.''

Yes, she's already on her way out over there. I've already checked. And Interfico isn't long for this world, either. So here's Mrs. Tighe, playing Eliza, crossing the ice, but instead of holding a baby in her arms, she's clutching this Jody Cassel project.

"How does Jody Cassel feel about that?'' I ask. "When you went down to deal with her, you represented Interfico. Is she going to let you go peddle it elsewhere?''

She shrugs. "I don't know,'' she admits. "I think we're friends, but I haven't told her yet. She's given me lots of oral history, she trusts me, and we made an agreement to agree. So I guess we can negotiate. There is one thing she's held out for. She wants creative control over any final script.''

"Only that?'' I ask. "Gotten pretty smart in her old age, hasn't she?''

"I guess she learned from you, Mr. Dawes,'' says Mrs. Tighe.

"Forget the flattery, dear,'' I tell her. "We had enough of that Sunday night at the banquet. Today, let's discuss reality. Here's a lady who hasn't been seen in front of an audience in years, who doesn't have an old TV series running anywhere, she hasn't even done a guest shot on "Love Boat,''—the kids never heard of her. She's one hell of a tough sell.''

"True, but her story would appeal to any kid who wants to make it in show business,'' she says. "Which they all do.''

"Maybe so,'' I say. "But you're hoping. You don't know.''

"Nobody *knows,*'' she says. "But I'm sure I'm right.''

"Of course you do,'' I say. "That's why you're here in my office, pitching. The question is, will the audience agree with you enough to lay down five bucks?''

I get up and walk over to the windows, open the blinds a little, look down at the Valley, spread out below in that great checkerboard sprawl. For a change, it's clear out there; today, you can even see the mountains.

. . . the same view I've seen ever since I first came out here. But now it's from the highest floor in the building. My building.

"Do you agree, Mr. Dawes?" she asks. "Are *you* interested?"

. . . am I interested?

Funny, yesterday morning, I probably wouldn't have spent five minutes listening to this lady's pitch.

But that was before I had my session with the doctor, out at U.C.L.A.

A lot of things change abruptly after a specialist tells you you're not on an open-end status any longer.

. . . How many months, then, Doctor?

Oh, don't think in months, Buck. If we handle the early phase with all the new techniques and the various drugs available to us, you'll go into remission, we can control it, you'll undoubtedly last a good long time.

. . . How many years, Doctor?

Buck, I don't draw up contracts with my patients; contrary to what a lot of people may have told you, I am not God. Try thinking of it this way. What you may have considered a finite term of life is a bit . . . less finite.

. . . Don't buy green bananas.

Beg pardon?

It's a joke, Doctor. The old man in the bank, negotiating an investment, the banker offers him 5 percent for a year, 7 percent for five years, and if you want to go to 2010, you can get 12 percent. 2010? asks the old man. I don't even buy green bananas!

I'm glad you can still laugh about it.

. . . Who's laughing, Doctor?

Now, suddenly, I've become very interested in Mrs. Tighe's project, to do a story about Jody Cassel in live TV.

And I know exactly why. Because it is history. *My* history. If I'm going, I'd like to leave it behind. Margaret's got her name on that clinic. Let them remember *me* for something.

It's history I made, damnit!

. . . I made Jody.

I turn around. She's waiting, her fingers playing with her empty iced-tea glass, she's very uptight, trying not to show how nervous she is.

"Okay, Mrs. Tighe," I tell her. "I am interested."

. . . Whew! she lets out a sigh. She can't help herself, that much emotion she has to show me.

". . . But, before we go any further, listen to me. I do not want to be part of any schlock operation," I tell her. "If that's the way it begins to shape up, Buck Dawes pulls out. From the minute I get involved in this project, it goes first cabin, all the way. Understood?"

"Explain to me what's first cabin," she says.

"It's the best, that's what," I instruct. "For a director, we go for somebody like Mike Nichols or Sidney Lumet—they both were there, they know the territory. Casting, we don't worry about until we have a script. But when it comes to script, we also go first cabin. Shouldn't somebody try to talk to Buddy Grimes?"

"He'd be a character in the script," she says.

"Probably," I say. "But he also is a class-act writer, and maybe we could put him together with somebody like Dick Hatch, he's another class-act—"

"I love it," says Mrs. Tighe, quickly.

. . . maybe a little too quickly.

I do not like people who buy on the first go. I want them to fight me a little.

"Honey, don't yes me until I've finished," I warn her. "Now, how about Ozzie Kaufman? Where does he fit in this?"

". . . I guess he'd be my agent," she says. "I wouldn't do it without him."

"Okay, fine. But does he represent Jody Cassel, too?"

She shakes her head. "I guess I'd have to deal with her direct. Let her find a lawyer."

"From where I sit, you've got a load of things to nail down, before you can even get started," I tell her. "Now, do you want me to get into this and start nailing them down?"

She hesitates.

". . . Unless you have a better deal," I say.

"No," she says. "You want to take over and run it, fine. I just want to see this thing happen so much—and if I end up with a fair piece of the action, okay, fine—"

"Don't sell out so fast," I tell her. "I'm not going to run things. You're going to do that. This is the age of the lady producer, so we'll be very fashionable in that department. Meanwhile, I'll sit here and get things expedited. I used to be pretty good at that . . ."

"You were the best, and you know it, Mr. Dawes." she says.

Today, I don't feel like arguing the point. She's absolutely right.

But why did she use the past tense?

She's still shaking her head, as if she can't believe what I've been telling her. "Partners," she says. "That's what you're proposing—a joint venture?"

"We'll worry about who does what to whom later," I say. "That's how our lawyers get richer."

She nods. Stands up.

". . . Wow," she says, half to herself. "Wowoweewewoh!"

"What's the matter?" I ask.

". . . Nothing, nothing at all!" she says. "I just cannot believe—I mean—this entire project could really *happen*. Do you have any idea how long I've been schlepping this thing around? Wow!"

And before I know what's coming, she's leaned over and popped me a convulsive kiss on my cheek.

"That's for telling me you're interested," she says, with a slightly embarrassed grin. "Couldn't help it. I feel as if I'd just acquired . . . a fairy godfather!"

I look at her.

. . . No, she's not making a joke.

Fine. She wants a fairy godfather, let her think she's acquired herself one.

Soon enough, she'll also find out she's gotten herself a boss.

Meanwhile, step one. "Go settle up with Mexico," I tell her. "An agreement to agree is nice, but as old Sam Goldwyn said, it's not worth the paper it's written on. Get to Jody and start setting up a legal deal."

"You don't want to be in on those negotiations?" she asks.

Hardly.

"No, leave me out of it," I tell her. "For now, I'm your invisible fairy godfather. You and Ozzie handle it. You want to be a producer—so produce."

". . . I still don't believe this," she says.

Funny. Neither do I.

*   *   *   *

Eileen Tighe:

So why were we in this air-conditioned Mercedes, protected from the bright sunlight by the tinted windows, headed down the highway from Mexico City, once again going to the Casa Lindo? Were we going to celebrate the successful closing of negotiations with Jody Cassel, which would lead to the preparation of a major motion picture, based on her career in live TV?

Hardly.

. . . If the Mexican immigration man had asked me what I and my companion, Mr. Dawes, had come to Mexico for, I would have told him we were the Coast Guard, here to rescue a floundering project.

Floundering? Perhaps sunk. For good.

. . . for a week after my first audition with Buck Dawes, I'd waited in my Interfico office, in a state of suspended animation. Smiling at the cadre of German accountants who were prowling the halls, going about my business (what there was of it, and keeping far out of the way of Sully Fischer and Klaus Dieterhelm. I wasn't ready to submit my resignation yet (don't be noble, never quit a job, my father once counseled me, always make them fire you, then they have to pay more.), no, not until everything was settled between me and Buck Dawes, and more importantly, until we had a deal set with Jody Cassel.

As soon as Ozzie had accomplished that, and closed it, I could get Sully annoyed enough at me to have Klaus fire me, and move over to Buck Dawes' offices.

But it's never quite that simple, is it?
Friday night, late, Ozzie reached me at home.
"The good news is, I finally reached your friend in Mexico," he said. "The bad news is, she's decided not to go forward with this project."
"Enough with the jokes, Ozzie," I said. "What kind of terms does she want?"
"Eileen, when it's business, I do not joke," he said. "Jody says to tell you, she likes you, she's very appreciative of all your efforts on her behalf, but NJ has decided she doesn't want to participate in the cult of OJ's nostalgia."
. . . I suddenly began to feel nauseous.
"What in hell does that rhetoric mean?" I asked him.
"Why don't you ask her?" he said. "I wrote it all down here, exactly as she said it to me, so I wouldn't misquote her. Tell me, is OJ orange juice?"
". . . It's too difficult to explain," I said.
Damn!
"What do you suggest I do now?" he asked.
"I'd better talk to her myself . . . I think," I said.
"Fine," he said. "What's NJ—New Jersey?"
". . . That's even more difficult to explain," I said.
"You know, it's funny," said Ozzie. "She doesn't *sound* like a flake. Not at all . . ."

I didn't get through to Jody until Sunday morning.
. . . after two sleepless nights.
"*Eileen!*" she said, happy to hear from me, as if nothing was wrong. "Nice to talk to you! How are things in L.A.?"
"Rotten," I said. "Ozzie Kaufman says you don't want to go any further with our deal."
"That's right," she said, cheerfully. "I hope it doesn't put

you out, toots, but I'm absolutely certain. It's not for NJ.''

"It *will* put me out," I told her, trying not to lose my temper. "I've made all sorts of plans—I've got partners—we've drawn up a paper—we agreed to agree—what's wrong with going forward?"

"I just don't want to," she said.

"Why?" I insisted.

"You know all those tape transcripts you sent me? The stuff you and I discussed while you were down here? Well, I sat and read it all, and the strangest thing happened. The more I remembered about OJ and what she'd done, how she behaved . . . the less I liked her. Actually, I got to the point where I really *hated* her . . . poor thing . . . you know?" she said.

"Fine," I said. "That makes her interesting, and she'll be interesting to the audience—"

"Do somebody else, Eileen," said Jody. "Please."

"No," I protested. "There *is* nobody else as interesting—"

"Ah, come on, baby, don't try to snow me, I've been snowed by the best," said Jody. You want to do this live TV thing, fine, go pick up some other big star who was there, there are plenty still around, you can use their story—"

"Damnit, Jody, it's not *possible*—" I said.

"Eileen," she said, "NJ has made up her mind. Now. You want to come down here and visit us? You're welcome any time. Doc says hello—Artie, well, he really misses you—"

". . . Have you discussed this with Doc?" I asked.

"Why should I do that?" she said. "He knows NJ is a big girl, she can make up her own mind. And she has."

We continued on a couple more go-rounds, like that, but it was absolutely no use.

I was, as they used to say, sucking wind.

When I hung up, I sat and took inventory. It seemed I had a deal set up to do a film with a very important partner—and a class-act potential writer for the script—and an equally class-act director—

—and one small problem.

I was missing what Groucho used to call . . . the body of the letter.

How to explain this to Mr. Buck Dawes?

"Tell him straight," advised Ozzie. "He doesn't relish any bullshit. Never shit a shitter."

I had Mr. Dawes' private home number, so I took a deep breath, dialed it, and got him. When I finished telling him about Jody's turndown, he didn't seem to be particularly upset.

In fact, he was chuckling.

"She's at it again," was his comment.

Meaning?

"It's her pattern," he told me. "Jody has to be wooed. She enjoys being seduced into deals. She gives you a lot of no, no-how-dare-you, and then she gives in."

". . . But that's OJ," I said. And I explained to him about OJ . . . and Doc Katzen's influence on OJ, and the emergence of NJ. "NJ is calling the shots, and NJ is saying no."

"You believe that?" asked Buck Dawes.

"I have to," I said.

"Why?"

"Because *she* does." I said.

". . . Tell me, Mrs. Tighe," he asked, "how many top performers have you gotten close to?"

". . . Only a few," I admitted.

"I've been around them a long time now," he told me. "All shapes and sizes, male and female, black, white—talls, shorts, uglies, beautifuls, gays, straights, talents, no-talents—outside, they're different. Inside, they all have one thing in common. They're crazy. Want to know what you're dealing with? Tall children."

"OJ may have been crazy," I said, "but this is NJ—and NJ is not crazy."

"Would you like to make a small bet on that?" he asked. "I've got five says she is."

"That's a bet I'd like to lose," I said. "Because if I did; it would explain why she's just turned down this project."

"She *hasn't* turned it down," said Buck. "Believe me—she's merely waiting for somebody to come down there, and make love to her, and seduce her into saying yes, take me!"

". . . Which somebody?" I asked.

There was silence.

Then, ". . . Could be me," he said.

. . . It was late in the day when our limo finally pulled up in front of the Casa Lindo, but there was still Mexican sunshine, and when we got out, after our air-conditioned ride, its heat hit us like a hammer.

The driver pulled out our overnight bags and followed us up the steps and inside.

At the front desk, there didn't seem to be anybody in sight. Not even Kitty . . .

I didn't know what I was expecting. A strolling mariachi band? A welcoming committee?

". . . Very casual joint," commented Buck Dawes.

"We didn't call ahead," I reminded him. I rapped on the counter several times, called out Kitty's name.

Then the office door was pushed open, and Doc Katzen peered out, blinking and yawning.

". . . Couldn't let a person take a nap?" he grumbled. "Oh—say, hello there, darling. Who's your friend?"

"This is Buck Dawes, Doc—Doc Katzen—Buck—"

"Dawes?" he said. "The name is familiar . . ." He extended a bony hand. "I may have heard a lot about you, I think, boy-chick . . ."

"Good or bad?" asked Buck.

"A little of both," said Doc. "So, what brings you down to our friendly hideaway?"

"We wanted to talk to Jody," I said. "A little business."

"She expecting you?" he asked.

I shook my head.

". . . Oh, you picked a bad night," said Doc. "This is her cabbage night. Don't interrupt her until she's finished stuffing . . ."

"Certainly," said Buck. "Let it be a surprise."

". . . Have you got rooms for us?" I asked. "We'll have to spend the night, and that includes our driver."

"For you and your friends, darling, always," said Doc. "You're an alumna, you got a special rate." Then he winked. ". . . By the way, I know somebody who'll be tickled to see you. Should I tell him you're here?"

"No," I said. "First let me wash up . . . *alone.*"

"That's her guru?" asked Buck, as we went upstairs.

"Not exactly a guru," I said.

". . . Then what?" he asked.

"It's hard to explain," I said. "Around here, there aren't any precise absolutes."

"There'd better be, before we leave," he said. "When we meet Jody, I'll do the pitch, understood?"

"She's all yours," I said.

The dessert was being passed around when Jody emerged from the kitchen, brushing her hair back from a somewhat perspired forehead, grinning expectantly.

". . . How was the cabbage, people?" she asked.

"*Olé!*" came a reply, from her diners.

"Glad to hear it," she said.

She came toward our table, passed it, then stopped. Turned. Peered at Buck, shook her head as if to say *no-no, not possible*— then took a look at me—on reflex—did a real wowser of a take! . . . A classic skull—a *double skull!*

Beautiful.

"*You* ate my cabbage?" she asked him. "I . . . fed *you?*"

Buck permitted himself a slight grin. "Delicious."

"If I'd known you were dining here, I'd've put in a little cyanide," said Jody, evenly.

His grin never faltered. He stood up, extended his arms in a Christ-like posture. ". . . I'm Mohammed," he said. "You're the mountain. I came."

"Not bad," said Jody. "Who writes your material?"

"The best," said Buck. "Always first cabin . . . How are you, Jody?"

"Who brought you down here?" she asked. She pointed a finger at me. "Eileen here? And why?"

"I was delighted to come," said Buck. "She told me about this TV project she's been preparing about you, and I think it's absolutely brilliant."

"Do you?" said Jody. "Use the past tense. It's over."

"I refuse to believe that," said Buck.

"*You* refuse?" she asked. "You flew all the way down here to tell me you refuse? It's *my* decision, not yours—"

". . . *Jody,*" said Buck, never raising his voice, "Of course it's your decision. We all know that. But there are other people to consider. Lots of people. People you *owe.*"

"*I* owe?" she asked. "I don't owe. Not any more. You think I owe *you?*"

"I didn't say that," he said.

". . . You'd better not," Jody said. "Because I could call in a few debts of my own if you did. Listen, Buck, it's late, I'm tired, I'm glad you had some stuffed cabbage before you go home tomorrow—because I certainly wouldn't have wanted you to make this whole trip down here without something to show for it—"

"The cabbage was delicious," said Buck, "but I came all this way to see you—"

"Now you've seen me," she said.

She started to turn away, but he reached out and took her gently by the arm. "Don't run out on me, Jody," he said. "We have a couple of things to discuss—"

"Fine," she said. "Discuss."

". . . Not here," he replied, softly, his face close to hers. "Somewhere else? Privately? We neither of us have all the time in the world left, do we? . . . *Please?*"

She stared at him for a long moment, then she chuckled. "Some things never change," she said. "Jesus, I never could resist it when you laid that sincere bit on me . . . Come on, Mr. Humble."

He followed her out of the dining room.

Doc Katzen came over to the table where I sat, alone. ". . . Didn't even eat his dessert," he said. Sat down and began to nibble at Buck's portion of cake. "So," he asked, "what do you think's gonna happen now?"

"I don't know yet," I told him. "Do you?"

". . . What am I?" he asked, his mouth full. "a mind reader? We'll have to wait. Meanwhile . . . a fella in the kitchen was asking for you. Give him a break and go in there, will you?"

. . . Artie and I lay on the bed.

. . . relaxing in the darkness.

First we'd had a nice warm bath, some pleasant water-play, and then some serious welcome-home screwing.

All very nice. I drowsed.

. . . but couldn't sleep.

What about Buck, and Jody?

Any change in the situation?

. . . I lay there in the darkness, turning over that scene in the dining room earlier. Those two people, who hadn't been near each other for all these years . . . twenty, no, closer to thirty—

—now they meet, in the dining room of this Mexican whateveryouwantocallit Casa Lindo—she's just cooked her speciality, stuffed cabbage, she doesn't know he's there, she couldn't expect him, and she walks out of the kitchen, there he is, actually eating her cabbage, waiting to tell her how good it is—

—pow—she does a take—

Him, here?

. . . what a wonderful opening scene for a script.

. . . sure, we could take it from there, right? It's a flashback, now we've set them up as they are in 1984, turn back to 1954, now she's a young girl, aggressive, he's the ambitious young agent—

That's how we start it—

Wait. Suddenly another thought sneaked in— *subtext*.

Maybe, back there, they might have had more of a relationship than merely agent and client, why not? She was young, and maybe a lot more attractive, that would be OJ, and Buck would be her father symbol, perhaps they might even have had an affair? my God, maybe they'd even had a baby together—

. . . Pretty Baby? Wow. Wowoweeweewoh.

. . . that's not a bad plot line, is it?

Oh, come on, Eileen, don't go too far. You can stretch coincidence just so much, but then it doesn't work, the audience will reject it—

I don't care. I still liked it.

In the warm darkness of my room, I chuckled.

". . . Mm what is it?" asked Artie.

". . . Just thought of how to open the picture," I told him.

"What picture?" he asked.

"One I thought I'd get to make," I said.

". . . You're going to do it, or not?"

"That's a good question," I said. "I don't know."

He pulled me over to him and began gently to nibble at my breast. ". . . Then do you mind if we went back to something important?" he asked.

Under the circumstances, an excellent suggestion.

*   *   *   *

Jody (NJ):

You would be proud of me, Doc. NJ's finest hour.

I never got angry at him. OJ might have, hell, she had every right to kick him in the garbanzos. But not NJ.

No, she sat calmly out there, under one of those trees, with a vast Mexican night sky hanging up above. Somewhere in the distance, the faint sound of a lonely dog barking—

—and she listened to Buck Dawes doing his pitch.

What a turnaround!

All those years I'd've given my left wisdom tooth for five minutes of Buck's private ear, to have him alone in an office, the phones turned off, so I could pitch myself to him (so would anybody in the whole damn business) . . .

And now, here he was, chasing after *me?*

. . . Softly telling me how this picture project of Eileen's would have to be the most exciting film in years, how he'd already worked out with her the precisely right way to present the Jody Cassel story—to guarantee to me, and the audience, it would be strictly first-cabin all the way—

Oh, he could still sell, could Buck Dawes. Even now, all these years since he first showed up in the mountains and handed us his card, he was still the absolute best I'd ever met. Never overpitching, always underplaying, hinting at more goodies to come, taking the pitchee (me) into his confidence, it would be Us, the good taste guys, against Them, the slobs—

We were all going on a Great Adventure together, we'd be making history. Tripping down the yellow brick road (yellow for gold, of course), along the way, we'd pick up Dick Hatch, da dum, da dum, and then we'd be connecting with Buddy Grimes, da dum, da dum, da dee, and arm in arm, we'd be off to see the Wizard—

He stopped pitching, to let it sink in.

Before he could go for The Closer—

". . . Buck?" I asked. "How's your wife, Margaret?"

Off in the night, a coyote joined in with the dog, now it was a strange sort of far-off eerie duet . . .

". . . Margaret?" he said. "She's a clinic."

"Is that a joke?" I asked him.

"Oh no, Jody," he said. "She died. Instead of her, there's a building—the Margaret Dawes Clinic for Battered Wives and Children."

There's such a thing as the too-easy gag.

". . . Your kids?" I asked.

The girl was married and living in Brazil; his boy was up in Vancouver. Doing what? "Farming," Buck told me.

"A helluva long stretch from show business, isn't it?"

"Indeed," said Buck. "How about you, and yours?" he asked. "What's become of . . . Pretty Baby?"

"When last seen," I told him, "she was in England, doing the intellectual bit, shrouded in Harris tweed and drinking sherry at faculty do's. Daughter, Melissa, very beautiful, loves horses, wants to be an astronomer. They all live in Cambridge. Very classy folks, eh?"

". . . Very far away," said Buck.

"A helluva long way from show business," I said.

"Did you ever figure your daughter would end up such an intellect?" he asked.

"Why not?" I said. "Her father went to Harvard, didn't he?"

Buck didn't answer.

Inside the Casa Lindo, there came old music. Doc's? It had to be one of his records. A Ruth Etting number he cherishes . . . "Love Me or Leave Me . . ."

". . . I would've helped you, if you'd let me," Buck said, softly. "You have to believe that, Jody."

"Ah, ancient history, amigo," I told him. "Forget it. *She's* forgotten all about it."

"She?"

"OJ. Old Jody . . . remember her? She's the one you want to immortalize on the giant screen, Buck. Not me."

"You're talking about her as if she were dead," he said.

"Absolutely," I told him. "She got it in the middle of a bullring. Terrific finish. A real blockbuster . . . There she was, out there on the dirt, running around, playing to the crowd, half stoned, not even knowing why she was there—with a real honest-to-God *toro* chasing after her ass—Oh boy, what a scene—the cops came and got her away just in time, dragged her out of there, kicking and screaming—the crowd roared—and then they locked her up—*Adios,* OJ!"

". . . This *happened?*" he asked.

"You should've been there, with cameras," I told him. "OJ's finest hour. Her finale."

". . . Christ, I never knew anything about that," he said.

And he sounded sincerely upset.

For Buck Dawes, that is.

"Ah, baby, would you have come down here to rescue OJ, if you had?" I asked.

He didn't answer.

Which was honest of him.

. . . and unexpected.

"Jesus, Jody," he said, finally. "How did you recover from all that?"

"Talk to Doc Katzen," I told him. "He was the one who saved OJ'S ass for posterity."

". . . I will," he said. "But first, Jody, let's get back to the project. Can I level with you?"

"Oh, God, please don't," I said. "I don't think I could stand any but-seriously-folks . . . Not from *you*."

"Hear me out, please," he said, and his voice had become urgent. "I want this picture made. I want to see it."

". . . Why?" I asked.

"Because *I* was there," he said. *"I* was part of it, remember?"

"Oh, I remember," I told him. "More than I'd like to. But that's not—"

"—and I don't have too much time left," he said, "before I end up as a memorial wing of Cedars-Sinai Hospital!" he said.

. . . Shit! What was he telling me?

"Explain," I said.

". . . You're a bright lady, figure it out," he said. "Or do you need to read the results of my latest CAT scan?"

Oh, God, I thought—I hate these scenes in the movies or on soaps. Always so maudlin, so phony, such an obvious piece of cliché shit—and here I am now, stuck in one—and who's this bastard sitting here under a Mexican tree, in the dark, under these hundreds of stars, telling NJ the bad news? None other than The Man You Loved To Hate—

Enough irony!

. . . Buck Dawes had just won the Academy Award for it.

How dare he pull this on me—

—then I had a random thought.

Sly bastard. Who's to say this isn't his way of snowing me? No.

Not even Buck Dawes could have come up with a ploy that fiendish.

". . . Mexico is full of phony clinics where they peddle cures, Buck," I said, softly, "but this isn't one of them."

"I know," he said. "I checked already. That's not why I came down here."

". . . You want to be a partner in OJ's immortality?" I asked him.

"Partly," he said. "I also wanted to see you."

"OJ?" I asked.

"OJ—NJ—*whatever!*" he said, irritated. "I *came*, didn't I?"

He had a point there. Damn him.

"Buck, you are not going to die on me," I told him.

". . . I'm not?" he said. "How do you prove that?"

"You had seconds of my stuffed cabbage," I said. "If you can survive that, you'll outlive us all."

. . . which got a laugh from both of us.

*   *   *   *

Eileen Tighe:

. . . The first fingers of morning sunlight woke me up.
I was alone.
No, I wasn't. Artie was already in the bathroom, showering.
He came back a few moments later, nudged me.
"Message for you," he said, and handed me a slip of paper.
'Under the door."
I took it and read, in a neatly printed hand:
"Dear Mrs. T: Breakfast meeting 8:30, re OJ project.
Dining room. B.D."

So he'd seduced her!

again.

". . . Good news?" asked Artie.
"Ask me a year from now," I told him.

THE END